The
Song of Hannah

The
Song of Hannah

A NOVEL

Eva Etzioni-Halevy

A PLUME BOOK

PLUME
Published by Penguin Group
Penguin Group (USA) Inc., 375 Hudson Street, New York, New York 10014, U.S.A.
Penguin Group (Canada), 10 Alcorn Avenue, Toronto, Ontario, Canada M4V 3B2
(a division of Pearson Penguin Canada Inc.)
Penguin Books Ltd., 80 Strand, London WC2R 0RL, England
Penguin Ireland, 25 St. Stephen's Green, Dublin 2, Ireland
(a division of Penguin Books Ltd.)
Penguin Group (Australia), 250 Camberwell Road, Camberwell, Victoria 3124,
Australia (a division of Pearson Australia Group Pty. Ltd.)
Penguin Books India Pvt. Ltd., 11 Community Centre, Panchsheel Park,
New Delhi – 110 017, India
Penguin Books (NZ), cnr Airborne and Rosedale Roads, Albany, Auckland 1310,
New Zealand (a division of Pearson New Zealand Ltd.)
Penguin Books (South Africa) (Pty.) Ltd., 24 Sturdee Avenue, Rosebank,
Johannesburg 2196, South Africa

Penguin Books Ltd., Registered Offices: 80 Strand, London WC2R 0RL, England

First published by Plume, a member of Penguin Group (USA) Inc.

First Printing, September 2005
10 9 8 7 6 5 4 3 2

Copyright © Eva Etzioni-Halevy, 2005
All rights reserved.

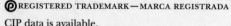
℗ REGISTERED TRADEMARK—MARCA REGISTRADA

CIP data is available.
ISBN 0-452-28672-7

Printed in the United States of America
Set in New Baskerville and Kbernhard Tango

PUBLISHER'S NOTE
This is a work of fiction. Names, characters, places, and incidents are either the product of the author's imagination or are used fictitiously, and any resemblance to actual persons, living or dead, business establishments, events, or locales is entirely coincidental.

AUTHOR'S NOTE

I follow in the footsteps of those who believe that books such as Psalms, The Song of Songs, and Proverbs are collections of writings composed by different people at different times. Thus, parts of these books must have existed before the figures of King David and King Solomon, to whom most of them are officially attributed, appeared on the scene. Hence, even though the historical period described in this novel preceded that of the two kings, it is not anachronistic to attribute to our heroines and heroes quotations from these books.

Hannah's Prologue

The tale of my son Samuel's birth and life has been told in a scroll that resides in the Temple, and in scroll rooms across the Land of Israel. The people will read it now and in all the generations to come. But it contains only a small part of that which really happened.

And so I suggested to my husband's first wife, Pninah, that we each write a book that would reveal all that could not be laid bare in the House of the Lord.

In her book, Pninah did not recoil from disclosing her innermost secrets: on how she was cast into the valley of the shadow of death, but chose life; on finding life in pleasure and in words and in laughter—even in sin. For she said that you, too, may have eaten from a forbidden fruit, or wanted to.

Nor did I hesitate to write down all that happened to me, for from beginning to end I had nothing to hide. Unlike Pninah, I had only one great love in my life, and there was never anything clandestine about it.

As for Samuel, we both told all we knew about him, so that you may realize that even exalted men are only human.

Of these two tales I wove a new one, which forms the scroll you see here before you.

By the time you read these words, we are no longer of this earth. But I hope that because of Samuel our memories live on in your hearts. So you will wish to know about him, about us, all that has been concealed so far and has been recorded in this book for the first time.

FIRST PART

In the Valley of the Shadow of Death

The Book of Hannah

What hurt before, no longer hurts. The grief of years gone by no longer clings to me. The pain I have inflicted and the pain inflicted on me then, the horrors of the wars—all these are long gone, overtaken by a new grief. Yet the memories are still as clear as the water that flows down the river Jordan, as strong as the blazing sun was on that day, in the month of the Festival of the Wheat Harvest, the day that determined my life.

I had slipped out of my house to walk in the vineyard, to be alone, balanced on the edge of the nagging doubts in my heart. What lay within my reach was beyond any maiden's dreams, yet my hand would not stretch out to grasp it. As if it were weighted with lead, I was unable to lift it up to take the man who was both rich and handsome and wanted me for his wife, as my father and mother ardently wished me to do.

Another father might have given his daughter, even against her will, to the man who had his seal of approval. But my father, and my mother as well, were of noble spirit and would not force me into that which I might find unbearable. But they bestowed their blessing on my suitor, Hanoch, and his offer. And the gentle words they uttered day after day, with the aim of convincing me to do the same, bore down on my soul as the massive stones in a press squeeze olives, to extract their precious oil.

I was determined that no one, not even my parents, would compel me to do something against my will. Yet I could not deny their claim that the decision could no longer be postponed, and this was the day on which I would make it.

The day before, Hanoch had paraded his riches before our eyes, tempting us, and I had not been impervious to their allure. He had brought us to inspect his house, a mansion of unequaled size and elegance. It was the only house in the entire hill country of Efraim that was built with two stories, an imposing stairway leading straight from the front yard to the second floor. In my mind's eye I caught a glimpse of myself as the mistress of this house, glowing like a star in the night sky in a bright tunic that shimmered in silvery splendor, standing at the head of the stairway, issuing instructions to a host of maids who would rush back and forth in haste to carry out my orders. And I knew myself to have the regal bearing necessary for this exalted position.

The apparition beckoned seductively and I was sorely tempted. But I banished it with the speed at which lightning tears the sky, for it held no merit and was unworthy of me. I resolved that if I became Hanoch's wife it would be not because he was rich, nor yet because he was tall and handsome and refined. Not even because he had stormed into my life like a whirlwind, as I had long dreamt that my husband would.

As I was treading the path through the vineyard, I vowed that my only consideration would be whether he was the man ordained for me, the one with whom I would be able to fulfill the secret mission of my life. If I wavered, it was because I was uncertain whether he was that man.

Ever since I was a child I knew that I was unlike other little girls; that in truth my life would be devoted to a special task, although its nature was shrouded in haze. I also had a premonition that my task would be connected to a man. A man who would be out of the common way, and would appear in my life in an unexpected manner, like a downpour of rain from a cloudless summer sky.

It had not escaped me that thanks to the rare beauty with which I was endowed, I stood out among the village girls. My hair was as black as a raven, straight and gleaming. A small part of it was braided, and fell over my right temple, while the rest hung heavily down to my waist. My skin was as white as milk and as smooth as marble, and my neck, long and slim. My eyes were of a deep brilliant green, enhanced by the green dresses my mother always made me wear.

The special destiny of my life, though, had nothing to do with my beauty, and I had no notion of why I of all others had been chosen for it. The Lord humbles the mighty and elevates the humble. But I was anything but humble; why I should have been singled out to be elevated was beyond my understanding. Nonetheless I knew that it was so. This was a certitude born not of visions or dreams or voices, but lodged in the essence of my being. As I knew myself, so I knew this to be true.

Although I foresaw that I would share my mission with a man, it was a riddle to me wherefrom this man would spring forth. I had spent all the fifteen years of my life in the village of Shaar Efraim, in the hill country of Efraim, and I was acquainted with every one of its fewer than six hundred inhabitants. I was as certain as I was that the Lord had created the heavens and the earth that the man destined for me was not among these six hundred. Where, then, was he concealing himself?

One day a caravan had arrived at the nearby town of Ramathayim, carrying rare goods: balm from Gilad and myrrh and cinnamon and saffron and all manner of other spices and healing ointments that were almost impossible to procure in our parts. My mother charged me with the task of purchasing some of these wares. Late in the afternoon, as the heat of the day abated, I asked my friend Pninah to accompany me on my expedition.

Ramathayim was barely a few hills away from our village, and we reached it, riding our donkeys, within a short time. It was a town spread out over several hills and the valleys between them, in which some ten thousand men, women, and children had their dwellings. The town square, where the caravan was encamped and its merchandise spread out, was located on the highest hill; and when we reached it, it was chaotic, filled to capacity with the many who, like us, had come to buy the scarce wares.

We slid from our donkeys, giving them into the hands of stable boys at the edge of the square, who took charge of them in return for a small payment of silver pieces. Then we joined the multitudes that were pushing and shoving to reach the stall on which the goods were displayed. We had no choice but to press ourselves forward as well, until our tempers ran short and our patience began to run out.

Suddenly we heard the noise of hooves pounding the ground. A whirl of dust arose and a dark horse racing at great speed came into view. Since our people, the Israelites, had not adopted the custom of breeding horses, I had never seen one before. But I had read in the Torah about the Egyptian Pharaoh's horses, those that had pursued the children of Israel after their exodus from Egypt. So I had no doubt as to what the animal was that now appeared before our eyes.

The crowd fell back in awe before the horse and its rider, a young man who reined it in forcefully until it reared and neighed. As I craned my neck to look up at him, he dismounted from the saddle with flair and tossed its reins to two youngsters who came forward to receive them.

The crowd had now parted to clear a path so that the man could approach the stall he evidently owned; and when the vendors caught sight of their master they bowed so low that their noses almost touched their knees. The young man disregarded them, and came to stand before us, his eyes riveted to mine.

"I am Hanoch, the son of Uziel," he proclaimed, "and you must surely be the most beautiful girl who has ever made a purchase at one of my stalls. What is your name?"

I met his gaze, and although he had ignored my friend, I told him both our names. He demanded to know what we wished to buy, and the vendors handed the wares to us without delay. His help brought great relief, for it released us from the necessity of jostling amongst the crowd. But when he refused to take payment, we simply placed the silver we had brought with us on the stall's counter and withdrew to make a place for the others.

Hanoch led us to the side of the square and asked where we had come from. When he learned that we were from Shaar Efraim he instructed the boys in charge of our donkeys to bring them out, and one from his own stable as well, as he wished to accompany us home.

In the ensuing silence I had an opportunity to observe him. He was undoubtedly the most handsome man on whom I had ever set eyes. He had straight hair, as dark as his horse's mane, and black eyes and finely sculptured features. His well-crafted linen garment and head covering were of the lightest shade of gray. His shirt had a fringe laced by a blue thread at its corner, as prescribed by Torah law. But unlike the other fringes I had seen, its tassels were laced with silver threads that shone in the sun, and there was an enormous golden seal hanging as a pendant around his neck. He uttered his words in a slightly nasal voice that oddly pleased my ears.

I remembered him proudly riding his horse a little while ago, and he conjured up in my mind an image of a prince from a distant land. I was deeply impressed with his looks and his noble demeanor, and when the donkeys were brought around I said, "We will be glad for your escort."

We rode out of the square, and when Pninah noted that Hanoch was smitten with me she fell behind so that we were free to talk. Hanoch recounted that he was twenty-six years old, his father's youngest son. "Since my father owns only one property," he continued, "the younger sons took up trading. Having prospered in trade, I bought a merchant ship, which, together with the trading caravans I own, is the source of my livelihood."

I was aware that Hanoch was the richest man in all the surrounding areas, for a kinswoman of mine had previously made a strenuous effort to catch this enormous fish in her net for me. But he had firmly declined her services, saying that he preferred to find his bride by his own efforts.

This memory brought a smile to my face. When Hanoch asked what made me smile, I gave him an account of what had happened.

He laughed. "I have tried to eschew my destiny, but it has nonetheless caught up with me and brought us together."

His words struck a chord in my heart, and I thought that perhaps destiny had caught up with both of us.

Several weeks passed since our first meeting, and during that time Hanoch, in his eagerness for me, had pledged himself to deliver into my father's hands a bride price so enormous that it would enable my family to live in prosperity all the days of their lives. As my father was not a rich man, the offer was tempting and he and my mother were keen to accept it.

I had to admit that, as they claimed, Hanoch was indeed as different from all the other young men who wanted me as gold was different from copper, precisely as I had hoped that the man in my life would be. Even so, I did not have the certainty about him that I had expected to have.

* * *

Even before I met Hanoch, I did not lack suitors. For years, boys, and later young men, had swarmed around me as bees swarm around flower blossoms. Sometimes they stood in front of my house for long stretches of time, patiently waiting for me. My four little brothers thought this hilarious. They would peer out of the front window together, tumbling over each other in glee, and with the un-thinking cruelty of children teased my admirers until my mother came along and chased them away.

This did not deter the young men. They continued standing with bent heads until I came out, and then accompanied me wher-ever I went. Surely, I said to myself, the man who was to be in charge of my life—as a husband should be—would not quake before me like a slave before his master.

At first I basked in the young men's admiration, even though I knew that there was more to me than just my beauty. My father im-bued me with love of the Torah, which he called the Tree of Life. Though a scholar, he had no inclination for teaching, and sent me for my lessons to another man's house. Nevertheless, he taught me to take pride in my eating the fruit of this Tree.

He also taught me that my family was a very unusual one. After the land of Canaan had been conquered by our people, many men and women from other domains settled amongst us. Many of those were the rough and tough of the earth and no one knew where they had come from. So there were many families in our midst whose ancestry was lost in the mist of time. My family was not of their number: it was one of the few that could trace its origin all the way back to Efraim, the father of our tribe. I was apprised that as the eldest daughter of a family of such noble descent, I had much to be proud of.

My mother was descended from one of the richest families in the land. She had her family's consent to marry my father, who was not their equal in assets, because of his impeccable lineage. As a woman, she had inherited little from her family, except her out-standing dignity, and her serenity and regal posture. But this was enough for me. I admired her greatly and emulated her. My mother, whom I resembled, reciprocated my love and admiration. This nurtured me, as the rain nourishes the lily of the valley.

As I grew, the persistent young men surrounding me no longer gladdened my heart but became a nuisance to me. Many pestered me with affirmations of love. Some attempted to edge me into dark corners. And many offered to take me as their wife, and I refused them all.

By the time I was fifteen years of age, I had a fair idea of what they all wanted of me. But I also had a good idea of what *I* wanted. I knew that I would not let them lead me into sin, nor would I become the wife of any of them. They were all worthy, but ordinary.

My mother became impatient with my obstinance. She scrutinized my followers and found three whom she pronounced to be worthy of me. When I rejected them all, she warned me, "Soon there will be no one in the village left for you."

"There are men in other towns and villages in our vicinity," I replied.

"But there is no opportunity for you to cross their way. Do not let your face crumple for lack of kisses," she begged me. "Do not to let your womb wither for lack of use; do not to allow your whole self to dwindle into a lonely old age."

As I was not even a woman grown, this possibility seemed remote.

But my mother insisted that marriageable girls were like starved animals in search of prey, and young men of worth were enticed into marriage by them so quickly that I would soon be a woman without a suitable man.

When she continued to reproach me, I spoke to her these words: "My mother, I honor you greatly and your words are a fountain of wisdom for me. Nevertheless I cannot do what you require of me, for I know that there is a man for me, and I for him, and I will take no other."

"My daughter," she retorted, "this is nothing but foolishness. Many girls look for the man who stands out amongst the multitude, but there is no such man."

"My honored mother, unlike these girls I am not looking for the man who stands head and shoulders above other men, but merely for the one who is for me. He may not be outstanding at all. But when I meet him, I will know it."

"And if he never comes?"

"He will come."

My mother regarded me as if I were out of my mind. She then

fell into dejection. I felt for her, and could only hope that it would not last long.

I cherished the sense I harbored about my mission, but buried it in the innermost recesses of my soul and did not reveal it to anyone but Pninah. She was almost of my own age, and I met her at the daily lessons at her father's house, where we, together with three young men, studied to become scribes.

Pninah was pretty. She had large blue-gray eyes that filled her face; and her thick, richly flowing, honey-colored hair spilled gracefully over her shoulders. Her body was slim, except for rounded breasts that pressed against her dress. She had well-shaped legs set off by slender ankles and small, dainty feet. But, as indicated by the young men's gazes on me alone, her prettiness paled before my beauty.

Still, we remained friends. Since childhood, Pninah, like me, loved Torah learning. She had fallen into the habit of walking home with me after her father's lessons. We talked about what we had learned, and about ourselves—confiding to each other even our innermost secrets—and so we became close friends, as only young girls can be.

I realized, though, that it was more than love of the Torah that led us to seek each other's friendship. She was attracted to me also because she was restless, while I had the tranquility and calm assurance, the confidence in my own worth, that she lacked. She felt that by being with me, some of it was passed on to her. I was drawn to her because I sensed that, although she was bright, she needed my guidance. By admiring my assurance, she strengthened it.

So it was also with regard to the mysterious goal of my life. When I spoke to her of it, she did not snigger behind a hand held over her mouth, as I am sure the other girls in the village would have done. When she asked what this goal would be I had to admit that it was not yet clear. Even so, she considered my words gravely, and so strengthened my faith in my as yet unnamed exalted aim.

Pninah was also the only one outside my family who knew of Hanoch. She had not only been present at our first meeting, but also knew that each day after I returned from lessons with her father, Hanoch frequented my house.

Whenever he came, we sat and talked in our front room. He told me that besides being a merchant he was also a seafaring man who had crossed the Great Sea several times in his own ship. He recounted the most wondrous tales about the peoples of the sea and their unheard-of customs.

He had not traveled all the way to the western edge of the earth, where the sun sets like a wheel of fire for the night; but he must have been very close to it. He had certainly traveled a greater distance and had a wider knowledge of the world than anyone else I had encountered. I was more strongly drawn to him each day.

He began to spin plans for our life together. "When we are married I will take you on a trip to faraway countries, so that we may enjoy their wonders together before our children are born."

My mother and father admitted they had been wrong in pressing me to accept the proposals of my previous suitors, as Hanoch outshone them in every way. He was the answer to their fervent prayers for me. And they had no doubt that I was poised to approve of him, and thus enrich us all.

Like my parents, I believed that Hanoch was indeed the embodiment of a dream. He had set out with a silver pouch as empty as if it were riddled with holes; he had amassed his riches with the power of his own brain and the diligence of his own hands. Yet he had the distinguished appearance of one who had been rich since birth. What more could any maiden ask for? But still I vacillated.

In the solitude of my walk amongst the vines, I finally made my decision: I resolved to consult Pninah. She had always relied on my advice, and I had given her the best I could muster. Now our lives had taken a different turn, and the time had come for me to seek help from her.

My decision to ask Pninah's advice was the most important one I would ever make. It was to lead me inexorably toward what fate had in store for me, which neither she nor I would be able to change.

The Book of Pninah

It was a blazing summer day and I was tending our flock on the hill under the scorching sun, when I saw a figure running toward me. At first the sunlight blinded my eyes. When I shaded them with my hands, I saw that it was my younger sister, Hagith, and I was deeply disappointed.

By that time I had been a shepherdess for a year, and in the valley of the shadow of death for a week, and it was someone very different I had been hoping to see. That someone was the man who had cast me into the valley. And when he'd found out, he had asked: "Can you not do anything about it?" Followed by: "I need some time to think it over." And finally: "Don't be in a worry."

Bitterly, I thought that this was like throwing a stone down a hill, then advising it not to fall.

As a shepherdess, I had had much leisure to gaze into the distance and spin dreams threaded with the gold of sunshine. The flawless lover, whose image I had conjured up in my restless mind, would not have required time to think it over; but my real lover did.

And time—five interminable days—had passed, but he had not returned. Had he now sent my sister to me with a message? I could not believe it. If he had something to tell me, he would do it himself. So apparently he had not thought it over, or else his thoughts had led him to abandon me in the pit in which he had placed me.

I had never heard of a disaster like this befalling any girl in our tribe. So while I was in the throes of fear, I could not yet name it.

For I could not imagine what my parents would do when they found out.

Would they give me up to the elders, to die by stoning as set out in the Torah?

Or even worse, would they submit me to the death of shame by keeping me at home to face my sin? Would they expose me to scorn, to be shunned by all, an outcast in the midst of my own tribe?

Whatever decision they made would still leave me to my fate, from which only my lover, and he alone, could rescue me.

With bitter regret I knew that it was not him, but myself, that I should blame. For when I had met him a few weeks earlier, I already knew how easily a girl's life could be destroyed. Yet I had let him convince me that it was not so.

It had begun one day in the third month of the year. The heat was already oppressive as I herded my flock toward the spring. This was one that would soon dry out, but at that time was still flowing. The rains had been plentiful that year and had continued to pour down even into the beginning of the summer, the time of the wheat harvest. A small pool of water had formed in front of the spring and the sheep and goats and lambs crowded around it to drink.

The hills were used for pastures, and this hill was set aside for our flock alone. So I slipped off my dress and my shoes and hung them on a bush beside me, making my way amongst the sheep's soft woolly bodies and plunging into the shallow water. I delighted in its coolness and drank from it out of my cupped hands.

When I came out, I was startled to see a strange man staring down at me.

He was tall, his head covered by profuse, bushy dark hair that protruded from his cap on all sides. He wore a light-brown garment with a fringe, laced by a blue thread at its corners. It was sleeveless and reached no further down than his knees, revealing his muscular body. He was holding a lamb under his arm and regarding me boldly, impudently.

I was hot with shame. I snatched up my dress and covered myself with it, clamping it to my body as if he were about to wrest it from me.

"I liked what I saw before much better," he said brightly, and I liked the sound of his laughing voice.

"Who are you?" I gasped.

"I am Elkanah, the son of Yeroham, your new neighbor. You must be one of the daughters of Elad, the son of Amihud, and Bathel. My father told me about you."

"Yes, I am the elder daughter, Pninah."

"You are like your name: a pearl."

Of course he had said this only to be polite.

My mother had named me "Pearl" in the hope that I would look like one; but she was disappointed. I had once overheard my father telling my mother that I was pretty and had a nicely shaped body. But no one had ever said that I was beautiful, or that I looked like a pearl. So I did not take what this man said seriously, but was merely embarrassed.

"What are you doing here?" I asked sharply.

He continued to stare at me. "Like you, I am tending the family's flock."

"But surely not here. These are the pastures for our flock."

He bowed deeply. "I apologize. One of our lambs went astray, so I came to retrieve it."

"You'd better go back to the rest of your flock, before it goes astray as well."

He laughed again. "I herded them into the enclosure before I came looking for this one." He nuzzled the lamb's nose gently.

"Turn around so I can put on my dress."

"May I put it on for you?" he offered, preparing to set his lamb down on the ground.

"No, just turn."

He showed me his back, and I drew my gray dress over my head, noting with even greater embarrassment that it was plain, ill fitting, and faded, and that my hair fell over my shoulders in damp disorder.

"Now, let's gather your flock into the enclosure as well, and then sit down in the shade of that tree."

We took care of the flock. Then, with water still dripping from my body, I walked with Elkanah toward the tree.

As we walked, my family's house came into view. It was one of the small houses of the village of Shaar Efraim, nestled at the foot of the hill.

The square houses, baking in the sun, were built of irregular little stones and plastered over with earth-colored clay. Each was surrounded by fig and olive trees, which cast shade on their front and back yards. Behind each house was a small vineyard, and then the rugged hills.

In the olden days, before the land of Canaan had been conquered by our people, the hills had been covered by forests. But the Israelites, who had come charging from the desert across the river Jordan, had been rich in livestock, yet poor in land. So the forests had been cleared for grazing. Now there were only a few trees and bushes left amidst the grass.

The leafy tree that we now approached was one of them. Under it I had left a bag filled with bread, a pouch of vinegar in which to dunk it, and a skin of grape juice for my midday meal, and we shared it.

I sat with my legs crossed in front of me, only partly covered by my damp dress, which was too short, exposing them to Elkanah's view.

He sat opposite me with his knees drawn up, restraining his lamb between them. And while we ate he surveyed each part of my body with probing eyes, and asked me questions about myself.

I had never been alone with a man before, so at first I felt tongue-tied and bashful. But he exuded a bold assurance; he was so much at ease that he made me feel easy, too. My shyness soon vanished and I talked freely. I told him that I was almost fifteen years old, and had one younger sister.

He told me that he was twenty-four, and that he had four sisters and one elder brother. Then he recounted how he had come to live near us.

Our neighbors on the large property next door had been a childless old couple. The woman had never borne the fruit of the womb, and as the man had recently died, she was left a widow.

Elkanah's father was the deceased man's younger brother. He had lived in Ramathayim. When his brother died, he came to his house to mourn him. As soon as the thirty days of mourning were over, he took the widow to be his second wife. This was so that he could sire a son in his brother's name, who would then inherit his uncle's property, as was the Torah law.

"Surely the widow is too old to bear a son," I said.

"That is even better, because now the property will belong to my father, and both my elder brother and myself will have properties to inherit. My elder sisters now have their own families, and they live some distance away," he continued. "And my elder brother and his family stayed to tend our other property in Ramathayim. Only I and my youngest sister have moved over here."

By that time the sheep and goats were getting restless in their enclosure, bleating noisily. I rose to my feet and told him that I must let them out.

He, too, arose, and before I anticipated his intent, he came close to me. For the first time, I inhaled the intoxicating smell of a man. My face almost touched his hairy chest, but he lifted my chin with his hand. He bent over me and his lips were hovering over mine, just barely touching them. An instant later, his hand and mouth were gone and he had left.

No man had kissed me before and I did not know whether this was to be deemed a kiss or not. Yet that night as I lay on my bed I felt a strange burning within me such as I had never felt before, nor had suspected that I could.

Although I had never experienced such a craving in my body, I had long known a yearning in my soul. My mother rebuked me in a plaintive voice for having a fidgety soul, for never being satisfied with all the good things with which the Lord had blessed me: plenty of fat food to eat, a softly padded bed to sleep on, and as many as four finely woven linen dresses to wear. This was a greater abundance than most other girls in the village could boast of, yet still I was sulky.

I could not tell my mother that she herself was the cause of my sullenness. Nor could I explain that I had no control over the strange yearnings in my soul, and that only vaguely did I know what I was yearning for.

But now I felt that if I could be close to Elkanah, I would find peace in my body and my soul. I did not know if he would want it to be so, for why should he when there were more beautiful girls in our village? Thus I tossed and turned for a long time, my sheet crumpled into a bulky heap underneath me, before I finally fell asleep.

In the morning, in the hope that Elkanah would visit me again, I arrayed myself in my best blue dress. The burning from last night was still in me, and I decided to extinguish it in the coolness of the pool. This time I looked around carefully. When I was sure that no one was there, I undressed and waded in, but it did not cool the fire inside me.

When I saw Elkanah stride over from the other hill, the flames were mingled with mortification. A man I had never seen before had barely touched my lips and I was trembling with desire to be close to him.

This time he carried no lamb under his arm, but a bag over his shoulder.

"Am I too late to behold the beauty of your wet breasts today?" he called in mock dismay.

I hardly had time to blush before his mood changed. "I've brought food and drink. Let us eat our meal together again."

He grasped me by the hand and led me to a big oak tree. It stood beyond the top of the hill, where we had a good view of the surrounding hills—on which the grass was drying out, taking on its summery yellow-brown color—but the village down in the valley was out of sight.

Elkanah set the food and drink out before us. It consisted of barley cakes and a honey nectar. While we ate and drank, I talked. I recounted that when my mother had given birth to my younger sister, Hagith, her womb had been torn to shreds and she could no longer bear children.

Elkanah listened only half-heartedly, not distracted from his purpose. Like yesterday, his kiss came suddenly. This time his lips enfolded mine, his teeth biting, until I felt my lips bleeding, as, clawing my shoulders, he gasped:

"Pninah, watching you naked yesterday has caused me to be crazed with desire for you. You must let me still it, or I'll go out of my mind."

My feelings were jumbled. I was reluctant yet eager, recoiling but lured, determined to push him away as I reached out to him, overcome both by his desire and mine. Fear wrestling with passion, fear vanquished.

Thus I succumbed to him, to my fate.

I let him lay me down on the ground, and remove my dress and his garment. Then his handsome face was above me, his strong body bearing down on mine. The fever inside me growing. His biting my nipples, bruising them until I cried out. Then his thrust, briefly halted by a barrier, then a piercing pain. Then his rapid movements inside me, his strength flowing into me, his shattering release. Then—nothing.

He withdrew from me, and we were both covered with blood.

"I have been wounded," I cried out in fear. For the wound that had been inflicted on me was obviously the punishment from the Lord for the sin I had just committed.

Elkanah laughed with his own special laughter, which I had grown to love. "No, my child, you have merely shown me that no man has known you before. Let's dip into the pool before we go on."

When we came back, I said, "I think we had better not do this again. I have been told that doing things . . . things . . . like this can cause a girl to become with child. I don't want that to happen to me."

"It does not happen so quickly," he soothed me. "It took my mother two years before she became pregnant."

I remembered that my mother had not carried me inside her until after she had been my father's wife for three years. I felt reassured, and then his mouth was on my breasts again.

This time I admired his muscular arms and shoulders and thighs, and then the amazing sight of his member growing before my eyes. I was mesmerized by my own power to cause this. My body squirmed, opening itself to his thrusts, heedless of the voice within me. Leaving his seed, leaving me behind.

I pulled my dress back down over my head, and told Elkanah that I had to return to my flock.

When he saw the disappointment of unreleased tension in my face, he held me back. "You did not enjoy this so much. I will do better next time."

I was puzzled. "Do women enjoy this?"

"So far I have known only the maids who work for us in the fields and women of easy virtue, and I was not concerned with their enjoyment."

These words piled up more confusion onto my confused mind. "What are women of easy virtue?" I asked.

"They are . . . I will explain it to you some other time. Meanwhile, I will consult with my elder brother, Nathanel, who has known numerous women. He told me that although many women don't enjoy the act of love, some do."

"Is what we were doing 'the act of love?'"

Throwing back his head he laughed with delight, and replied: "It is called so. Nathanel and his family will be arriving today, to stay for the sabbath. I will ask his advice. And when we are together again on the first day of next week, I hope that the act of love will also become an act of joy for you, as it is for me. In the meantime, may the peace of the sabbath descend upon you."

But the peace of the sabbath did not descend upon me. For throughout this holy day, my blood was racing so that I could almost hear it bubbling inside me.

On the morning of each sabbath, it was the custom for a small part of the Torah to be read in our village square. My father was the one to read, and he expected me to be there to listen.

He was a tall slim man with a deep rich voice that seemed to emanate from a body heavier than his. I usually enjoyed his chanting of the sacred words, but that day my thoughts were roaming around in other domains.

I encountered my friend Hannah in the square. She had recently attracted the attentions of a wealthy young man about whom she had much to tell me. But she accused me of not listening to the Torah reading, or to a word of what she was saying to me, either. She was right: I attended neither to my father's voice nor to hers. I was listening to a much more insistent voice inside me.

When I met Elkanah the next day, it transpired that his brother had taught him exceedingly well. This time he took time to caress my breasts with his tongue and my most secret parts with his hand, leading me slowly up the slope of need, before he came into me. His breath came in stark gasps, but still he restrained himself, holding back the rush of his blood. Only when I was being carried on a surging wave did he set himself free. Then I felt a joy rocking inside me, and the flame that had been burning there was finally extinguished.

But not for long. The deep calm that overcame us soon gave way to renewed lust, and we enjoyed the fruit of Elkanah's brother's instruction again and then a third time.

During the two weeks that followed, we met every day except the sabbath; our flocks were sadly neglected. Lust, love, and fulfillment entwined together until we could no longer tell them apart. There was perfect harmony in the rhythms of our bodies, as they poured their love into each other.

Then the sabbath came, and the first day of the week, and Elkanah did not come.

At first I was not overly worried. I thought he must have some matters to attend to that he had not known of before. But when he did not appear for an entire week, I had to face the truth that he no longer wished to see me.

I could not fathom it. We had been so happy with each other. He had never said that he loved me, but he had shown it in his eagerness for me, as fierce as that of a lion for his rutting mate. So I had thought. But in truth all the love and happiness had been on my side alone.

Each night I pined for him, aching for his touch, and telling myself that the next day he would come. But when the next day came, he did not. There was no sign of him. Nothing.

One night, as I lay on my bed, I felt a strange sensation in my breasts. They were hard and swollen, and ached at my touch. I was frightened.

The tiny bedroom that was mine and my sister's faced the backyard. It contained only our two beds and a plain wooden case. From my bed underneath the window I had a view of the moon, emerging from behind some shallow clouds. It shed its pale light over our yard, and over the vineyard beyond. I shivered with fear.

Each month, my flow came at the first light of the new moon, when it was still a sliver in the sky. Now the moon was almost full. Yet the rags that I had laid nearby to absorb my blood were still untouched, piled up in the wooden case, staring at me accusingly for failing to use them. I got out of bed and shoved the rags even deeper into their dark corner, so that Hagith would not notice them waiting there in vain.

The next morning, as I sat down for my meal, the sight of the freshly baked bread laid out on the table was repellent to me and I left it untouched.

I tended the sheep, but brought them home early, and threw myself down on my bed. Hagith came in and looked at me in worry.

Although she was a year younger than I was, she knew what had befallen me, but kept her knowledge in her heart.

When I awoke in the morning, I was overcome with nausea. I ran into a remote corner of the backyard and was sick. I felt drained of strength, and sought refuge in my bed.

Soon my mother came in to inquire why I had not taken the flock out to pasture. When she saw me lying on my bed she was puzzled, as I had never been ill in my life. She studied me grimly with her eyes and I could tell she was suspicious, so I jumped out of bed as fast as I could.

I hurried to the sheepfold, nudged the flock with my rod and began guiding it up the hill. As I walked through the shadowy vineyard that lay between our house and the hill, I thought of how stupid I had been not to have protected my own vineyard. For when I met Elkanah, I had known already what a girl's vineyard was, and why it must be guarded.

I had not always known. I had heard girls in the village sing:

They put me to guard the vineyards,
my own vineyard I have not guarded.

I had believed that these words meant what they seemed to mean. Until, one evening last summer, I was sitting in our backyard in the cool of the evening breeze, when I heard my parents' voices from a distance. My father said that the man who had been tending the flock would now assist in the fields instead. "Our daughters," he added, "are big enough now to do this, and they will take turns."

My mother decreed: "Pninah is almost fourteen. She will tend the sheep."

"Hagith is almost thirteen. She is big enough, too," my father said.

"Hagith cannot do it. She is too beautiful."

My father did not deny this. Hagith's creamy skin, light copper curls, dark, almond-shaped eyes, and her body, mature beyond her age, entranced everyone.

"Men stare at Hagith's shapely body," continued my mother. "If she went up that hill on her own, men would flock around her. One of them might invade her vineyard and make her pregnant."

My father took up my cause. "Pninah, too, is pretty and has a nicely shaped body."

Then I heard my mother's words distinctly, too distinctly: "Men don't look at her as they look at her sister."

"Give her time to bloom and there will be men who look at her."

"Then the workman must continue to tend the flock." My mother's voice was becoming shriller. "Certainly not Hagith."

My father remained silent and I knew that, as usual, my mother had overruled him. He had the power with which our tradition endowed him, but she had a loud, piercing voice and he was a peace-loving man. Apart from tending our farm, he was a scribe and a scholar. And only in peace could he pursue the studies his soul craved.

My ears stung from the words I had heard. I crept away to my room like a beaten dog. I had gained a fair notion of what this vineyard of Hagith's was that my mother so adamantly insisted on guarding. As for mine, she did not even mention it, for it was of no value to her. I cried inside myself. From that day forward, and until the time she died, I no longer had a mother.

Since that day a year had passed, but I had never met anyone and had never had an opportunity to guard anything. Until the day Elkanah watched me emerge from the pool. Then, like the girl in the song, I failed to guard my vineyard. Now I was paying for my stupidity.

Yet I had some hope that Hannah, whose mother talked to her and instructed her in everything, might know something about the trouble I was facing. Perhaps she would be able to help me get rid of the infant in my belly, and all would be well again.

In the late afternoon, during my father's lesson, I saw Hannah regarding me thoughtfully. Recently she had been so deeply engrossed in her concern over Hanoch, that she'd had hardly any thoughts to spare for anything else. But now she turned her attention to me. When I accompanied her home, she said, "Pninah, I'm afraid that there is something very wrong with you. Have you not heeded yourself as you should have?"

I nodded in shamefaced silence.

"Who is the villain?" she probed.

"He is Elkanah, the son of Yeroham, and he is not a villain."

"I don't know him."

"He has just moved here from Ramathayim."

"Get him to marry you," she advised.

I sighed unhappily. "He does not want to marry me."

"Does he know that you are carrying his child?"

"No."

"So then . . ."

"Hannah, tell me: Is there a way to stop this pregnancy?"

"I do not think so. But there is a woman who knows more about these things than anyone. Her name is Binah and she is like her name, a wise woman. She lives close by. Go and visit her."

I proceeded to the home of Binah. She was a tall, straight-backed woman of advanced years with large brown eyes, through which she regarded me with kindness.

I told her my concern and asked: "Is there anything that can be done to release me from my trouble?"

"Yes, but it is dangerous."

"Can you do it for me?" I persisted, for what choice did I have?

"I can, but I will not. There are women who do such things, but banish any thoughts of going to them. You could be borne from their home straight into your grave. Get the man to take you for his wife."

"He doesn't want me for his wife."

Binah's eyes revealed her compassion. "Get him to want you. Entice him. Beguile him. Dangle your charm before him. Kindle his desire, but don't satisfy it. Let your eyes and your body promise much, but deliver little, until you are safely ensconced in his home as his wife."

That night when everyone was asleep, I stepped out into the backyard to contemplate my fate. I felt the sharp stones on the ground cutting into my bare soles like a punishment for my sin.

I decided that the nothingness of death by stoning would be preferable to the death of dishonor. And both would be better than becoming the wife of a man who, though feeling obliged to marry me, did not love me.

Then I knew that I was truly in the valley of the shadow of death, and into my heart came the words of the psalm:

The Lord is my shepherd . . .
even though I walk
in the valley of the shadow of death
I fear no evil for you are with me . . .

Having recited the words, I was overcome with a feeling of comfort, as if in some strange way I had come close to God.

My fears momentarily laid to rest, I went back to my bed and slept. And in the morning, I strode over to the next hill to seek out Elkanah, as I had not dared to do before.

My heart began pounding when, still at a distance, I saw a head of bushy black hair among the sheep. Only when I came closer did I see that it topped the head of a girl who resembled him, his sister.

She told me that the first-born brother, Nathanel, had now been put in charge of the family's larger property here, as was his right. Elkanah had moved back to Ramathayim to manage the family's other property there.

I retraced my steps to our hill, and later when I came home I wrote a letter to Elkanah. Then I headed for the village gates, where I found a messenger and, handing him half a silver shekel as payment, gave him my letter to deliver.

Sitting on the hill the next morning, it was not long before I saw Elkanah approaching. I arranged my hair becomingly over my shoulders and sprang up to meet him. As before, I was conscious of his dark eyes and the muscular build of his body. My heart gave a leap at the sight of my lover, but my body tensed in uncertainty.

He came close, touched my lips with his, and the fire flared up inside me. He tugged at my dress, but I halted him, saying that I had to speak to him.

Breathing heavily, he retorted: "Yes, you told me so in your letter. But how can I talk when I am overwhelmed with desire? We'll talk later."

My resolve crumbled. Overpowered by our hunger for each other, we reached happiness together. Only then did I remember

Binah's advice. After we dressed, I tried to devise the best way of conveying my tidings.

He made it unnecessary. "You have no need to tell me. I understand what has happened."

I was eager to learn what his response to my pregnancy would be, but the moments spun by and he did not give any response at all. Then my heart fell as I heard him say: "Can you not do anything about this?"

I told him that I had already consulted a wise woman, who had advised that it was too dangerous.

There was no joy in his face. He was frowning, a deep scowl on his forehead. Finally he spoke in a strained voice. "This is sudden. I need time to think it over. In the meantime, don't be in a worry."

Then, my mind still reeling from his words, he overwhelmed me once more with his desire. When he rose up I sought reassurance in his eyes, but he had already turned from me.

Only later did it occur to me that he had not accounted for his long absence. He had recounted that he had previously known maids who worked in his family's fields. Now that he alone was in charge of the property in Ramathayim, all those maids would be at his disposal. Had he found one he particularly favored? Was she the reason he had tossed me out of his mind? As the days crept by, I was tormented over what I should do if it was so, and if Elkanah never came back to see me.

I thought of confessing my perfidy to my father and throwing myself on his mercy. Once, when I caught his eyes dwelling on me kindly, I almost blurted out the secret I kept tightly locked in my womb.

My father was strict in his observance of the law of Torah, which flatly condemned what I had done. I had flagrantly transgressed that which he cherished. But he loved me as no one else did, and had taught me that our God was a God of mercy. So perhaps he himself would be as forgiving as the Lord and take pity on me.

I could not imagine how he could help me, but he knew much that I did not. Perhaps he would be able to guide my steps.

All of this was darting through my mind as I saw Hagith skipping uphill toward me.

"Pninah," she shouted, panting from the effort, "go home quickly. You are wanted."

"Who wants me?"

Still breathless, she said, "Our father has sent me to fetch you. Elkanah and his father Yeroham have come to call. I'll take care of the sheep. Just go."

As I began walking downhill, Hagith came running after me and kissed my cheek and whispered, "You have been in a bad way, but now all will be well."

I was not so sure, for I was assailed by a new doubt. Once again I remembered Elkanah's words of a few days earlier. These had not been words of love, and their memory made the nausea well up in me. I was violently sick in the thick of a bush. Then I felt calm in my belly, but not calm in my heart.

If he preferred another girl and would marry me only because he did not want to have my death on his conscience, our life together would be nothing but constant torture.

Yet now they would all be sitting there together, so how could I find out? As I entered our backyard, I decided what I must do.

A table and some chairs stood against the back wall of our house. Elkanah and his father, Yeroham, clad in their festive garments, sat with their backs to the wall, opposite my own father and Bathel. The table was laden with sweet cakes and jars of grape juice.

I approached and bowed. Yeroham, who was the image of Elkanah, smiled benignly. And Elkanah looked at me gravely out of his beloved dark eyes.

After I sat, my father cleared his throat impressively and embarked with unnecessary pomp on the speech he had prepared: "My daughter, Elkanah's esteemed father has come to request that you become his son's wife. I thought that I could do no better than respond in the words: 'Let us call the girl and ask her.' So now we would like to hear your response."

I felt confused, for I had never received so much attention from so many people before. But I had already decided what I must do. I gathered my courage and spoke: "My father, I beg for your indulgence, for I would like to talk with Elkanah the son of Yeroham alone for a short while, before I give his honored father my reply."

Elkanah arose, and we went to sit at the boundary of the backyard. Conscious of our parents' eyes upon us, I sat modestly. My legs were bent sideways, covered by my dress as far as it went, my feet tucked demurely underneath me, and my hands folded primly on my lap.

"Sir," I said, "a few days ago you asked if I could rid myself of the infant in my belly. Yet today you have come to take me to be your wife. What has led you to change your mind?"

I was pleasantly surprised, as he retorted: "You have not heeded my advice, I hope."

I shook my head from side to side, and he seemed relieved.

"I said that because I was stunned. I had not previously considered becoming a father. But after further reflection I decided that I would like it very much."

I still had some concern. "I know that there are more beautiful girls than me in these parts, and you are a man of wealth and good looks. You could find a wife who would please you better than I could."

He laughed his heart-melting laugh. "I have gloried in the knowledge of you. You please me very much, Pninah."

"Perhaps there is even a maid who pleases you more than I do," I persisted, hinting at my suspicion.

"You please me more than any maid," he replied evasively.

I looked at him intensely, willing him to say the words he had left unsaid, to voice his love for me. But he did not.

So I prompted: "Yet you don't say that you love me."

"Would I want you for my wife if I did not love you?"

I had hoped for a more ardent declaration of his love, the kind the lover of my imagination would have voiced. Still, I was content. I sighed, and tears of thankful relief gathered in my eyes. I chased them back inside me and said, "I, too, love you very much."

He regarded me boldly. "I have had no doubt of this. You have shown it very clearly, up on the hill."

Elkanah helped me to my feet, opened a pouch he had been carrying, removed a golden bracelet from it and clasped it on my wrist. Then he put his arm around my waist, and together we approached our parents, who welcomed us with blessings and kisses. Afterward, Yeroham paid my father the bride price for me, and we were betrothed.

That evening I stepped out into the stillness of the night. Looking at the misty outline of the hills with mist of my own in my eyes, I blessed the Lord for leading me out of the valley of the shadow of death.

My cup was flowing over. I foresaw that Elkanah and I would always be close to each other in our bodies and our souls. We would live to see our children and then our children's children around us. Even when we grew old we would still love each other as we did now, and only death would pry us apart.

The Book of Hannah

Lately Pninah had changed from a girl who was floundering helplessly into a confident young woman whose life was set out clearly before her. I knew her well enough to realize that this was not merely because she was no longer in danger of bringing disgrace to her family, but because she loved very deeply the man she was to marry. Perhaps from her newly gained knowledge of love, she would be able to advise me.

I went to her house and found her crouching on the floor in her room, assembling the sheets and pots and bowls she planned to bring with her to her husband's house. When she saw me she abandoned her task, and after she offered me refreshment we stepped out for a stroll along the path that wound its way through the village.

Little houses lined both its sides. Sitting in front of them, old men and women basked in the last rays of the setting sun, placidly watching half-naked children, their little bare feet caked with brown earth, playing noisily. Mothers with babies on their hips stood in doorways, calling their children in to be fed, scolding the ones who tarried. Men, returning from the fields, walking slowly, weary from the day's toil, called out greetings to wives and children and neighbors.

Turning away from this familiar scene, I inquired of Pninah, "Tell me—when you met Elkanah did you know immediately that he was the man for you?"

"I have long harbored an image of a lover in my mind," she replied, "a handsome young scribe and scholar who resembles my father. Elkanah is nothing like that image. But when he kissed me, I instantly forgot the creation of my fertile imagination. I felt a burning inside me, and knew without a shred of a doubt that only by being close to him could I find peace in my body and in my restless soul."

Guessing the purpose of my question, she inquired how I fared with my own admirer. I had to admit that I was not sure, and that he had never kissed me.

She reflected on this for a while, and finally gave me her advice. "Hannah, I know that you will never be as stupid as I was, and let a man make you pregnant before you are his wife. So you will not let Hanoch come to you. But you should let him embrace you and kiss you. Otherwise, how will you know whether you like him well enough to be at his side in bed for the rest of your life? If you marry him, you will be the greatest lady in all the surrounding areas. But even a great lady lies with her husband, and if you cannot stand having his arms around you, how will you be able to bear it?"

I later turned this advice over in my mind in the solitude of my room, and thought it sensible. So I told my mother that the next time Hanoch came, I would go for a walk with him. When she insisted that the maid must accompany us, I replied: "My revered mother, out of the depth of your knowledge of me you must surely trust me not to do what is wrong in the eyes of the Lord."

We argued over this for a while, and finally I made it plain to her that if I had no chance to be alone with my suitor, I would never be able to make up my mind about him. In the end, she gave in.

Soon Hanoch arrived, and we did as I had planned. I guided him to a path that led up the slope of the hill. Once we had reached a secluded spot, between a massive rock and a dense bush, I halted expectantly.

He could tell that I wanted him to kiss me, but hesitated. Apparently he deemed it improper to do so, as we were not yet betrothed; but I would not budge. He realized that he would not get me to move from the spot unless he bestowed a kiss on me, and finally he did. Apart from touching my lips with his he also thrust his tongue into my mouth, deeper and deeper, as if he were bent on digging a well in it.

Once he had his intrusive tongue back in his own mouth, he declared, "I love you, Hannah, and wish to make you my wife. Let us not delay and set the day for our wedding soon."

I gave no answer.

His kiss had held no attraction for me. It had even been distasteful. I'd had an overpowering urge to pull away from him, to have my mouth out of the reach of his, and I had no wish to have his kiss repeated. Certainly I felt no burning in my body or in my soul. I realized how narrowly I had escaped the abhorrent fate of having to endure his embraces all the days of my life.

And in my heart I blessed Pninah for her advice.

The next afternoon I sat at our front room window, immersed in thought, when Hanoch arrived. By that time I had resolved that this man, whose embrace had been so repulsive to me, could not be the man ordained for me. I was about to apprise Hanoch of my decision not to become his wife, when he forestalled my words with his own.

"My father invites you, together with your father and mother, to visit his house," he announced, "so that we may all be acquainted with each other."

I was on the verge of declining, for there was in truth no need for us to be acquainted. But just then my father came in, followed by my mother, and they both pounced on the invitation as if it were rich war loot from an enemy king's castle.

I began to feel uneasy, as if a trap had been laid for me, and my parents had been joined with Hanoch in laying it. So their eagerness bolstered up my resolution to refuse.

But Hanoch said, "The food has been prepared, the table has been set, and my father and mother are waiting. They would feel deeply insulted if you failed to honor them with your visit."

My father supported my suitor by calling me aside and whispering that he could see no harm in a simple visit during which I would not be coerced into anything. I gave in.

As soon as we entered Hanoch's father's yard in Ramathayim on our donkeys, I realized to my chagrin that my suspicion had been well founded: I had been trapped. For what met my eyes was not one set table but five, at which sat what was apparently Hanoch's entire—and sizable—family. Of course I could not draw back, and we sat down with them.

Once pleasantries had been exchanged, and the enormous meal of spiced roasted meat, and fowl, and fish from the Great Sea and sweet wine had been consumed, Hanoch arose. There was a ripple of attention at the tables, as he extracted from his belt a pouch, from which he removed a necklace of flawless pearls, each more shimmering in its whiteness than its neighbor.

He was about to clasp it to my neck, and I was overcome with dread. It would be unthinkable for me to shame Hanoch by rejecting his gift in plain sight of his relatives. Yet if I did not do so, I had no doubt that the scroll in which he had set out the bride price he would pay for me would be handed to my father at greater speed than the drop of an apple from a tree. Then he would recite the words, "you are betrothed to me forever," and I would be irrevocably tied to him.

I was in a panic, unable to think of an appropriate manner to extricate myself from my entanglement without giving offense, yet without forfeiting my life. But in that flicker of an instant, much to my own surprise, I found a way out.

I took the only course open to me: I fainted. Or feigned it, slumping limply to the ground, which was enough to cause a big uproar in which the necklace was forgotten.

I was transported to a room to lie down on a bed. When Hanoch came in to inquire about my health, I spoke to him in a low voice in case we were overheard, blaming him bitterly for having failed to consult me before bringing forth his necklace, thereby bringing embarrassment down on both our heads.

"Since yesterday you rejected neither my kiss nor my offer to become my wife," retorted Hanoch. "I had no reason to believe that both were anything but welcome to you."

My low voice dropping to a whisper, I told him, gently yet firmly, "I will not take your necklace, because I cannot become your wife."

Hanoch's face fell but he retorted with grim determination, "I am not a man who bows to defeat. I will continue to try to convince you."

I insisted that it would be useless.

Just then my mother came in; when she heard my words, she shed silent tears.

Having no doubt that she and my father had conspired with Hanoch to visit this shame on me and on him as well, I was as deeply disappointed in them as they were in me. Yet on the way home, my father swore that he and my mother had had no inkling of what Hanoch intended to do. Although he admitted that when the invitation came it was to their liking, he stressed that (as he had promised) I had not been coerced. In any event I could not entirely blame him or my mother, for Hanoch was the man all parents of unwed daughters in our parts longed to have for their son-in-law.

Once we were home and I had recuperated from my unpalatable experience, I told my mother, "Have no fear, for the man I am waiting for will surely appear."

Though I eased my mother's heart, there was no ease in mine. I nurtured a fear of my own, one which I did not disclose to her. A fear so horrendous, I did not have the courage to admit it even to myself.

After Pninah was betrothed, her father decided that our lessons with him should come to an end. We had studied with him for ten years, and we were now as well versed in the Torah as anyone he had ever taught.

As was the custom, he sent us to see the most highly regarded scholar and scribe in our tribe. This was Joash, the son of Nimrod, who also lived in Ramathayim. This white-bearded and awe-inspiring scribe invited us into his huge scroll room. He made us read for him aloud, and instructed us to copy and interpret difficult passages from the Torah. Deeming our knowledge to be sufficient, he placed the palms of his hands on our heads and, in front of two witnesses, proclaimed us to be accomplished scholars and scribes.

I began to teach children reading and writing as well as the stories and laws of the Torah. Pninah's father now spent much of his time with the elders at the village gates, and as he could no longer teach the children he had taught before, he sent them to me instead. I taught two groups of five boys; then a mother came and requested that I teach her two little daughters.

Not many women were well versed in reading and writing, but it was not unheard of. Deborah, the wife of Lapidoth, who had been a famous judge and prophetess some years before, had been highly revered by both men and women. And although apart from me and Pninah I did not know of any women scribes, my father told me that in his youth he had known two, who had copied holy Torah scrolls with their own hands.

There were a few mothers who thought that if a woman could do great deeds in Israel as Deborah had done, there was no reason why their daughters—if they learned to read and write—should not be destined for great deeds as well.

So I agreed to teach the girls. Knowledge of my teaching both boys and girls soon spread, and three more mothers brought their little daughters to me. Thus I taught a group of girls; and thereafter I always taught girls as well as boys.

At first the children's fathers were apprehensive. Since they had never met a woman scribe before, they doubted that a woman could do a man's work. But when they saw that the children learned their lessons, their doubts were dispelled. Not so mine.

My doubts did not concern my teaching, in which I found joy, but the man who would share this joy, and my life's other joys and sorrows with me.

Slowly the assurance I had always harbored began to wane, and I began to face a new overwhelming fear. I had no doubt that the man who was for me existed and that he would appear. But what if by that time he already loved another woman?

I was certain that even if this were so, I could lure him and make him love me, instead. Still, if my life was destined to have a unique purpose, I had to be worthy of it. If I coveted a man who belonged to another, this would be in breach of one of the Ten Commandments. If I enticed him away from her, causing her misery, would not the Lord punish me by depriving me of the very destiny for the sake of which I was so keen to meet this man?

My impatience to encounter the one I was waiting for grew from day to day, and so did my trepidation. And every day that passed without his turning up on my doorstep became yet another disappointment to me.

The Book of Pninah

My memories of my wedding celebration are disjointed, like those of a dream. I remember the colorful bridal dress and the many jewels that were lent to me; I recall my kinswomen dressing me and painting my face. I felt as if I were clad not in a dress, but in a cloud of happiness; as if I were borne to my wedding not in a litter, but on the wings of my love.

I retain the memory of Elkanah standing in the huge front yard of his house in Ramathayim, helping me to alight. Of his fingers lifting the heavy, gold-threaded veil from my face, then gently replacing it. Of the embroidered canopy under which we stood, and the priest who faced us. Of Elkanah's placing the ring on my finger, and softly kissing my lips to seal the ceremony that made me his wife. Of his whispering into my ear that the main ceremony was still to come.

Then came the feast, of which I could not partake due to my excitement, and then the singing and dancing.

When the guests prepared to leave, Elkanah led me into the bridal chamber, which was to be my bedroom. It was dark, and he lit an oil lamp that stood atop a table. In its dim light I saw that the room was sparsely furnished. It contained only a bed flanked by empty shelves, and an old table surrounded by some odd chairs. The pale walls were bare, but I resolved to change all this and make the room habitable.

Looking out of the window, I saw that although by now the guests had left, Elkanah's father and mother, and my own father and Bathel were still there. I thought this was odd and asked Elkanah why they had not departed.

He laughed. "Pninah my bride, I have bad tidings for you. I will now have to cut your finger with a knife."

"Cut my finger?" I repeated in disbelief. "Why?" I balled my hands into fists and hid them behind my back.

"Because we need some blood on that sheet. It is what our esteemed fathers and mothers are waiting for."

"Then we must cut *your* finger, since it's your fault that my blood won't be on that sheet tonight," I said, jokingly.

"Nevertheless it's your finger that we will have to cut. I am the one who must carry the sheet out to them, and they would be surprised if I did so with a bleeding finger."

He took up a small knife that had been resting on a shelf. We sat down on the bed, and I shut my eyes. He did not have the courage to cut me forcefully enough, and I had to take the knife from his hand and cut my own finger.

When enough blood had trickled onto the bedclothes, Elkanah replaced it with a clean one. Then he went out carrying the bloodied sheet on his arms. Just as I began to unclasp my jewels, I heard cheers from the yard and knew that all was well.

After Elkanah returned, we lay in bed quietly, inhaling the air thick with the summery scent of trees from the yard, the moonlight spilling in through the window over our nude bodies. When we heard the sound of donkeys' hoofbeats trotting out of the yard, we turned to each other.

It had been some weeks since we had been together, and we knew each other with the crazed impatience bred by our long waiting. That night I wept out of sheer pleasure.

For the next week our life revolved around the act of love. In the morning my husband went out into the fields. But he came home as early as he could. As soon as he had washed the sweat off his flesh, we withdrew into my room. After the evening meal we reveled in each other once more. And after we slept for a while we woke up and came together again.

Now that we were husband and wife there was an unrestrained closeness in our togetherness. Our hands and mouths roamed freely, studying each other's bodies, each other's wants, learning the little gestures that led us to even higher levels of arousal and delight. Night after night, the silvery moon shone its countenance upon us, blessing the joining of our bodies. More and more we melted into each other and became one flesh. Yet it was more than the pleasure of the flesh. It was the bliss of love—of knowing that through it, we were building our house in Israel.

Some evenings, we sat in the yard, Elkanah propped against the trunk of a tree, my back leaning against his knees. And he proclaimed that this was yet another celebration of our togetherness, in which the sky was our canopy, the moon a priest officiating at our ceremony, and the stars our invited guests. Later, as I lay under the tree, nestled in Elkanah's arms, the rush of the wind in the leaves lulled us into a peaceful sleep. And when we awoke in the morning we stretched ourselves contentedly, and Elkanah kissed my hair, still damp with the dew of the night. And those were the days and nights of our greatest happiness together.

A happiness soon to be sacrificed on the altar of another love.

Before long my belly began to swell. Elkanah no longer came to me each night, and when he did, he was as eager to stroke my belly as he was to perform the act of love. I did not mind, because as my belly expanded, my need for him shrank and gradually melted away.

I now found contentment in my new home. Elkanah's house was large. In truth, it was more than just one house: It contained three whitewashed four-room houses, adjacent to each other. And its front yard boasted fig trees and olive trees and almond trees, whose branches would burst into white blossoms in the winter.

The front room was oblong and spacious, with a large table in its center, to accommodate what we hoped would be the growing number of our children. Also, it had something that was to be found only in the homes of the wealthy: a hearth, built on a brick platform. In the my mind's eye I saw myself and Elkanah sitting in each other's embrace in front of it in the winter, when a fire would be lit to ward off the chill.

In my father's home the food was cooked in a roofed courtyard. Here there was a cooking room set aside for these tasks. In my father's house the woman who gave birth to me arranged everything to suit her wishes. Now, I had a home of my own to do with as I saw fit.

Since Elkanah was well off, we had maids to draw water from the well, and to cook our stews on the cooking stones and grind flour and knead the dough and bake the bread, and do the cleaning and laundering. My task was that of supervising them, ensuring that the stews were well-seasoned to please Elkanah's choosy palate, and that the house was scrubbed clean.

This left me some free time so I, like Hannah, took on the task of teaching children. I enjoyed it—and the silver that flowed into our coffers from the wealthy parents who paid the large fees that I demanded. Elkanah had a wooden box made up for the silver, and he was pleased to see it filling up.

I also relished spending the sabbath with Elkanah. On this day I did not teach and he did not go out into the fields, nor did his workers. Clad in festive garments, we would head for the Ramathayim town square to chat with our friends and listen to the Torah being read.

The weeks passed pleasantly. But as they went by, I noticed a change in Elkanah. He now formed the habit of carrying a set of clean clothing with him to the fields. I asked him about this, and he retorted with asperity that the work made him sweaty, and he liked to wash and don new garments before he came home.

Also, he began coming home later. I asked him about that, too, and he retorted testily that he had something important to attend to. He did not say what it was, but when I noticed his irritation, I decided not to pester him with further questions.

I suspected that he was engaging in some illicit activities with one of his field maids. Once I had visited him there, bearing a basket of sweet red grapes from our vineyard. The workmen had already plowed the fields, and the maids were sowing wheat and barley in row after row of newly tilled earth, under Elkanah's supervision. As they worked, the maids would raise their eyes from their labor and look at him, eager for his approval. I saw how young and pretty they were, and how the shapes of their bodies were revealed to Elkanah's gaze in the course of their work.

The threshing floor, which had a secluded shed for the storing of ploughshares tucked away at its corner, stood close by. A few doves busily picked at forgotten kernels of grain that the threshers had left behind. These doves might well be privy to dark secrets, but they did not share any with me.

Could it be that when the workday was finished, Elkanah utilized the shed for a purpose that had nothing to do with the storing of ploughshares? But why did he take with him a change of garments, if all he needed to do was to take off the ones he had on?

I could make no sense of it.

Elkanah was always home for the evening meal, but he became more and more absent-minded and withdrawn. I talked to him of matters that I thought would appeal to him. Of the prospects for our crop of grains and lentils and olives, and of how our neighbors fared with their farms.

But he rarely responded, sometimes merely grunting in reply. He was as stingy with his words as if each was worth its weight in gold. I pined for them; but he had almost none to give me. We began to while away our evenings in an awkward silence that hung heavily in the air and became more ominous by the day. Yet he occasionally came to me at night, and this kept my fears at bay.

One morning, before he set out for the fields, Elkanah told me that this night he would come home only after the evening meal, as he planned to visit his father and mother. Before that, we had always visited our parents together, and I asked if it would not be proper for me to accompany him. But he replied that this time he needed to confer with them by himself.

This, too, seemed strange, and I began to wonder what he wanted to discuss with his parents. Was it something to do with one of his sisters? Would he tell me about it when he came home?

I sat up late, waiting for him. Listening for his familiar footfalls. Looking out of the front room window, trying to discern his tall figure in front of me. But the stillness of the night remained undisturbed. While I sat there I felt a blast of cold air sweep in, chilling me. As I shuttered the windows, the walls of the room, and my loneliness, closed in on me.

In the end, it grew late. I went to my room before Elkanah came home.

The Book of Hannah

The first time my eyes rested on Elkanah was at his and Pninah's wedding. I still recall that evening, the true beginning of my life, in vivid detail.

I knew how desperate Pninah had been before Elkanah had offered to make her his wife, and how happy she was afterward. I was happy for her, and I looked forward to the celebration. Indeed it was all that any bride could hope for.

When I reached Elkanah's house in my mother and father's wake before sunset, I saw that around the edges of the front yard several long tables had been set, while in its center the guests, preening in their finery, were assembled.

Then Pninah arrived, followed by her father and mother, friends and relatives. As she looked at Elkanah, her tear-filled blue-gray eyes were more sparkling than the jewelery that adorned her. And when I saw how tenderly he regarded her, I wept with joy for my friend's happiness.

It all began after the ceremony, as the guests lined up to bless the couple. Previously, I had regarded Elkanah merely as Pninah's bridegroom. Now he stood before me as a man.

My heart gave a thud and I stood before him with my lips parted in stunned admiration. It was some time before I could recall the blessings I was to recite. And even as I was reciting them I looked at him for longer, and he looked at me more appraisingly, than was proper for the occasion.

When I relinquished my place to others, I was still reeling from the encounter. The truly unusual man had made his unusual entrance into my life.

Presently the guests seated themselves around the tables. Elkanah led his bride to the place of honor, and an expectant hush fell on the guests as he stood up to address them:

"Hear me relatives and friends. Those who bless us, I bless. I present to you my bride Pninah. She is like her name: a pearl. She is not only beautiful, but also a woman of valor whose price is far beyond pearls. Together we will build a house of love and peace and friendship in Israel. Be blessed for sharing in our joy."

Men exclaimed at the speech, women shed tears, and they all cheered noisily.

The tables were weighed down with baked meats, round cakes of fine wheat flour, figs dunked in delicate rare spices, and wines and strong spirits. While bellies were being filled, singers chanted lewd love songs replete with veiled images of the way of a man with a woman, to nudge the bride and the bridegroom into what was supposed to be their first night of love. The guests smirked and winked at each other indulgently, though some young girls hid their faces in their hands in shame.

This prompted the bride and bridegroom to look into each other's eyes meaningfully. But occasionally Elkanah's eyes strayed in my direction, and I could feel his gaze on me.

Then Pninah brought Elkanah around and presented my parents and myself, honoring us by announcing that we were as a second family to her. As the couple moved on, Elkanah's arm brushed mine. He regarded me with a piercing glance, which I returned.

Then the dancing began. We danced to the sound of lyres, flutes and drums. There was a moment when I felt Elkanah's arm encircling my waist. And as we resumed our seats still breathless from the dance, I knew that this was not the last time that Elkanah's arm would rest there. He had touched me but twice, and I resolved that no other man ever would. He alone would be the lover who would enter my locked garden and eat from its fruit.

When the feast was over, and the bride and bridegroom had withdrawn to the bridal chamber, I sat with my father and mother at the edge of the yard waiting for Elkanah's parents and Pninah's parents, who had not as yet relinquished their seats at the table, for we were to ride back to Shaar Efraim together.

Presently Elkanah emerged from his seclusion with Pninah,

proudly bearing on his arms a spread-out, bloodied sheet, which both pairs of parents duly welcomed with cheers. I had no knowledge of how the false stains on the sheet had been produced, but in my heart I wondered what the fathers and mothers would say when their grandchild came into the world a mere seven months after they had seen the blood with their own eyes.

On the way home, Elkanah's image, and the looks we had exchanged, rose before my eyes again. I became aware that I had gleaned a glimpse of heaven. But this was merely the beginning. Before long, heaven would open its gates to me, and I would enter it and dwell there forever.

For the next few weeks nothing was heard of the new husband and wife, but I was not perturbed. I was certain that soon Elkanah would come to claim me for his wife.

One day Pninah came to visit. We sat in my parents' front room drinking milk and honey, and words came bubbling out of her mouth—about her new home, her teaching, and the preparations for the arrival of her child.

I was quiet. She noticed my silence, and thought it had to do with Hanoch, for she inquired about him. I told her that I had refused to be his wife, and that her advice had been crucial in my decision. She looked grave, and asked if I had anyone else in view. I blushed, but made no reply.

When the sun was sliding toward the crest of the hills, Elkanah came to collect Pninah. As I placed bowls of dates and almonds on the table, he regarded me with a smile, wooing me with his eyes. I looked into his eyes steadily, until I saw the smile in them fading. Thus I knew that he understood my message, as I understood his.

A week later, sometime before sunset, he arrived by himself, as I had known he would. I was not surprised, but my mother was. He invited me to go for a walk with him, and my mother insisted that the maid accompany us.

Before we could leave the house, though, something untoward happened. The door to the front room opened and Hanoch stood on the threshold.

Since the day I had refused to become his wife, he had visited me several times, each time renewing his offer, each time meeting with a rebuff. I had believed that he would eventually resign himself to the rejection. It now seemed that he had more perseverance than that with which I had credited him.

For a while, my two suitors stood facing each other. The one outstandingly tall and handsome, slim and nobly refined. The other half a head shorter yet still tall, broad-shouldered and muscular, his entire being oozing muscular power. The first leaving my heart as icy cold as the frost that covers the ground on the mountains during the long winter nights. The other causing it to flutter like a bird straining to burst forth from its cage.

They regarded each other with such fury in their eyes that they seemed like two dogs ready to pounce on each other.

Then Hanoch spoke in a scathing tone. "Is your wife Pninah, who is Hannah's friend, accompanying you on this visit?"

Elkanah made no reply.

"Having seen her from afar recently and beheld the size of her belly, I know her pregnancy to have begun before your wedding. Are her days close to give birth?"

Elkanah clenched his hands into fists. "Your mouth spews forth filth like a troubled sea. Unless you cease, the might of my arm will soon cause you to be sprawling on the floor."

This gave Hanoch pause. But then he took heart again. "I did not intend to cast an insult at your wife but merely to warn Hannah, a gracious lady who deserves a better fate than to join Pninah in misery." He aimed his gaze at me and added, "With me she will not be dishonored before she becomes my wife. And afterward she will remain the only one. I will never take, nor will I ever love, another."

"We were about to go out for a stroll," said Elkanah coolly. "Is the maid ready yet to accompany us?"

I strode forward behind Elkanah, who was purposefully heading for the doorway that Hanoch was blocking.

My mother, who had been watching all this from the far corner of the room, now came forward and spoke gently. "Hannah, my daughter, it would be unthinkable for you to leave. The father of our people, Abraham, was renowned in the land for the hospitality he extended to anyone who came to the shelter of his abode. You must follow his example and welcome both your honored guests to our home. Pray, make them sit down in the shade of our fig tree, and bring them grape juice to drink."

These words brought both of my suitors to their senses, and me as well. Before long my father joined us. Having exchanged a glance with my mother, he sat down with both men and interpreted for them at great length the passage from the Torah in which Abraham's hospitality toward strangers was depicted, until they began yawning under their breath. Then, one after the other, they left.

On the following day I was determined to avoid a repetition of yesterday's confrontation. Knowing that Hanoch would visit me again, I prepared to flee the house well before the sun approached the hills. My mother, whose eyes were so alert that hardly anything escaped them, thrust the maid upon me, but did not prevent my flight.

I set out to intercept Elkanah by climbing up the hill behind our house that overlooked the path by which I anticipated that he would arrive. When he approached I skipped down the hill, with the maid trotting behind me, to meet him.

To my chagrin, I saw Hanoch arriving by another path. I turned from him to face Elkanah, but he caught up with me and halted me by touching my shoulder, and said in a trembling voice: "Hannah, you have scorned the heart and riches I have laid at your feet. You have done so in favor of a man who has an established household, to which you will form but a small addition. You will repent your foolishness all the days of your life."

I had no reply to those words, but Elkanah did. "Unless you leave us alone this instant, you will repent your foolishness for many days of *your* life."

Since Elkanah's muscles were visibly more powerful than Hanoch's, I could not blame him for turning on his heels and leaving as fast as his feet would carry him.

As I began climbing the next hill with Elkanah, he asked in a low voice how we were to rid ourselves of the maid. I replied that we were not to be rid of her at all. But I did request that she remain at a distance, so that we could talk.

I asked about Pninah's health, and he assured me that she was well. Next I inquired after his parents' health, and he responded that they, too, were well.

For a while he was at a loss, and then he said: "Hannah, I will not speak to you of things of no importance. Instead I will say what I came to say—that you are the most beautiful woman I have ever beheld, and that your beauty is beyond this world. It is not merely in your face and in your body, but also in your mind and in your soul. I came to tell you that I love you and want you, and that, one way or another, I will have you."

At these words, a glow of warmth suffused me. I asked him what he meant by one way or another, and he answered that one way was to send the maid home and climb farther up the hill, and the other was for me to become his wife. He intimated that there was also a third way, which was a combination of the two.

I laughed at his words, but told him that all three courses posed grave difficulties, the chief of which was Pninah and my friendship with her. We talked of this for a while, and then I declared that it was time to go home.

Thereafter, Hanoch no longer treaded the path to our house, but Elkanah came every day after work. Since the maid was always in view, we could only talk. Of what we had done yesterday, of what we planned to accomplish tomorrow, of our past years, of the years to come.

Elkanah told me that his wish was to coax his land to yield its strength to him, to extract large crops from the fullness of the earth. He would sell part of the harvest to buy more land, to grow even larger crops, to buy even more land.

He required all of this land because he wanted to sire multitudes of children, and they would all need sustenance. When they grew, the sons would need properties of their own and bride prices for their wives, and the daughters would need other assistance to smooth over their moves into their husbands' homes. He wanted to be able to give them all they needed and, in return, they would beget children's children for him.

I said that I, too, wanted to have many children. But I also had another dream. I wanted to write a tale and a poem that the entire people of Israel would read or hear about. Something that would be passed down from generation to generation, to all the generations to come.

I told him that lately I had begun writing stories about people I knew, and poems in praise of the Lord. I had a way with words. I could spin yarns and weave tales as other women wove cloth. They delighted the eye of the reader and pleased the ear of the listener. And as the heavens and the earth spoke the glory of the Lord so, in their small way, did my poems. I read some of these stories and poems to Elkanah, and he enjoyed listening to them. For, as he said, my writings were the gateway to my soul.

I said that what I dreamt of writing one day would be much different from what I had written before. It would concern something of great importance to our entire people, of which I alone would be aware.

Elkanah was incredulous, though he was also impressed with my vision. He told me that the beauty of my face and of my body could not equal the beauty of my soul. He added: "Hannah, you are the great love of my life. I want to be close to you in mind and spirit. I want to be not only your lover, but also your friend."

"I have never thought otherwise," I replied.

The next day, as we wound our way through the hills, he came back to the same topic. "Hannah, I love everything about you. You are exalted above any woman I have ever met."

"And you are above any man. I will never look at anyone else."

"I have never thought otherwise."

On one of our strolls, Elkanah recounted a dream he had the night before. "In my dream, I was clasping a golden necklace studded with six precious stones around your neck. Then I woke up and felt happier than I had ever felt before."

"We would need Joseph," I said, "the forefather of our tribe, the great dreamer and interpreter of dreams, to explain this to us."

"Can you picture in your mind what Joseph would have seen in the dream?" he asked.

With certainty, I declared, "My husband to be, when you clasp the necklace around my neck, this will tie me to you. And after I am yours, you will give me six precious presents: They will be our children."

"Only six?" he retorted in mock disappointment, "I will try to dream better than that tonight."

Thus we marveled over Elkanah's dream and counted it as a blessing from the Lord. Around it we spun more dreams, in which we endowed each one of our as yet unborn sons and daughters with fine attributes, and envisioned what each of them would look like.

Elkanah also revealed a family secret to me. He and his brother had in their possession scrolls that traced their family's origins all the way back to Efraim. Hence he was directly descended from Efraim's father Joseph the dreamer, who had dreamed himself into a pit, from which other people's dreams had retrieved him.

I was elated. I told him that my father, too, could trace our family's origins to Efraim. Our children would be among the very few of whom it would be known with certainty that they were descended from the father of our tribe, on both their father's and their mother's sides.

I explained that I had long known that my life would have a special purpose, and that it would be tied to the man I married. It now appeared that this mission, and the tale I would write, would be connected to our children and their very unusual, noble descent.

With a bemused expression on his beloved face, Elkanah said, "It is not possible to divine what will happen to us in the years to come."

But we both knew that his dream, which had shown us those years ahead, had brought us even closer together than we had been before.

As the days went by and Elkanah continued to visit me every day, my mother became anxious. She was afraid that he wished to take me for his second wife.

When I did not offer words that assuaged her fears, she made me privy to more of her wisdom: "Hannah, it would be foolish of you to become his second wife. If you do, you will have a rival in your home. You will have to share your husband and house with her, and as she is the first wife, you will have to defer to her wishes and abide by her whims. Would it not be a hundred times better for you to take the handsome and wealthy man who loves only you? You would be the most revered lady in the area and have scores of servants to do your bidding. You would be clad in finery and decked in precious jewels. And you would have a husband who adores you, who would be yours alone."

But my mother's entreaties could not sway me from my chosen path. I agreed with every word she said, but added: "Still, I can no longer conceal from you that Elkanah is the man I have been waiting for."

My mother was taken aback, and asked me when I had realized this. I admitted that it had been at the moment at which I had blessed him and Pninah for becoming husband and wife.

And for the second time in the last few months, my mother burst into tears.

The Book of Pninah

O n the evening after Elkanah had visited his parents, a heavy rain lashed at the ground. During the meal Elkanah told me nothing of what he had talked about with his mother and father, and I was reluctant to ask.

Later we sat near the window in the front room, looking out at the torrents of rain that offered the blessing of abundant crops from our fields. Behind us the fire in the hearth was burning. The heat and the soft glow of the flickering flames made the room warm and cozy, the perfect backdrop for our love.

I touched Elkanah's arm gently, letting my fingers convey my love for him. I told him how pleasant it was to be sitting close to each other, our love as forceful as the water battering the yard before our eyes.

He nodded his assent, but added, "Soon we will have someone else here with us."

I smiled softly and looked down, my hands stroking my swollen belly, where I felt the flutter of life.

Elkanah followed my gaze, then swung his chair around to face me, rested his arm on the table at his side, and drew a sharp intake of breath before he spoke. "Yes, there will be the child. But there will be someone else as well."

I stiffened in anticipation of his next words.

"Pninah, I am taking a second wife."

I was dizzy with shock. The rain had stopped and all was still. The fire had dwindled and now lit only the middle of the room, leaving its corners in a cold darkness that chilled me to the bone. I sat rigid, my eyes fixed unseeingly on the wall behind Elkanah.

It took some time before I could collect enough strength to

speak. "A second wife?" I finally repeated in horrified disbelief. "Why, sir? Have I not been a good wife to you?"

"You are a good wife."

"Then why?" I asked again. "If I no longer please you it is because of my pregnancy. I assure you that after the child is born, we will revel in each other again as we did before."

"I know this. I have reached incredible heights of pleasure with you, and so it will be in the future."

"Then why?" I pleaded, "Do you no longer love me?"

"Hear me, Pninah," he replied. "You are still young and innocent, and you don't yet understand matters as they are. There is a difference between a man and a woman. A woman will love only one man all her life. A man can love more than one woman."

"How do you know this?" I asked in doubt.

"See how many men in Ramathayim have taken second wives."

"But most are content with one wife," I said in a low voice.

He shrugged.

"And how do you know that a woman loves only one man?" I queried, in rising agitation.

"I have never heard otherwise," he responded with deep conviction.

"By our laws a woman is not allowed to marry two men. But the heart is reckless and knows no laws. If a woman loved and knew a man who was not her husband, do you think that she would tell you of it?"

"Such would be a deviant woman, her deeds punishable by death," he said scornfully. "If there were such women in our midst, we would have heard of them. It need not concern us. I know that you will never love another man, and that is sufficient for me."

In my anger I blurted out words that, though I did not know it yet, foreshadowed that which was to be my future. "Your loving another woman might drive me to it."

At this his own anger flared up and turned into a massive rage. He slammed his fist down on the table. Drops of sweat sprang out on his forehead and his eyes narrowed threateningly. "Pninah, beware of what you are saying. I will not put up with such insolent words from you. A woman is ruled by her husband and must submit to him. At all times. In everything."

He waited for me to acquiesce to his words, but as I did not react, his fury was funneled again. "You will resign yourself to what I am doing with good grace and without demur," he fairly shouted at me.

I recoiled, and fearing that I had pushed him too far, I muttered placatingly, "I will not speak of this to you again, sir. And now, who is this woman whom you are taking for your second wife?"

He calmed down, hesitated, then answered. "It is someone close to you."

My body began rocking back and forth like a leaf battered by a storm. "Is it Hagith?"

He laughed. "No, of course it's not Hagith. It is Hannah."

Nausea rose up in me. "I cannot believe it," I flung at him. "Hannah is my friend. She would never do this to me."

"Your friendship ought to make you welcome her. You will have much to say to each other, and you will get on well together."

I rose from my chair and stood behind it, gripping the back tightly until the knuckles of my hands turned white from the strain. "You're crazy," I whispered almost inaudibly, but I could tell from the flicker of his eyelids that he had heard me.

For a moment I glared at him, my eyes flashing, then I stormed from the room. The nausea welled up into my mouth. I vomited, then ran to my room and locked the door and shuttered the window.

I did not light the lamp. I did not take off my dress. I just threw myself down on the bed and closed my eyes.

The air in the room was stifling, but I hardly noticed it. I was sucked into utter emptiness.

On this night my girlhood dream of love and happiness died and, though I continued breathing, I died with it. There was only a mournful melody that sounded in the distance, floating through the night, lamenting my loss.

The Book of Hannah

Ten days after my mother's outburst of tears, as I was climbing the hill with Elkanah, I noticed that the maid who always accompanied us had disappeared. I wondered aloud what could have happened to her, and he murmured, "Silver pieces have a wondrous quality: They make people lose their way, and stray from the path of righteousness."

Then he kissed me long and lovingly, and said with a husky voice that betrayed his excitement: "Hannah, my love, you cannot imagine how much I have been waiting for this moment. I will make you mine now, and we will obtain God's blessing later."

Unlike Hanoch's kiss, Elkanah's was like wine on my lips. But when he attempted to lead me to a hidden spot among the bushes, I resisted. "I will not be subjected to Pninah's fate," I told him. "My virginity," I added, "will be taken only on my bridal bed and the blood on my bed-cloth will be genuine."

Holding me with trembling hands he demanded: "When will it be?"

Henceforth Elkanah would be in charge of my life, and I would be ruled by him. "Whenever you wish," I replied.

Elkanah extracted a little pouch from his belt. He removed from it a beautiful golden necklace studded with six fiery precious stones.

He put it around my neck, and announced, "I give you this necklace so that it may bear witness to my love for you. So that all men and women may know that you are tied to me. And in honor of the six children we will beget through our love."

Then he kissed me again, and our love grew wings and soared and proclaimed itself to all the four corners of the world.

* * *

The next few days were given over to drawing our parents to our side and bringing them together to settle the bride price. The meeting, which was our betrothal, turned into a congenial social gathering that went on merrily late into the night.

Then came the difficult task of telling Pninah. Elkanah later told me that he had performed the task as gently as he could, but that she had taken it badly. She had even threatened him with loving another man. Her disrespectful words had made it necessary for him to reprimand her, which was not what he had wanted to do when she was so deeply distressed. After that she had locked herself in her room and refused to speak to him.

He proposed that I talk to her. Knowing her as well as I knew the palm of my own hand, I thought that whatever I might say to her would only make matters worse. But I was loath to reject his request, so I did as he asked me to do.

I came to his house and stood in front of Pninah's room. "Pninah, it is me, Hannah," I called to her through the locked door. "Let me in, I want to talk to you."

There was no reply.

"I know that you are angry, but please listen to me."

No sound came from her room.

"I am your longtime friend, and at least you must hear what I have to say to you."

Silence.

I turned away from her room, and for the first time in my life, I was boiling with rage. But I was not sure whether I was angry with Pninah for refusing to open her door, or at myself for coming to speak to her, or at Elkanah for making me humble myself before her.

I knew that by coveting my friend's husband I had not only sinned but had also inflicted great pain on her. The Torah commands anyone who has sinned unwittingly to atone by making a guilt offering as a sacrifice to the Lord. Had I felt guilty, I would have fulfilled this duty. Yet in my heart I felt no guilt—only compassion for my friend.

My earlier misgivings about coveting the husband of another woman were overshadowed by the conviction that my purpose in life was inextricably linked with Elkanah. In tying him to me, I was merely following my destiny.

At times I wondered whether this notion might not be a figment of my imagination, whether I had not invented it to justify the sin of coveting my friend's husband. But I was certain that Elkanah was the only man for me, that there would never be another. And even for Pninah's sake, I could not give up the great love, the only love of my life.

I did not then foresee the evil that would arise from the misery I had caused Pninah to suffer. Perhaps if I had, I would have felt guilty, or at least ashamed or regretful. But all this was still to come, and I had no inkling of it.

The Book of Pninah

I don't know for how long I lay on my bed. Once again I was in the valley of the shadow of death, but this time it was closed in by high mountains, with no way out.

When the sun rose the next morning, I felt the infant kicking against the walls of my belly and a gnawing hunger. The child was reminding me of its need to be fed. I knew by the angle of the sun that Elkanah had left, so I stepped out into the glaring light of the yard. I headed for the cooking room, where a jar of milk stood on the table. I drank it, then returned to my room.

Before long, an unusual noise broke through my torpor, and I went to see what it was. I found three men at the other side of the house unloading a cart of building materials and immediately beginning their work.

I returned to my room, but soon it was time for one of my lessons. I did not have it in my heart to dismiss the children. I taught my lesson, drank more milk, then went back to my room. There I stayed until the next morning, when it was time to teach again. And so also in the coming days.

Two days later, at dusk, Elkanah tried to enter my room, but it was locked. "Let me in, Pninah, I wish to talk to you."

I did not reply, and he went away.

The next day Hannah came and she, too, demanded to talk to me. I ignored her.

Time passed, and in the solitude of my room, there was little to mark off one day from the next. Binah came and discerned the infant's heartbeats by holding her ear to my belly. She noted how emaciated I was, but did not ask why, because she knew. She warned me that if I did not begin eating again, I would not have the strength to deliver the baby. I was determined to give life to my child, so I began chewing a few pieces of bread and honey each day in my room.

I had grown so accustomed to the racket the builders caused, that when it finally ceased, I felt something was missing. I went to inspect the fruit of their labor. It was a room, huge and full of light. The ceiling was made of Egyptian bricks. Pillars of cedar from the Lebanon interlaced with marble formed the walls. The room was furnished with a large bed, an ornate table and matching chairs, and an elaborate sideboard. Elegant rugs covered the bed and the floor and vividly patterned tapestries decorated the walls. All manner of fine pottery was on every surface.

It was a room fit for a queen.

As I viewed these luxuries, I remembered sadly how bare my room had been, until I had decorated it myself. But I was beyond weeping.

I went into Elkanah's room. Against one of its walls stood a cupboard. It was locked, but I knew where the key was concealed. Inside the cupboard sat the wooden box that had been filled with silver pieces from the fees for my lessons. With fumbling fingers I opened it. The box was empty.

Later in the day, I heard Elkanah rattling my door. "Let me in, Pninah."

I made no reply.

"Then I will speak to you from here. The wedding will take place on the third day of next week. You will attend the celebration, wearing a suitable dress."

The next day the house sprang to life and erupted into bustling activity. Leaves were being raked from the front yard and tables were set up. Traders scurried back and forth, delivering food and spices and wines and strong spirits. The noises and smells penetrated my room. I tried to shut them out, but I could not.

At first I resolved not to attend the wedding. By taking another woman so soon after he had married me, Elkanah was proclaiming to all our relatives and friends, as clearly as if he had shouted the words into their ears, that he had tried me out and had found me wanting. At the wedding, my humiliation would be paraded before our entire tribe. I did not wish to be there to witness it. Nor did I wish to be the object of the guests' looks of thinly masked derision and pity.

Yet it would be much worse not to appear and to be scorned behind my back. Besides, in the eyes of our friends and relatives Elkanah was merely doing what by law and tradition he had the right to do. I must be seen to acquiesce, for doing otherwise would bring even greater dishonor on me.

In the end I decided to brave my degradation.

Before the wedding was due to begin, I slipped on a dark red dress and went into the cooking room. I found a jar of wine the color of my dress, and gulped down two large cups of it. Next to the wine was a jug of strong spirits, and I forced myself to drain two cups of the evil-tasting liquid as well.

I had never indulged in strong spirits before, and my first taste of this liquid left bitter remnants in my mouth and seared its way down my throat. But it warmed me to my toes, imparting a rosy glow to my cheeks and a dizziness to my spirit. I felt as light as a bird floating through the air. I stepped out into the front yard, and when the guests arrived, I looked and acted as cheerful as if it had been my own wedding.

Elkanah, whom I had not seen for a long time, was a different man from that he had been before. Somehow, in a manner I could not comprehend or describe, he had changed from my husband into my master—my imperious, ruthless master.

He looked me over with an insulting sweep of his eyes, as if I were some merchandise he had to decide whether to sell or to keep for his own. My head dropped in shame to be so slighted. He turned back to his guests.

He must have been satisfied with my appearance, though, for when the time came, he honored me by leading me to a seat on his right-hand side. Only then did he turn back to bring his new bride to her place on his left.

I stared at Hannah in her many-colored wedding dress and the profusion of jewels around her neck, arms, and ankles. Her green eyes glowed with a peculiar light, like those of a tigress. I had always admired them for their beauty, but now their glitter was the gleam of evil. I could hardly believe that this girl had been my childhood friend. As speedily as a lizard moves, I averted my eyes from hers, and kept them averted for many years.

Throughout the meal I sat next to Elkanah, my shoulders square, my body rigid. My degradation masked under glazed eyes and a thin smile, as stiff as if it had been carved in stone.

After the singing and dancing, as the guests prepared to disperse, I caught a glimpse of Elkanah wrapping his arm around Hannah's waist with impatient eagerness. Then, accompanied by the guests' cheers, he led her toward the bridal chamber, the room he had built for her.

I stared after them blindly, hard pressed not to scream out my mortification. Feeling the guests' eyes like daggers on my back, the air still swimming with the fuzzy sounds of their cheers, I staggered to my room. I slid into bed and immediately fell into a deep stupor.

When next I tried to open my eyes, I squinted at the sunlight that penetrated the cracks in the shutters. Thus I lay for a while, dazed, my senses still dulled by strong drink.

Vaguely, I perceived a man, as superbly beautiful as an angel, looming over me, his body pressing down on mine, our arms and legs entwined, and I moaned with pleasure and bliss.

Then I woke with a start, bathed in sweat. Sighing wistfully, I realized that I had experienced a glorious dream. It had enfolded me in the twilight between sleep and wakefulness, but it had faded, defeated by the light of the day and the grim reality of my life. The angel-like man was nowhere in sight and in truth it was my husband's body that was pressing down on another, and not on mine.

I rubbed my eyes, which were swollen from months of unshed tears. I saw the valley of the shadow of death stretching out interminably before me for all the weeks and months and years to come.

During the next few weeks I continued to keep to my room, except for the time at which I taught my lessons. I had no words for Hannah, nor she for me. I tasted my bitterness toward her even in my dreams. I never looked at her, so I did not know whether she looked at me. On my way back from my lesson, whenever I caught a glimpse of her crossing the yard, I turned the other way and quickened my steps, slamming the door of my room behind me.

Nonetheless, when my time to give birth came close, she intercepted me in the yard, and proposed that she take over my lessons until I recuperated. I had wondered already how I would cope with the lessons during the coming weeks. My animosity toward her momentarily laid aside, I agreed.

In the early spring, when the ewes were heavy with lamb, I was heavy with my own child. And in the first month of the year, the month in which the children of Israel were delivered from their bondage in Egypt, I was delivered of my first-born son.

Despite Binah's skills, as I squatted on the birthing stones I melted into a hell of pain, the like of which I had not previously imagined. I could not afterward remember how long it lasted, but the moment came when the midwife announced that I had given birth to a son; and then, back in my bed, I felt Elkanah's lips kissing every part of my sweaty face.

Looking at the infant that had just been thrust from my body, I felt a surge of tenderness, of bliss spreading through my limbs, like that which follows the drinking of sweet wine.

It was the custom to hold a party as large as a wedding in honor of a boy's circumcision on the eighth day after his birth. Thus, for the third time in a few months, Elkanah's house was the scene of a lavish feast.

If our guests recalled that our wedding had taken place only seven months before, they did not mention it. If there were any raised eyebrows, I did not see them. Instead, they shouted their eagerness to hear what the boy's name was to be.

I announced that I had named our son Elroy, for I said that the Lord was my shepherd, and that when I had been in the valley of the shadow of death, he had sent this boy to comfort me.

The priest who was to perform the circumcision stepped forward and took my barely-born infant from me. The child's looming ordeal tugged at my heart, but no sooner had I averted my eyes than I heard his outraged squall, and the priest had thrust him back at me. With practiced hands he dressed the infant's wound. I cradled him in my arms and pacified him with a drop of sweet wine on my finger, followed by my breast.

Then the priest called out that the boy who had now been entered into the covenant of our father Abraham, his name in Israel would be Elroy. Our guests clapped their hands to welcome my son into the congregation of Israel, and my face came alight with renewed joy and pride in my firstborn. My father stood beside me and blessed the Lord for having kept us alive, and sustained us, to reach this time of joy.

Elroy, with his dark eyes and bushy dark curls, was created in the image of Elkanah. I loved him not only for himself, but also because I saw in him the Elkanah I had loved, before he had bestowed his own love on another woman. Against my will the infant called me back to life. My sorrow was heavy in my heart, but I was no longer immersed in emptiness.

I continued to confine myself to my room. Only now I enlarged my quarters to include the adjacent room for my little son, and it was impossible to keep Elkanah out.

When he came from the fields, he sat in the child's room and watched me suckle him. When I was done, he would rock him in his arms, whispering promises of a good life into his tiny ears, long after he had fallen asleep.

I could no longer be in total seclusion, but in my heart I still was. So it was a surprise to me when, after Elkanah had placed Elroy in his cradle, he led me into my room. He told me that from now on I would take my meals in the front room with him and Hannah. I said that I had no wish for it and that he could not force me.

He regarded me grimly in his new masterly fashion and threatened, "I certainly can, and I will. So far I have let you have your way, because you were in distress and pregnant and weak. But this has gone on long enough. You will now act like any other woman and eat your meals with your family."

There was something ominous in his look, in his overbearing voice. I was worn out by my months of loneliness and weakened by my delivery. I shrank from confronting him, and replied in a subdued voice, "I will do as you order me to do, sir."

He smiled smugly. His nostrils flared up in conceit, demonstrating that he savored my helplessness before him as if it were a fragrant flower that pleased his senses.

The next moment, though, he relented. He took my hands into his and whispered: "Pninah, before the child was born I hardly saw you for several months. I have been hungry for your soft body under mine." He cupped my chin in his hand and kissed me. "Soon it will be time, and I will lie with you and enjoy you again."

For one blissfully intoxicating moment, happiness enfolded me like a blanket, as smooth as the one in which I swaddled my child, and I smiled shyly up at him. Then I recalled his love for Hannah and the joy drained from my heart.

From then on, I ate in the front room. I listened to Elkanah and Hannah chat with each other, but I did not look at Hannah and I said little, as there was little I had to say.

Hannah wrote stories and poems; and sometimes after our meals she would read them to Elkanah. I had no wish to listen, and the first time she began reading I tried to slide away silently. But as I reached the door Elkanah took two swift strides, caught up with me, whirled me around and scowled at me.

"You will remember that you belong to a family," he chastised me.

When I tried to pull myself from his grip, he looked at me so ruthlessly that I flinched. I ducked my head, came back obediently, and sank into my chair.

After that night I always listened to Hannah in meek silence. When she finished reading he would fondle her, and praise her to the clouds for her beauty and for her writings.

It was as if I did not exist. In his eyes Hannah was a cedar, reaching tall and proud into the sky. I was merely a bit of moss, growing in a hidden crevice of a forgotten wall.

At night, I created images in my mind of what they were doing together on the other side of the house and my heart would throb endlessly with jealousy.

As long as the bleeding from my delivery continued, Elkanah did not visit me, since I was forbidden to him by Torah law. But as soon as the proper time came, he entered my room.

I lay on my bed and he sat down and began removing my night garment. I bolted up, incensed at his presumption that he could do as he wished with me. In a rush of indignation, my chest heaving, I said defiantly, "I will not share you with another woman."

Not backing down in the least, he reminded me of the commandment that a man who took a second wife must also continue to have carnal knowledge of his first wife. "You have an obligation to help me fulfill this commandment, or else I will take you by force."

I had no doubt that his harsh words would be followed by harsh deeds, that he would make good his threat. I did not want to have my body battered, so I abandoned my resistance.

On this night and the many that followed it, as I felt his muscular arms around me, his hairy chest against my mouth, the hard promise of his member against my body, I was seized by a frenzy of unsought passion, which called forth his own. My thick hair loose and flying wildly about me, I would wantonly explore the secret parts of his body with my mouth. I was brazen, without the restraint of feminine modesty, shyness, or shame. In his excitement he would do the same to me and I would follow his lead to astonishingly shattering peaks. Then we would lay drained in each other's arms and tears would flow from my eyes.

Thus it was with us, but only in bed.

After a few weeks my sickness was upon me again. I disclosed nothing to Elkanah; but one morning as we were eating our meal, he saw me clumsily scramble out of my seat and bolt from the room.

He stepped out into the yard to await my return and said: "This child must have been implanted in your womb when you were in one of your frenzies of passion. I am delighted."

When my sickness subsided, I resumed my teaching, though I took on only one group of children. I found great joy in the wonder of my infant. Yet underneath that joy, there was the pain of my loss of Elkanah's love, which weighed down on me as heavily as a stone on the mouth of a well. It was impossible to dislodge. As my pregnancy advanced, my frenzies of desire again disappeared. When my belly grew, Elkanah's lust for me also abated and he no longer came to me.

During the months of this pregnancy, Hagith married. A man of wealth from the town of Bethlehem in the domain of Judah had come to visit a kinsman; he beheld Hagith, and loved her. She preferred him to all the others who had wanted her for their wife, so she moved to the faraway city of Bethlehem, and thereafter we saw little of her. Bathel fell into dejection, for Hagith was the delight of her life.

Long before winter blossomed into spring, my second son made his way into my life. He looked like Elkanah in all except his large blue-gray eyes, which were mine. I called his name Elhanan, for I said that God had endowed me with him to restore me to life.

Yet it was a life of desolation, and I began spinning wild thoughts of escaping from it.

The Book of Hannah

When I became Elkanah's wife, I did not forget that as a house is built on its stone foundations, so my good fortune was built upon Pninah's bad fortune. But my bliss was so intense that it swept away everything before it, even the way in which she turned from me whenever our paths crossed. At first I was still eager for her friendship, but I was not about to plead for it, and in time I came to ignore her as she ignored me. There were no noisy quarrels between us, merely hostile silence.

Pninah had divested herself of her household duties by keeping to her room. So I became the mistress of Elkanah's house as I had become the mistress of his heart. Because of this, Pninah's bitter face notwithstanding, my happiness was boundless.

Elkanah's first knowing of me had been painful. He penetrated me slowly, soothing me with sweet words of love. But though I willed myself to open for him, I tightened up. My body repelled his thrust, the passage to my womb coiling itself, drawing backward out of his reach. Finally he thrust his way in and broke through my barrier. Then came the pain and the bleeding, and I felt sore and had to beg him to desist for an entire week.

After that it was no longer painful, but neither did I enjoy it as much as I had hoped I would. The closeness of Elkanah's body was as soothing to me as the balm of Gilad. His kisses were as sweet as dates. Yet his caresses did not entice me to anything else. And his penetration offered me nothing but the assurance of his love, and the prospect of motherhood. Should there have been more? I was not sure.

Nothing Elkanah did moved the inner recesses of my body. He tried various ways of pleasing me; but they were all the same to me.

Soon he gave up and reverted to the simple way in which he had performed the act on the night of our wedding.

For me it was an act of love, but not an act of passion, for I felt none. Was lust reserved for men alone? On one occasion I took heart and asked Elkanah this very question, but in response he merely laughed. Perhaps he did not know himself, for I was not sure whether he had ever come to any other women other than Pninah and myself. I was reluctant to ask, and he did not divulge this of his own accord.

At first, none of this bothered me, for my bliss with Elkanah derived from things more important than mere passion: the closeness of our spirits, his love for me and my tenderness for him. In all these things Pninah had no part.

Over time, however, I could not help wondering. I saw how sorrowful Pninah remained, except on those occasions when Elkanah had visited her at night. They would emerge from her room in the morning holding hands, and Pninah would look as if she had just been in paradise. What had he done to make her look so? And Elkanah would look as if he had just known an angel or, perhaps, a witch. What did she do to him to so bewitch him?

When I understood how much my husband enjoyed himself with Pninah, this chafed me, and I asked myself why he did not experience that same pleasure with me, or I with him. Although Elkanah never complained, I began to fret over the possibility that he was disappointed in me.

There was no one whom I could ask what was amiss—not my mother, nor Binah, and certainly not Elkanah. Occasionally I even had the notion of consulting Pninah, but always I rejected it; I could not demean myself before her in that manner.

Against my will, I began to envy Pninah her carnal pleasure with Elkanah. I was ashamed of my feelings, and locked them up tightly inside me. I was not one to show feelings like that, and I was determined that neither she nor Elkanah would ever know of them.

Elkanah was always attentive to me. He never praised Pninah in my presence, and he talked to me incessantly. From day to day the closeness of our souls deepened.

Still, as time went by, my bliss evaporated as it became clearer by the day that I could not bear a child. Had it not been for Pninah, Elkanah would have come to me more often than he did, and I believed that I might have conceived on one of the nights he now spent with her.

She was getting to be a nuisance to me, like a weed in a carefully tended garden. I thought of how much better it would be if she were no longer there to vex me with the bitterness of her face, and the pleasure she bestowed on my husband's body, and the fear that he might implant in her womb the seed that would allow me to conceive. I began to search for a way to be rid of her.

One day I raised with Elkanah the matter of his giving Pninah a book of divorcement and sending her away from his house. But for the first time in his life he regarded me coldly and spoke to me in a rough voice: "I will give you all you wish for, Hannah, but in this I will not heed your request."

"Why are you so set upon keeping Pninah?" I asked.

He dodged my question, and only said in a determined voice, "She is my wife, and will remain so."

Perversely, just as I was plotting against Pninah, I began to be plagued by guilt for the suffering I was causing her. My jealousy and grudges and guilt were strangely interwoven, like the three strands of a braid. In time, guilt came to dominate my soul, weighing me down as would a yoke around my neck. I began to believe that my closed womb was a punishment from the Lord for the suffering I was inflicting on her.

I was not going to give up Elkanah for Pninah's sake, but I cast about for another way to atone for my misdeeds. I resolved to do what I should have done long ago—to bring a guilt offering to the Lord, in the hope that it would lead him to cast away my sins to the depth of the sea, open my womb, and grant me a child.

I sought out a priest, bearing with me an unblemished ram and a large measure of fine flour and choice olive oil. I lifted my face heavenward in supplication, and cried out to the Lord to accept my gift and regard it with favor.

The priest spread the fingers of his hands before me and bestowed on me the ancient triple blessing written in the Torah, beseeching the Lord to bless me and keep me, to be gracious and shine his countenance upon me, and to grant me peace. Then he added: "Through this sacrifice may you find life, and give life."

I charged the priest to carry my guilt offering to the House of the Lord in the town of Shiloh. There he offered it up on the altar, and for a while this set my mind at ease.

But it did no good. My sin was not forgiven, my womb remained closed; my guilt was a heavy door, barred and locked.

Each month I waited in trepidation. My flow was due when the moon was full. I prayed that the moon would wax and wane, and that I would still be dry. But each month I was disappointed. Long before the moon disappeared to gather strength for its rebirth I felt the warm wetness of blood staining my thighs, the dull ache in my loins, the emptiness in my womb, and an ever greater distress in my soul.

One morning I finally felt the sickness that I had been longing for. Elkanah had just left for the fields when I was overcome with nausea. As I had seen Pninah do so many times, I ran to the edge of the yard to be sick.

When I came back, I was drained of strength, yet overjoyed. I lay down on my bed and began spinning dreams of motherhood. Soon I had to be sick again, and my joy grew.

At noontime I was not hungry. But I went to the front room, where the midday meal of roasted lamb spiced with garlic was set out, because I knew that Pninah would be there and I wanted to consult her.

She was in her second pregnancy, her belly sticking out in front of her like the underside of a huge bowl, and her face was puffed up. When I entered the room she immediately looked out the window as if something of great importance were going forth in the yard. I knew that it would not be easy to talk to her, yet I forced myself to do so.

I told her of my nausea, and I asked her anxiously if she thought that I was pregnant. I was afraid that she would ignore me, but she was surprisingly kind. She asked me when my bleeding had been due. I told her that it was due now, and she cast her eyes down.

Finally she said, "With me, the sickness does not begin until a few weeks after I am late with my bleeding. But I know nothing about these things. Would it not be best if you went to see Binah?"

I replied that I was too weak to ride all the way to her house. Pninah suggested that she send a message to her to come to me.

Then, for the first time in more than a year, she looked squarely into my face. "You are flaming red in the face," she exclaimed. "You have a fever. Perhaps it would be best if I called the woman healer, who knows all about soothing herbs, to come to you."

She barely finished speaking when the door opened and Elkanah came in. He never returned from the fields at noon, and we both looked at him in surprise. He, too, was flushed and drained of strength, and he sat down wearily and complained of nausea.

My face fell, my hopes shattered. I did not want Elkanah to know how stupid I had been, and I looked at Pninah pleadingly. She shook her head at me silently, and said that she would send a message to the healer to come and see us both.

When I needed her, Pninah had extended a helping hand to me, as though we were still the friends we no longer were. I was grateful to her and decided that I would remember this act of kindness.

Elkanah came to my room, and we lay down on my bed to rest. By the time the healer had made us drink her potions and had left, I was crying. Elkanah took me in his arms, but I would not be comforted. For I knew that only a fertile woman is like a blossoming vine. Her husband blesses her for giving him sons to carry forth his name. But a barren woman is like a withered vine. Her husband bemoans her, and though she is a beauty, a scribe, and a writer, she is nothing.

I came to be seized by the fear that as I was nothing, so I would remain—barren all the days of my life, to descend into the grave without issue from my womb. When I disclosed my fear to Elkanah, my husband remained silent.

The Book of Pninah

By the time my two sons were born, I began thinking of leaving Elkanah's house, for I did not want to remain an unloved wife forever. Yet, strange as it was, I still loved him and could not envisage my life without him. I was trapped in my life by my love, like a fly in a spider web.

I found it more and more difficult to sleep at night. Often I would sit on one of the big stones in front of my room and gaze at the dark outline of the hills.

Once I remained there until the night began to brighten into dawn. The birds in the treetops were already singing when I heard the stealthy opening of a door and the muffled murmur of voices.

My eyes open wide in disbelief, I watched Elkanah, accompanied by a cloaked female figure, emerge from his room and walk to the stables. Soon he returned alone and his eyes alighted on me.

He was startled and approached me warily. I rose to my feet and bowed to him.

Having regained his composure, he spoke to me sternly: "Pninah, why are you sitting here?"

"I am not able to sleep."

"What did you see?" he thundered.

"Yourself and a woman wearing a cloak," I replied, subduing the quake in my voice.

"You will forget what you saw," he hammered at me.

"I will do as you say."

This meek reply did not appease him; he became vexed with me. "You do not reproach me, nor are you upset. Why is that?" he flung at me accusingly. "Do you not love me?"

I was, in truth, deeply upset. Now that the suspicion I had long harbored about Elkanah had been confirmed, I felt the sharp pang of a dagger through my heart. Yet I did not wish to show how humiliated I felt, so I responded in a hollow voice, "I love you, sir. But since you already love another woman, it hurts me only a little if there are more of them."

The affirmation of my love cast him into a pensive mood. "I certainly don't love this maid," he mused. Then his tone became imperious again. "But if Hannah were to find out it would grieve her very much, so your lips will be sealed."

"Whatever you command, I will do."

"And now, go to sleep."

"I still cannot sleep."

"I will see to it that you sleep." With these words he put his arm around my shoulder. I was distraught at his brazen design, but by then he had battered down my pride. I obeyed the pressure of his hand as he led me to my room.

A faint feminine aroma, offensive to my nostrils, still clung to him, so I proposed, with some embarrassment, "I think . . . I feel . . . I mean . . . it would be well if you took a bath, first."

Laughing his special laughter, which I still adored, he agreed.

I brought forth the tub I had stowed away, and poured pitchers of water into it. He undressed, sunk his large body into the cool water and said easily, "Since it is you who wanted me to wash, you might as well wash me."

I did, and then I dried him. While I toweled his muscular legs, I looked up into his face and saw that it had broken out into the triumphant smirk it always wore when he had subdued me. I detested it, yet when he touched my breasts, I gasped with pleasure.

By then we were both more excited than we had ever been before, and afterward I fell into a dreamless sleep. All too soon I was called back from it by the hungry whimper of the children.

Later, I felt shamed by my docility. I had no wish to remain servile. But Elkanah was as blind to my distress as a Canaanite idol. If I ranted and kicked up a storm, it would be futile. And if I nagged at him, demanding that he cease his ways, it would have as much effect as if I insisted that the wind stop blowing.

Clearly, sooner or later, one of the maids would become pregnant from Elkanah. I asked myself, would he feel obliged to marry her, or would he abandon her to her shame? And how would Hannah react when she found out?

As autumn faded into winter, long before the time of the rebirth of life, I myself gave birth to new life. My third child was a daughter. She had Elkanah's dark eyes, but my face. I was overjoyed to see myself in the little infant, so I called her name Gilah.

Before I would have believed possible, I was pregnant again. The summer had barely approached its end when my pregnancy came to term. More than a month before my days were full, I gave birth to my second daughter. She was tiny, golden skinned, and lovely—and, most importantly, healthy. I called her name Nehamah, for I said that in her I had found consolation for my sorrow.

Yet, as birth followed pregnancy, and pregnancy followed birth in rapid succession, I felt my strength seep out of me with the milk my infants sucked from my breasts. When the bleeding from my last delivery ceased, I knew that soon I would be pregnant again, so I went to seek help from Binah before it was too late.

It was not necessary to tell the wise woman what was wrong with me; as usual, she knew. As she sat with me in her yard, she said, "You are an uncommonly fertile woman, Pninah. You cannot go on as you do."

"Can you help me?"

"It is help that depends on you."

She stepped into the house, and returned with a small pouch made out of a cow's derma, with a string laced around its edges. "Before your man comes to you," she explained, "you must place this inside you to cover the mouth of your womb. Then you must pull the string and tie it."

The wise woman continued: "There is more that is wrong with you. Your husband has taken another wife, and there is no remedy for this. But you have fallen into despair and that is wrong."

"What can I do?"

"You must cause yourself to look well, to make him love you again. You have beautiful eyes and hair and a sensuous mouth. And you had a shapely figure. If you regain it, your husband will not be able to disregard you."

"What can I do?" I repeated.

"There is a Canaanite woman named Bathanath, who makes women look well. She lives at the outskirts of the town of Sdeh Canaan, one of the Canaanite towns left as an enclave within the domain of the tribe of Efraim. Go to her. She will help you."

Binah then took me into a heavily draped room. She made me lie down on the bed that stood in it, gently drew my legs apart and taught me how not to have children anymore.

On my way home, I looked at the hills of Efraim. Even in their rugged, early autumn's dryness they were more beautiful than I would have thought possible. They spoke the power of the Lord to bring forth beauty even from desolation. I prayed that he might endow the dryness of my life with beauty as well.

For more than three years the misery of my existence had been so deep that I had not even had the strength to reach out to the Lord. But now I took my prayer as a sign of his mercy, and of a brighter future that seemed to beckon from the horizon.

Two days later, I arose at dawn and saddled my donkey. The three older children waddled into the yard, and when they saw me ready to go, their little faces puckered and they broke into loud wails.

Elkanah emerged from Hannah's room. He was annoyed and called out, "What is this?"

The children, who stood in awe of him, fell silent.

"Sir, I must go on a brief trip and the children are unhappy."

Irritably he asked, "Where do you wish to go?"

"To visit a woman in Sdeh Canaan, for there is something important that I must learn from her."

He was disgruntled. "You should have asked my permission."

Somehow I found the courage, and exclaimed defiantly: "I am not a slave."

He was exasperated. "You are the mother of my children; and before you go, I must be sure that they are well cared for."

"Since you did me the honor to make me the mother of your children, sir," I rushed on before my courage gave out, "you must also do me the honor of entrusting me with their welfare."

I had hardly ever spoken to Elkanah so boldly before, and I could not believe that I had uttered those words.

Yet the world did not collapse, and Elkanah replied, "Go in peace."

I sighed with relief. "May God be with you," I responded, and bowed to him.

Hannah, who had come out of her room, stood next to Elkanah, her hair tangled and her feet bare. He looked at her tenderly, encircled her waist with his arm, and led her back to her room.

Her eyes, resting on the children, had been heavy with anguish—the sorrow of a fruitless woman, confronted with the issue of another woman's too-fertile womb.

Had Hannah still been my friend, I would have grieved with her and searched for words to console her. But she was not my friend. My heart was hard, and I had no words of comfort for her.

I called to the nurse to take charge of the children. I lifted myself onto my donkey and left.

As I rode, the morning dawned brightly. The moist smell of the night's dew, still clinging to the plants at the side of the road, filled my nostrils. I inhaled deeply and immersed myself in the joy of leaving behind me the house I no longer considered as my home.

I felt that I was at the beginning of a long journey, although I did not know as yet where it would lead me.

SECOND PART

A New Existence

The Book of Hannah

After I had believed myself to be pregnant and was disappointed, the days dragged by even more slowly than before. Woman has been cursed by the Lord to give birth in pain, yet the curse was also a blessing, of which I was deprived. When almost three years had passed since my wedding and still I did not conceive, my life came to be a heavy burden to me.

My mother, who shared this burden with me, prepared a hot brew of crushed dried mandrakes—which, she assured me, had helped to implant me in her womb—and made me drink this nauseating concoction morning and night until my belly was bloated, but not with child. My many kinswomen visited, one by one, each offering a failsafe remedy to open my womb, all of which failed miserably in their purpose. Their only effect was to oppress my spirit even more.

Each month when the moon was full and round and heavy as a fruit, my bleeding began, as did the pain in my heart. I stared at the moon, whose face stared back at me and mouthed soundless words: "You are neither a maiden, nor yet a woman. Your husband knows the pleasure of the flesh and the joy of fatherhood with another. You are worthless to him in every way."

Elkanah never blamed me. Never berated me or voiced his disappointment as husbands of other barren women were wont to do. But I could not delude myself. I sensed that he was even more downcast than I was, as he realized that the dream we had spun of begetting six children together would never come true. I knew that even now he still yearned to sire more sons and daughters, and it would not be surprising if he decided to take a third wife. This would be no more than I deserved, for had I not brought upon Pninah's head precisely the bitter fate that now loomed before me? Still I felt that if it came about I would prefer to die.

One night, as I was lying in Elkanah's arms he murmured, "My beloved Hannah, don't distress yourself."

"It's the emptiness inside me. My life is as empty as my womb."

His voice was a caress as he asked, "Do I not fill you to your satisfaction?"

"When you are inside me I am filled with your love, but when you leave, my husband, I am as empty as before."

"I can only repeat what our father Jacob told Rachel when she came to him with this same complaint. 'Am I in the place of God, who has withheld from you the fruit of the womb?'"

In my distress I blurted out, my voice cracking, "You are disappointed, and in the end you will take another wife."

His forehead creased. "Such a thought never entered my mind."

But in the flicker of an instant I could see that now it had. In my stupidity I had placed it there. Soon he gave me proof of this. "Indeed, when Rachel was barren, she gave her husband her slave girl and urged him to come to her. Have you no suitable maid that you would like to give me? I could go to her, and you would have sons through her."

"No," I fairly shouted at him, "I have no suitable maid at all."

"Then I will have to find one myself."

"Don't inflict this humiliation on me." The words were uttered in my heart, but I did not have the strength to bring them forth from my mouth. He did not know that I had spoken, and when tears fell from my eyes he slept deeply in my embrace.

My thoughts wandered into the domain of happiness where only mothers dwelled, and from which I was barred. When I drifted into sleep, the necklace Elkanah had given me before our wedding seemed to hover before my eyes, its six precious stones—my six unborn children—having grown tear-studded eyes, which regarded me accusingly for not having endowed them with the breath of life. When I awoke, my heart was heavy with my dream, and I could almost feel my womb shriveling inside me.

A few evenings later, Elkanah summoned me to his room. He made me sit, then handed me a drink of water mixed with honey, an act that made me immediately suspicious. While I sipped it, he announced that he had found a maid he favored. She was young and sturdy, still a virgin, and willing to do his bidding. He would go to her that night, and she would bear a child on my knees, and I would be happy again. He spoke these words in a festive voice, as if he expected me to be immensely grateful to him.

The sweet honeyed water turned to vinegar in my mouth and the cup slid from my hand, breaking into little pieces and spilling its contents as it hit the floor. I rose and staggered forward, embracing him convulsively and pleading with him not to burn my life to ashes.

His face showed clearly that he had already set his heart on having the maid. But he would not reveal her name, and when he saw how distraught I was, he said, laughing reluctantly, "Hannah, my darling, I was merely joking," but I knew that this was not the truth.

Once again, I wished to consult Pninah. I wanted to learn what she thought of this, and whether she, too, had been troubled by the possibility of Elkanah's taking a third wife. But I was so deeply mortified that I said nothing.

I began wondering which of the six maids who served the household and Pninah's children was the one he had singled out, and meant to foist on me. If I could establish who she was, I would send her away to find her sustenance elsewhere, as our mother Sarah had done with her handmaiden, Hagar.

In the following days, I scrutinized the maids but their faces were as bland as the clouds in the sky, and showed nothing but reverence for me. They were all young and sturdy, and there was no telling which one of them was still a virgin and willing to do Elkanah's bidding. One seemed to have a sly smile and, too often for my taste, hooded her eyes. She was as mute as a fish in the sea, and I was convinced that she had much to be mute about. But this was not sufficient to condemn her, and naturally I could not ask.

I then pondered a new notion, and it was good in my eyes. I procured other posts for all of our young maids, and replaced them with elderly ones. In the coming days I watched Elkanah intently to see whether he disliked what I was doing, but he seemed not to have noticed anything at all.

The next time Pninah and I ate our midday meal together in the front room, she suddenly abandoned her usual custom of averting her gaze from me and spoke. "Are you worried, Hannah, that Elkanah's eyes may be straying to other women?"

I stared at her. "Of course not," I said with a tremor of wrath in my voice.

"Then why did you suddenly replace our young and pretty maids with old and ugly ones?" she persisted.

"That was because . . . because . . . he had the thought of taking a maid for his third wife so that she could bear sons for me—for the sake of my own happiness," I retorted, reproaching her silently for being so obtuse as to have failed to understand this on her own accord.

"It does not seem to me that he is eager to take on the burden of caring for another wife."

"Once he realized how much his notion of taking another wife distressed me, he abandoned it."

Pninah seemed not to have heard my words. "And the maids he would have in his view are not the ones that work here under your supervision, but the ones that work for him in the fields," she said dourly.

I scoffed at her words. "As he has decided not to take another wife, he has no maids in his view at all," I retorted firmly.

Pninah's face twisted into a sour, inscrutable smile, and she said nothing. I was puzzled and wondered what it was that she had on her mind, but soon her eyes were glued to the window as they always were, and she made it plain that she had no wish to share any further thoughts with me.

That night, when Elkanah was lying at my side in bed, he said, "Many barren women have children in the end. Perhaps you will, too. You once told me that you would consult with the wise woman, Binah. Did you go to her?"

"Yes, but she gave me such odd advice that I took it for witchery and disregarded it."

Binah had indeed acted very strangely. She asked me the most prying questions, not only about the monthly flow of my blood, but also about when it was that my man came to me each month, and how he made his seed penetrate my womb. I lost all patience with her. Then, instead of providing me with a beneficial potion to drink, as she should have done, she instructed me as to the precise nights on which my man was to come to me or refrain from doing so (as well as to Pninah) and on how he should go about it. I resented this very much, and left her house in anger.

After that, I wanted to hear no more from this woman whose name, meaning wisdom, no longer suited her, whose mind had clearly been addled by old age.

She had even linked the times at which Elkanah should know me to the precise size of the moon. And while I was present, she approached two white doves settled on her window sill and gave them some crumbs from her hand. She muttered and cooed to them, and I could have sworn that she was mumbling an incantation. I feared that she might have fallen under the evil spell of witchery, an unpardonable sin by Torah law.

Still, after some hesitation, I said to Elkanah: "Even so, by now I am so desperate that I am willing to do anything."

"What was her advice?"

"That from the fullness of the moon, the onset of my monthly bleeding, you must keep away from all women, both me and Pninah. From the eleventh day after the moon's fullness and onward, when the moon is nothing but a sliver in the sky and then disappears, you must know only me, and do it once every night for seven nights in a row."

"It is indeed odd advice," he mused. "Nonetheless, we will try this," he promised.

So it came about that on the eleventh night after the onset of my way of women Elkanah came to my room. He let his love for me take over, and my hope soared.

But the next day Pninah went to visit a Canaanite woman for some mysterious purpose of her own. I have no knowledge of what transpired, but when she returned, the oppression of spirit that had plagued her for almost three years had miraculously disappeared. The morose female with whom I had shared the house was no more. Pninah was a new woman.

She wore a new dress that was too tight for her and made her breasts stand out like watchtowers in a city wall; and during the evening meal she sat as straight and proud as an oak tree. Elkanah talked to me, but leered at her; and I knew that he would not be keeping his promise to come to me every night for a week.

And my hope plummeted like lead in deep water.

The Book of Pninah

Having left Elkanah's house early in the morning, it was not difficult to find my way to Sdeh Canaan. The road I took wound through a narrow valley that opened into a much wider one. There the tranquil town came into sight, a hodgepodge of little houses dotting the landscape, set in pleasing disorder amidst all manner of trees and shrubs.

From the outside the houses resembled ours, but I wondered what was in them. Apart from some merchants who passed through Ramathayim occasionally, I had encountered no Canaanites. I knew only that they worshipped idols, which the Torah requires us to regard as an abomination.

Some women chatting idly in the street directed me to Bathanath's house, the biggest on the street. It had a front yard abounding with citron trees, the branches weighed down by their tangy yellow fruit, welcoming me with their spicy aroma. As I entered the yard, a boy took charge of my donkey's bridle, then showed me to Bathanath's room at the front of the house.

It was a large room, filled with the fragrance of woman, a temple to the beauty of the female face and body.

In the center of the room stood a square table on which rested a mirror surrounded by bowls of scented oils and ointments. Wooden shelves adorned the room, graced by statues of Canaanite goddesses.

The woman who came forward to meet me was about thirty-five years old, tall and slim. She had grey eyes, light skin, and straight copper-colored hair with a red tint to it. She was delicately good looking.

She spoke the Hebrew language well, and after we greeted each other, I told her my name and that Binah had sent me to seek her help.

"She did well."

Bathanath left me in no doubt as to the meaning of her words. She reached out her hand to my shoulder, held me at arm's length, then pronounced judgment on my appearance: "You look like a woman who has abandoned hope. Your dress is drab and shapeless like a sackcloth, as if you were in mourning."

"I *am* in mourning," I replied.

"For whom?"

In a sudden wash of self-pity I whispered, "For my life."

My eyes brimmed over with tears that blurred my vision but lightened my burden.

Or perhaps the relief was caused by Bathanath, for I saw much kindness in her eyes. She was a stranger, a woman not even of my people, yet I could feel her open her heart to me. She hushed me by rubbing her cheek against mine, and murmuring soft words of comfort into my ear.

Suddenly a side door opened, and I saw a young man in the doorway.

"Arnon, go from this room," she admonished him.

The man disregarded her command and came closer. Even through my tears I could see that he was very tall, broad-shouldered and lean. And like Bathanath, who was apparently his sister, he had clear gray eyes. Unlike Israelite men, who wore their caps inside a house, his head was uncovered, revealing copper-colored hair with the same red glow as his sister's. His skin was lighter than that of the men of our tribe, and he was disturbingly handsome.

Speaking in my own tongue, he tried to encourage me. "It's not shameful to cry. Especially when the tears make your eyes shine like stars." He took a piece of white cloth from the table and dabbed at my eyes and nose. "Who are you?" he inquired.

"I am Pninah from Ramathayim, and I am an ugly woman."

"No, you are beautiful. But you need my sister to help you reveal it."

"Arnon, go," Bathanath repeated.

"When you are finished here, walk through this door and I will show you things that your eyes have never seen before."

With these words the man stepped out, and Bathanath and I sat at the table. She picked up a jar and poured a light-green liquid into two cups, then offered me one. It was cool water mixed with herbs, and it was delicious.

"Tell me," she prompted, "who has destroyed your life? Your husband?"

I poured forth my tale of woe, and the weight in my heart lightened even further.

Bathanath listened in attentive silence, and said, "Men are wild beasts, in dire need of taming."

"Women, too."

"But your husband and your rival cannot rob you of your life."

"I am sick of my life."

"We will change that. We will make you eager to greet each dawning day."

"How?" I inquired dubiously.

"First we must make you look desirable again. The rest will follow. Your breasts are heavy with milk and are beginning to sag. Your shoulders, too, are sagging. Your belly is as round as a heap of grain, as if there were a child in it still. It should not be so. When delicacies are set before you, you must purse your mouth."

"I am nursing my infant. I must eat so that she will be satisfied."

"You must drink milk to make your own milk flow, but eat little. And you must use this cloth to swaddle your belly, to deceive the eye, to make it look smaller."

She led me to the back of the room and rummaged through some wares she kept on shelves there and handed the cloth to me, along with another one. "And you must swaddle your breasts with *this* cloth so that they do not sag."

She looked me over once more. "And you must never wear that brown sackcloth again. Who would look at a woman clad in this abomination?"

"I don't want anyone to look at me."

"That also must change."

She took up two linen dresses that were laid out there. "These should fit you. Put one on after you have swaddled yourself, and take the other one home. Throw the sackcloth away."

One of the dresses had blue and white stripes, and the other had stripes of many colors. I chose to wear the first, but it was cut low and too tight over my breasts.

Bathanath pronounced it to be beautiful, adding, "Breasts are nothing to be ashamed of—they nurture infants and passion. Now let me look at your face. Your skin is like a pouch of leather."

She gave me a container of fragrant oil, and instructed me to rub it into my face morning and night. She warned me never to let the sun spot my face, for it was a vicious ravisher of women's beauty, leaving skin as parched as the earth after a drought. Then she took the pouch of silver I held out to her, invited me to come back to learn more from her, and gently pushed me toward the side door, through which Arnon had disappeared.

The door led to another large room filled with merchandise, where Arnon was suddenly beside me.

On the right-hand side, there stood statues of gods and goddesses, shaped out of clay, wood, and bronze. I slid by the repugnant idols hastily as if I were chased by a demon.

"It is well that you turned away from these statues, else they might have cracked from the scorn in your eyes. Let's look at the other wares instead," he invited.

My eyes took in wonders: there were shelves laden with pieces of painted pottery decorated with colorful birds, animals, and palm trees. Other shelves were laid out with gold and silver bracelets and necklaces. Further down stood transparent, yet elaborately painted, bowls and cups.

Following my gaze, Arnon said, "These are utensils made of glass. They are brought here by caravans from the east, or by merchant ships from across the Great Sea."

All the wares on display were artfully crafted, giving voice to their creators' eloquent souls. I declared, truthfully, that I had seen nothing to equal them in our land.

"Your people are interested only in scrolls. The crafts are nothing to them. The written words are their sculptures."

"It's true," I conceded. "I am a scribe myself."

He was impressed, and asked if there were many woman scribes in Ramathayim.

"No. Apart from myself, I know only one other, and she is . . . she is . . ."

"Yes?"

"My husband's other wife."

"And your rival?"

I bowed my head.

He selected a particularly exquisite bracelet and clasped it around my wrist. I returned it to him. "I have no silver shekels left with which to buy it."

"You can give me the silver whenever you have it, or perhaps never."

I expressed my gratitude but refused the offer.

He led me through an inner courtyard to an eating room. A table was set and he invited me to share his meal. I declined, saying that his sister had admonished me to stop eating so much.

He laughed. "No, you misunderstood. My sister did not intend you to fast from the beginning of the day to its end. The meal we have here is very small, only salted fish from the Great Sea and quail's eggs. You will find them pleasing."

He led me to the table, pulled out a chair and made me sit down, adding, "If you don't eat, I'll have to feed you."

"You are kind, sir, but I have been feeding myself for many years now."

We began eating and he asked, "How many years?"

"I am eighteen and I have been eating by myself since I was three years old."

"I am twenty-six, and I began feeding myself immediately. My mother told me that I was squeezing the milk out of her breasts as soon as I was born."

I laughed and he approved. "We must keep you cheerful."

He demanded to know how long I had been married and how many children I had. When I told him, and he wondered about this, I admitted that my firstborn arrived seven months after my wedding, the others came one after the other, and my little one was born before my days were full.

Then silence fell. I regarded him, and he looked back at me, and an unspoken message passed between us.

Even a short while before I would not have believed that I could exchange such intimacies with any man but my husband. I blushed and lowered my gaze. When I raised it again, I saw him smiling at me, gently mocking me with his eyes, enjoying my confusion.

For the rest of the meal I sat, wondering why a woman still disfigured from her pregnancies, as fat as a ewe grazing in juicy pastures, should have captured the notice of so handsome a man as Arnon.

Then I rose from my chair, thanked my host for the meal, and announced that I had to ride home. Arnon told me that he would accompany me.

As we left Sdeh Canaan behind us, Arnon inquired why I had been crying so pitifully before. "Even though I know what your sorrow is, I would like to hear it from the beginning."

So I spilled out my tale at even greater length. I even mentioned that I had threatened my husband with loving another man, his angry response, and his certainty that there were no such deviant women amongst us.

An amused smile spread over Arnon's face. "Your husband is wrong. There are quite a number of such women in your tribe."

"How can you be sure of that?"

"Because I have known many myself."

"Do you mean known in the sense of . . ." I said in breathless embarrassment.

"Yes."

For the second time that day my face was flushed in confusion, for apart from Elkanah, I had never mentioned the act of carnal knowledge to any man.

When my blush subsided, I said, "They are deviant women by Torah law."

He laughed. "They seem to have forgotten that."

"Why would they . . . Why did they . . ."

With a renewed smile in his eyes he suggested, "You must ask them yourself."

"But I don't know who they are."

"You won't learn that from me."

"No," I conceded regretfully.

Finally Arnon said, "All that need not concern us. What is important is that from now on, Pninah, you are no longer alone, because I am your friend now and forever."

I swallowed my tears of gratitude, and asked why he should wish to befriend me.

"It is too early to tell you this today," he replied.

I rode on beside Arnon in puzzled silence, then inquired about his life and his family. He told me that his brother-in-law spent much of his time crossing the Great Sea on merchant ships to buy merchandise from the sea peoples, and brought them to be sold here. His own task was to buy wares from peoples that dwelled nearer by.

I then found the courage to inquire whether he had a wife. He disclosed that he'd had one until a short while ago, but no longer. She had spent her days in the potter's workshop painting bowls and, as he found out, also in his bed. He had sent her back to her father's house.

By that time the sun had begun its retreat in the sky and Ramathayim had come into view.

"I must ask that you turn back now," I said, "or else my husband will spot us, and think *me* a deviant woman."

"We must give him reason to think it then," he replied, delighting in my third bout of blushing confusion. He urged me to visit again soon.

His purpose was obvious, but I did not recoil, for whatever Arnon wanted me to do with him Elkanah had given me plentiful reasons for doing it. So I agreed.

"But you cannot travel alone, for you may be set upon," he said. "If it suits you, we will set the second day of the week after next for your visit. I will send two of our people to meet you on this spot early in the morning, to guard you on the way."

With these words he brought his hand around to the opening of my newly acquired low-cut dress. He traced the line of skin that bordered my dress, skimming it with his fingers, until he reached the cleavage between my breasts. Then he let his hand trail the line of my dress up again on the other side.

A rush of heat seeped from his roaming fingers into my skin. But he merely kissed me lightly and, without saying another word, turned his donkey around and left.

It is then that the grief that had been plaguing me for three years was washed away as if by water from an overflowing spring. In the space of one balmy day, I had stumbled out of the valley of the shadow of death, and onto the mountain of the light of life. And the fire, which during my pregnancies had been almost extinct, flared up and burned in my bones. If Arnon had demanded that I lie with him there and then in the field, I would not have refused him. But he had left. So I spurred my donkey to greater speed, and rode home.

After stabling the animal, I ran into my room, changed into my spurned old dress and hurried to see my children. I felt my milk flowing, and immediately nursed the fretting infant, Nehamah. While I held her to my breast, I cuddled the older children in my arms. Sucking greedily on their thumbs, they snuggled themselves to me. As I felt their little bodies against mine I laughed out loud in joy. I talked and talked to them, speaking words that contained little sense but much love, until there were no more words left in my mouth.

I wore my new dress again for the evening meal. I peeked at myself in the copper mirror, and decided that the woman who gazed back from it was not so shapeless after all.

I swept into the front room with more confidence than I had had for a long time. Elkanah and Hannah were there already. He was rolling strands of her black hair around his fingers, kissing them with ardor, and whispering words of love into her ear. But when I came in he turned around and halted in mid-sentence. His gaze ran down the length of me, caressing my body and my legs.

We sat down to a meal of red-lentil stew, of which I partook only sparingly. During the meal, as they continued talking with one another, Elkanah shot me looks which intimated that he would come to me that night, the first time since the delivery of my youngest child.

Later, between one panting breath and another, Elkanah told me that he needed me badly. From the day I had met him until this night, all the use he had ever had for me was to calm his lust between Hannah and one maid or another. I had married him hoping also for love and friendship, which he reserved for Hannah only. Soon I forgot this, as I myself was overtaken by fits of desire, and we knew each other three times that night and the fire inside me abated.

Yet the Canaanite's image was already engraved in my soul. In the morning, when I followed Elkanah out of my room and watched him standing at the threshold of Hannah's room embracing her, my yearning for Arnon became overwhelming.

I lay down on my bed again and relived every moment I had spent with him. I pondered the words he had said to me, those I had said to him, and those I might have said but did not utter, as well as the touch of his hand on my skin and that of his lips on mine.

Arnon had barely entered into my life, yet my pain had dissolved, as darkness lifts with the rising of the sun.

The Book of Hannah

O n the evening on which Pninah returned from Sdeh Canaan I found it impossible to sleep after I watched Elkanah slip into her room. My indignation grew from moment to moment. When they emerged from her room in the morning, and I saw the smile of bliss on her face, I was very angry indeed. If I did not conceive that month it would be, without doubt, Pninah's fault.

When Elkanah saw the tears of anger in my eyes, he came over to calm me. It was to no avail. I reentered my room, and stayed there until evening.

That night when Elkanah came to me, he confessed guiltily that on the previous night he had known Pninah three times. It was no wonder that we had great difficulty getting him to spill his seed inside me, and I was greatly incensed.

Once again the thought struck me: How much better it would be if Pninah were not there to share my husband with me!

The next week was the festival of Sukkot. The Torah commands us to rejoice in our festivals, and I have always done so. There is no more joyous festival than this one, when we commemorate our ancestors' sitting in tabernacles during their wandering in the desert; and also when our yearly pilgrimage to the House of the Lord at Shiloh takes place. In years past, before I knew that I was barren, I enjoyed the week we spent there more than any other part of the year. Since then, I no longer found any joy in it, for in Shiloh my flat belly was shamefully displayed before our entire tribe.

Even my mother regarded me there with undisguised pity. And this year, the week in Shiloh was the most harrowing I ever lived through.

It began with the tumult of the preparations for our journey. Pninah was busy with her children, so the preparations were all left to me. By the time all was ready, I was not only exhausted, but irritable as well.

As soon as we arrived and set up our tents and tabernacle in the compound set aside for the tribe of Efraim, Pninah became unbearable. She had vexed me on our pilgrimages in previous years, but this time she surpassed herself. She was clad in another one of the dresses she had brought back from Sdeh Canaan. And, blooming like a wildflower in the spring, she gathered her children and their nurse around her and began strutting through the encampment, greeting all the people she knew.

She showed off her children as if they were precious stones, which Elkanah had given her as tokens of his love, and which he had refused to bestow on me. This of course was far, very far, from the truth. But Pninah was determined to spite me by making me look like the unloved wife.

She came back in time to help prepare the evening meal, which we laid out in the tabernacle. She upset all the arrangements I had made by bringing forth a dish of honeyed barley cakes that I had not intended to serve until two days later.

I was aware that it was I who had brought sorrow into her life, not she into mine, but it now seemed that she was determined to get even with me in petty ways, and I was furious.

The next day, Elkanah rose early in the morning and took the lamb and the fine flour and the oil he had prepared for the sacrifice to the Lord and set out for the Temple, which stood at some distance away. He was detained for a long time, because thousands of other men were waiting for their sacrifices to be offered up before his. When he returned, the sun was low in the sky.

He brought with him the part of the sacrificial lamb, and the flour cooked in oil, that the priests at the Temple had left over for us to eat. And he set out the food on a cloth on the ground of the tabernacle.

When we sat down for our meal, Pninah did not leave the children to eat with the nurse, as was her custom. Instead, she brought them along to eat with us, even though the infant was too young to partake of any solid food at all. People who passed by peeked in to greet us, thus affording her another chance to flaunt her children, and call attention to the absence of mine. She would not let pass such a splendid opportunity to slight me; she was reveling in my misery.

Elkanah, who distributed the food, spooned some into Pninah's bowl, for her and for the children. But when he noted my humiliation at her hand, he glared angrily at her. Then, to spite her, he put a double serving into my bowl. I was so despondent that I could not touch a morsel of it but I felt vindicated.

That night, when Elkanah came into my tent, he found me sitting on the ground, my low seat a sign of my low spirits. He raised me and gathered me into his arms and murmured, "Hannah, why are you weeping, and why are you not eating, and why are you grieved? Am I not better for you than ten sons?" Then he covered my face and my hands with kisses, but the tears streaming from my eyes told him, more loudly than words could, that however much I loved him, he could not take the place of sons I did not have.

As the next morning dawned, I decided that Binah's witchcraft could do me no good, that only God's help could lift me out of my despair; and that I must perform a deed of my own to seek it. Had he not redeemed the children of Israel from the house of bondage in Egypt? Why, then, should he not redeem me from my own bondage?

The time of our pilgrimage to the House of the Lord marked the most auspicious time for me to present my petition to him. So I arose while Elkanah still lay asleep. I ate and drank, then made my way to the Temple to offer prayers there.

The Temple was a large stone building. In its center stood the sanctuary, with the Ark of the Covenant placed on a raised platform against its inner wall. In front of it hung a heavy, richly embroidered curtain, which separated the ark, the holiest of holies, from the rest of the sanctuary.

To one side stood a table with two large loaves of bread on it, and on the other stood the large, seven-pronged golden menorah that was always lit in the evening. In front of it was a big incense burner, from which the scent of holy incense spread to the entire sanctuary.

Around its inner walls were stone benches, where worshipers sat to await their turn to approach the ark. The ceiling was covered with a huge goat-leather sheet, modeled after that of the Tent of Meeting, which had accompanied the Israelites during their travels in the desert and afterward.

Adjacent to the sanctuary's entrance was a roofless space, closed off by walls. It housed another raised platform with a sacrificial altar on it, which only the priests were allowed to approach.

Behind the sanctuary, several other structures had been added over the years. These included the priests' living quarters and their eating room, as well as a sizable scroll room, where the people of Israel's most treasured scrolls were kept, and copied many times over. In the midst of this welter of structures there was a spacious courtyard where priests and visitors could meet.

When I approached, I saw that the huge square in front of the Temple was already packed, the Temple besieged by thousands of people waiting to offer their sacrifices or to pray. After wandering about desolately for a while, I found a stone in the shade of a tree and sat down on it.

As I sat, it dawned on me that despite Pninah's contemptible conduct since our arrival in Shiloh, I had sinned against her more heavily than she had sinned against me. And the Lord would never open my womb as long as I searched for ways to undo her life even further than I had already. I resolved not to contemplate evil against her ever again.

I continued to sit there, watching the crowd until it thinned. This did not happen until evening, by which time I realized that although I had not eaten since morning, I felt no hunger or thirst. When the multitudes dispersed I approached the Temple. Its candlelight spilled out into the encroaching darkness, and I was overwhelmed with awe.

The sanctuary was empty, and as no one halted me, I entered and approached the curtain in front of the ark. I bowed down until my forehead touched the ground, and began to weep silently. Then I raised my head and knelt, and in a whisper that came from the bitterness in my heart, I recited this prayer:

> God of Israel, I know that you have closed my womb as a punishment for my wrongdoing, for I have inflicted sorrow on

another woman and I have nursed unkind thoughts about her. But have I not suffered enough to atone for my sins? My man and I are one flesh, thus I cannot undo the pain I have caused my rival. But henceforward I will banish all malevolence in my heart toward her and I will cause her no further harm. Therefore I beg you to forgive me and endow me with life and open my womb and give me a son.

Everything around me seemed to fade away as I took a vow:

God of hosts, if you pay heed to my suffering, and if you will remember me and not forsake me and give me a son, I will give him to God all the days of his life.

When I lifted my gaze, I saw the high priest Eli standing at the sanctuary's threshold, regarding me. He was an old man, more than eighty years of age, but his eyesight had not dimmed, and when he peered at me with narrowed eyes, he perceived that my lips were moving, though my voice could not be heard.

Hence Eli thought that I was drunk, and he was angry. "How long will you go on drinking? Put away your wine from you!"

"No, sir," I said, "I am a woman in sorrow. I have drunk neither wine nor strong spirits, but have poured out my soul before the Lord. Don't take me for a worthless woman, for I have been speaking out of grief."

Eli seemed convinced, for he answered benignly, "Go in peace, and may the God of Israel grant your request of him."

Under his richly decorated, elaborate priestly garb and cap, Eli looked much like any other old man. His head was bald and he had only a few teeth left in his mouth. Nevertheless he was the most elevated of all men in the land, closer than all others to the one who reigned in the heavens and the earth, the one whose favor I came to curry. So as soon as the high priest's words penetrated my ear they worked their magic on me.

In that instant, my mood changed. There was a new spirit upon me, and a new light illuminating my soul. I felt the moment, tangible like the smile on Eli's face, in which heaven opened its gates to my prayer. I was lifted from the depths of despair to the height of exultation. My fallen face was no more and my eyes were gleaming with joy.

I stepped backward so as not to turn my back to the ark, and thus approached the Temple's exit. As I looked out into the dark, I saw a young Cohanite priest peering at me with the admiring look with which young men usually regarded me.

"Lady," he said softly, "it's dark outside, and you will have difficulty finding your way back to your own tabernacle. To which tribe do you belong?"

I told him, and he offered to guide me back to our encampment. I gratefully accepted his offer.

When we approached the compound, I caught sight of Pninah sitting cross-legged at the entrance to the children's tent. She saw me with the young priest, but barely answered my joyous greeting with a slight smile. I thanked the priest for his escort then entered the tabernacle, where the remnants of the evening meal still awaited me.

Suddenly I was ravenously hungry. I ate, I drank, I ate again, then I drank some more. When I finished my meal, I raised my eyes to see Elkanah standing there silently regarding me in a blind rage. Apparently my zest and my radiant face did nothing to calm his fury, but quite the opposite.

"Hannah, come with me, I wish to speak to you," he said menacingly as he approached me.

He pulled me to my feet and led me out of the tabernacle and pushed me, none too gently, into my tent.

"Where have you been?" he began, his voice trembling with wrath.

"I was praying at the Temple," I said numbly.

"All day long?" he asked incredulously.

"No," I replied as convincingly as I could, "I was sitting outside and waiting for the other worshippers to leave, and this took all day."

"You did not say a word to me."

"No. I did not know it would take so long. I ask your forgiveness, sir."

"And what was this young priest doing with you?"

"Nothing, nothing. He merely escorted me back here to show me the way."

Elkanah's face was twisted with rage. At the peak of his wrath he raised his hand, as if he were about to lash out at me, and I winced and held up my arm to shield my face. But with great effort he restrained himself, the veins bulging and throbbing in his temples.

"Swear to me by God that this is the truth."

"I cannot take the name of the Lord in vain, but I assure you that it is the truth. I don't even know his name."

Instead of hitting me, Elkanah forced me down onto the blanket on the ground. He lifted up my dress and lay down on top of me, knowing me in a manner that indicated that this was to be the punishment for my misdeed, which had taken place only in his mind. It was painful and made me as sore inside as I was when he had ruptured my virginity. It even spotted me with blood.

But I did not cry out. I even welcomed the pain and the blood, for it consecrated our act. I thought that perhaps it would be from his hurtful knowing of me that my sin toward Pninah would be atoned and my child would come into the world.

By the time we were ready to leave, a few days later, Elkanah was reconciled with me. On that day we arose early in the morning. We passed by the Temple, bowed down before the Lord, and recited prayers. Then we set out on our way home.

As we rode, I raised my eyes to the heavy clouds in the sky and watched patches of sunlight penetrating them. I hoped that soon the rays of sunlight would also penetrate the dark clouds of my life.

When we reached home, as soon as we had settled in and eaten our evening meal, I stepped out into the front yard. What had been a mild, overcast day had given way to a clear, chilly evening. The moon was rising, gaining luster as it rose, and I rubbed my arms to dispel the cold. Presently I saw Elkanah leaving his room, heading for Pninah's quarters.

I intercepted him and said, "You mistake, beloved husband. My room is not here, but over there, on the other side."

He laughed but retorted, "I was not planning to come to your room."

"I beg that you will, though, just this once. I feel that it is still important. Please oblige me in this tonight only, and then you will be free to do as you wish."

So Elkanah came to me that night and he knew me.

While we were in Shiloh, my monthly flow had been due to begin, but there was nothing. Even in the following week there was no onset of my way of women, and I rejoiced in the Lord. He had let his countenance shine upon me, and in his infinite mercy he had endowed me with a new existence.

I decided to concentrate my being on my impending motherhood. For I knew that soon everything else would pale into insignificance.

But Elkanah's passion for Pninah continued to bother me. I had expected that over time it would abate, but instead it was growing stronger. Previously, I had searched for a way to put an end to it by removing Pninah from our midst. But at the Temple, having begged God's forgiveness for harboring unkind thoughts about her, I had promised to abandon any wish to harm her.

Yet it was only a short while after I made this promise that I had the ability to do precisely what I had resolved never to think of again.

The Book of Pninah

On the second day of the week after our return from Shiloh, I arose before the sun. On the spot appointed by Arnon I found a young man and woman waiting for me, and we immediately started on our journey.

As my donkey trailed theirs, I gave free rein to my anxiety. Arnon was, after all, a stranger. I found it difficult to imagine what it would be like when he touched me, and when he— Here my thoughts would advance no further. Yet neither would they turn back. It was as if I had crossed some invisible line in my soul, from which there was no return.

We arrived in midmorning, and I entered Bathanath's room. She hugged me briefly, ushered me into the room in which I had eaten with Arnon two weeks before, then disappeared.

Now only a jar of wine and two silver goblets were set on the table, next to which stood Arnon. His lips curved into a smile, soft and inviting, as his head bent in a gesture of silent welcome, and I walked straight into his arms.

He bent over me, tilting my head backward, his lips fastening on mine. My hair hung loosely behind my back; and he played with it gently with one hand, as he embraced me with the other.

"Pninah, these last two weeks have passed slowly," were his first words.

"And I have yearned to see you, Arnon."

Still holding my waist, he poured wine into the goblets and handed me one. We drank silently. The wine, though of a pale golden color, was intoxicating. I felt my head swim and my body heat up in hunger for him.

Arnon, who sensed this, waited no more and said, "Come."

As his bedroom windows were heavily shuttered, only a crack in the shutters enabled me to see that the room was large and square and had a huge bed set against its inner wall. This was covered with a light blue bed-cloth, and two large pillows awaited our heads.

I let my dress slip to the floor. As I lay down on the bed, I thought briefly of the other women who must have lain on it with Arnon before. Then I forgot everything. Arnon explored my mouth and my breasts with his lips, and my secret spot with his hand, wanting to prolong the joy before the joy. But my need for him was too urgent to allow for this. He excited me beyond sense and, astounded by my own wanton response, I pleaded with him to come into me at once.

As he entered me I drowned in delight. My moans, my joy, and my spasms came almost immediately. Then, with slow deliberation, he prolonged his roaming inside me. I cried out as my joy came again, and when it happened for the third time, it overcame us together. Thus I was initiated into the art of repeated delights, and I lay in Arnon's arms in a state of utter well-being.

I was the first to speak. "I am a deviant woman now."

"Did you enjoy the act of becoming one?"

"So very much," I sighed in contentment.

"As I enjoyed making you one."

After we dressed, Arnon went out and returned with a tray laden with food and wine. We were famished with the hunger that only lovemaking can produce, and we ate and drank until not a crumb was left on the tray.

While we ate, Arnon said, "Pninah, don't feel badly about lying with me. A man who treats his wife as your husband treats you has no right to expect otherwise."

Suddenly a fear I had been unwilling to face reared its head. "By our law of Torah, what he is doing with Hannah is totally acceptable, but what I am doing is punishable by death. If Elkanah suspects me, he will drag me before the priests and they will kill me."

"No, no." There was a gleam of the amusement I loved in his eyes. "Having had some dealings with suspicious husbands, I know that the priests will merely make you drink some bitter water. It has a nauseating taste, but it's harmless."

"He will give me a book of divorcement, then, and send me away from his house."

"Yes," he conceded, "and perhaps this would be a good thing."

I looked at him in surprise.

"I love you," he said, "I want you to be mine, and I want to be yours. For our entire lives."

"I love you, too," I replied, but I did not react to his offer.

We returned to bed, and knew each other again and again with as much passion as if each had been the first time. Then passion gave way to weariness, and we dropped into a sleep of exhaustion.

When we awoke, Arnon led me into an adjacent room, set aside for bathing only. There a large stone tub had been filled with warm water by unseen hands. We bathed in it together, lulling languidly in the warm water, while Arnon tried to calm my anxieties: "You must not be afraid that Elkanah will find you out. If he comes in search of you, Bathanath will say that you are visiting with her and have just stepped out to attend to your needs."

My fears were not laid to rest. If Elkanah came, would he believe Bathanath's words? Would he not prefer to find out for himself what I was doing?

Yet meeting my lover had infused me with a sense of being wanted not only for bodily pleasures but also for my soul. I had no intention of breaking away from him and we arranged our next meeting for the second day of the second week.

When I mounted my donkey, Bathanath was beside me, mounting hers, intending to accompany me for a while. As the guards were also ready we set out together.

Bathanath praised me for my improved appearance. Happiness, she added, did more for beauty than any of her oils or perfumes. Enjoining me once more to hide my face from the sun, she brought forth a head-covering with a wide rim and placed it with both her hands, like a blessing, on my head.

As the way home to my town wound before us, we found much to talk about, until she decided that it was time for her to turn back. Before long we approached Ramathayim, and my escorts left me on my own.

This was the moment I had been waiting for, the moment to praise the Lord once again, for coming to my aid and giving me a previously unknown existence.

The Book of Hannah

At first I thought that I should keep my own counsel for a short while—my pregnancy a secret shared only with the Lord—but my joy was too great to contain. As soon as I was completely sure I hugged and kissed Elkanah until he could bear it no longer.

I took hold of the rags I kept prepared to absorb the monthly flow of my blood, and with great pomp carried them out to the backyard. I dropped them one by one into a heap, over which I poured pure, choice, olive oil, as if it were a libation on the altar of the Lord. Then, calling to Elkanah to witness my deed, I set fire to them. And we both watched the flames that rose forth from them with glee.

Next I rode over to Shaar Efraim to convey the glad tidings to my mother and father and my young brothers who lived with them, and we shed tears of joy together. Even my brothers' eyes were moist as they hugged me between the four of them, until I had to warn them to be careful of crushing my suddenly exceedingly precious belly.

As I rode back from my parents' home, it was raining gently. The rains had begun early that year, and the leafy trees on the sides of the road were fresh and green and strong, their branches pointing heavenward as in a prayer of thanks for the libation. For a while I, too, raised my face toward heaven, saying a silent prayer of gratitude and praise to the Lord. The rain continued and the earth was absorbing God's bounty, as I was drinking up his mercy on me.

When I reached home, I even hugged Pninah, who smiled brilliantly, yet in truth barely noticed me, and seemed immersed in a happiness of her own.

Two more weeks passed, and my elation was now tinged with the sickness that hung over me every morning. I could no longer manage the house as I was accustomed to. I had to ask Pninah to take the task from me, which she did.

One evening two months later, as we were sitting around the table for the evening meal, I decided that it would not be right to keep my other secret from my husband. I revealed that I had taken a vow that if I bore a son, I would give him to God all the days of his life.

A long silence greeted my announcement. Elkanah looked anything but pleased. After he composed himself, he inquired uneasily: "What does that mean?"

"It means that he will grow up at the Temple and devote his life to the service of the Lord."

Elkanah set down the cup of grape juice he had just brought to his mouth and looked at me. The love in his eyes was intermingled with what looked distinctly like concern for my sanity. "Hannah, my loved one. You cannot be serious. For years you have been yearning for a child. And now that you are finally about to bear one, you want to give it away?"

"Only if it's a boy," I said, although I was already certain that it was.

Running his hand distractedly through his hair, he asked, "Will you not miss him?"

I could hardly deny this. "Of course I will miss him. I can feel the pain of separation in my heart already. But I have made a promise to the Lord, and I cannot turn back from it."

I could see the relief in his face as he replied, "By Torah law I can release you from it, and I will do so right now."

"Of course your wisdom greatly exceeds mine, and I would never set my will against yours, but, in truth, I don't wish to be released from my vow—I want to keep it."

"Hannah, you have not considered this." He now spoke with the pained patience he usually reserved for his sons and daughters when they were naughty. "What do the priests in the Temple know about caring for children? And why should they make the effort?"

"I will hire a woman to take care of him, naturally," I said with rising assurance.

His patience now ran out and he was exasperated. "The priests will never permit a woman to live in their midst. It would look as if she were a harlot."

"I will choose an elderly woman, and she will bother no one. I will suffer, but that cannot be avoided."

"And so will the boy suffer. What is the purpose of it?" he pleaded with me.

"When he grows up, he will forget his sufferings and he will do great deeds in Israel." I felt certain of what I was saying, although I did not know the source of my conviction.

Elkanah remained unconvinced. "What great deeds?"

I had no hesitation in proclaiming haughtily, "He will be a prophet, a leader, and a judge, and he will live on in our people's memories forever."

"This is nothing but foolishness. Besides, I don't want him to be a prophet and a leader and a judge. I just want him to be healthy and happy like my other children."

This did not rattle my confidence. "It's his destiny."

Pninah now intervened. "Are you a prophetess yourself, then?"

"No. But this I know."

Elkanah seemed to be swayed by my confidence, and in the end he said with a sigh of resignation, "Do as is good in your eyes."

Still, he remained seated in his chair long after the meal was over, scowling at the table in front of him. And I could tell that his doubts as to what might befall our as yet unborn son when he came to reside at the House of the Lord—far from us, and at the mercy of strangers—had not been laid to rest.

As my belly expanded, Pninah's contracted. As I became broader, she became slimmer, until she was as well shaped as she had been at the age of fifteen. Her skin, which had been dry and of a very ordinary olive color, had become as smooth and light as alabaster, with pink roses of the valley blooming in her cheeks. This made her large eyes, aglow with happiness, all the more outstanding. Grudgingly I had to admit that she looked more beautiful than ever.

Elkanah looked and saw, spending more nights with her and fewer with me. I could see the gleam of lust in his eyes whenever they alighted on her. Yet I sensed that it was more than her looks that attracted him. And I wished, as I had many times before, that I knew what she was doing to incite such insatiable lust in him.

As my pregnancy progressed, I became more and more engrossed with the life growing inside me. I paid less attention to the world outside, even to Elkanah and Pninah's carnal pleasures. But I did continue to be perplexed about her evident happiness, which had appeared even before Elkanah's passion for her had reawakened. I found this incomprehensible until, one day, a kinswoman of mine, Efrath, came to visit me.

As we sat drinking milk and honey and chatting under the sheltering leaves of a fig tree, she told me an odd story.

She had long been a widow, and over the years the youthful smoothness of her face had faded. She had just come back from Sdeh Canaan, where at Binah's behest she had gone to visit a woman named Bathanath to revive her beauty.

There she had seen Pninah, sitting and drinking herbal water with the Canaanite woman. The account of her visit—of the handsome brother she had spotted there, and Pninah's vanishing as soon as he appeared—explained all too well my rival's new happiness to me.

When Efrath departed I continued to sit under the fig tree, distraught at Pninah's misdeed, mulling over what I had just heard, weighing in my mind what next I must do.

Was this Pninah, my childhood friend, who had known nearly nothing about the way of a man with a woman, and now knew twice as much as she should? The very thought that a man other than Elkanah would touch me disgusted me. How could Pninah bear to be naked to the gaze and touch of two men, to gather the seed of a man other than her husband into her womb? Had she no womanly modesty, no shame?

All this was beyond my understanding. But of Pninah's activities, there was no doubt. I had to decide how to respond, and my thoughts clashed with each other. If I told Elkanah, he would undoubtedly hand Pninah a book of divorcement and I would finally be rid of her, as I had longed to be. But I had promised the Lord never again to think unkind thoughts about her, let alone harm her. If Elkanah knew of her misdeeds, it would not merely harm her, but destroy her. He would never forgive such a slight to his honor. She would be shamed before our entire tribe. He would punish her even further by keeping the children and never letting her see them again. I did not want to be the one to tear a mother away from her children. I also still had a commitment to Pninah, to make amends for the sorrow I had caused her.

Yet if I did not tell Elkanah, I would be guilty of letting his wife dishonor him. It would be as if I were dishonoring him myself. I loved Elkanah in a way that overwhelmed all else, and colluding with Pninah behind his back was inconceivable.

I could not decide between my two obligations. My reflections only led me to suffer a piercing, throbbing headache.

The Book of Pninah

A rnon's body thrilled me in a much different manner than Elkanah's. My husband compelled me into submissive passion and shamelessly delighted in my meek surrender. But Arnon and I abandoned ourselves to our mutual lust, neither of us subdued by the other. Arnon told me that of all the women he had known, I was the most lustful. Casting down my eyes in shame, I asked whether that was good or bad. He kissed me softly, then held my face away from him and replied, "Very good."

Beyond lust, there was love. Not having experienced a man's true love before, I felt like a shriveled flower that, having been put into water, flourished again. Arnon gave me not merely the heat of his lust, but also the warmth of his friendship. All the words that were buried inside me, which Elkanah showed no wish to hear, sprang forth from me much as water gushes down from the mountains of the north after the snows have melted. They streamed into Arnon's receptive ears, and they brought forth his, as gifts from his heart.

One day I found on my side of the bed a pouch, which Arnon bade me open. It contained a golden necklace studded with a multitude of sparkling, precious stones. He clasped it around my neck, and declared that from now on my eyes would outshine not only the stars.

I looked into the mirror standing nearby and laughed with happiness, for I had never owned anything that beautiful. Yet I resolutely removed the necklace from my neck and gave it back to Arnon, explaining that if I accepted this expensive gift I would feel like a harlot who exacts payment for her favors.

Arnon restored it to its pouch quite roughly and placed it on the shelf next to my side of his bed. He announced curtly, "It will be waiting for you there until you change your mind."

Later, as we were lying in bed, calm after love, Arnon once again broached the topic of our marriage: "Leave your husband, Pninah. Come here and be my wife. My *only* wife."

"I have children, Arnon, and they are the light of my eyes."

"Bring them along with you. I will love them and raise them as my own. We will buy a house, and you can have all the maids and nurses you wish for."

"Their father will never let me take them. And he will have the priests and the elders and the judges on his side. Besides, they are Israelites and I want them to grow up as Israelites."

"Then come here by yourself, and go and visit them as much as you like."

"Elkanah would never let me near them," I said in agitation. "Besides, the priests and the elders would curse me. My father would scorn me. I would be ostracized by my people."

Arnon drew me to him and held me close. "Don't be upset, my love. I won't press you to do what you don't want to do."

I was relieved.

All that I had told Arnon was the truth, but I had not revealed that despite the manner in which Elkanah degraded me, I was still bound to him by ties of love. I did not wish to leave him.

My friendship with Bathanath was flourishing as well. Often riding with me on my way home, she would tell me of her husband, who was roaming over the seas, and of her twelve-year-old twin sons, who were growing up without a father. She hinted that she did not spend all her nights alone, as there was a priest who worshipped her body more ardently than he worshipped the god Baal. I listened and shared her concerns, but did not have as much advice to offer her as she gave me.

She bade me never to cast my eyes at butter and honey and dates and figs. She gave me aromatic substances, extracted from rare plants that grew in hidden nooks and crannies, the eating of which would cause my body to assume its previous enticing shape. "For," she added, "there is a shapely woman lurking inside you, waiting to emerge if only you will let her."

She also supplied me with subtle scents that would exude from the most hidden parts of my body, oils and bay laurels crushed into nectars to render my skin soft and smooth. And herbs to chew on, to ensure that my breath was sweet at all times.

One day, when I entered Bathanath's room to greet her before I proceeded to meet Arnon, she requested that I stay with her for a while, since Arnon was busy with a merchant who had come to him from afar. The morning was chilly, so the steaming hot herbal water she offered me was welcome.

I was still savoring it when the front door opened and a woman came in. I recognized her as a kinswoman of Hannah's named Efrath. Our hostess invited her to drink with us. As she sat, she recognized me and inquired after my family.

Then Efrath looked out of the window into the front yard, where Arnon was standing with the foreign merchant. Upon learning that he was Bathanath's brother, she nodded. "Yes, there is a great resemblance between you."

As Arnon walked back into the house, Bathanath said that she knew me to be in a rush to get home. She escorted me to the back door from which, she claimed, I could more easily reach the stables.

As I stepped into the corridor to meet Arnon, I felt uneasy. For although there was nothing improper in my sitting with Bathanath, it would have been better if Efrath had not seen me there.

Arnon, and later Bathanath, made light of my worries. But when I reached home, a nagging fear crept into my heart, and I was no longer at ease with myself.

The Book of Hannah

The morning after Efrath visited me, I saw Elkanah off into the fields, then I turned back to look for Pninah.

She had a penchant for cleanliness. The floors in her quarters were always painstakingly scrubbed. She bathed her children morning and night without fail, so that their little bodies always smelled of the fragrant liquid soap she lavished on them. I found her in the boys' room, where she had all the little ones in a big tub. She was kneeling beside it and scrubbing them with a cloth dunked in soap until their soft skin shone pink.

"When you are finished here, Pninah, I would like to speak to you," I said and watched her grow pale.

A short while later she entered my room, and when I bade her sit down, and sat down opposite her, she said with what was obviously feigned courage: "Speak, for I am listening."

I found it difficult to say what I had planned to say. But my protruding belly and the gathering heaviness of my swelling breasts increased my confidence.

Finally I began: "My kinswoman Efrath came to visit me yesterday."

"Yes?" Pninah strove to appear calm, but I saw that she was clenching and unclenching her hands in her lap.

"Yes. She was on her way back from Sdeh Canaan, where she had visited Bathanath. She said that she saw you there, sitting with the Canaanite woman."

"True, I sat with her."

"She told me that there was a younger brother. A tall, handsome brother, with a red tint to his copper-colored hair."

"Yes, that is Arnon, he is a merchant."

"She also prided herself on having discovered a shortcut from

Sdeh Canaan, for you left Bathanath before she did; and yet you were not back when she arrived here."

"She may be right."

"Pninah, don't play with me," I warned her. "You may think that I am stupid, but I am not."

"No one has seen me with the brother, and no one will." She tried to keep her voice steady, but it had just the slightest tremor in it, and it was not difficult to divine that she was shaken.

I retorted, "It is not necessary for people to see you together to have a good guess of what you are doing. And if Elkanah finds out . . ." I let my words trail off.

With a stricken look on her face, Pninah asked, "Are you going to voice your suspicions?"

I hesitated for a while, letting her fret. Then I replied with deliberate hesitation, "No . . . but the tale may reach him in other ways; and then your life and your children's lives will be destroyed."

Her hands were now visibly trembling. Yet she sat there, sullen and defiant. The forward tilt to her chin told me, more loudly than any words could have, of her resolution to continue in her grievous sin.

I noticed, as I never had before, that despite her delicately built body she had a spine of iron, a soul as sturdy as stone. It would not be easy to make her change her ways.

Still I tried. "What if you become pregnant and bear a child with a red tint to its hair?"

"I will not bear a child with a red tint, or any other color, to its hair."

"So you have been to see Binah, and she has beguiled you with her witchery."

"You know well that Binah never deals in witchery."

"Even if it's not witchery, you must surely know that what she gave you doesn't always fulfill the hope you may pin on it."

By now Pninah had regained her spirits, and she said with courage that was no longer feigned, "It will do what it should for me."

"Are *you* a prophetess, then?"

"No, but this I know."

"If nothing else weighs with you, will you not consider that you are breaking one of the Ten Commandments?"

"Don't lecture me on the commandments," she flashed back. Suddenly her voice was loud, and shaking not with fear but with wrath. "You may not be aware of this," she added scathingly, "but there is also a commandment not to covet what belongs to your friend. Yet you have coveted my husband, and you have both committed adultery."

"I coveted your husband, and I regret it," I said, to appease her. "But we have not been adulterers, for I never let Elkanah know me before I became his wife."

"It's still adultery in my eyes," she fumed, the longtime bitterness in her heart finally bursting out of her, coloring her voice.

"But not in the eyes of Torah law," I replied calmly.

"A law that permits a man to know a woman other than his wife but does not permit a woman to know a man other than her husband is unjust," she continued her litany.

Her blistering tirade left me unshaken. "Who put you in charge of pronouncing judgment over the Lord's laws as laid down in the Torah, and deciding whether they are just or not?" I asked.

Suddenly Pninah rose and began striding back and forth in front of me, her hands clenched into fists at her sides, as she ranted, "Even Abraham, the father of our people, questioned the Lord's decrees about Sodom and Gomorrah, when he said to him, 'Will not the judge of the entire earth do justice?'"

"You may not be aware of this," I said as scathingly as she had spoken to me before, "but you are not Abraham. And neither am I. We must accept the Torah laws as they are. They were given to us on Mount Sinai, and they cannot be changed."

"This law can be changed, and it *will* be changed."

I remained unconvinced. "Are you prophesying again?"

Though still agitated, Pninah resumed her place and sat silently with her head bent, regarding her own knees. Strands of her honey-colored hair fell down over her temples, and her mouth pouted in the manner of a little girl who has just been scolded severely by her mother over a small prank.

Then she shook back her hair and raised her face to mine. She regarded me somberly, and there was a vengeful gleam in her eyes. For a moment it seemed as if she were about to reveal something of great importance.

"Besides, Elkanah also . . ." she said, then stopped herself in mid-sentence. The vengeful look faded from her eyes and she fell silent again.

"Besides, Elkanah also?" I prompted her to continue.

"Nothing," she said and once more cast her eyes down.

I wondered what she had been about to reveal. It was evidently something designed to hurt me. But what?

Given what had just passed between us, I did not want to press her. We sat in silence for a while, and I realized that any further attempt to bring her around to my way of thinking would be futile. I told her that I had said all that I had to say to her, she rose to her feet and turned on her heels and stalked out of my room.

A few weeks later, when my days to give birth were full and my labor pains began, I panicked. The preparations for the birthing had been made, but I knew that much could go wrong.

There was a midwife in Ramathayim, and Elkanah wanted her to deliver the baby because she was closest. But my mother insisted on Binah, even though it might take her longer to get to our home. In the end, both women were engaged. I foresaw that there would be strife between them, as each would wish to display her superior knowledge, and that this might well make the birthing more difficult. This did nothing to enhance my peace of mind.

The first to arrive, the midwife who lived close by, brought the birthing stones with her. Elkanah arrived next, called back from the fields. Then came my mother and my father, and finally, Binah. The two midwives wanted everyone else out of the room, but I begged to have my mother beside me to hold my hand, so they allowed her to stay.

I had heard Pninah scream with pain during her first delivery. She began shrieking when the sun had set in the sky and did not calm down until the middle of the night, when the infant was born. I had promised myself that when my time came, I would comport myself with more dignity and stifle my shouts inside me. That promise was forgotten as soon as the pains increased.

Miraculously, the two midwives got on well with each other. The one from Ramathayim began chanting incantations and pouring libations over me to chase away evil spirits and coax the child out of the womb. But Binah, whom I had apparently maligned unjustly, speedily put an end to this witchery, and after that peace reigned.

At first, the two women attempted to alleviate my pains by stroking my belly and rubbing an oily ointment into it. Then they measured out a potion for me to drink, made of crushed poppy seeds as black as night, but just as the pains were at their strongest, and almost continuous, they gave me no more of it because soon I would have to push, to help the infant come out.

In the brief intervals between the pains, I heard them whisper between themselves, saying that the baby had turned around, and that its head was not pointing downward as it should. They said it was a large infant, and that it would be difficult for it to make its way through the passage.

I recalled the women I knew who had died while giving birth to dead infants, and now I faced a horrendous fear for both the child and for myself.

As I squatted on the birthing stones, the local midwife knelt down behind me and made me recline backward onto her knees, bidding me to push. The more my pains increased, the more she demanded that I push.

Binah was crouching in front of me, her hand and knife below me between the two stones, and I felt her cutting inside me, attempting to enlarge the opening of my womb and trying to turn the child around, in oder to ease its passage. The pain from her doing so was beyond anything I imagined possible, too strong to bear.

Binah called on me to push even more vigorously, and it is then that I began to scream with so much force that all of Ramathayim must have heard it. I did not care whether my mother was beside me or not, I just screamed and screamed until my strength and my voice failed me and I could scream no more.

Later I was told that Elkanah and my father had been sitting on the ground in front of the door, sweat pouring down their bodies and tears from their eyes, pleading with the Lord on my behalf and on behalf of the child. And when they heard me stop screaming, they became so panicked that they burst into my room to make sure I was still alive.

Finally I felt the water washing out of me and the baby's body tearing me apart, then a sense of great relief; there was Binah's voice announcing that I had delivered a son, then my sinking into a pit, and then—darkness.

When I drifted hazily back into awareness, I was lying in my bed drenched in sweat. The washed and swaddled infant lay at my side, and Elkanah and my father and mother were sitting around me, reciting psalms and weeping tears of gratitude before the Lord.

I was too weak to pick up the infant myself, so Elkanah held him and gave him to me to see. I kissed his bushy dark hair, before I drifted back to sleep.

When next I awoke, I heard Elkanah and my father and mother making plans for a huge celebration in honor of the boy's circumcision. I was too exhausted to speak, but I shook my head, and I saw the lack of comprehension in their eyes. It was only much later that I could utter a few words, and explain that I wanted to invite only a few close relatives for the circumcision, but that we would hold an enormous feast for his weaning.

They disliked my plan, since it was not the common way. Yet they knew that it was what our father Abraham had done when his son Isaac was weaned. Also, they did not feel that they could deny my wish, after all that I had been through.

We did not reveal the boy's name to anyone until the circumcision. Then I asked the priest performing the ritual to announce this: The boy who had now been entered into the covenant of our father Abraham, his name in Israel would be Samuel, for I said that I had asked him from the Lord.

I had feared that the infant would not live to draw a single breath, but here he was—the first issue of my womb, a sign for the many others yet to come. A token of the Lord's mercy for me. The son I had promised to him.

A promise the consequences of which I still had not the slightest notion.

The Book of Pninah

After the incident with Hannah, a cloud hovered over my life. I visited Arnon as often as before, yet during our acts of love I was jumpy and even the faintest noise startled me. Afterward, my eyes would dart across the room, as if I expected someone to leap out of a shady corner and into our bed.

At night my dreams were shaped by my fears. I had a recurring nightmare in which Elkanah burst into Arnon's room, grabbed me and dragged me naked through the streets to lead me before the priests. The people lined the streets, their outstretched fingers, glittering like knives, pointed at me, as they knew me for what I was, a deviant woman. And in the morning my heart was heavy with the memory of my dream.

I sensed that Arnon's heart, too, was heavy. One day he said mournfully: "It is unfair that he, who does not love you, should take you whenever he wants. Yet I, who love you so much, can show my love for you twice a month only."

I concealed from Arnon that Elkanah now came to me three or four times each week, and on these occasions we ravished each other time after time. I feared this knowledge would lead him to believe that my love for him was diminished in some way. But I reiterated that I could not tear myself away from my children.

Running his fingers up and down the inside of my thighs, he complained, "The nights are cold and lonely without you."

He rolled over to lie facedown and, stroking his back, I admitted that although it was very sad, there was no other way but for him to take a wife.

Abruptly he turned around to face me, revealing the copper-colored hair on his chest, which narrowed tantalizingly toward the lower part of his body. He knew me to be aroused but ignored this, and his eyes hardened as he said, "How would you feel if I took a wife and we never saw each other again?"

I replied with a sob that it would be agony for me, but that he must nevertheless live with a woman who would be at his side at all times.

On another occasion, as we lay in bed, Arnon returned to that which lay heavily on his heart. "Pninah my loved one, I must tell you the truth. Performing the act of love with you every second week is not enough to satisfy me."

My response was that to come to him more often would make my husband suspicious, but between our meetings Arnon could do whatever he wished.

He replied, "I am grateful for your permission." Then his face tightened and he added: "But I would remind you that the act of love sometimes involves feelings of love. Not always, but it may happen."

There seemed to be nothing to say in response, so I buried my face in his broad chest, and clung to him and whispered words of love into its hair. He closed his arms around me and took me with a ruthless desperation he had never shown me before, as if he wanted to ingrain his power, himself, in my memory.

At that time another dark cloud gathered in the sky of my life. It was the illness of the woman who gave birth to me.

Ever since Hagith had moved to the faraway town of Bethlehem, our mother had been wasting away. She was getting thinner, her hair had lost its luster, and she looked old beyond her years, which were no more than forty.

But it was only later that she was beset by her illness. Defying her womanly being, her breasts became as hard as stone, but as they did not pain her, she was not worried.

Later the pains began, then spread to other parts of her body. At first they were slight, but their strength increased until she could bear it no more. Bathel was now bedridden and needed constant care.

My father engaged a maid to care for the sick woman, but she was a stranger, and Bathel felt uncomfortable with her. My sister had small children to care for, and it was difficult for her to come home often. So to me fell the major burden of caring for the woman who, even if I did not think of her as such, was still my mother.

I sought out renowned herbalists and healers who gave her potions to drink and mixtures to rub on her skin. But their remedies were as useless as abundant rain to a felled tree.

All that was left was for me was to give Bathel yet another poppy-seed drink to alleviate her pain, and to see to her needs and wash her, while she stroked my ministering hands in mute gratitude. I watched her sink into despair as life gradually drained from her body.

Time dragged on, and Bathel's state worsened even further. I could no longer keep up my visits with Arnon. Twice I had to dispatch a messenger to Bathanath to tell her that I would not be able to come, and so I did not see Arnon for a month and a half.

Finally I sent word to Hagith that it was time to come. She replied that she would arrive in two days' time, so I sent a missive to Bathanath, advising her that I would visit on the day Hagith was due to arrive.

I found Arnon hungrier for me than ever. He once told me that there were mountains that erupted and spewed forth fire and a hot liquid. Our reunion after such a long parting was what I imagined such an eruption to be.

But no sooner had our bodies parted than I heard a commotion outside the room and a fierce rattling of the door.

I jumped out of the bed as one bitten by a snake. I broke into a profuse sweat, and began dressing myself with trembling hands.

The Book of Hannah

As Samuel grew, so did my love and admiration for him. I would not let any maid touch him, and did everything for him myself. I hardly ever let him lie on a blanket or, later, sit or crawl on the carpeted floor, as Pninah used to do with her children. Instead, I held him in my lap as much as he would allow. Only when he demanded it did I let him down to play on his own. I permitted his father and his grandparents to fuss over him, but after a while I always got impatient and drew the infant back into my arms.

My mother warned me that he would become so demanding of my attention that there would be no bearing him. She was wrong. He never demanded anything. He was never cranky, he never shuffled about restlessly, and he was never bored.

Samuel's hair was dark and curly like that of Elkanah's other sons. But his eyes were green like mine. He was beautiful.

Since I never cooed to him but talked to him incessantly as if he were able to understand my words, he very soon did comprehend them; he learned to speak at a very early age. Yet he did not prattle on as other children did, and seemed often to be engrossed in his own thoughts.

I recounted fables, making up enthralling tales of miraculous adventures spun out of childhood dreams. At first he would listen, gaping at me in openmouthed wonder, but as he neared the age of three, his eyes widened with what looked distinctly like disbelief. Once, I was so disconcerted that I cut off a tale in the midst of telling it, and thereafter told him only of events that had truly happened.

Each year, when it was time to set out on our pilgrimage to the Temple in Shiloh, Elkanah urged me to come and bring the child along, as Pninah was always doing with her children. But I declined, preferring to spend those days alone with my son, for I knew that the time of our parting was drawing near, and my heart was aching at the thought.

Elkanah said, "Do as is good in your eyes."

When Samuel approached the age of three, the time of his weaning, I looked about me for a suitable woman to be his nurse at the Temple. My kinswoman Efrath was the one I chose for the post. She was old enough to live among the priests without being taken for a harlot, yet young enough to care for a child. Being a widow she needed sustenance, and she gladly accepted my offer. I invited her to come and live with us so that she and the child could get used to each other, and they grew fond of one another.

My next step was to send a messenger bearing a letter to the high priest Eli. In it I reminded him of his blessing for me, told him of my vow, and requested his permission to have the boy reside at the Temple.

The messenger was detained for several days, and finally he came back with a missive from one of the ordinary priests. It was curt and informed me that there was no place for a child at the Temple, but that I would be permitted to bring him to visit from time to time.

It was clear to me that I must speak with the high priest face to face. I decided to bring the boy with me, thus making it more difficult for him to refuse me.

Before I could go, I had to wean the child from my breast and arrange for the large party that we were to give in his honor. Bit by bit I replaced my breast milk with cow's milk and solid food, and began preparing the party.

It was during this time that an incident occurred. Pninah's mother was severely ill, and I knew that she was now spending her days at her mother's side. I was therefore surprised when a messenger from her father's house appeared early one morning to tell us that Bathel was on the verge of death, and that Pninah must come to her immediately.

She had left the house some time earlier, and I presumed that she had set out for her mother's house already. But the messenger assured us that she had not arrived there, nor had he encountered her on the way.

Elkanah, who was about to leave for the fields, was annoyed. He said testily that she had probably gone off to visit the Canaanite woman again, and that he would have to ride over to fetch her.

My thoughts chased each other rapidly and I foresaw disaster. I pressed my hands to my temples in an attempt to calm myself, as I decided what I should or should not do.

While I was vacillating, agonizing over my decision, I became conscious of what I had not been conscious of before: since I was no longer barren, my previous jealousy of Pninah had gradually diminished. It had not vanished, but right now, I was concerned for her.

Had this incident occurred before I became pregnant, I would have had no doubt as to what I should do: I would have done nothing. I would have let events take their own course to bring about her doom.

I knew that what she was doing was utterly wrong, and that if Elkanah came upon her unawares she would get her just desserts, but the great bliss I now felt due to motherhood prompted me to feel more generous toward her. I felt a flare of compassion, and of guilt. For I was as sure as I was of the rising of the sun in the morning that her misdeeds were the result of the sorrow I had brought into her life.

Her welfare was important to me. It would be unbearable to see her lose her mother, her husband, and her children at the same time. Unbearable to see her perish in the new sorrow I would bring down upon her simply by doing nothing.

I told Elkanah that I would ride to fetch Pninah in his stead. He replied that he could ride faster than I could and bring her back more quickly. All my entreaties to let me go were to no avail. I tried to stall him with words, but he would not hear me. He said that if he did not go quickly, and Pninah was too late to see her mother, he would not be able to forgive himself. He prepared to set out for Sdeh Canaan.

I rushed back to my room to get dressed and ordered Efrath to take charge of Samuel. As soon as I saw Elkanah leave, I ran to the stables and told one of the stable boys whom I knew to be a Canaanite that he must ride with me to Sdeh Canaan and find a shortcut that would get us there quicker than the wind. The boy was surprised, but saddled his own donkey while I saddled mine, and off we went.

In my impatience it seemed to me that our donkeys hardly outpaced turtles, even though we spurred them to move as quickly as possible. The boy led me through a narrow trail between the fields, which few had trodden before. He also knew Bathanath's house, and when we entered its front yard on our exhausted animals, I instructed him to repair with them to the stables and stay out of sight.

I entered the front room, seeing its many aids to female beauty, inhaling its sweet scents of women, and knew myself to be of their numbers. Thus I was strengthened in my determination to help Pninah.

Bathanath did not know me and came forward with a friendly smile.

"I am Hannah from Ramathayim," I said, and her face darkened. "I've come to get Pninah."

"Yes, she is here with me, but she has stepped out for a short while to attend to her needs. Please sit down, and I will get her."

"I know well what needs she is attending to. Get her quickly. Her mother is dying and her husband will be here soon to fetch her."

I spoke with urgency, and although Bathanath tried to appear calm, I could see that she was not. She took hold of my hand and led me into another room, shuttered it so that Elkanah would not see me when he came, and told me to lock it from the inside, then hurried away. Before long I heard voices in the front yard, and I knew that they heralded Elkanah's arrival.

I could only hope that Bathanath would be able to fetch Pninah from wherever she was with her lover before Elkanah understood what was taking place.

The Book of Pninah

The commotion outside Arnon's room was followed by Bathanath's voice calling to me to come out because my husband would arrive soon. My heart beat in my ears. While I fumbled with my shoelaces, I shot a distressed look at Arnon, who smiled reassuringly. Then I left the room.

Bathanath told me what had occurred. I ran out to the room in which Hannah was waiting, and when she let me in, I blessed her many times over for what she had done for me. She said that I must compose myself, and step into Bathanath's room to meet Elkanah.

When Elkanah entered, barely a few moments later, he found Bathanath and I sitting primly at the table, demurely inspecting material for a new dress. Elkanah conveyed the bad tidings to me, and I pretended to be surprised. But I did not pretend to be shattered, for I truly was. I offered him a cup of herbal water, which he pronounced to be vile, but still gulped down thirstily. Then I led him to the front yard, and we set out.

Elkanah was in a thunderous mood. We were hardly out of earshot of the house, when he could no longer contain his wrath. "What were you about to visit that woman now, when you knew your mother to be in such a bad way?" he snarled at me.

I was painfully aware that he was right in his rebuke, his accusation irrefutable. "It was ill done of me," I admitted. "I regret to have put you to so much trouble, sir."

Elkanah's ferocious rage began to dissipate, giving way to pity on account of my mother's impending death. He reproached me no more and the rest of the journey was accomplished in silence.

Only when we approached Ramathayim did I speak, requesting him to accompany me to Shaar Efraim. I did this to ensure that Hannah would have time to reach home before he did. He agreed reluctantly, entered Bathel's room with me to pay his respects, then left.

The shutters of Bathel's window were closed to protect her from the glare of sunlight, and a suffocating smell of decaying flesh hung in the air. She was lying on her back, her eyes were sunken, and the crinkled skin on her face had assumed the gray color of the sheet on which she lay.

I bent over her and asked if she was in pain. With many pauses to catch her breath, she whispered hoarsely that the pain had left her, but she could hardly breathe. She motioned my father who was sitting with her to leave, then drew me down to sit on her bed. Though her breathing was labored, she managed to murmur, "Pninah my dear daughter, you always thought that I only loved Hagith, but I did love you with all my heart."

"Don't distress yourself. Just rest and get well again."

"Even now you don't call me mother."

"Don't distress yourself . . . my mother."

My voice cracked, and as I uttered these words, the jealousy of Hagith, that had festered like a sore inside me, vanished. All the feelings for my mother that I had kept inside for years were released in a torrent of choking sobs.

"Please be healthy again, my mother. I love you so much."

I hugged her, and wept until her face was a blur before my eyes.

My mother's breaths were growing more rapid and shallow. Still she insisted on talking. "Be blessed my child in the triple blessing of the Lord. And may this blessing come down also on your children and on your children's children."

At this moment Hagith rushed in and hurled herself into her mother's arms, almost choking her. I left them together and sat down in front of the door. Soon Hagith called me in.

By now Bathel was no longer able to whisper. All we could do was lie down on either side of her and kiss her cheeks while she stroked our hair, until she fell into a deep sleep from which she did not awake.

After three days of wheezing in her sleep, we witnessed my mother's last sigh, a sigh of relief. She died with my father, Hagith, and me sitting around her bed. When we saw that her struggle had ceased, we arose and, with tears stinging our eyes, followed the ancient ritual of mourning, tearing our garments.

We buried my mother in the family plot. Then we removed our shoes, dressed in sackcloth, strew ashes on our heads and sat on the ground in the yard to mourn her for thirty days.

Hagith was devastated, but I thought that my grief was the heavier, for I could not forgive myself for not forgiving her until it was too late. I had lost my mother just when I had found her.

The first to arrive to comfort me was Hannah, who sat by me on the ground and told me that my children were well cared for and that she would take over my lessons until I could return home. After that, silence fell.

Finally I collected my strength and asked her why she had exerted herself so much to help me.

She replied, "I know you don't think so, Pninah, but despite everything, I still love you and I am still your friend."

My grudge against her was forgotten, as if it had never existed. I embraced her warmly and kissed her cheek. I felt that through her kindness we had been reconciled.

Elkanah, who approached us at that moment, looked puzzled and pleased.

Then our friends and relatives arrived, and with them all the people of the village. Talking to so many people lightened the burden of my mourning.

Back home, Elkanah spent the first night after my mourning with me, and extinguished some of the fire that had been burning within me. But my yearning for Arnon was not put to rest.

I had previously advised Bathanath of my mourning and now I prepared to send her a letter advising her of my next visit. But before I could dispatch the courier, Elkanah approached me and demanded my help in the preparations for Samuel's party, which was to take place in ten days' time. After all that Hannah had done for me, I could hardly refuse. So my visit to Arnon was further delayed, and my yearning for him had turned into a dull pain in my chest.

I did not attend the party, but the noise that emanated from the front yard lasted until shortly before dawn. As soon as it died down, in the first pale light that heralds the dawn, I set out for the stables.

Having advised Bathanath of my visit, my guards were waiting for me. We reached Sdeh Canaan in good time, and I entered Bathanath's room to greet her briefly, before going to meet Arnon.

But she detained me, requesting that I sit down with her. I told her that much as I loved her, I was impatient to see Arnon, but she repeated her request.

Warily, I lowered myself into a chair. She said that she had bad tidings to convey. I asked whether they concerned Arnon and she admitted that it was so.

My neck stiffened with alarm. "Is he . . . is he . . . ill?"

"No, it's not an illness."

Then I knew; and I felt the color draining from my face.

After a brief silence, Bathanath said, "Arnon has taken a wife."

My body shook in all its parts, precisely as it had done on the evening that Elkanah disclosed his intention to take Hannah as his second wife.

"I know how much this must distress you," she added, "yet I cannot blame him. Lately he has been lonelier than ever, and this is the result."

As Bathanath had always been unfailingly kind to me, her severe words stung. Feebly, I rose to leave. Bathanath handed me a cup of herbal water to drink, but my throat was so constricted that I could not swallow anything.

I embraced her briefly, and expressed the hope that she would come to visit me. She agreed, then said that Arnon would ride with me for a little while on my way back.

I had not the strength to face him, but when I came out into the front yard he was there already, holding the reins of two donkeys.

I mounted my animal in silence and we rode out of the yard. The guards kept their distance, and Arnon recited the speech he had prepared. "Pninah, I still love you, but during the last three months I have seen you only once very briefly. I was unbearably alone, and as you know from you own life, loneliness is a fertile breeding ground for a new love."

I could not condemn him. It took me time to swallow the lump in my throat, but I finally managed to say, "True. But could you not have advised me of this in writing, rather than having me come here to hear these words?"

"You know well that would have been impossible. My missive might have fallen into your husband's hands."

Then he continued, enunciating his words carefully, as if he wished to impress them in my memory. "You may rest assured that I shall guard your secret. I cherish the memories of what has transpired between us. You will always retain a place deep in my heart, and even if we don't see each other again, I will remain your friend forever. If you should require help in anything, advise me of it by letter and I will do all I can."

I wished him happiness with his wife, then reined in my donkey, indicating that I expected him to turn back. He brought his donkey close to mine and prepared to embrace me, but I eased away from him, and stretched out my hand in a gesture of refusal. Without uttering another sound, he rode away.

I turned my head a few times and caught glimpses of his figure fading into the distance—disappearing from view, but not from my heart.

I stared dully between the ears of my donkey, and gradually dissolved into tears. I let the crisp morning breeze brush at my damp face and dry them off.

When I reached home, I hurried into my room and slid down onto my bed.

For a second time, my dream of love had been torn to shreds, and my life had been ripped apart.

The Book of Hannah

As soon as the remnants from the party had been cleared, I set out for Shiloh. Apart from Samuel and Efrath, I took with me a maid, two guards, and various offerings for the Temple.

On the way, the joy of the party faded from my mind as grave misgivings began to tear at me. I knew that by bringing Samuel to the Temple I was fulfilling the purpose of my life and his. I was certain that I was doing right. It was his destiny to grow up at the Temple, but I was now far from sure that he would not suffer direly. The path in front of me was strewn with little rocks and gravel that had gathered there over time, and they churned under my donkey's hooves as the pain of the forthcoming separation started making its way through my body.

For a brief moment, I had the hideous thought that my actions were similar to those of Abraham, the father of our people, who had led his beloved son Isaac to a designated spot, there to be sacrificed as an offering to the Lord.

Like Abraham, I, too, was affirming my faith in the Lord. Still, it horrified me to think of the fear that must have gripped the child Isaac at the sight of the dagger that was to slit his throat.

Yet, Samuel, straddling the donkey in front of me, appeared anything but frightened. Even though I had told him that I would be leaving him at the Temple, he seemed to be unperturbed and was enjoying the ride.

I had brought with me some carobs, which I handed to Samuel one by one, and he nibbled at them happily. He was rapturously absorbed in his surroundings, asking me the names of the trees and shrubs we encountered on the way, and what fruit they produced. From time to time he fondled the head of the donkey, and bent forward to whisper soft blandishments in its ear.

Samuel was still very young, barely more than three years of age, and he had never spent as much as one day away from me. The Temple was a holy place and it should have an elevating effect on his spirit. But would he be aware of it? And what would I do if I found that he was scared of the strange surroundings and the unfamiliar priests, and began crying and refused to be left behind? I decided that I would not force him to stay against his will. I would take him back home and try again in a few months' time.

We reached Shiloh at dusk and I sent the maid to find accommodation for us. Then I took Samuel and Efrath and the guards, together with the offerings I had brought, to the Temple. A priest intercepted us at the entrance, and inquired as to our purpose. I knew that if I was to succeed, I must not show my misgivings but speak with confidence.

I announced in the most serene voice I could muster that I needed to speak with the high priest. But this priest acted as if he were the angel guarding the gateway to the Garden of Eden with a blazing sword. He blocked my way, and replied scathingly that the high priest was not available at this time. I insisted on seeing him, and he persisted in his refusal.

I said stiffly that I had met Eli already and that surely he would not refuse to receive me. Then I made known my intention of camping at the Temple's threshold with the child, until the high priest should see fit to meet me. The priest asked for my name and withdrew.

Eli soon appeared, then angrily informed me that he had never seen me before. He was about to leave when I reminded him that I was the woman who had prayed here for a child almost four years ago, and to whom he had given his blessing. I lifted Samuel over my head, presented him to Eli and proclaimed: "This is the boy for whom I have been praying, and the Lord has granted my request of him. And so, I will lend him to the Lord for his entire life."

I bowed to Eli and then, before anyone could stop me, I entered the sanctuary. I approached the Ark of the Covenant and set the child down on the floor beside me. The many glowing candles enfolded me in their heat and light. I bowed down until my forehead touched the ground and my song, a hymn of praise and gratitude, came pouring from my heart:

My heart rejoices in the Lord . . .
I am gladdened in your salvation . . .

While I recited my prayer aloud, Samuel looked around him in awe. He remained silent, as if he did not dare disturb the solemn occasion. As if he understood that any sound he might make would only jeopardize my mission.

The high priest regarded this curious scene with astonishment, but eventually he must have recalled the occurrence of which I had reminded him, for he let me finish my words. He called me back, and proclaimed that he was happy to learn that his blessing had helped fulfill my prayer. I told him of the offerings I had brought with me. He praised me, instructed a priest to take charge of them, and dismissed me with a friendly wave of his hand.

I begged to see him alone for a short while. He sighed, and wearily guided us into a small room and bade us sit down.

"Exalted priest," I began my prepared speech, "when I petitioned the Lord for this child in the Temple four years ago, I vowed that if my prayer were answered, and I gave birth to a son, I would lend him to the Lord. I have brought him now to fulfill this vow."

He listened with kindness in his face, but said that the Temple was not the right place to bring up a child and, besides, there was no free room for him.

I had come prepared for this response. I informed Eli that I would make a handsome donation to the Temple, to enable those in charge to build a room in the compound for the child and his nurse. I removed my belt from my waist, and extracted several pouches from it. These contained a considerable number of round gold shekels, which I rolled onto the table. The high priest bade me wait while he stepped out for a consultation.

Soon he returned with his two sons, Hofni and Pinhas, at his heels. Pinhas ogled me lasciviously, and I pointedly disregarded him. But Hofni's attention was aimed at the gold pieces on the table. He announced that the priests would accommodate the boy, provided that they would not have to look after him. I agreed to this with a sigh of relief. Hofni collected the gold pieces. An understanding had been reached.

Hofni and Pinhas were handsome and their priestly garb made them look distinguished, but I quickly took their measure, and I despised them in my heart. Their bearing tarnished the image I had held of the priests at the Temple. I could only hope that with God's mercy Samuel would have as little to do with them as possible. I prayed that worthier priests would surround him and the Temple's holiness would envelop him.

I waited while a room was made ready, where Samuel and Efrath would be accommodated until the new room was built for them. Before I left, Eli placed the palms of his hands on my head and blessed me. Then he bade me convey this further blessing to Elkanah:

May the Lord give you seed from this woman,
instead of the boy whom you have lent to the Lord.

I bowed and backed respectfully out of his presence. I took leave of Samuel, relieved to see that he was content to be left behind with Efrath. I promised him that I would be back tomorrow, then went out to meet the maid at the Temple entrance.

She had found comfortable accommodation for us in a family's home, for which I had to pay with silver pieces. The next morning, when I came to the Temple with Samuel's belongings, I saw him sitting in the courtyard with two elderly priests, who were fussing around him and teaching him to recite the "Shma" prayer.

Samuel ran up to me, caught my hand, and led me to the priests, saying with touching childish pride, "This is my mother. She can recite the whole 'Shma.'"

I sat and watched them for a while. But when I saw that my boy and the priests were engrossed with each other, I said that I would leave but would be back tomorrow.

On my way out I encountered Pinhas, who seemed to have been lying in wait for me.

"Hannah," he murmured huskily, placing his hands on my shoulders making no attempt to disguise his purpose. "Before you gave birth to your son, you were barren. I can bestow upon you my priestly blessing, which has been known to be most beneficial for barren women whose husbands cannot make them pregnant." His voice now dropped to a whisper: "Come with me, and I will show you how beneficial my priestly blessing, my *triple* priestly blessing," he added suggestively, "can be."

Pinhas had spoken brazenly, without even blinking, as if he had recited holy words entirely proper for a priest at the House of the Lord. He glared at me gleefully, certain that he had whetted my desire with his lewd speech. But I had nothing but contempt for him. Worse than that—he was so shamelessly crude that my flesh crawled at the very idea of his touch.

At first I thought that I would merely shake off his hands as one shakes off a fly, and walk on, pretending not to have heard him. But I was afraid that this might prompt him to wreak revenge on me by harming my son.

Hence I decided to instill in him some fear of Samuel and, with deceptive sweetness, I prevaricated. "Exalted priest, I am eager to obtain your beneficial blessing, only I cannot, for it would put you at peril of your life."

There was a flicker of unease in his eyes, and I continued, lying without compunction, for Samuel's sake. "My son is only a little one. But already he can invoke the Lord's power. Anyone who thwarts him is bound to suffer a dire fate. If he casts his spell on a man, even if he is a holy priest, and foretells his death, this man will surely die. I would not wish this fate to befall you."

The priest removed his hands from me and quickly withdrew. Inwardly I laughed, for he reminded me of a dog who had been beaten by his master and retreated with his tail between his legs. I proceeded on my way, and he never accosted me again.

In the evening I repaired to my room in the home in which we were lodging. There I took out a scroll I had brought with me, and recorded the tale of how my prayers to give birth to a son had been answered. At its end I wrote down the hymn of thanks that I had poured out before the Ark of the Covenant the night before.

The next day I saw Samuel with the same two priests, who were now teaching him the Torah's account of the world's creation. Again, Samuel took me by the hand and led me to them. A close scrutiny of their time-battered faces revealed nothing but kindness. Reassured, I returned to my room in Shiloh, and sat down to copy the scroll I had written the night before.

I took the copied scroll with me to the Temple the next day. By this time, the priests were used to seeing me with Samuel, and they let me move around freely. After searching for a while, I found the scroll room and entered it. It was a very long room, lit by several windows along one of its walls. The other walls were lined with shelves, all of which held scrolls packed closely together. In its center stood a large table, at which sat a number of priestly scribes busily copying scrolls.

The head scribe rose to meet me, and asked what my request was. I told him that I was Hannah, wife of Elkanah and the mother of the boy Samuel, who had been accepted by the high priest to grow up at the Temple. I added that I had written a scroll in which I had recorded how it had all come to pass. My request was that this scroll be placed in the Temple's scroll room.

The priest was taken aback at my presumption. "A woman scribe?" he queried doubtfully, with a condescending smile. "I've never heard of one before. I don't believe that women can write well enough to have their writings placed for keeping at the Temple."

"Exalted priest," I retorted with unshaken confidence. "It does not matter who wrote the scroll. My son will be a prophet and a great leader, remembered in Israel forever. It is important that his story be recorded for this generation and for all generations to come."

The scribe looked skeptical. Yet he was impressed by the assurance in my voice. He hesitated, then said: "Leave the scroll with me and return tomorrow."

I thanked him and went to search for Samuel. He was sitting in his customary place with the two priests, and did not come forward to meet me. But when I approached, he told me that he had just learned that Cain had killed Abel, that killing was a terrible sin and that the Lord should have killed Cain in retribution. The two old priests looked at me as proudly as if Samuel had been their own son.

On the following morning, when I came to the Temple, I went directly to the scroll room. The chief scribe made me sit down and announced: "Hannah, the wife of Elkanah, I have read your scroll." Permitting himself half a smile, he added, "For a woman, you have written it fairly well. But how do I know that what is written is the truth?"

"I am prepared to swear before God that every word in it is true."

"This is good. But I am not the one to decide which scrolls are to be stored in the Temple. The great assembly of elders will have to make a decision."

"How many of these elders are there?"

"Seventy."

I felt disheartened.

"They come from all tribes, and they convene here only twice a year. I will have your scroll copied nine times over, so that ten elders will read it at the same time. Even so, it will take a number of years for a decision to be reached."

This was discouraging, but I thanked him for his help and headed for the courtyard. On the way I met Efrath, carrying a pile of Samuel's laundered clothing on her arm. She told me that Samuel was spending all his time with the two priests, so that there was little for her to do. I made it plain to her that I expected her to show herself in the courtyard several times each day to ensure that the boy was well. And if anything untoward happened, she must send a messenger to advise me of it immediately.

When I came out into the yard, and Samuel saw me, he leapt to his feet and bowed. He said that he had just learned that a son must honor his father and his mother, and that from now on he would always rise and bow to me whenever he met me and whenever he left me. I praised him for this resolution, and told him that I must go home to his father. To my relief he accepted this. I gathered him up in my arms and hugged and kissed him.

When I put him down, one of the priests admonished: "How do you bless your mother when she leaves?"

"Go in peace," he said, and bowed once more.

"May the Lord be with you," I replied, hastily departing before he could see the tears flooding my eyes.

By the time I reached home, the elation I had felt at Shiloh had left me and my spirits had plunged. When Elkanah saw me he hugged me, and we were joyous at being together. But by then my vision of Samuel as a great prophet had faded. Instead, I envisioned all the vile things that might befall a helpless little child among strangers, two of whom I knew with certainty to be evil.

I had charged Efrath to apprise me if anything were to happen, but now I had no trust in her either. Least of all was I confident of her ability to defend Samuel against the evil designs of known or unknown villains.

Dark shadows invaded my soul, and I felt sick with longing and fear for my child.

When I saw Pninah, I realized that her state was worse than mine. During our meals she sat with a stricken face. The light had vanished from her eyes, and the rosy blush had waned from her cheeks. She wrapped herself in a cloud of almost total silence. Elkanah spoke of this to me. He put it down to her mourning for her mother, but I knew better.

I went to her room to talk to her. I said she must have realized that her connection with the Canaanite man could not have lasted forever, that sooner or later Elkanah would have found out about it. So she was better off now than she had been before.

But all she would say was, "You may think that I am alive, but in truth I am as dead as the Sea of Salt, the sea of death."

I tried to distract Pninah from her sorrow by talking to her of my trepidation over Samuel's plight at the Temple. But she hardly listened, and finally I gave up and left.

Elkanah now had two dejected women, and he did his best to comfort us, each in a different way. He spent endless stretches of time holding me in his arms, but when evening fell, I saw his eyes light up with lust for her. He came to me occasionally, but he spent most of his nights with Pninah. I thought bitterly that, whatever she might be doing to excite such passion in him showed that she was not totally dead, after all.

I had promised Samuel I would visit him again at the harvesting of the grapes. But before I could carry out this plan, while the grapes were still hanging heavily on the vines, a new pregnancy was upon me. My sickness bore down on me every morning, and I could do nothing but fret about my child from a distance without an inkling of what was going on in his life.

The Book of Pninah

I had intended to relegate Arnon to the corner of my soul reserved for sweet memories from which one draws strength, but I could not. Far from bringing peace, memories of him came back to torment me, deepening my sense of loss.

During the day I came alive only when I was caring for the children, and at night I was revived only when Elkanah came to my bed and touched me. To his delight, at those times I was seized by a shameless passion, doing his will and more, thankful of his delight, and of mine. But as soon as our act of knowing each other was over, even though he slept beside me, I hovered between death and grief.

In my longing for Arnon I believed that if only I could see him once more, it would be easier for me to bear my separation from him. I had the notion of requesting his help in some matter or other. This would entail a meeting between us and, afterward, my longing for him would be eased. But the only matter in which I required his help was that of restoring his love for me. And this was not something in which he would be willing to extend his assistance.

One night I began spinning wild thoughts of riding to Sdeh Canaan and hiding myself in the thicket of dense bushes in his front yard so that I could get a glimpse of him when he appeared. Yet when the morning dawned, I did not find the courage for this venture and my plan came to naught.

Some three months after my last trip to Sdeh Canaan, Bathanath came to visit me. She saw that I looked unwell, but made no comment. Instead she told me of herself and her family.

My unspoken question hung in the air. She answered it, recounting that Arnon's wife was pregnant, and that he was looking forward to becoming a father. I wondered how a heart that was broken already could break once more.

When she rose to leave, I did not invite her to come again. And when we embraced each other in parting we knew that, most probably, we would never see each other again.

I did still manage to find something new to fill my days. As many scribes were wont to do, I took up writing letters for people who were willing to pay me for my effort.

I wrote letters for women whose husbands had expelled them from their homes, who pleaded with those husbands to take them back. For women who had left their husbands when they had taken second wives and now asked to be taken back on any terms. For parents whose children had moved to faraway places, who had to inform them that they were ill, and much more besides.

I wept with the people whose missives I wrote, and by sharing their sorrow, I shed some of mine.

My letter-writing soon came to be linked with my own life in a surprising way.

One morning, a girl of about sixteen years came to my room. She was dark and pretty and timid, and this is the letter she asked me to write:

Hear me, my master. This is your maidservant Maaha writing to you.

When you came to me for the first time I was a virgin, and I asked you to take me to be your wife. Though you refused, you continued to know me.

But now I am pregnant and if you don't marry me, I will be shamed before my family and my tribe.

If you make me your wife, I will not bother you or your wives in any way. I plead with you: I will do anything; only don't let me suffer shame.

When I finished writing the letter, the girl told me that she was poor and had no silver with which to pay me. I said that it did not matter. She rose to leave, and I noted that the letter was still on the table. I handed it to her, but she would not take it.

I sensed that there was trouble to come.

"What do you wish me to do with the letter?" I asked.

Looking straight into my eyes, she replied: "Give it to your husband."

I agreed as calmly as I could.

"And will you support my request of him?"

I was unsure of my response, so I replied, "This is between my husband and myself."

"I swear that I will be no trouble to you. I will just work for you, for nothing."

"Go in peace, and I am sure that he will come and talk to you."

"He has already talked to me," she retorted in a plaintive voice, "but he said only that he needed time to think it over. Since then time has gone by, and he has forgotten me."

"The letter will remind him."

At that, the girl stepped outside, but instead of walkng toward the street she turned toward Hannah's room.

I blocked her way and shoved her back into my room, shutting the door. "What are you doing?"

"Since you will not help me," she said petulantly, "I will talk to your husband's other wife."

Hannah had recently given birth to a daughter and since the birthing she had not been well. I advised the girl of this. "She is ill and cannot see anyone."

"I will stay with her for only a short while."

After Hannah had helped me so much, I had come to feel in charge of her welfare. So I held the door closed behind my back and leaned against it, preventing the girl's exit. I said adamantly, "You will not stay with her at all. I will not let you harass her."

By this time the girl's timidity had evaporated. Her voice rose in anger and she shouted, "You cannot stop me."

I felt the door opening behind me and Elkanah came in. Someone must have apprised him of the girl's visit. He had a furious look in his eyes as he issued his order to her, "Wait here."

He led me out of the room and whispered, "Go to Hannah and don't let her come out of her room until I get there."

"I will do so, sir, but please have pity on the girl. She is in trouble, and I know how she must feel."

His wrath gave way to a thin smile. "I understand you. Now go, and let me deal with this in my own way."

Hannah was weak from her illness, and I was determined to protect her from the knowledge of this dismal occurrence. I went to her room and asked her how she felt. She replied that she had not improved, but she would nonetheless get up from bed to eat her midday meal in the front room.

Frantically, I searched for a way to stop her. I asked to see her baby girl. We went into the infant's room where I took the child in my arms and praised her beauty. Then I tickled her tummy to make her smile.

Hannah was getting impatient. She instructed the nurse to take charge of the baby. Then she prepared to step out into the front yard.

In desperation, I asked her to wait, as there was an urgent matter of which I needed to speak to her. She replied that we could talk while we ate.

I reminded Hannah that in the front room the maids could overhear us, whereas I wanted to talk to her alone. She gave in, and in her weariness returned to her room, stretched out on her bed, and shut her eyes.

I closed the door to the child's room and sat down on a chair next to her. I told her that since she had a fever, it would be best to hire a wet nurse for the infant, which I offered to do.

If Hannah was surprised at my deeming this to be of such urgency and secrecy, she did not show it. Time passed as we discussed the qualities to be looked for in a wet nurse, until, to my relief, Elkanah came in.

That night he came to me, and once our passion was spent, he reminisced. "I recall that when I knew about your pregnancy, it took a few days before I decided to take you for my wife. Those days must have been hell for you." Already half-asleep, slurring his words, he added: "I am glad that I made the right decision, though. Even then I had incredible pleasure in knowing you, and this pleasure has grown all this time."

With these words his eyelids drooped and he crossed over into sleep. So it was not until the morning that I could raise the matter of the maid with him. As we sat down to our morning meal of freshly baked bread and olives, I asked him what he had decided to do about her.

"It's not your concern," he replied brusquely.

"I realize it, sir," I conceded meekly, "but I would like to know."

With the juicy olives he favored in his mouth, he replied, "I found among our young workmen one who is willing to take her for his wife, in exchange for a piece of land I will buy for him."

"And was she happy with this arrangement?"

He removed the pits from his mouth and said pensively, "I forgot to ask her."

"But she accepted it?"

"Yes. It's a common arrangement. It enables poor people who have nothing to become owners of land."

"You mean that you have done it before."

"Only once. But I know several wealthy men who have done the same."

Elkanah's words did nothing to raise my spirits. It was as clear as a sunny day what must have happened when I had advised Elkanah of my pregnancy. He had told me that he needed some time to think the matter over. Now I was sure of what he had been thinking about. Doubtless, he had considered dealing with me in the same manner in which he now dealt with the maid.

In the end, he had married me not because he loved me but because he wished to have me at his, rather than another man's, disposal. Or he had not been able to find anyone willing to marry me in his stead. In my realization of this my dejection deepened even further.

A few days later, as I entered the front yard, I was astounded to see Bathanath descending from her donkey. Many months had passed since her previous visit, and I was sure that I would never set eyes on her again. I felt a surge of light working itself into the darkness of my soul. And while I dragged her into my room, I puzzled over what might have brought her to me.

The Book of Hannah

My second delivery was much easier than the first. I gave birth to a daughter whom I called Tirzah, because I wanted her so much. But after her birth I was seized by a fever, which raged inside me for many weeks. Binah knew how to alleviate it but was unable to cure it.

Pninah took on herself the task of finding a wet nurse for my daughter. This woman was so exalted in her own eyes that she would do nothing for the baby but nurse her. As I could do hardly anything myself, Pninah found another nurse experienced in caring for small children. She also supervised the three women, and frequently came by to see to the infant's needs and to ensure that she was well. She also took charge of the household.

All this Pninah did on top of her own chores. She was busy from dawn to dusk with no respite. But after what I had done for her, she was eager to help me in every way she could.

It was several months before I regained my strength. As a result, I did not see Samuel for more than a year, and when I did, it was only for a short while.

When I reached the Temple, I saw instantly that he was blooming. He told me of all he had learned, and showed me little scrolls on which he had written down words. He promised that from now on, he would be writing us letters.

It seemed that my fears as to Samuel's fate in the Temple had been groundless. Hofni and Pinhas notwithstanding, the Temple had proved to be a holy House of the Lord. I realized with surprise that although the void left in my heart by Samuel's absence was still there, the pain of longing had eased.

Thereafter we received little letters from him through messengers, and I savored all the scraps of knowledge about him that they contained. I went to visit him every two months, and Elkanah and I both saw him during our yearly pilgrimages to Shiloh.

Three more years passed, and then came my third pregnancy. I had some bleeding, and although it was slight, Binah warned me that I would have to remain in bed until the delivery, or else lose the child. Lying there for months, I felt like a heavy stone that was getting bulkier by the day. But it was not in vain, for in the end all went well. I gave birth to a son, whom I named Efraim, after the father of our tribe. Only after the naming ceremony could I visit Samuel again.

Once more it had been a year since I had seen him, and he was much grown and changed, though he was not as happy and carefree as he had been. I asked whether Efrath was good to him, and he said, "Yes." I asked whether the priests were dealing kindly with him, and he said, "Yes." I was puzzled, and asked him what was wrong, but he would not tell me. I begged him to speak, but he would not. I reminded him of his obligation to honor his father and his mother, and he was unable to refuse.

He took me utterly by surprise when he exclaimed in his still childish yet strangely compelling voice: "Bad times are ahead, my mother. The people of Israel are not heeding the commandments as they should. Many in their midst are worshipping the gods of the peoples around us. Therefore trouble looms."

"What trouble?" I voiced my surprise.

"Wars. Terrible wars. Many will die."

"Against whom?" I asked in a shaky voice.

"I do not know," he admitted.

"Wh . . . when?" I stuttered.

"I am not sure. Not right away. There is time left for the people to return to the Lord. But if they don't change their ways, the wars will come upon us."

Doubtfully, I queried, "Where does your certainty of this come from?"

He remained silent.

I persisted, and he said, "This I cannot explain even to you, my mother, because I don't know myself."

While we were talking I sat with Samuel in the Temple courtyard, and presently I saw a man of advanced years approaching. His head-covering and flowing mantle were white, the color of purity, holiness and wisdom. We honored him by rising and bowing to him, but he motioned us to sit, and sat down beside us.

"Who is this boy?" he inquired.

"He is Samuel, the son of Elkanah and myself, and we come from Ramathayim. I am Hannah. And who are you, sir?"

"I am the head of the great assembly of elders, which is convening here this week," he proclaimed. Then he turned to Samuel. "I overheard what you said to your mother, my son. I know that you spoke truly and I believe you, but others will not. I counsel you to say nothing of this to anyone until you grow in years and learning and wisdom."

"Yes, sir," replied Samuel, bending his head with becoming modesty. "I was thinking so myself."

My head was reeling from what I had just heard. The head of the great assembly of elders did not scoff at Samuel's dire prophecy, but believed in it! Thus, I myself began to be convinced of its truth.

When I entered the Temple on the following morning, I encountered the head scribe. He summoned me into the scroll room and announced with great pomp: "A meeting of the assembly of elders was held last night, and the scroll you left with me some years ago has been accepted for deposit at the Temple."

The elation I felt when I first wrote the scroll again overcame me, and I asked: "Will I have to swear to the truth of its content?"

"No, that will not be necessary. The head of the great assembly testified of hearing you talk with your son last night. He would not tell us what was spoken, but it convinced him that all you have written is true. The high priest, too, has testified that he remembers some of the events you have recorded."

"My blessings to you, sir, and to the head of the great assembly, and to the high priest and all the priests and elders."

"Of course your scroll will have to be rewritten in more proper language," he cautioned condescendingly, no doubt meaning that a man would be rewriting it. "But once this is accomplished, it will be copied many times over. One hundred copies will be stored here, and hundreds of copies will be dispatched to scroll rooms around the land of Israel, even to the new scroll room that has been recently constructed in Jerusalem, the town of the Jebusites. Your scroll will become part of our heritage, and it will be remembered in Israel forever."

These tidings exceeded all my expectations and I bowed my head in gratitude. A large part of my mission in life had been fulfilled, and I could not fathom why I, of all women, had been so favored by the Lord.

I found Samuel, and we talked for a while of the family. Then I took up the topic of the wars, which had been troubling me.

"Samuel," I began, "are you sure of what you foresaw yesterday?"

His beautiful green eyes seemed to have lost their brilliance and to be gazing inward into his own soul, as he said, "Yes, my mother."

"Yet you don't know when the wars will come about?"

"Unless the people change their ways, they will probably occur in a few years' time, but I don't know precisely."

"By that time your elder brothers, Elroy and Elhanan, will be grown, and a while later, you will be grown as well. You may have to go into battle."

"Yes."

"What will happen then?"

"I don't know. When the time comes, there will be grave danger for all young men."

A film of cold sweat broke out on my brow. "Can you enlighten me no further?"

"No." There was a note of finality in his voice, and I decided not to press him any more.

When I reached home, Samuel's prophecy still rang loud in my ears. Sitting with Elkanah on my bed, I told him all that had come to pass. He was pleased that my scroll would be deposited in the Temple, but when he learned about my talks with Samuel, he was deeply troubled, though not for the same reason I was.

"This is nothing but foolishness," he objected. "You have put it into the boy's mind that he is a great prophet, and this is the result."

"I have never spoken a word to him about this," I gasped.

"Then he has sensed it from the way you treated him," he said with asperity.

Clasping both my hands in his, he continued: "Hear me, Hannah. I am a good Israelite. I keep the commandments as best as I can. I remember the sabbath to keep it holy, and I see to it that all the people who work for us, and even the animals, rest on this day. I let the poor, and the widows, and the orphans, and the strangers in our midst roam our fields after the harvest and collect all that the reapers have left behind. And if this is not sufficient, I open my hand to them and give them enough for their needs. I have never worshipped other gods, but only the Lord our God, and I offer him all the sacrifices that are required of me. But nothing will lead me to believe that God speaks to some as one man to another and apprises them of his plans for the future. Some people proclaim themselves as prophets, but they are false prophets."

I resented the aspersion he had cast on our son. "Samuel is too little to have made up what he said to me."

Elkanah continued holding my hands in his, but he remained firm in his objection to Samuel's prophecy. "Wherever his words come from, I don't want him to speak them. I want him to be like his brothers and sisters."

"How can he be like his brothers and sisters when he is growing up at the Temple?" I asked reasonably.

"And whose fault is it that he is growing up at the Temple?" he replied indignantly.

This was the closest Elkanah and I had ever come to having a dispute. Of course I could not let a quarrel break out between us, and I had to cede to his greater wisdom and let his view prevail. In any case, I began to weigh the possibility that Elkanah might be right in his reproof. I did not doubt the truth of Samuel's prophecy of disastrous wars, but what benefit could come of foretelling them, when he was still a young boy and nothing he could do would prevent them?

Like Elkanah, I now had dire misgivings about having brought Samuel to the Temple. I no longer feared that he would suffer maltreatment from the priests. Instead, I agonized over the possibility that, by bringing him there, I had condemned him to a life of dark forebodings in which he would never find rest for his soul.

The Book of Pninah

As soon as I got Bathanath to my room, I obliged her to sit down at the table and inquired if she was well. She said she was. Then silence fell, for neither of us could decide what to say next. To overcome the awkwardness, I said that I would get something for her to drink.

But she would not let me. "Leave the drink alone, Pninah, for I have come to talk to you."

I waited.

After fixing her clear gray eyes on me, which reminded me painfully of Arnon's, she voiced her concern. "You look poorly. Are you not well?"

"No."

"Arnon has sent me to ask after you. What shall I tell him?"

"Don't tell him the truth."

"But he wishes to know."

As I did not comprehend what her mission from him to me might be, I asked, "What does he wish to know?"

"If you miss him."

I did not want Arnon to know that my love for him had not dulled, but there was no sense in denying what was so evident in my face. Instead of answering, I lowered my head, and the tears that streamed from my eyes formed my response.

"Arnon was hoping that this would be your reply, because he, too, misses you beyond words."

"Are things not going as they should with his wife?"

"They are going well. She has given birth to an infant son whom Arnon loves very much. But his craving for you has become so intense that he must see you."

At first I was stunned. Then, in the fleeting instant that followed, as if by a miracle, I was recalled from my pit of sorrow. I heard myself whispering, "I want to see him so much—but how?"

Bathanath told me that when Arnon's baby was about to be born, he had bought a property in a village close by, and had moved there with his wife. But he still came to their house in Sdeh Canaan regularly to do his trading. We could meet there, as we had done before.

I invited my friend to share my midday meal, which I brought into my room on a tray. Since my head was in the clouds, I almost tripped on the threshold, and only Bathanth's deft intervention saved me from spilling the tray's contents on the floor.

While we ate, Bathanath recounted that she and Arnon had bought two carriages, and that in the future I would be conveyed to her home in one of these vehicles, in which I could recline in comfort.

"A carriage?" I was thunderstruck, for I had never seen one.

"Yes. We Canaanites have a long tradition of building them, not only for warfare but also for the use of the rich among our people. Here, in the hills of Efraim, they are constructed so that they may be drawn by mules, which are preferable to horses in this hilly terrain."

"But their cost must be in the sky," I protested.

She laughed. "Arnon and I have amassed large fortunes, and now you will enjoy the fruits as well."

Later, after seeing Bathanath off, I ran into Hannah. She watched Bathanath's retreating figure, then noticed my flaming cheeks. She gasped, "The ways of the Lord are wondrous." Then she strode into her room.

And I ran into my room and gave thanks to the Lord for his wondrous ways.

As I approached the meeting place through the mist of dawn, I caught sight of the carriage awaiting me. It was a vehicle of unsurpassed luxury. Its body was of iron, but the seats were lavishly upholstered with soft wool covered by brown leather and it was topped by a leather roof.

The guards helped me climb into the back seat. Then they

leaped up, and took the reins and the carriage moved forward, slowly at first and then at a brisk pace. Leaning back in my seat, I delighted in its pampering comfort.

It was early spring. The cool morning breeze was rustling my hair. Yellow and red wildflowers carpeted the green grass, white and pink blossoms covered the trees, and spring blossomed inside me as well.

I felt no guilt regarding Elkanah, for he who casts stones deserves to have stones cast at him. But Arnon now had a wife, a wife who had done me no harm and deserved none. Yet, unlike Lot's wife, I proceeded with never a backward look. I was led inexorably forward by a force too strong to resist, the force of life. I'd had my fill of death and I would have no more of it. I would lie in Arnon's arms and live.

He was waiting for me in the eating room, his shirt carelessly open, a silent invitation in his eyes. Without uttering a sound he led me into his bedroom. He locked the door, took me into his arms and I melted into him.

His kiss was insistent and inflamed me so much that I tore at him, attempting to pull him down onto the bed. But now I perceived a change in my lover: He stood his ground and prolonged the kiss.

When Arnon finally removed his mouth from mine, his eyes still staring into mine, he reached out his hand to the shelf behind him and brought forth a pouch. It contained the necklace with precious stones that I had refused to accept before.

He spoke for the first time: "My beloved, I have been desperate for you. Since I cannot place a ring on your finger, I am placing this on your neck as a sign between us that you belong to me now and forever, and that there will be no parting again."

As he fastened the necklace around my neck, I decided not to argue about it any more. I thanked him for it and said, "Arnon, my love for you is stronger than I had thought possible. There will be no parting for as long as you want me."

I felt that all that needed to be said had been said. I removed all I had on except the necklace. Then I ran my hands up his arms, his shoulders, his neck, and pulled him down with me onto the bed, and he no longer resisted.

When later I remembered our togetherness, I realized that Arnon's way of knowing me, too, had undergone a change. He was not as desperately starved for the act of love as he had been before, and of course I knew why. When I got impatient, and pleaded for him to enter me, he still delayed, playing with me.

Thus, when he finally came into me after so much waiting, and I felt his presence swelling up inside me, my joy was so great that I cried out piteously as if I were in the throes of delivering a child. I wailed his name, then my breath shuddered in a sigh of relief.

Later, as we lay in each other's arms, Arnon said softly, "Pninah, of all that I have missed about you, I missed your eyes the most. You have the most beautiful eyes I have ever beheld. I would lie awake at night and recall how they clouded over with passion before we began, how they sparkled like stars during the act, and how they became like clear, still pools of spring water afterward. I thought that I must have imagined it, but now I see that my memories did not lie."

He kissed my eyes for a long time, and when I cried with happiness he kissed away my tears.

We knew each other for a second time, and again after our meal, and so also in our future meetings on the second day of every second week. Each time, Arnon whispered passionate endearments into my eager ears, assuring me that I was the shining sunlight of his days and the sparkling moonlight of his nights.

We had always talked with each other, but now we talked even more. In between our meetings I stored up my words inside me, and when we met I poured them out to him. And each time I hoarded his words to me, as bees hoard honey in the hive, to nourish me during the next two weeks. When I was alone I would bring them forth from their hiding place one by one, and taste their sweetness.

One day during our meal, when he talked about his trading, he paused, unsure whether he ought to continue, but finally he said, "You know that we make part of our wealth from selling idols. Recently this trading is bearing plentiful fruit among the Israelites, like citron trees in the autumn. More and more of your people buy large imposing statues of our gods, to be placed on shrines near altars on hills and under leafy trees. There I have seen them bow down and drink wine and beat drums and fornicate in honor of our gods and goddesses, whom they believe to be deities of joy and love and fertility."

I was pale with shock, but he continued with a gleam of amusement in his gray eyes. "I have resolved to make a huge donation to the Temple of your God at Shiloh, to atone for the sins of his people."

My food stuck in my mouth. "Only those who have sinned can atone for their sins."

His amusement grew. "I was merely jesting," he said lightly. But when he saw how deeply troubled I was, his amusement disappeared and he calmed me by stroking my face. But I knew myself to be no better than those idol worshippers. The only difference was that they transgressed the second, and I the seventh, of the Ten Commandments.

On another occasion, Arnon informed me that from now on we need not be confined always to his room. This pleased me, but worried me as well. For there was the constant fear that Elkanah might follow my trail to Sdeh Canaan, as he had done before. What excuse could Bathanath offer if he came and I was not there? Still, I did not dare to disappoint Arnon. I could only trust that there would be no reason for Elkanah to come to my lover's house.

Following his new resolution, Arnon took me in his carriage to a thermal bath in the Canaanite city of Ishkar, a fortified city encircled by a heavy wall. We approached it through a noisy and dirty neighborhood, which lay outside the wall, in which the poor people had their dwellings. The streets were narrow, the houses nothing but hovels. Dirty children in tattered garments played in front of them, and a mixture of noxious smells emanated from inside their doors.

Arnon said that he wanted to show me this part of the town only once. The next time we came, he would take me straight to the neighborhood of the wealthy, but he felt it important that we not forget how blessed we were to live as we did.

The wall through which we entered the more prosperous part of the city was thick enough to shut out the uncouth noises and evil odors from the outside, while keeping in the pleasing fragrance of garden flowers. The carriage rolled along the streets, rattled by the cobblestones that paved their ground. Elegant houses were painted in soft shades of pink and blue and green, and overhung with rare climbing plants.

The building that housed the thermal bath was large and ornate, but its purpose was well concealed. The guards stationed at its entrance, scrutinizing all newcomers, greeted Arnon respectfully as they ushered us in.

My lover led me down a long passage with many doors, one of which he opened with a key. We found ourselves in a little room, with paintings of men and women in the various stages of the act of lust on its walls, and a bed in its center, on which were laid out special garments for bathing.

We dressed ourselves in them and went to a huge hall with a thermal pool in its center. It was surrounded by pillars that supported the ceiling, with couches between them. The walls of white marble veined subtly with brown lines held niches in which there stood nude gods and goddesses, with the parts of their bodies that should have been concealed prominently exposed.

We sunk ourselves in the warm water that came bubbling up, which the earth spewed forth from a hidden spring, apparently with the express purpose of pampering the rich. We inhaled its heavy odor, which bore in it the strength of the core of the earth, until its power was coursing in our veins.

Then we returned to our room, where a tub of fresh warm water awaited us. We washed ourselves and, invigorated by the thermal water, we knew each other in ways we had not previously explored.

I asked Arnon if some of the people who frequented the pool were Israelites, and when he said they were, I voiced the fear that they might recognize me and bear tales about me to Ramathayim.

He attempted to put my mind at ease. "The bath is set aside for a select group of rich men who pay dearly for the privilege of coming here with women who are not their wives. It is a rule among us never to speak on the outside of what occurs on the inside."

Yet I was not reassured, and whenever we went there, I looked furtively around me to make sure that I had not been recognized.

Several years passed and nothing untoward happened. But then one day as we came out of the pool, I sensed that there was someone watching me. I looked around and saw a tall man with wet black hair reclining on a couch with a woman beside him. He was leering at me with an insolent smile on his face.

I looked back at him in pained recognition. He was Hanoch, Hannah's suitor from years ago, before she had rejected him in favor of Elkanah. When I had seen him in the past, his attention had been riveted on Hannah, and I thought that he had not even noticed me. Now it seemed that he had.

When we reached our room, Arnon said that Hanoch, an exceedingly rich merchant, posed no danger to me. His scathing glance told me otherwise.

We decided not to come to the bath for a while. But the damage had been done, and I could only wait to see what it would be.

Arnon also took me to Ishkar to visit the home of a very expensive seamstress, whose unique dresses were made to cling to the wearer's shape to show off her most hidden charms. I selected five pieces of material for my dresses, which were to be ready for me in two weeks' time.

When we came to collect them, I removed from my belt a pouch of silver shekels to pay the seamstress. But when Arnon's eyes alighted on the pouch they flashed with anger. I put it away, and he brought forth his own pouch instead.

From among the dresses that awaited me, I chose one that was of a brick color and low cut, and clung to my breasts more tightly than anything I had ever worn. After I put it on, Arnon said briefly, "Let's go." When we reached his bed he did not delay.

These dresses were disgraceful, but when I looked at myself in the mirror I was so entranced that I decided to wear them also in Ramathayim.

The next time we were invited for a wedding, I slipped into one of a golden color. As we made our way toward the house of the feast, Elkanah was chatting with Hannah as was his custom, and took no notice of me. Only when we reached our destination did he realize that something was out of the ordinary, for several men began staring at me with undisguised intent.

Elkanah surveyed them, then me. I saw the ominous wrath gathering in his eyes and the menacing look he directed at me. His mouth tightened, and I could almost hear his teeth grinding in his mouth. Leaving Hannah behind, he took me home and summoned me to his room.

Barely keeping his temper in check, he read me an angry homily on the proper conduct to be expected of an Israelite woman. "An Israelite woman," he lectured sternly, "may show off her body only to her husband. When she appears before others, she must be dressed modestly. The shape of her body must not be seen through her dress."

I made an effort to appease Elkanah. "I was not aware of this, sir, as I should have been," I said in a placating voice. "From now on, I will be modest as befits an Israelite woman."

He was mollified. But when he looked at me with narrowed eyes, it did not escape him that I had a mischievous look in my eye and this infuriated him more than anything else.

Suddenly, his fury turned into lust. He stared at my body as the men in the square had done before, and went to lock the door and shutter the windows. Then he clutched my arm and pushed me down onto his bed. And without bothering to caress me, he entered me again and again and again.

Only afterward did he become aware of the noise of the children playing in the yard, and grinned ruefully.

By the time we got up, the grin had faded from his face. He made me face him and commanded: "Pninah, you will never wear a dress such as this outside the house again."

In meek acceptance of his domineering manner, I said, "It will be as you say, sir."

Then he added magnanimously, "But you are permitted to wear one at home, when we have no visitors."

Since then I took to putting on one of my new dresses whenever I had no lessons, and to my delight they drove Elkanah wild with a lust and passion that I shared.

The Book of Hannah

My pregnancies now came more frequently than I desired. In addition to Samuel, I gave birth to three sons and two daughters, each one as shiningly lovely as the precious stones on the necklace that had been Elkanah's gift to me before our wedding, each a jewel in the crown of my life, my motherhood.

Our house and yard were always filled with the welcome sights and sounds of children playing rough-and-tumble. Of boys wrestling with each other and girls chasing each other and pulling each other's hair.

Yet, after my sixth child came into the world, although my womb was not worn out yet, I hoped that I had brought forth its last issue. I was grateful to the Lord for having redeemed me from my barren state and having made me bear plentiful fruit, but having known the fullness of the womb six times, I was content for it to remain so. And I was grateful to Elkanah for confining himself to kisses, and for hardly ever coming to me any more. I silently rejoiced in my good fortune.

During the years of my pregnancies and deliveries my health had been poor, and Pninah had been surprisingly helpful to me. I had done her a kindness by saving her from an ugly fate, but she had repaid it ten times over. She not only managed the household, but even cared for my children, feeding them and dangling them on her knees, handling them as affectionately as if they were her own.

From the rising of the sun to nightfall she had no moments of rest. Each weekday she worked as hard as if she were still a Hebrew slave in Egypt, but she was never fatigued. She was imbued with a strength that enabled her to cope with everything.

I knew well wherefrom this strength derived, and I had meant to admonish her, as I had done once before, but I knew that it would be pointless, so I kept my peace.

What Pninah was doing with her Canaanite man was unforgivable, and I still harbored some jealousy over Elkanah's continuing passion for her, but I was deeply indebted to her for all the help she had given me. Thus I resolved that it was my duty to shield her. Soon this resolution was put to the test.

While my pregnancies and illnesses lasted, I was not able to frequent the town square on the sabbath for the reading of the Torah. But once they ceased, I slowly regained my strength and resumed doing so. It was then that I encountered a man there whom I had not seen for years—Hanoch, son of Uziel, the one I had almost married before I met Elkanah. I had not encountered him since I became Elkanah's wife.

One sabbath, as I stood in the square exchanging gossip with some of my relatives, he approached and asked if I remembered him. I was momentarily taken aback, but I promptly recovered. He had changed, but I easily recognized him by his nasal voice, tall stature and refined features, which I remembered of old. I asked him of his life since we had last seen each other.

He told me that he had been traveling on his merchant ship for some years. He had since settled in another town and taken a wife, with whom he had begotten sons and daughters. Recently he had returned to Ramathayim, in order to be close to his aging parents.

He looked at me in a measuring way and then led me aside. With hardly a pause, he announced that he had never ceased loving me and that he had kept track of my life. He pronounced it a shame that I should have married a man who already had a wife, and voiced the certainty that I would have been much happier with him.

He peered into my eyes and added in a honey-coated voice that did nothing to endear him to me, "It is not too late, Hannah my love."

I was not sure whether he was implying that he still wanted me for his wife, or that clandestine meetings were his intent. Whichever it was, I thought his words impertinent. I was about to turn from him, but his next remark halted me, for he said that he had something to impart about Pninah. I could hardly ignore him, but I said nothing as he continued in a jeering voice, "I've seen her where she should not be, with a man with whom she should not have been."

Once more, I wanted to turn my back on him. But I was curious to find out more, so I waited.

A stinging contempt colored his voice as he added, "At a place of whose very existence a lady of refinement such as you should be unaware."

I was incensed at his words. "Yet you were there yourself."

"I am a man," he stated coolly.

I felt nothing but disdain for him, a feeling undisguised in my voice as I replied, "If it was so uncouth a place as you make it out to be, you must have been there with a woman."

"But not with a refined lady."

My wrath rising, I asked with deceptive sweetness, "Does your wife know about this?"

His lips thinned, and the nasal tone of his voice became disgustingly pronounced. "I can only promise that had you been my wife, I would never have rested my eyes on any other woman."

The sticky sweetness of honey in Hanoch's mouth did little to conceal the evil spite of the poisonous snake in his heart. "In truth," I said dryly, "what do you want?"

"As I told you, I still love you. If I cannot make you my wife, at least let me do something for you. It must be very uncomfortable for you to have a rival. If your husband were to be advised of what I just told you, you would have a rival no longer."

Hanoch was evidently intent on causing trouble, so I said scathingly, "Be blessed for your solicitude, but pray confine it to your own life."

"And if I do not accept your advice?" he threatened.

I was more determined than ever to defend Pninah from his malevolent designs. I asked angrily, "How would your wife respond if she were advised of your clandestine visit to that secret place?"

At that moment Elkanah approached. I shot Hanoch what I hoped was a devastating glance, as my husband took hold of my arm possessively and led me away.

There was no doubt in my mind that Hanoch would have been as unfaithful to me as he was to his present wife, and that this would have reduced me to sheer misery. I knew that in this, as in everything else, Elkanah was as different from Hanoch as light was from darkness. I was jubilant for having rejected Hanoch's offer to marry him. And I was fervently grateful to Pninah, whose advice had saved me from this loathsome fate.

When later I questioned Pninah about where it was that Hanoch had spotted her, she replied that it was merely a thermal pool. As I looked at her sideways in disbelief, she admitted that it had little rooms attached to it. "Rich men rent them, in order to . . ." At this point she paused, for like Hanoch, she apparently believed that this was something that I should not know about.

On the next sabbath Hanoch appeared at the town square again. During the week he must have experienced some disquiet about my threat to reveal his illicit activities to his wife, for he now approached me and apologized for his words of the previous week. He added feebly that he had no intention of displeasing me, and he promised that he would not interfere in my life.

I saw Pninah standing some distance away, regarding us anxiously, and I could only hope that Hanoch would keep his promise.

But before long, I came to be immersed in other cares. Chief among them were Samuel's continuing prophecies of doom and the looming wars. Pninah's sons were almost grown men now, and Samuel himself was maturing quickly. I was terrified, and my dread over what would befall our sons in the coming wars overshadowed all else.

THIRD PART

Sons in the Battlefield

The Book of Hannah

As soon as I was fully recovered from my pregnancies and deliveries, I took over the running of the household again. But while I was kept busy with my children at home, uppermost in my mind was Samuel and his increasingly troubled soul.

I visited my first-born as often as I could, bringing him new jackets and other garments, which I had sewn myself, whenever I went. He was growing into a tall, handsome boy who no longer needed Efrath's care, so I proposed that she come home and help me with the other children instead, and both she and Samuel were content with this.

I talked to Samuel and watched him in his surroundings. He had come to be much involved in his studies with the priests and in the Temple service, but although he was busy he was unhappy. I could not understand this, since the priests were kind and had a high regard for him. When I asked him what was weighing on his heart, he would only say that he had already told me.

I did not press him to speak of his visions again, since I knew that Elkanah would frown on them. But one day, as we were sitting in the courtyard after our usual fashion, he broached the subject himself.

"My mother," he began, "I can no longer conceal from you that the terrible disaster of which I talked to you before is drawing near."

My ears stung from his words and I was at a loss for a reply.

"There will be wars. Thousands and more of our people will be killed."

I was rattled to the core by his dire prophecy and, as I had done before, I asked about what was closest to my heart. "What about your brothers and yourself?"

"I do not know."

"Samuel, my son, how is it possible? Our land is at peace now. We have no enemies."

His gaze seemed to turn inward and he said: "The Lord will appoint enemies for us, in accordance with his own design."

"Why?"

"Do you not see what is going on around you? Many of our people worship other gods. The poor and the widows and the orphans and the strangers in our midst are left with insufficient food and clothing. Men lie with women who are not their wives, and women lie with men who are not their husbands. Israelite men lie with women from the peoples around us, and Israelite women lie with men from the peoples around us."

"Who are those men and women?"

"I cannot tell you, because that would be in transgression of the commandment 'You shall not bear tales among your people,' but some of this you know yourself."

He regarded me with a piercing look. I was sure that he was conveying a message to me about Pninah and about Hanoch as well. "How can you know all this?" I queried.

"My mother, each day when I finish my duties at the Temple I follow the lure of the hills and walk among them. There the future has its own sights and sounds, and the distance has its own views and voices. They are reflected inside me. I watch and listen. But I see and hear so little. So very little."

I shivered at his account of that which defied the nature of things.

After a while he went on: "I have only to look around me to see that even here at the Temple some things happen as they did in Sodom and Gomorrah. Some priests take more of the sacrifices for themselves than they are entitled to, and so many Israelites no longer wish to offer sacrifices to the Lord. Those same priests lie with the women who assemble at the Temple to worship."

Because of my previous experience with Hofni and Pinhas, I knew who he had in mind.

"I see the calamity approaching, unless the priests and the people return to God. Yet I can do nothing to convince them to change their ways."

"I am helpless, too. If I were to admonish the persons who . . . who . . . I would not be heeded."

"I know this, my mother, and I am not asking it of you. It is not only one person, or even two—there are more in your vicinity. But I am most concerned with the people of Israel as a whole and with the Temple, which should be the holiest of all places, which should remain standing on its place forever. Yet now it is doomed for destruction."

In an attempt to ease the burden in his heart, I said, "Samuel, you are still a boy and you cannot be your brothers' keeper. So why be unhappy?"

"I *am* my brothers' keeper. Soon I will have to speak up. I am merely waiting for a clear . . . a clear . . . message."

As he spoke those words, his face was flushed and hot and he buried it in his hands. I took him in my arms, and put his face against my chest. I stroked his curly hair and whispered, over and over again, "My child, my child," as I had done when he was an infant.

And I could feel his tears on my dress.

I resolved to say nothing of this to Elkanah, since I knew that he would be greatly displeased. But when I came home, my husband looked at me and knew that something was lying heavy on my heart. He pressed me to tell him and, in the end I gave in. I reported my talk with Samuel word for word, leaving out only the part that had to do with adultery in our vicinity.

Elkanah was deeply distressed. "Hannah," he said, "it's as clear as can be that the boy is becoming mad. You will go and take him out of the Temple, and bring him home before it's too late."

"I have taken a vow, my husband."

"As long as Samuel was a child, you were responsible for keeping him at the Temple, which you have done. You have fulfilled your vow. But he became thirteen years old a few months ago, and in the eyes of our law he is now a grown man, able to participate in the reading of the Torah, and in all the rituals. Now he, and not you, is responsible for his deeds. He has taken no vow and he can leave the Temple at any time he wishes."

"He will not wish for it. He will not come with me."

"Then we will go together. Even if he is thirteen he still has an obligation to honor his father and his mother. He will have to do so by accepting our decree."

And so, with a heavy heart, we began the preparations for our journey to Shiloh to bring Samuel home.

In the coming week Elkanah would be busy with the farm, for the harvest of wheat and barley had been rich that year. The grain had been stocked in neat piles in our storerooms, and it was ready for grinding. Traders would be coming around to buy what we did not need for ourselves. So we set the time of our journey for the week after that.

We reached Shiloh as planned, but what we encountered there was so odd that our scheme had to be abandoned.

The Book of Pninah

One day I arrived at Sdeh Canaan to find the house in turmoil. Several carts were lined up in the front yard, being loaded with provisions.

When I reached Arnon's room, I asked him what was happening, but he only said, "Later."

When 'later' came, he told me that what I had seen were preparations for a journey to be undertaken in a few days' time. He and Bathanath were about to embark on a journey to the city of Ashdod in the land of the Philistines, to visit relatives of his defunct mother who had been a Philistine, and to do some trading. The trip would last for about a week.

"I call on you to join us," he continued. "You have never left your country, or seen the Great Sea. The time has come to do so."

"Why?"

"When you see it, you will know. It's overwhelming."

I could not conjure an image of a stretch of water so vast that it went on and on and on, with nothing beyond it for as far as the eye could see. Yet how was I to go?

"Will not your wife be coming?" I asked.

"No. The children are still small, and she has decided to remain at home to care for them. We will spend the nights in each other's arms."

The prospect was alluring, but it would not be so to Elkanah. I said doubtfully, "I will have to ask permission from my husband and he may not grant it."

"Press him. Make him feel guilty for all he has done to you. We will not budge without you."

That evening, when I came to Elkanah's room and raised the

matter of the journey with him, I described it as Bathanath and her family's excursion, which indeed it would be.

Elkanah's forehead creased in disapproval. But instead of refusing outright, he searched for a way to deny my request without seeming to do so. "Pninah, it's not necessary for you to go with the Canaanite woman. We'll go on a journey of our own," he tried. "Next week I must go with Hannah to Shiloh to bring Samuel home. But after that we will set out to distant towns and villages, until we reach the Great Sea."

"Who will be the travelers on this journey?"

"Me and you and Hannah."

I braced myself to follow Arnon's advice. "Sir, I would never dare to question your decrees. For, of course, your wisdom exceeds mine in every way." In the hope of having appeased him in this manner, I rushed forward. "Yet I have no wish to go with you and Hannah, and watch you kissing and hugging her all day long."

Elkanah seemed to vacillate between wrath at my insolent words and his own guilt, because he could not but recognize their truth. Finally he replied. "I may hug her during the day, but at night, and sometimes even during the day . . ."

He let the words taper off, and I could see the familiar gleam of lust blossoming in his eyes.

"What we do in bed is a great joy to me, sir, as you surely must have noticed. But it's not enough."

He was taken aback at my rebellious response. "I was hoping that the enmity you felt for Hannah would have abated, and that you were content with your lot. I see, now, that it's not so."

"I feel no enmity toward Hannah."

"Toward me, then."

"No, sir. I love you deeply, and I have accepted all you have done." He seemed pacified, so I pressed on: "Only I will not go on a journey with you and Hannah."

His guilt and my flattery and words of love seemed to have found their target, for he asked, "How many people will be going on this trip?"

"I don't know precisely. At least twenty."

The large size of the traveling party reassured Elkanah. He

sighed heavily in resignation, rose to his feet, dismissing me from his presence with the words, "Go in peace."

Two days later, at the first light of day, Arnon's carriage collected me and brought me to join the caravan that was waiting for us at an appointed spot. There, the staff was told that, as I was a woman scribe, I had dealings of my own in the land of the Philistines.

All was in readiness, and in no time the whole caravan moved forward. It was headed by several guards mounted on donkeys, followed by Arnon's family's two carriages, trailed by the provision-laden carts, with the aides and several more guards on their donkeys bringing up the rear.

To avert suspicion from the real purpose of my trip, Bathanath was my traveling companion. But as we pitched our tents for the night, places were switched in the dark and I found myself with Arnon beside me.

It was the first time that I did not have to agonize over Elkanah descending upon us. So I abandoned myself to passion, and we drank the wine of love until the darkness was chased away by the dawn.

The next morning, Arnon rode beside me. We headed west and south at a vigorous pace. Before long, as we emerged from a narrow creek, the terrain widened and flattened and stretched itself out before us. We had reached the southern plain.

The wheat had been harvested already, and for a while nothing met our gaze either near or far but the naked, blistered, brown earth, as parched from the summer's dryness as an old woman's skin.

Arnon explained that we were entering the land of the Philistines, a people with origins across the Great Sea, who were now as firmly settled in their land as were the Israelites in theirs.

Yet I hardly looked or listened, for my tired eyes closed of their own accord. My head kept rolling onto Arnon's shoulder and he had to push it gently away, so that my reputation as a Hebrew woman scribe with dealings of her own in the land of the Philistines could be preserved.

We caught sight of our destination well before dusk, and suddenly I was wide awake. I saw the interminable expanse of the Great Sea, its ever-moving blue water shimmering in the receding sunlight, stretching out into the endless distance until it met the blue of the sky. It was breathtaking.

So, too, were the waves, topped by white crests that swelled out of nowhere, overtaking each other, as they broke with roaring splashes against the sandy beach before they slid back into the depths of the sea.

We plunged into the water, splashing around among the waves, playfully warding them off, as they sprayed torrents of salty water over our heads. Some boats in the vicinity were swaying like drunkards and we swayed with them.

I had been traveling in a simple dress that could withstand the dust of the road. But I had packed a bag with elegant dresses, one of which I took out after our dip in the sea. It was crumpled, but I shook it out and made it presentable. My hair hung in wet strands down my face, but I combed it and arranged it neatly over my shoulders.

Later I was glad that I had done so, for I learned that Arnon's kinsman, Patrussim, who we were to meet, was one of the Philistines' chief leaders and a high officer in their army. I was happy I could present myself to such an exalted man in my finest attire and not in my drab, shabby traveling dress.

Patrussim and his family resided in an affluent neighborhood on the outskirts of Ashdod. Their residence was an opulent, imposing mansion built on pillars near the seashore.

This we now entered, to find the entire family assembled in the large entrance hall to welcome us. The hall was beautifully appointed, with statues of the family's ancestors on pedestals along the marble walls, and lush carpets on the floors.

The family was large, and while I could not distinguish its many members from each other, the head of the household stood out both for his glimmering blue silk tunic as well as for his more advanced years and air of assurance.

When he learned that I was a Hebrew scribe, he was favorably impressed. So, after gifts had been exchanged and lavishly praised, he had me seated on his right, and Arnon on his left, for the evening meal.

Sumptuous dishes were placed on the table by light-robed servants, who moved about in utter silence. I selected the ones that I was allowed to eat by Torah law, mainly fish, delicately cooked in rare herbs. The meal was enhanced by the choicest wines, served in elaborate silver goblets. It was the finest meal of which I had ever partaken.

At first I felt awkward sitting beside such a great commander of men. But Patrussim, who spoke my own language, had considerable experience putting persons at their ease when he wished to do so. He apparently did wish it, for soon I was chatting with him as if he were a close kinsman. But before long he stopped talking idly, and the words he spoke came as an utter surprise.

"Pninah," he began, "I must tell you that bad things are happening between your people and mine. There have been wars between us in the past. But for many years now we have been at peace. This peace seems to be drawing to an end."

Perplexed, I asked, "How is that?"

"Two towns, Beth Shemesh and Azakah, are in dispute between us. Your sword-bearers have now occupied them, even though we demanded that they refrain. No good can come of this."

"What is the importance of this, sir?" I queried.

"We are a peace-loving but proud people," he responded gently but with a chill in his voice, "and we will not cower to anyone nor sit by and suffer others to nibble away at our land. If your warlords don't withdraw, we will meet for battle. Our men and your men will draw their swords and masses of young men will face bloody deaths."

I drew a sharp breath and my words almost withered in my mouth as I asked, "When will this happen?"

"It must never happen," Arnon interrupted; then, seeing my ashen face, he turned to speak of other matters and I fell silent.

Soon it was time to retire for the night. I was led through a maze of corridors to a well-furnished room with a bed underneath a window that looked out over the sea. Against two walls there were low cabinets, on which stood pottery jars adorned by colorful flower and animal designs. A statue of the Philistine god Dagon graced one of them. On the other walls were immense murals depicting hunting scenes.

I sat on a chair in deep distress until Arnon came in. He took hold of the repugnant idol of Dagon and put it in the cabinet. Then he took me to bed, enfolding me in his arms as I clung to him. He placed my face close to his chest, covering it with the palm of his hand, until I ceased trembling. I fell into a fitful sleep, but long before the break of dawn I awoke to the noise of the roaring waves lashing at the shore below my window.

When we sat down to our morning meal, Patrussim perceived that I was heavy-eyed, and I admitted that I had spent an almost sleepless night agonizing over the words that he had spoken the night before.

"Since you have been so deeply affected by them," he remarked, "you will be all the more willing to help me prevent this cruel slaughter."

I voiced my doubt. "What can I do?"

"You can help me write letters to your leaders, to appeal to them to stop your mindless warlords in their recklessness. I can speak the Hebrew language, but I cannot write in it. You will transcribe my words."

When the others went out to do their trading, Patrussim ushered me into his scroll room. We sat at the table, on which were laid out some small scrolls, an iron pen, and an inkwell. My host had me write a letter to our high priest, Eli, and several to other Israelite leaders. He pressed his seal on them, and then I made copies of them for him to keep.

When the sun was almost ready to slide below the horizon, Arnon came to fetch me for a stroll on the beach. It was the eve of the sabbath, when I usually felt more at peace with myself than at any other time. Today, however, peace would not come.

During the evening meal, Patrussim inquired after my family, showing a gratifying interest in my sons. He asked what their names and ages were. When I told him that they were seventeen and sixteen years old, he looked grave and fell silent. Suddenly I realized the purpose of his questions, and I was seized by forebodings of disaster.

He pressed my hand reassuringly, and said, "Have no fear. All will be well."

I was not pacified, but he said no more to me.

Patrussim now shifted his attention to Arnon. While they talked, I looked across the table at Patrussim's two eldest sons, who were only a few years older than mine. I caught sight of his wife, a glimmer of furtive fear in her face, which vanished as quickly as it had appeared. I wondered whether, in the seclusion of her own soul, she was trembling with apprehension for her sons, as I was for mine.

Before Arnon and I retired for the night, we cast our eyes at the silvery moonlight reflected in endless points skipping across the Great Sea. Beneath the glinting beams, the water was dark and deep and frightening. Patrussim said that the sea could be savage in its storms. It held the secrets of the wreckage of countless lives of seafaring people, who had sunk with their ships into its depth. And I prayed that the sea would not one day hold the secret of the wreckage of our own lives as well.

During the morning meal Patrussim announced that he wished me to write for him directly to the Israelite warlords, to bring them to their senses.

As it was the sabbath, I demurred, explaining that this was a holy day of rest, and that I would write for him tomorrow.

There was a surprised silence around the table. Noting my confusion, Patrussim said helpfully: "Yes, of course. It is well known that the Israelites have strange—that is, *interesting*, customs. No matter. One day will make no difference."

Following the meal, as I sat in my room, I succeeded in convincing myself that this nightmare of war could never become reality. Human beings, those created in the very image of God, could not be so stupid as to kill and be killed over nothing. This comforting thought gave me respite from my fears, and the peace of the sabbath finally descended upon me.

Arnon and I cherished every moment of the rest of our stay in Ashdod, for we did not know if we would ever have so much time with each other again.

On the way back, I reflected on what the staff had been told about me. Inadvertently, the lie had come true: I did have dealings in the land of the Philistines.

At home I found Elkanah and Hannah busy preparing for their trip to Shiloh. I had intended to apprise them of the bad tidings I had brought with me, but when I saw how deeply immersed they were in their worries about Samuel, I kept my peace.

All the same, what I had learned in Ashdod occupied my mind incessantly. My trust in the wisdom of human beings had fled, and I spent sleepless nights nursing dark fears for my sons.

The Book of Hannah

As soon as we reached the Temple in Shiloh, we saw that something out of the ordinary was happening. Thousands of people were milling around in the square in front of it. This seemed strange, since the day was not the sabbath, nor was it a festival.

We must have looked lost, for one of the priests standing at the edge of the crowd noticed us and asked what our request was. Elkanah told him that we were the parents of Samuel, and we had come to see our son. The priest looked at us in a peculiar way, and the crowd fell back to let us pass.

"Is anything wrong?" I asked, apprehension darting into my heart.

"No, no," the priest replied to my relief. "Come, and you shall see your son. But if you will honor me with your trust, let me speak to you before I call him."

In great astonishment we followed the priest into a secluded chamber, where he invited us to sit down, gave us some cool water to drink, and began. "It will be good for you to know what has transpired here. You may not believe it, but I have seen and heard everything myself, and I assure you that it is the truth.

"The day before last, on the sabbath, Samuel read the Torah aloud in front of the crowd, as was his custom. In the afternoon he left the temple to wander around on the hills, as he often does. He did not come back until nightfall, when we had all retired to our rooms.

"As is our habit in the hot summer nights, we left our doors open to let in the night breeze. I was asleep, but I was awakened by the noise of footsteps. When I peered out of my room, I saw Samuel. Despite the heat, he was dressed in his jacket, and he was running across the courtyard toward the Temple. I followed him and saw him lying down near the Ark of the Covenant. Then I went back to sleep.

"Just before dawn, I woke up again and saw that Samuel, still in the sanctuary, was also awake. He seemed to be listening, and suddenly I saw him run toward the high priest's chamber. Like the other rooms, this room stood open, and I heard Samuel call, 'I am here, for you have called me.' Eli responded. 'Go and lie down, I have not called you.'

"So Samuel returned to his place to lie down, but soon he rushed back to Eli's chamber and called once more, 'I am here, for you have called me.'

"Eli said, 'I have not called you, my son. Go and lie down again.' This was repeated a third time, and Samuel once more went to lie down in his place.

"In the morning, I heard Eli come out of his room. As you know, he is old, his eyes are dim, and he can hardly walk. Yet he rushed toward the sanctuary as if he were a youngster. There he stopped and called out to Samuel in a voice shrill with anxiety, 'Samuel, my son.'

"Samuel replied: 'I am here.'

"Eli said, 'I know that the voice you heard last night was that of the Lord. What is it that the Lord has been saying to you? Do not leave anything out.'

"Then Samuel spoke out in a clear voice, which carried from one end of the Temple to the other. 'The Lord will do a deed in Israel, and he will punish Hofni and Pinhas for their sins. For they have taken more than was their due from the sacrifices, and they have lain with the women who came here to worship, and you have not restrained them. And so the Lord will bring death to both of them on the same day.'

"Hearing this, Eli bowed down in agitation and cried with a trembling voice: 'He is the Lord and he will do as is good in his eyes.'"

When the priest finished his account, we sat speechless for a while.

Then Elkanah demanded imperiously, "Where is Samuel now? I wish to speak to him immediately."

The priest rushed out, and Elkanah whispered to me, "It is as I feared. The many years at the Temple have confounded his wits. The boy is now mad, and it may be too late to cure him."

While he spoke, I looked out the window and asked in wonder, "What are all these people doing here?" But just as I uttered these words, I saw them begin to disband.

Samuel came in and bowed, first to his father, then to me. He inquired if we were well, and I moved forward to embrace him.

Elkanah did not embrace him, but spoke to him sternly. "I have heard the most incredible tale. What is this? It cannot be true that you have claimed that you have seen the Lord and that he has spoken to you."

"No my father, I have not seen the Lord, nor have I claimed to have seen him. The Lord is everywhere and nowhere, and no human being can lay eyes on him and live. Only Moses could see, not the Lord, but the light that emanates from his glory. I have seen nothing."

"But you claim that the Lord has spoken to you, and that you have heard his voice?"

"At first I thought that I had heard a voice from across the yard, but that was because I was confused and sleepy. I then realized that it was inside me. It was still a message, and I had to convey it."

Elkanah now spoke in an appeasing tone, "My son, there are many people who believe that they hear voices, and that they carry messages from the Lord. It then transpires that they are ill. This may be the trouble with you. We have come to take you home, so that we can care for you and you can be cured."

Samuel demurred, though respectfully. "My father, what I hear from inside me is true. I will give you a sign to prove it. I do this because I honor you and love you, and I don't want you to grieve in the belief that your son is mad."

"What is this sign?"

"I see things that are happening in your—in our—family, even though I am not there. I will tell you one of these, and you will go back and you will find that it is as I say."

I was afraid that Samuel was about to destroy Pninah's life. I shook my head at him in silence, and he acknowledged my little gesture by shaking his head at me in return.

He continued: "Go home now, my father and my mother. And when you do, my father, visit your own father, Yeroham the son of Elihu. You will find that he has contracted an illness. It is a lingering disease that will make his body deteriorate slowly, a disease from which he will not recover."

Elkanah's gaze was fixed on Samuel, a look of incredulity on his face.

I intervened. "If you know this, can you not cure him?"

"No," Samuel replied regretfully. "I cannot work miracles."

"What were all the people doing here before?" I asked, still puzzled.

"Yesterday, when I conveyed . . . the . . . message, I was forced to foretell death for Hofni and Pinhas. The rumor of this spread quickly. The two priests are widely hated in these parts. Thousands of people came to bless me. They sent a delegation to ask me to become their judge and leader."

"What was your response?"

Samuel was unperturbed, unmoved by the turmoil and admiration he had stirred up amongst the people. "I told them that I was too young to be their leader, but if they came back tomorrow, I would have a message for them."

"And what will that be?"

"I have to wait until tomorrow to be sure. I think that I will have to tell them the truth—that if the people do not return to the Lord, there will be terrible wars soon." He paused. "And now, my honored parents, go in peace, test the truth of what I told you, and I will come to visit you shortly. Then we will decide what is next to be done."

With these words he bowed again. We embraced him and he left.

This was the last time we visited the House of the Lord in Shiloh. We were never to set foot there again.

We set out from Shiloh in the heat of the day, the sun's rays spreading out from behind a small cloud, beating on our heads. Elkanah brought his donkey close to mine. He told me that we now had to consider how best to cure Samuel of his illness.

I tried to lighten his burden. I said that the oppression of spirit from which Samuel had been suffering for years had lightened. It was as if, once he had finally received the message he had been waiting for, a burden had been lifted from his heart.

Elkanah retorted, "Yes, mad persons usually are not burdened in their hearts. It's the people around them who suffer."

Instead of going home, we made our way directly to the home of Elkanah's father. Yeroham lived in Shaar Efraim with his two wives and Elkanah's elder brother and his family. It was our custom to visit them once a month. We had not done so for almost that long, and it was time that we went there.

When we approached the house, we saw Elkanah's father and his mother as well as Yeroham's second wife sitting in companionable silence in the shade of a large fig tree. Elkanah's brother Nathanel and his sons were out in the fields, and his wife was not at home.

Elkanah's mother saw us first and her face was wreathed in a broad smile. She jumped up and came forward to embrace us, enfolding us in her plump arms. We then bowed to Yeroham and to his second wife.

We sat down, and Elkanah inquired respectfully if they were all well. Yeroham said that, yes, all was well. We were relieved to hear this, but my husband also looked at me, as if to say: "Did I not tell you that the boy is crazy?"

Nathanel's daughters came out to greet us, and one of them brought refreshments. While I sipped my grape juice, I observed my father-in-law. His body had thinned. His left hand was resting in his lap, while his right hand was holding it down.

"Honored father-in-law," I inquired, "is there anything wrong with your hand?"

"No, no. It's merely shaking a little."

My mother-in-law intervened. "Yes, and most of the time he is tired."

"True, but it's nothing. A renowned healer has given me an excellent potion and promised that I would soon regain my strength."

My mother-in-law again intervened, recounting that this had been two weeks ago, and since then things had worsened. I consoled her by saying that it sometimes took a long time before the beneficial effects of a potion became evident.

Then silence prevailed, until Elkanah asked, "My honored father and mother, have you visited the Temple in Shiloh lately?"

"The Temple in Shiloh?" Yeroham seemed surprised. "No. We only go there for the festival of Sukkot. Since then, almost a year has passed."

"Has our son Samuel visited you?"

"Samuel? No, we only see him when we go to the Temple."

"Have you written him a letter?"

"Elkanah, what strange questions you ask. You know well that neither I nor your mother know how to write."

"Have you perhaps asked someone to write a letter to him for you?"

"We have never done so in all our lives."

"Then perhaps you have sent a message to him through some-one who visited the Temple?"

"No one we know has visited the Temple recently."

Yeroham ran the fingers of his right hand through his thinning gray hair as if he were cudgeling his brain and, leaning forward in his chair, asked in a puzzled voice, "Elkanah, why are you asking all of these questions? You seem to have a purpose."

"It's only that we have visited Samuel, and he spoke of you."

"What did he say?"

"He merely mentioned you. It's nothing."

We soon took our leave, and when we were out of earshot, Elkanah reminded me of a neighbor of ours, who had suffered an illness that began with the shaking of his hand and had ended, a few years later, in his death. We remembered the many fail-safe potions that had been administered to him and that they all had been useless.

Elkanah's thoughts then reverted to Samuel. "It's very puzzling," he mused, "yet you don't seem surprised. How is that?"

"I have been aware for some time that he is a seer, that he sees things with the eyes of his spirit."

"What does that mean?"

"He is aware of events that happen at a distance from him. Even though he is at the Temple, he knows things about us that we have never told him."

"What things?" he asked dubiously.

"Various things," I replied evasively.

"Tell me about them," Elkanah persisted.

"You may remember that some time ago Tirzah broke her leg. When I came to visit Samuel he spoke of this, even though I had not mentioned it before. Then, too, when I was last pregnant, I came to see him before I was aware of my pregnancy. As soon as he greeted me, he said that he was proud of his parents who were, once again, fulfilling the commandment to be fruitful and multiply. I said that he was mistaken, since I was not with child. But he said that when I came home I would find that I was, and it was so."

"Why did you not speak of this to me?"

"My beloved, on the one occasion on which I did speak of it, you were so displeased that I did not dare broach the subject again."

When we reached home, we lay down on my bed to rest. Elkanah held me and whispered that perhaps it was time for us to fulfill the commandment to be fruitful and multiply once again. I said that it was all in the hands of the Lord. But I was thankful that he showed no intention of transforming his words into deeds, and in weariness from our long trip we fell asleep in each other's arms.

As soon as I woke up in the morning, my thoughts were with Samuel again. There was no doubt in my mind that the wars he predicted were imminent. I was terrified of what might happen to our other sons and, most of all, to him, in these wars.

The Book of Pninah

When Elkanah and Hannah returned from Shiloh without Samuel, they spoke little. They would only say that he was to come for a visit shortly. Nine months passed before he arrived.

During these months it became evident that war was approaching. In our worry we even cancelled our yearly pilgrimage to Shiloh, and many of our friends and neighbors did the same.

Patrussim advised Arnon that the letters I had written for him had called forth nothing but belligerent responses. He had lost all hope of a peaceful resolution to the conflict, and he had continued to build up his army.

Bad tidings came from inside the land of Israel as well. Our leaders regarded the towns in dispute as part of our own land. They were affronted by the Philistines' demands, and showed no inclination to accede to them.

Because of the impending war, the prospect of Samuel's visit had all but slipped my mind. But when he came, the manner of his arrival, and what he had to say, was so surprising that I forgot all else.

It was in the morning, and Elkanah was about to go out into the fields, when we saw Samuel entering the yard. He bowed to his father, then saw his mother coming toward him and bowed to her. After that he bowed to me, but only briefly, and quickly averted his gaze.

It seemed that Samuel had taken an aversion to me, and I was hurt. Apart from brief greetings on our pilgrimages to the Temple, we had never spoken to each other. Thus there seemed to be no explanation for the manner in which he regarded me.

While he greeted his father and mother, I had the opportunity to observe him as I had never done before. He looked more mature than his fourteen years warranted, and he now matched Elkanah in height.

He had dark, profuse hair, too wild for my taste, which was only partly contained under his head-covering. He wore a light brown garment with fringes, laced with a blue thread at its corners, and it was well suited for the almost adult shape of his body.

He was handsome in a rugged way, his bronzed arms and legs corded with muscles. But what was most striking about him was the piercing look in his green eyes, which seemed to penetrate one's innermost being. It was not a look designed to make one feel at ease, and although he had directed it at me for an instant only, I felt disquieted. I found his whole bearing intimidating, and turned my gaze away from him.

As we headed for the front room, curiosity made my eyes stray back in his direction. I could not help but notice that he radiated an unusual strength, which emanated not only from his body but also from his soul. It struck me that in some inexplicable way he irresistibly drew the eye, and would stand out in a crowd of thousands as easily as he did here.

Samuel's arrival was followed by that of a group of young men of all sorts and demeanors. It was not clear why they were following him or what they wanted of him; they were simply there. When he entered the front room, they sat down in the yard to wait for him, and Samuel requested that refreshment be sent out to them.

Hannah bade her son sit down at the big table, so that food and drink could be brought for him as well. Elkanah sat next to him, and the older children came in and arrayed themselves around him. As I was intrigued and curious to learn what he had to say, I sat down as well and continued to study him.

Bread and oil and and a skin of grape juice were set before him; and while he stilled his hunger and thirst there was total silence. When he had finished his small meal, Elkanah plied him with questions, and we listened to his answers in rapt attention.

Elkanah's first question pertained to the people in the yard, and Samuel said that they had set their hearts on becoming prophets. Hence they had gathered around him, and had been following him for the last several months.

Elkanah was far from pleased. "Where precisely have you been wandering during those months? Your missives were never clear."

"My father, you may remember the people who were assembled in front of the Temple when you came. The next day, I had . . . I had . . . a message for them. After that, more and more people assembled every day, and I had to speak to them, too. Then some elders came, and announced that people across the land wished to hear me speak. I thought that while I came here to visit you, I might stop on the way and speak to them. Only, whenever I stopped at one town or village, people from adjacent ones demanded that I come there. So the journey took much longer than I had anticipated, and I deeply apologize for the delay."

At that, a babble of voices burst forth, as Samuel's brothers and sisters began talking to him all at once.

Elkanah subdued them by raising his hand, and Hannah asked, "What message are you spreading to all of these people that they are so keen to hear you?"

"I call on the people to return to the Lord, to cease worshipping other gods, and to heed the commandments, or else horrible wars will break out, in which thousands will be killed."

"And what is their response?"

"Multitudes listen to me. They claim that my voice is loud, and even those standing at a great distance can hear me. But they say to each other: 'Let the boy play in front of us,' and take no notice of what I say. And now, my father and my mother, war is near, and I no longer have much hope that it can be averted."

I was seized with fear for my boys, and I could not contain myself. "I have visited the land of the Philistines, and I was told that our warlords have invaded Beth Shemesh and Azakah, and if they halt those warmongering deeds, the Philistines will let go of us. Then we will continue to sit, each man under his vine and his fig tree, and there will be peace in the land."

Samuel jerked his head around to face me. "Pninah, you cannot have considered," he said tersely. "These towns are part of the land the Lord has promised our fathers to give us. We could not give them over to Philistine rule."

But I persisted. "What would be the damage?"

"They would bring their worship of Dagon into them, and the Israelites living there would worship him. Israelite men would lie with Philistine women, and Israelite women would lie with Philistine men. And they would be cut off from Israel."

"If they are truly Israelites," I retorted, "they will not worship other gods. And Israelite women would never lie with men from the peoples around us . . ."

I felt Samuel's smoldering gaze on me. I realized the stupidity of what I had said, and my voice fizzled out.

My elder son, Elroy, now raised his voice. "My mother, I honor you deeply, but the truth in Samuel's words cannot be denied. We cannot abandon our brethren in the two towns to the mercy of the uncircumcised, as we would not wish them to abandon us if we were in their place."

Samuel resumed: "If the sins of our people continue, the Lord will bring this bloodbath upon us as surely as he brings autumn after summer. I cannot even be sure that death will pass over our house."

By then, Hannah's face was as pale as mine must have been. She exclaimed that Samuel was weary and needed to rest, and we dispersed.

I went to my room, but before I could close the door I heard steps behind me. I turned around and to my utter surprise, I saw Samuel following me.

"Pninah, I want to speak to you."

I could not imagine what he might have to say, but I invited him in and he closed the door behind him.

Facing him, I asked in some disquiet, "And what is it that you want to talk about?"

I did not have to give lessons on that day, and so I wore one of my revealing dresses from Ishkar, this time a violet one. Samuel's eyes strayed to it, to my body, his gaze lingering there. He appeared to be confused, and I blushed furiously and became hot and uncomfortable. Then he looked at my face and his eyes locked with mine. Finally he collected himself and resumed the thread of his thought. "Pninah, return to the Lord, your God."

I was taken aback. "Why do you speak these words?"

"You are well aware of why," he said bluntly.

"I am aware that you hold me in aversion," I blurted out, "but . . ."

"You are mistaken. I don't hold you in aversion, only what you are doing."

I felt a new rush of blood into my cheeks and my ears, as I realized that Samuel knew about me. I was dumbfounded, for I could not fathom how this had come about. For a while I stood there, my head bent, my hair tumbling down over my face, staring at the ground in deep shame.

I thought that he might have pried my secret from his mother, so with my head still low, I said: "Has your mother spoken to you about me?"

"No," he replied forcibly, "and if she did, I would not listen to her. It would be in transgression of the commandment 'You shall not bear tales among your people.'"

"And will you speak to your father about me?"

"No, that would be in breach of the same commandment."

Somewhat reassured, I raised my head slightly to look at him, and said bitterly, "Samuel, no one can understand—"

"Pninah, I *can* understand." He looked at me sternly, yet not unkindly. "I understand how horrifying it was for you when my father took my mother for his second wife, and loved her more than he loved you. Something similar had happened to you with your mother, and this made my father's deed all the worse. And I understand how desperately you love the Canaanite man with whom you are sinning."

I now delivered a gentle rebuke of my own: "In what manner are you concerned in this?"

He gave me a scalding look. "If you wish to keep your sons, my brothers, safe, this is the way."

"Are you telling me that if I mend my ways there will be no war?"

"No. I am saying that if the people as a whole mend their ways, there will be no war. And each and every person of Israel must bring this about."

Tears sprung to my eyes. "I can stop this no more than I can stop breathing."

But Samuel was implacable. "You must find the strength inside you. I cannot help you with this." After a pause he said, "May you find your way back to the Lord; and may the Lord be with you."

With these words he bowed and spun on his heels to leave.

I gathered my courage and called him back. He turned to face me again and waited.

"Do you think that a man has more of a right to commit adultery than a woman?"

He gave me a penetrating look. "No, but when a man commits such acts, this does not justify his wife in doing the same."

After that he stood and looked into my eyes for a long time. Little by little, reluctantly, the harsh expression in his face melted into a smile. "I regret, Pninah, that things are as they are. You are worthy of a man who would love only you."

"There will never be such a man."

Samuel's eyes had laughter lurking in them. "You would not make a successful prophetess." As soon as he had spoken those words the laughter in his eyes faded as if it had never been there, and their look became stringent again.

Having made this unfathomable remark he bowed once more and, his features still etched in harsh lines, he departed, leaving me in bewilderment. I should have asked about the source of his knowledge of my innermost feelings, and what he had meant by his last remark, yet I knew it would have been useless. He would not have told me.

During the evening meal the subject of the war cropped up again. Elroy and Elhanan were gripped with a strange zeal. They declared themselves willing to go out in defense of the land of Israel whenever they should be called on to do so, and the horrendous forebodings of the last months overwhelmed me.

Once Samuel had left, I spoke to them. "My sons," I admonished them, "this is all happening at a great distance from us. We dwell in the remote hills of Efraim, and it has nothing to do with us."

But Elhanan spoke to me thus: "My mother, we, the Israelites, are many tribes but one people. When the need arises, we stand together before the Lord and against our enemies."

Elkanah forbade our sons to join the army. Had they been twenty years of age, it would have been their duty, as set out in the Torah. But as they were not, they were compelled to bow to his decree and stay home.

Elroy explained that he and his brother were as tall and sturdy as any man of twenty. As both of them were, in fact, taller than Elkanah, this claim could not be denied.

Since they had been infants, I had been close to my sons, and they had confided their little joys and sorrows to me. But now I felt that a gulf was stretching out between us.

Each day, my daughters and I sat for a long time hugging each other in silent trepidation.

The Book of Hannah

Although Samuel had promised to come see us after our return from Shiloh, he was in no hurry to keep his promise, and I was angry at him for failing to honor us with a visit. But when he finally did so and I saw how exhausted he was, my anger dissipated. All I wanted was for him to eat some food and to rest before he decided what he must do next.

As word of his arrival was passed from mouth to mouth, Samuel's visit caused an uproar not only in our family but in our entire neighborhood. His words conveyed a heavy sense of the impending war, bringing our fears to a new peak.

Then he did something unexpected: He went to speak to Pninah in her room. I waited in the front yard, but it was some time before he reappeared.

When he did, he looked shaken, as if he had undergone a harrowing event. My heart wrenched in my chest for him. Wrapping my arm around him, I led him to a room behind mine, which I had prepared for him, and asked, "My son, what has happened to you?"

With his face hidden, he replied glumly, "My mother, what could have happened? I merely talked to Pninah for a short while."

I gave him a sideways look. "What was your talk about?"

By that time we had reached his room, and he made this an excuse for failing to answer my question.

But I was not so easily put off, and as we sat down on his bed, I eyed him again and continued to probe. "You have never spoken to Pninah before."

"No."

"Then why now?"

"There was something that needed to be said."

Though I knew what this "something" was, his words did nothing to clarify why he looked so stricken. "Samuel, did she say anything unkind, anything that hurt you?"

This time he looked at me unflinchingly and shook his head vigorously. "No."

"Then what has upset you?"

His face turned stony, as he replied, "My mother, you know well that the upcoming war is the source of my upset."

"You are more perturbed now than you were before you entered her room."

He did not respond, and I realized that he would tell me no more, so I rose up and left. When I gazed through his window a while later, he was lying on his bed, with his hands folded on the cushion I had placed there for his comfort, his head resting on his hands, deep in sleep.

He slept for a long time. When he finally emerged from behind the closed door, it was twilight. But he did not seem refreshed. His eyes looked as heavy as the windless air that hung about the yard. The trees that grew at the edge of our backyard were casting their lengthening shadows on the vineyard beyond, shadows that were reflected in Samuel's wan face.

I took him to my room, made him sit down, and gave him a cup of apple nectar. But he hardly drank anything.

Before long Elkanah came in, and sat down and asked, "Samuel, what will you do now?"

"I will continue what I have been doing."

"Do you still have any hope of averting this war?"

"No. Still, I have no choice but to try."

"You are tired." I sighed, "Stay home for a few days before you exert yourself again."

"My mother, I would much prefer to stay with you and with . . . but I cannot. The time to try to stop the war is running out, and I am compelled to resume as soon as possible."

Elkanah said sternly, "When the war breaks out you will come home directly."

Samuel raised his cup to his lips and drank from it, making no reply to his father's words, but Elkanah persisted. "I demand that you come home the moment the war breaks out."

"My father," Samuel answered respectfully, yet unyieldingly, "I cannot promise."

Speaking for both of us, Elkanah said, "We forbid you even to approach the battlefield!"

Samuel bent his head in silence.

By now the veins on Elkanah's forehead were pulsing, his hands were clenched into fists, and in his wrath he shouted, "Did you hear my words?"

"I heard your words, my father," Samuel replied.

Elkanah's face was suffused by a dark red color, and he readied himself for another outburst. I placed my hand on his arm soothingly, and at that moment the door opened and Samuel's younger brothers and sisters crowded the threshold, noisily demanding his attention. I hoped that they might distract him from whatever it was that had befallen him before, so I told him that he could go with them.

I watched them sitting in the yard, Samuel fondly patting their cheeks and pressing them against his, while they touched his garment, his arms, his face, with doting hands.

Elkanah stayed behind in my room in scowling silence. He bent forward in his chair and covered his face with his hands and sat there, groaning, as if in pain. He must have been thinking that he would soon have three sons in the battlefield. I hugged him and tried to calm him. I could say nothing reassuring about his and Pninah's sons, as it was obvious that they would join the army as soon as war broke out. But I reminded him that Samuel, barely fourteen years old, would certainly not go into battle.

But on that day I had come to know my firstborn son better than I had known him so far, and I placed little trust in my own words.

The evening meal prepared in Samuel's honor included all manner of delicacies from the fullness of the land to tempt his palate. The roast set before him was made of the choicest cut of veal. The stew was subtly seasoned with rare spices and the honey-and-date cakes were sweet and soft and baked to perfection. Following his lengthy travels, I had expected him to be as famished as a wolf long deprived of prey. But he ate sparingly and paid no heed to these treats. I had hoped that the meal would be festive, but because the looming war was once more discussed at length, it was somber.

During the meal I searched Pninah's face, hoping to glean what had befallen my son in her presence. But there was nothing there to enlighten me. Although the violet color of her dress attractively set off her eyes, these eyes revealed nothing but anguished concern over the upcoming war, and her sons' fate.

In the morning, as Samuel prepared to leave, I embraced him, still ignorant of what tugged at his heart.

After he had gone, with his followers at his heels, the front yard was left strewn with all manner of litter, but I did not mind. For the hope soared inside me that, with the sweeping of the debris from the yard, the war would also be swept away.

This hope proved to be unfounded. Quite the opposite—in the coming weeks the winds of war blew even stronger, and swept everything before them.

When travelers came by, they recounted that our officers had begun assembling the army. They were passing through towns and villages, calling on all young men to do battle with the Philistines in the name of the Lord.

By that time we had almost lost touch with Samuel. We asked the travelers who bore the tidings of the call-up if they had encountered him. Some said they had; some had listened to his speeches. But then he had moved on and, because they did not know which way he had headed, we could never be sure where he was. And we were still uncertain of what he intended to do once we were at war.

At night, I would lie on my bed, gazing into the dark, screaming silently inside myself. The dawn that banished the night's darkness did not dispel the dark terror in my soul.

Then one bleak winter day a caravan carrying merchandise from the Great Sea came by. While the travelers stopped for rest we besieged them with questions, hoping to learn the latest news. They told us that they had seen officers calling up the young men from the tribe of Efraim for the army, and that they were approaching Ramathayim.

Elroy and Elhanan ran to their room to gather up the provisions they had prepared for themselves. I got hold of a stableboy and, barely able to keep my voice from trembling, charged him to bring Elkanah back from the fields at the speed of an eagle in the sky.

Then I rattled the door of Pninah's room.

The Book of Pninah

When I heard the rattle of my door, I had little doubt as to what it signified. As I came out, my sons were already standing in the front yard, with their provisions.

I made a last attempt to prevent them from going. I threw myself at Elroy's chest, then at Elhanan's. I cried, I pleaded, I screamed, but they stood before me in implacable silence.

Elkanah, who entered the yard, reproved me. "Cease, Pninah. What you are doing is useless. You cannot prevent them from going. You only make them leave with a heavy heart, for worry of you." After a pause, he said, "Elroy, come and stand in front of me, to the right-hand side. And you, Elhanan, do the same to the left. And you, Pninah, come and stand beside me."

I came, and regarded the boys: tall and broad shouldered, and the most handsome young men I had ever beheld.

They bowed their heads, and Elkanah placed my right hand on Elroy's head, and my left hand on Elhanan's head. Then he placed his hands over mine and, my voice rent by sobs, we recited the ancient triple blessing of the Lord:

May the Lord bless you and keep you.
May the Lord make his countenance shine upon you and be
    gracious to you.
May the Lord turn his countenance to you and may he grant
    you peace.

When the boys rode out of the yard, I trailed them on foot, my red eyes staring blindly at the ground before me, avoiding the anguished looks of the other mothers crowding the streets, escorting their sons to the town square.

There I saw the captain of a thousand, whose name was Ahiassaf, with his aides and his banners flying high, shouting out orders. Around him stood ten captains of a hundred, each assembling the young men under their command. Elroy and Elhanan were ordered to join the captain of a hundred whose name was Pnuel. He mounted his donkey, and my sons, along with many of our friends' and neighbors' sons, fell in behind him.

In another part of the square was another captain of a thousand with his captains of hundreds, and at some distance there was another one, and another.

Soon the exodus began, as each officer led his squad toward the road bound for the land of the Philistines.

When my sons left the square, I continued to stand, my eyes straining to follow them until, rounding a bend in the road, they disappeared from my sight.

I stood still; but my heart, ripped out of my chest, followed them.

I returned home, where I sat in my room battling despair. Soon I threw a few belongings into a cloth bag. When I saw the clouds threatening a downpour, I took out my sheepskin cloak and hung it on my arm. Then I went to look for Elkanah.

The Book of Hannah

After Elroy and Elhanan had left for the square and Pninah had followed in their wake, Elkanah remained standing in the yard, as one paralyzed by a deadly disease.

My heart went out to him. I touched his hand gently and led him to the front room, where we sat down for a belated midday meal. My mouth was parched, and I felt as if my throat was knotted into a coil. What little food I put into my mouth would not go down, and Elkanah left his meal untouched.

When we stood up, Elkanah prepared to return to the fields, but Pninah came in and halted him.

"Sir," she began, "before you go, I must tell you that I am going up to the top of the hill that overlooks the road bound for the land of the Philistines. I will sit there until our sons return from the war."

"What is this?" he shouted.

She flinched, but remained silent.

"Don't we have enough mad people in this house that you need to be crazy as well?" he thundered.

Pninah was apparently so overtaken by fear for her sons that her usual fear of Elkanah had dissipated, and she was able to stand up to him. "I'm not crazy," she retorted with a tremor in her voice, yet forcefully.

"Certainly you are, if this is what you mean to do," he ranted. In a more subdued voice he continued: "And you mean to sleep out under the sky?"

"Yes."

"It is beginning to rain—you will be soaked and die of the wet and the cold. Hear me, Pninah," he now forced himself to speak patiently to her, as to a little child. "My anxiety for the boys is no less than yours, and I could suggest we go and sit there together, but what good would it do?"

"When they come back, I want to be the first to welcome them."

"What if they never come back?"

"Then I prefer death to life. I will stay there and die."

He was incensed again. "And leave me to grieve for them alone, and for you as well? You will not do this to me."

Their daughters, Gilah and Nehamah, who had entered the room, now came forward to hug her, and Gilah cried, "Mother, we need you alive."

"My daughters," she responded, "I love you more than my own life but even you cannot keep me back."

Elkanah placed his hands on the girls' shoulders, and drew them away from their mother. He came close to her and declared sharply, "Pninah, I forbid you to leave this house until you have come to your senses." Then he commanded, "Go to your room, and I will come to comfort you."

"Sir," she retorted, "I honor you greatly. Under ordinary circumstances I would do as you order me, as I have always done, but now I cannot."

"You will not dare to flout me."

She gathered up her belongings and began walking to the front door. Elkanah blocked her way by force. "You are truly deranged," he pronounced in a shaking voice.

Indeed, Pninah seemed to be crazed with despair and defiance. Her madness lent her strength, and she struggled in Elkanah's embrace like a lioness robbed of her cubs. In the end, he was stronger than she was. He placed his right hand around her back, and his left hand under her knees and picked her up in his arms. With some effort, he began carrying her to her room, while she kicked and scratched and bit his flesh to break free.

I had been standing in the background watching this harrowing scene in silence, but now, compelled to intervene, I stepped forward and said with feigned assurance, "No, my husband. What you are doing is not good. Let her go. She will feel relief when she has done what she has set out to do. And she will not die, because we will pitch a tent for her on the hill. We will supply her with food and drink, we will have our people guard her, and we will visit her as often as we can."

And Elkanah relented.

The Book of Pninah

My two daughters and two old men who worked in our stables escorted me up the hill. The men brought two goatskin tents with them, pitching one for me close to the point that overlooked the road, and their own at a considerable distance, allowing me some solitude.

By that time the menacing clouds had dispersed, taking their load of heavy rain to be shed in other domains. The girls sat with me in front of my tent, our gaze riveted to the road below, where row after row of young men were riding by.

As the sun set the flow thinned out, then ceased altogether. We sat watching the sun slip behind the hills, the clouds reflecting it in a grayish pink before melting into a deepening darkness, like that of my forebodings. We continued to gaze down on the empty road until, engulfed in the blackness of the night, it became invisible.

Later Elkanah came with a basket of food on his arm. He sent the girls home, and spread out the food on a cloth in front of us. He attempted to coax me to swallow a morsel of one or other of the dishes, but I could not.

Elkanah spent the night with me. The clouds rolled in again and the rain resumed, and we lay in each other's arms listening to it splatter on the roof of the tent, our throats choked, our tears mingling. Although I felt Elkanah's lust stir against me, I told him that I felt numb, and for the first time ever, he heeded my objection.

The next morning, after he had left for the fields, Hannah arrived. After some hesitation, her eyes on the verge of tears, she revealed that she had no notion of where Samuel was at this time.

I understood what she was driving at. "If you are worried that Samuel will be going into battle, you need not be. No officer would take him into his contingent at his age."

My words seemed to comfort Hannah, yet I harbored doubts. Samuel was tall and looked far more mature than his years. He was forceful, and none would dare oppose him. I did not give voice to these thoughts, but felt nausea rise up in me.

As we spoke, rain began to fall, and a gust of cold wind blew, causing us to withdraw into the tent.

The flow of young men on the road had resumed, and we could see them man next to man, man behind man, riding their donkeys, wrapped in their sheepskin cloaks. My heart was wrung for them, as I asked myself which among them would never return into his mother's arms.

We sat watching for some time when, to my astonishment, I caught sight of a familiar carriage. It halted at the side of the road, and Bathanath alit from it and began ascending the hill.

I brought her into the tent, and helped her out of her wet cloak.

She greeted Hannah, and turned to me to say, "How is this? I came to your home and was told that you were here. Are you out of your mind?"

"Bathanath, you are my dear friend. I have been told already that I'm crazy. Is it necessary for you to tell me, too?"

"I will say no more. I have brought up some warm milk with honey from your home. Drink it before it cools off."

"Honey? Have you not instructed me never to touch honey all the days of my life?"

"Your daughters tell me that you have refused food since yesterday morning. Drink this and don't argue with me."

Bathanath had traveled from a distance, she had made an effort to be helpful, and I could not say no. I forced myself to drink the milk but it lay heavy as a stone in my stomach.

Silence fell, and Hannah, perceiving that Bathanath wished to be alone with me, left. As soon as she was out of earshot, Bathanath told me that Arnon was preparing to set out for the land of the Philistines.

"Don't say these words," I responded with a wail. "Do I now have to be sick with worry for him as well?"

"Certainly not. He has no intention of going into battle. Arnon will visit Patrussim to see what he can do for your boys."

"What can he do?"

"Perhaps nothing, but he will try. He asked for the name of the captain of a thousand and of the captain of a hundred under whose banners the boys will go to war."

I told her, and she wrote down the names. I added that Samuel might also have gone into battle, and requested that Arnon do what he could for him as well. But when, in response to her question, I admitted that I did not know which contingent he had joined, she said that there would be no way for Arnon to locate him. Then she left in a hurry to convey to Arnon the names I had given her.

In the evening Elkanah appeared with the familiar basket of food. As we sat, I saw that his face wore the pallor of death. Although I looked at him, he did not look back at me. The certainty was growing inside me that he was concealing something horrendous. I asked if he had heard anything about our sons; he replied that he had not.

"Then what is it?"

At first he would not speak but, after much begging and pleading and cajoling, I got it out of him. Some travelers who had come from where the troops were assembled reported that our men were greatly outnumbered by the Philistines, who were equipped with ominous weapons. Our commanders expected defeat and enormous casualties.

I began shaking, my teeth chattering, as if I were in the throes of a deadly fever. I wished myself to unconsciousness, but the opposite happened: My senses were sharpened, and I began to conjure visions of inescapable doom.

My state worsened when Elkanah revealed that the travelers had encountered Samuel there, and that he had sent his greetings. On this, at least, I tried to reassure him: "Surely our officers will not let him fight at his age."

"He is willful and stubborn and does only what he wants to do."

"Does Hannah know this?"

"No. I said nothing to her. And you will not do so, either."

That night, as we lay in each other's arms, our despair was so deep that there were no tears left to shed. Sleep would not come, and with the dawning of the day, there was no dawning of hope for us.

The next evening, when Elkanah came, we sat at the entrance of my tent. I could still vaguely discern the empty road, and in my imagination I saw it winding itself into the distance, all the way to our sons.

I began to recite the "Shma" prayer, the basic affirmation of our faith:

Hear O Israel
the Lord is our God
The Lord is one . . .

We lay down on the sheet inside the tent, and I finally slept.

As dusk followed dawn and dawn followed dusk, I ceased counting the days. It might have been a week since I began my vigil, or eight days, or even nine. The sun had slid behind the hills, but it was not dark yet. I sat, my empty gaze scanning the road, only an occasional bleating of sheep disturbing the silence, when I spotted four men approaching on donkeys. There was nothing unusual in this, but still I continued looking. I heard indistinct voices floating up from the road.

At first I could not be sure, then I was. I wanted to scream, but no sound escaped my gaping mouth.

I raced downhill in a wild tumult, my eyes blurred by tears. I tripped and pitched forward and crashed to the ground and bruised my knees and scrambled to my feet and lurched forward again. I saw two of the men running up the hill. When they reached me, they lifted me up in their arms and carried me down between them, their faces against my smudged one, my tears wetting their cheeks, and I was born again.

Two other men stood on the road beside their donkeys, and I recognized them as being in Arnon's employ.

They bowed, and one said, "Lady, we have delivered your sons safely into your hands, and we bid you farewell."

I thanked them over and over again, and invited them to put up at our house for the night. But, as their orders were to return immediately, even if it meant riding through the night, they left.

Only now did I look at my sons through my tears, and I noticed that Elhanan's left arm was bandaged, and that they were both red-eyed for lack of sleep. I took them into my arms and kissed them, together and separately, and then together again. They bore it with great patience, until it began to rain. Then Elroy wrapped me in his cloak, and ran up the hill to advise our men of their arrival.

I began pelting Elhanan with questions. Occasionally wincing with pain, he replied that he was eager to recount the baffling tale of their rescue, but it would be best if we reached home quickly, and talking would only delay us. He merely reassured me about his wound and about Samuel, and as soon as Elroy returned we set out.

Before long the homecomers had to endure more tears and embraces from their father and their siblings. I sent Gilah for a healer to tend to Elhanan's wound. It could be seen that both he and his brother were filthy, and two tubs of water warmed in large kettles on the cooking stones were brought to their room for their bath.

When they came out, the healer was waiting for Elhanan. After she bandaged the wound anew, the evening meal was placed on the table. An expectant hush fell as we waited while the boys satiated their hunger. I could only hope that, whatever had happened, their tale would not reveal Arnon's part in it.

Soon words rushed forth from their mouths, but as they were both speaking at once, it was impossible to understand them. So the honor of telling the tale was bestowed on the firstborn, and Elroy began.

The Israelite army had assembled at Even Ha'ezer, the Philistine army was camped at Afek, north of Even Haezer. There was little time to train the Israelite men for warfare—they were merely provided with swords and shields. Before long the Philistine army was advancing toward them. The Israelite captains flew their banners, sounding the ram horns and trumpets, and they charged into battle.

To their surprise, they saw Samuel riding across the battlefield, shouting words of encouragement to the warriors. The Philistines tried to get to him, but he was soon lost from sight.

When Hannah heard this, she slid down limply in her chair. I gripped her hand tightly, and Elkanah wrapped his arms around her. But Elroy assured her that Samuel was unhurt, and she brightened a bit.

At first, chaos reigned. They could not make out what was happening. Their instructions had been to stay close to Pnuel, who was standing in their midst shouting out orders, which no one could hear and no one heeded.

It did not take them long to realize that the Philistines were a bloodthirsty lot, their murderous rage clearly visible in their angry, bulging eyes. The Israelites plunged at them with their swords. But this enemy thrust far superior swords back at them, and also protected itself with massive, round shields. It was impossible for the Israelites to pierce those shields with their own paltry blades, or to protect themselves with their own dismally small shields.

Their little contingent was surrounded, and the Philistines began to wreak havoc in their midst. In the bloody confusion, through the haze of sweat that blurred their vision, they saw the men around them felled, screaming in agony, their wails piercing the air as they sunk down into agonizing death. Those who did not die quickly lay whimpering on the ground, pleading for help that would never come.

Defeat was imminent. Fury overcoming their fear, they resolved to fight to the end. One murderous Philistine attempted to thrust his sword into Elhanan's chest, and almost succeeded, but fortunately Elhanan turned around, and the sword lodged in his left arm. He was overwhelmed with pain, blood began streaming from him, and he collapsed to the ground.

It was at that point that one who seemed to be a Philistine commander rode into the battlefield on horseback. He shouted an order that our sons could not understand, but they heard it being passed from man to man.

Suddenly the Philistines ceased their charge. Instead, they held out their enormous shields and moved forward, pushing the Israelites back. Pnuel bellowed hoarsely to keep on fighting, but they were forced to stagger backward and Elroy dragged Elhanan with him.

As the Philistines continued to move forward, Elroy, too, stumbled and fell to the ground. They were sure that they would be crushed under their enemies' feet. Strangely, the Philistines did not tread on them, but turned them over to lie face down. They then grabbed their garments from behind, and dragged them over the bodies of the dead and the wounded until, smeared with blood, they were clear of the battlefield.

Elhanan, blood still gushing from his arm, weakened by the moment until he fainted. Elroy took off his own shirt, tore it to pieces and bandaged his brother's wound, tying it as strongly as he could to stifle the blood. The bleeding stopped, but Elhanan lay senseless on the ground.

The commander on horseback shouted to them in Hebrew that if they lay down their weapons no further harm would befall them. Pnuel, whose voice had almost given out, managed to hiss that it was a ruse, and that if they gave up their weapons they would be killed to the last man.

The Philistine officer signaled his men to deal with Pnuel. Swiftly they subdued him and wrested his sword from his hands. Then they hauled him away and forced him to sit down with his men.

When the Israelite men saw that their captured leader had not been harmed, they let their swords and shields drop to the ground. They were led away from the battlefield, Elroy forced to carry Elhanan over his shoulder. When they had moved some distance, they were ordered to sit and the Philistines brought them water. Elroy leaned Elhanan against his shoulder and poured water into his mouth. Elhanan coughed some of it out, regaining consciousness although his face was contorted with pain.

Elroy now surveyed the men around him, and of the hundred that had formed their group, only some seventy were left. He shuddered to think what had befallen the rest.

Soon another Philistine officer appeared, and he announced in Hebrew that each Israelite would be required to state his name and each of these would be registered on a scroll. Then they would be called upon to take an oath before their own God that they would never come back to do battle against the Philistines, and this would be written down as well. After that, they would be escorted to the border of their land, where they would be released.

By now, Elroy was exhausted from telling the story, so Elhanan took over.

"We had no choice but to do what the officer demanded, and it all happened as he had said it would. But when it was our turn, after they had noted our names and we had sworn our oaths, two men grabbed us and led us away. We were sure that they were leading us as lambs to the slaughter. We were sweating in panic as they guided us to an elevated spot, where the commander who had given the order to save us stood waiting for us with another man.

"The commander, whose black hair was grizzled with white, was no taller than most men; but he had a commanding bearing, as one used to having others at his beck and call. He examined us closely. 'So you are Elroy and Elhanan,' he said. 'I am Patrussim, and I have heard of you before.'

"At hearing these words, we were sure that our fears were being confirmed. Because of all the blood I had lost, my head swam and I was on the verge of fainting once more. Elroy wrapped his arm around me and so I remained standing, only my head bent forward.

"Patrussim raised my chin with his hand, and we had an enormous surprise as he announced: 'I would have you know that your mother, whom you resemble, is a very fine lady and I hold her in high regard. In her honor I have spared not only your lives, but the lives of all the young men still left in your contingent.'

"His words revived me, and Elroy found the courage to inquire: 'Sir, you know our mother, then?'

"'Yes, she once visited our home and told me about you. And she wrote letters for me to your leaders to try to prevent this futile slaughter. It was to no avail, but we did what we could.'

"So far he had spoken kindly, but suddenly his face became harsh. He raised his voice and his words assumed a threatening demeanor. 'You will now go back to your land. But you will do well to remember that you have sworn an oath never to return to wage bloody battles against us again. If you show your faces here, except with a banner of peace, it will not bode well for you.'

"We thanked the Philistine for sparing our lives and, once more, swore not to do battle with the Philistines again.

"The expression on Patrussim's face remained stern for some time, then softened and became fatherly as he continued. 'I believe you. And now, I have tidings for you from your mother. She is waiting for you on top of the hill overlooking the road leading into Ramathayim. Her heart goes out to you, so don't delay. First, a healer will bandage your arm properly, Elhanan. And here are new shirts and donkeys and two men to escort you. They have provisions with them, and you will eat and drink on the way.'

"I became aware of the another man standing beside the Philistine commander. He was tall, with hair of a copper color and a red glow to it. He regarded us with tears in his eyes, but did not say a word.

"There was nothing left for us to do but bless the Philistine, bow to both men, and step over to the side of the hill, where the healer was waiting for us.

"As we crossed the border, we saw scores of wounded men lying on the ground, and Samuel, along with some others, caring for them. He waved to us, and though we wanted to stop and assist him, our guards forced us to proceed."

Throughout the telling of this tale, we sat in stunned silence, hardly moving our eyes from the boys' lips. Only when Elhanan mentioned the second man's coppery-reddish hair did Hannah look at me sharply, and I braced myself so as not to blush.

For a while, silence reigned. Then Elkanah spoke to me. "Pninah, you never spoke of those letters."

"No, sir. When I came back from the land of the Philistines, I found you and Hannah so engrossed in your worries about Samuel that I decided not to burden you with the bad tidings I bore."

Elkanah spoke again, this time to the boys. "Did you not ask the name of the other man who was standing there, and did you not inquire what part he had played in your rescue?"

"No, my father. For we were dazed, and only later did we puzzle over this."

Elkanah now quizzed me with his eyes and asked, "How did the Philistine know where you were, and what contingent the boys were in?"

For a moment the air was brittle with tension and I was thrown into confusion; but Hannah, who had regained her usual serenity, said calmly, "These are puzzles that will probably never be solved. It's enough that the boys are all safe. Let us rejoice and praise the Lord."

I sighed with relief and directed a grateful look at her, which she acknowledged with a faint smile.

One question remained: What had happened on other parts of the battlefield? The boys replied that before they had been dragged away, matters had not looked good. But the battle was still raging, and they had no way of knowing what happened afterward.

By now, Elroy and Elhanan were falling asleep in their chairs, their heads dropping forward. I put my arms around them, made them get up and led them to their room. When I turned back, I saw Elkanah waiting to lead me to mine.

We lay down on my bed embracing each other. Once again our tears mingled, only this time they were tears of relief. Then I felt a tremor of excitement run through me at the same time that I felt Elkanah's lust stir. This time I was ready for him, for his fierce movements inside me, and we soared to delight together.

Later Elkanah murmured, "I have missed being inside you more than I can tell," and immediately he fell into the heavy sleep of utter relief.

In all the years since I had met him, Elkanah had not changed. All he ever missed about me was the knowing of me. Yet I, too, was content. I whispered a silent prayer of thanks to the Lord and then followed Elkanah into sleep. And I did not stir all night long.

In the morning I sent word to Bathanath that I would like to visit her, but for some days there was no reply.

The Book of Hannah

During the coming days, despite the joy of Elroy's and Elhanan's homecoming, our spirits sank again, for horrendous tidings reached our ears. The battle had been an inconceivable disaster for the Israelites. Our army had been defeated, and four thousand of our men—no, our children—had been killed.

Names began to be mentioned. Mothers and fathers tore their garments, wore sackcloth and strewed ashes on their heads, sat on the ground and broke into pitiful wails. Many visits to comfort the bereaved needed to be made, and many tears had to be shed.

Samuel came home again, his followers behind him. He said nothing of his prophecy having been fulfilled, or of his bravery on the battlefield. He merely sat down in the town square, weeping with the rest of Israel and refusing to be comforted.

Later, when he came to our house, his face was still stained with tears, but he was calm as he stood next to me in silence. When he saw Pninah cross the yard, he stepped forward and said quietly, "Pninah, my brothers are safe and you will see to it that they remain so."

"You have been careless of your own safety," I protested.

"I tried to prevent the war, but I could not. When it came, I tried to encourage our warriors but I was not successful and we were defeated. And there are more defeats in store for me."

"So the wars are not over yet."

"No."

"Then you must not repeat what you have done on the battlefield. It was madness, Samuel. You must never to do it again."

He looked at me, but did not respond. I realized that it would be futile to press him to speak of something he had no wish to talk about. So I said no more.

Before the evening meal, he sat on the ground with a group of his admirers. Then the maids brought out refreshments for them, and he joined the family in the front room.

During the meal, he broached the topic that was close to his heart. "I will continue to call on the people to return to the Lord, but I'm afraid that I will not succeed. If so, the disaster that has befallen us is but a trifle compared to what is still to come. Twenty times as many men will be killed. Twenty times as many mothers and fathers will tear their garments and strew earth and ashes on their heads, and sit on the ground and wail. I know this but I am powerless to prevent it, because the people will not listen to me."

I begged Samuel to stay home for some time and rest. But he replied that he must continue to try to avert further disaster. On the next morning, he left.

Before he set out, our morning meal over, the family stood outside among the mild morning rays of what would soon turn into a sunny day, to take leave of him. First he turned to me, and I perceived that his mood had changed overnight. His face was pale and tears were streaming down his cheeks.

I exclaimed, "Samuel, you are in distress."

"Yes, but at least I no longer have to be apprehensive about my brothers."

Pninah, who was standing at our side, had tears in her eyes as she asked, "What about yourself? You cannot be thinking of going into the battlefield? You are not of the proper age."

Evading her question, he replied, "It is not myself, but the people of Israel that I am worried about."

"You must promise," I said in a suffocating voice, "not to go near . . ."

"My mother, I make promises only to the Lord."

He bowed, and as I knew that any further words would be useless, I said: "Go in peace," and Pninah reiterated my blessing.

He replied, "May the Lord be with you."

Now his brothers and sisters overwhelmed him with embraces,

and after he had mounted his donkey, Elkanah accompanied him out of the yard.

As soon as he had left, Pninah and the children and I returned to the front room. There we sat, hugging each other in fear for Samuel, until Elkanah came to take the boys to the fields.

The Book of Pninah

It was ten days after my sons' return that Bathanath's reply, inviting me to visit her, finally arrived. So I knew that Arnon had returned from the land of the Philistines.

With my sons back home, and Samuel's visit, and the many visits to the bereaved that had to be paid, I'd had little time for solitude until then. But as I reclined in the carriage conveying me to Sdeh Canaan, I found ample time to reflect.

I remembered my talk with Samuel before the war. I recalled his warning that only the mending of my sinful ways could help save my sons. Yet the opposite had happened: It was through my sin that my children had been saved. This did not make sense.

There was no doubt in my mind that Samuel was closer to the Lord than anyone, for his prophecy of doom for the people of Israel had come true—all had transpired precisely as he had foreseen. Also, he had known things about me that no one of flesh and blood could have told him. And he understood my life as no one else of his age could.

Yet, as to my sons' destiny, he had been utterly wrong. I weighed this in my mind for a while, and finding it too puzzling to understand, concluded that the ways of the Lord were unfathomable.

I met Arnon in the eating room. I flung myself into his arms, wishing to bless him and thank him, but he would not allow it. He accepted the letter of thanks that I had written to Patrussim, and promised to have it conveyed to its destination. But beyond that he would have none of my gratitude.

He sat down near the table and drew me down into his lap. I was wearing the blue-gray dress from Ishkar that I knew he favored more than all others because it matched the color of my eyes, and the sparkling necklace he had given me adorned my chest. He kissed my eyes and my mouth, then ran his lips along the line between my skin and my dress. It was no secret to him that this, more than anything, made me crazy with desire; but when I began dragging him toward his bedroom, he refused to comply, halting me with these words: "Not yet. I cannot be at ease until I have said what I must to you."

He placed me in a chair beside him and said, "Pninah, you have two outstanding sons. They have always been precious to me, because they are yours. Now that I have seen them they are even more precious. It is for this reason that I must speak painful words to you, words that I would prefer not to utter."

With some apprehension I asked, "What are those words?"

"That you cannot let them back onto the battlefield again. They have taken an oath that they will never return to the land of the Philistines in enmity, and the Philistines have given them their lives in exchange. The Philistines may occasionally show mercy to their enemies, but they will never show mercy to traitors. If they discover your sons at war against them again, they will suffer *a fate that is a hundred times worse than death*. And no intervention of mine will save them."

I was shaken and instantly promised: "They won't go again. And now you must let me thank you for giving me back my life. What you did is beyond words, but you must surely know what is in my heart."

Once again he refused to listen. Instead, he filled the silver goblets on the table with glowing red wine. We drank deeply; he made me get up and with the speed of a lizard led me to his bed. Then we forgot all that prevailed in the heavens and on earth, except each other.

When I reached home, I led my sons into my room. I told them of how the Philistines would deal with those who went back on their oaths. Mercifully they were so deeply shocked that they asked only once where my knowledge had come from. When I failed to reply, they forgot to ask again.

I demanded that they take a vow before the Lord that they would never again fight against those who had preserved them from a horrifying death. They did so, and they kept their vow all the days of their lives.

*   *   *

A few months after the first war, Samuel arrived for another visit and, once again, he had changed. He had left his boyhood behind, his body assuming a pronounced manly shape. He was taller than his father, a broad-shouldered young man whose vital strength was more evident than ever before. His short garb finished well above his knees, and clearly showed his thighs and legs, which, like his arms, were hairy and muscled.

When I saw him shortly after his arrival, he was standing in the front yard conferring with a group of his followers. They, too, had changed. While previously they had all been boys and young men, now there were many girls among them.

At my approach he bowed to me. Then he glanced at his followers. They understood the message and withdrew to sit at the edge of the yard.

I had just come back from Arnon, my body tingling with the memory of our pleasure. I was wearing one of the dresses he had given me, this time a red one.

Samuel's stared at me, still as a statue, unable to move. I felt my cheeks burning with the flush of shame.

Finally he raised his gaze from my body to my face, and said: "My father has been called back from the fields, and will be here shortly. If he sees you like this . . . It would be well if you went to your room."

With my eyes downcast, I followed his advice.

Later, as we sat around the table for the evening meal, Elkanah asked Samuel about his female followers, about what they wanted of him. He replied that, like his male followers, they were troubled and being around him seemed to make them feel easier.

Hannah voiced her disbelief. "Samuel, are you sure that being around you is all that these girls want of you?"

Samuel seemed ill at ease and did not respond. It occurred to me that it would indeed be strange if a young man of his age, who had all those adoring girls around him, were to live in abstinence.

When he saw me regarding him, he looked into my eyes, studying them as if he were exploring my thoughts. It seemed that he tried to gauge my unspoken response to his mother's query and to his own silence.

After the meal we stepped into the front yard, and I found myself with Samuel, in the faint light of a sliver of the moon, a little way apart from the others. He spoke to me in a low voice: "Pninah, I have not forgotten how dismally I have failed in my advice to you in your room before the war. I cannot clear my mind now, but I intend to speak to you of this when the wars are over. In the meantime, I am glad that at least on the matter of the girls you don't judge me harshly."

"Samuel, how can you know?"

He merely laughed. Truly, he had an unfathomable power to divine everything about me, but he could not be enticed into revealing what he did not want to reveal about himself.

The Book of Hannah

The months that followed were filled with sadness for the past and alarm for the future. Presentiment of disaster soon became certainty, as the next war broke out.

Although we did not know it at the time, Samuel was once again involved in it, and also in the third one that came upon us some time later. And after each war he came home and told us about it, his followers filling in what he left out. I wrote down their words, so that the people of Israel would know and remember these atrocities forever.

When the second war broke out, the council of elders thought that they had devised an infallible way of defeating the Philistines. They resolved to fetch the Ark of the Covenant out of the Temple and bear it onto the battlefield, so that it would save them from the hand of their enemies and lead them to victory.

Samuel warned them not to do anything so foolish. He told them that this was as if they were trying to force the hand of the Lord to do what they wanted him to do. Not only would it not help, it would bring down a terrible disaster upon their heads.

He added that the only way to enlist the help of the Lord was to leave the ark where it was and, instead, for the people to return to him in their hearts, to destroy their idols and worship him alone, to refrain from committing adultery, to remember the sabbath to keep it holy, and to open their hands to the destitute. The elders listened to him attentively and praised him for delivering a fine, elevating speech.

As soon as Samuel left, they sent word to Hofni and Pinhas to bring the ark along. When it was carried into the camp, the warriors welcomed it by raising a great shout.

When the Philistines heard the noise, they realized that the Ark of the Lord had arrived. Suddenly of the belief that God had come into the Israelite camp, they were afraid. Who would deliver them from the wrath of this mighty God? But the Philistine officers appealed to their soldiers' pride, calling on them to acquit themselves like men and fight, lest they become slaves to the Hebrews. The officers' call whipped up the Philistines, so that they fought as fiercely as bereaved bears.

The Torah commands us to do battle by stealth, but our officers had forgotten this injunction and had laid no devious plans. Instead, they sent their soldiers out to confront a far superior enemy head-on. Not so the Philistine commanders, who were not only fierce but as cunning as foxes, craftily employing ruses, laying traps for our warriors, appearing where they were not expected, taking our men by surprise. Our officers were outwitted and our soldiers were left helpless.

Despite our pleading with Samuel to be careful, he once again charged onto the field, and when he arrived, our soldiers cheered almost as loudly as they had cheered the ark. Samuel did not join any contingent, but formed a contingent of his own. As before, he rode on his donkey, and could be seen from afar. Thus he was an easy target for our tormentors.

They charged at him but he struck down his attackers at the edge of his sword. Defying all danger, he shouted words of encouragement to the men, so as to raise their spirits: "Heroes of Israel. Go forth and stride to victory, for the sake of our God and our people and our land." But again, he was unable to prevent disaster.

Once again our troops suffered a crushing defeat. Israel was roundly beaten, our army in shambles. There was unbelievable slaughter—thousands of our foot soldiers were slain and the rest fled. Only afterward did the full horror of the battle become evident.

In truth, it had been not a battle but a nightmarish hell, its results too dreadful to contemplate. The ground was strewn with our young men's lifeless bodies, the soil soaked with their blood— strewn also with the wounded, whose gashes remained untended, whose screams floated piteously through the air, until the Philistines came by and stabbed them to death.

The blood of our boys screamed from the earth on which it had been shed. It rose to heaven, but its voice was not heard. Their flesh remained, to be eaten by the animals in the field and the birds in the sky. Vultures circled above, preparing to swoop down on their prey.

Israel was vanquished not only in battle but also by grief. There was no consolation to soften the blow. Bereaved mothers and fathers howled bitterly like jackals in the night.

But the Philistines were jubilant. They gazed triumphantly at their hands, stained with our blood. And they despised and sneered at our God—the one they had feared so much before—seemingly defeated along with his people. In the course of the battle they had captured the Ark of the Covenant, and they kicked it and abused it as if it were a pile of garbage.

Hofni and Pinhas, who were carrying the ark, were both slain on the same day, as Samuel had foretold. By that time their father, Eli, was ninety-eight years of age. When he was apprised of his sons' slayings and of the capture of the ark, he staggered backward off his chair and broke his neck, joining his sons in death.

The Philistine warriors took the ark to Ashdod. As they entered the city in triumph, the blood of our warriors still on their garments, the people of Ashdod lined the streets and gave them a heroes' welcome. The Philistine women rejoiced, singing and dancing in the streets, beating drums and swaying in ecstasy.

Yet our enemies could not humiliate the God of Israel with impunity. Afterward, fearsome tales were passed from mouth to mouth, awesome tales of the utter humiliation the Lord had inflicted on Dagon. According to these tales, the Philistines brought the Ark of the Lord into the temple of Dagon that stood there and placed it at Dagon's side. Still inebriated by the joy of their victory, they broke into coarse laughter, and some of their leaders shouted derisively: "Let this inferior god face our mighty one. Let this dismal box, and the powerless god inside it, wrestle with our all-powerful Dagon and let us see how he will fare." Others responded with glee: "He will fare no better than his miserable people, whom we have just reduced to piles of bodies and rivers of blood."

They sat around in the temple courtyard and caroused, imbibing strong spirits, their cheerful boasts bubbling out of them, until they fell into a heavy, drunken, sleep.

But when they entered the temple on the next day, they saw that

Dagon had fallen onto his face before the ark. Uprighting their idol, they restored him to his previous place on his pedestal, but when they entered the temple the next morning, Dagon was on the ground again. This time his head and both of his hands lay severed on the threshold, and only the trunk was left.

After that, the ark's presence wrought havoc amongst the Philistines. The people of Ashdod were afflicted with a devastating plague, in which thousands died. Death passed over hardly a house. Even the noblemen and the rich, who could afford to call in the best healers in the land, found no relief. The smell of death was everywhere, in the houses, the streets, the bazaar, and the seashore where the bodies of the dead were being piled up. Masses of people began to flee from the plague.

When the leaders of Ashdod saw what had befallen them, they decided that the ark of the God of Israel was to blame. They resolved that it should not remain in their city, and ordered that it be transported to other towns. But wherever the ark dwelled disease was rife, and many Philistines died.

The ark remained in the land of the Philistines for seven months. As the plague knew no respite, the leaders were once more seized by a mortal fear of the God they had previously scorned and humiliated. Resolving to rid themselves of his malevolent ark, they summoned their priests and officers, and instructed them to send it back to Israel in haste. But they also wished to appease the vengeful God, and did not want to send his ark away without an offering to accompany it.

So they constructed a cart and laid the ark on it. They placed animals crafted of pure gold around it, and carried it to Beth Shemesh. There they bowed down, prostrating themselves before it. Then they backed away, and fled from its presence as fast as their feet would carry them.

At the sight of the ark the people of Beth Shemesh cheered and rejoiced. But they, too, were afflicted with disease, and thousands died. They sent word to the people of Kiryath Yaarim, to come and collect the ark.

At first, the inhabitants of this town were scared for their lives, and refused to do as they were bid. But Samuel traveled there to talk to them. He disclosed that it was the Lord's decree that the ark be placed in their town, and pledged that its presence would cause no evil to befall them. They came to fetch the ark, and the plague finally ceased.

The people of Israel now lamented those who had died of plague. All of Samuel's prophecies had come true. He was devastated, and rent his garments. He visited us, but did not stay long. Instead, he immediately went to the town square. There he sat on the ground with the rest of Israel, removing his shoes, donning sackcloth, and covering his hair with ashes. Rocking back and forth, he sobbed and recited lamentations. A wail rose up in the square. And the men and women gathered around him to hear his wails, and to take comfort from him.

In the wake of those terrible wars, the Israelites banished their idols and returned to the Lord. When it became clear that they would not resume their idol worship, Samuel assembled masses of people in Mizpah. There he prayed to the Lord on their behalf, and his prayers were answered.

Thus, when the passing of time had erased the awesome deeds of our God from the Philistines' memory, and fear of him from their evil hearts, they came to fight Israel again. Again the hand of the Lord was heavy on them.

When the Philistines mounted their attack, the Israelite warriors were ready for them. Springing valiantly into battle, they were lighter than eagles and fiercer than lions, fighting like true heroes. This time, too, Samuel rode through the battlefield to encourage the men. And this time the Philistines were crushed like the earth under our warriors' feet.

Those Philistines whose souls were still in their bodies fled the battlefield in disorder. But our soldiers gave chase and caught up with them. Thousands of their number were killed, three thousand were seized and became captives of the sword.

The Israelite towns that the Philistines had conquered during the last war were recaptured. The Philistines did not come back to do battle against Israel for a long time.

The elders of Israel now wished to take the Ark of the Covenant from Kiryath Yaarim and restore it to the Temple in Shiloh. But Samuel would not let them. He proclaimed that the Shiloh Temple had been desecrated by all of the sins that had been committed there. It had lost its holiness, it was doomed for destruction, and the Ark of the Lord would never again be placed there. It would have to be left in Kiryath Yaarim until the Lord chose a new place for his name to dwell.

The last victorious war should have brought Samuel some consolation, yet he did not seem to recover, his bleak mood clinging to him. There was peace in the land but no peace in his heart.

Was he still mourning our casualties? Did his soul still linger on the unsettling talk he'd had with Pninah before the wars? Or was he stirred by a new sorrow? I could find no answer to these questions.

In time he became a judge, and he judged the people of Israel in Mizpah. Once a year he would make the rounds of various towns and cities and judge the people in those places. But even his prominent position at such a young age did not bring him comfort.

Only much later did I discover that there were shady corners in his soul, dark temptations he had to confront. And at the time he became a judge, these tribulations in his life were just beginning.

FOURTH PART

✧

Samuel's Torment

The Book of Hannah

The wars had left us all with tormenting memories; yet gradually these began to fade. Those of our relatives and friends who had not lost their sons regained their fortitude and became cheerful again. Only Samuel did not recuperate. When he came to visit, he no longer permitted his followers to accompany him. Apart from chatting with his brothers and sisters he spoke little, engrossed in his own thoughts.

His life in Mizpah appeared to be good. He was highly regarded as a judge, and the people now took his words seriously as they had not done before. It was difficult to understand what was bothering him. I besought him to reveal his secret to me, but he refused.

Frequently I puzzled over this with Elkanah, and one time I asked Pninah for her opinion. I confided to her the feeling I had that Samuel's existence was not what it seemed to be. I suspected that something evil had taken hold, and he was bent on concealing it from us. Although Samuel frequently talked to her, she could only admit that she had no solution to the puzzle either, and that she was equally perplexed.

Surely there were many pitfalls to trap a young man alone in a strange town. Had he fallen victim to such a trap? Was there some murky secret, some deed he had done, that he was keeping from us? Or perhaps an illicit act that he felt compelled to commit?

I began harboring a suspicion that Samuel's state must have something to do with a woman. Someone in Mizpah, perhaps, whom he loved and who did not reciprocate his feelings.

I turned this idea over in my mind and spoke of it to Pninah, but in her opinion, by all she had seen and heard, this could not be so: There was no woman whom Samuel could want who would be able to resist him.

I agreed, but thought that he loved a married woman, whom his conscience would never allow him to approach. The women of Mizpah were renowned for their beauty and charm, and many stirring love songs had been written in their honor. It would not be unheard-of for a young man to fall under the spell of such a woman, even if she was a man's wife. Could Samuel have been so ensnared? Of this, too, I spoke to Pninah, and she admitted that it was possible.

From day to day this notion solidified in my mind. My son might well pine for a woman to whom it would be sinful for him to go. Frequently there was a wistful look in his eyes, as if he mourned a missed joy, something that could have been but would never come to pass.

He was a living riddle to me. I was determined to solve it, to pry my way into his being, to help revive his soul, but could find no pathways to it.

Digging my nails into Pninah's arm, I made her promise solemnly that she would search for an opportunity to speak to Samuel about his trouble. She promised, but added that she could not imagine that he would be willing to tell her any more about himself than he had told me.

It was at this time that Elkanah's father, Yeroham, died of the illness that had plagued him for several years. His sons and daughters and their children, and also Samuel, came to his house in Shaar Efraim to mourn him. As I entered the house's front yard to comfort the family, my eyes were met by a few score of people clad in sackcloth, sitting on the ground. Since Yeroham's death had been long in coming, there were no loud lamentations. But male eyes were cast down in gentle sorrow, and female eyes were brimming over with silent tears.

I soon perceived that Samuel was immersed in a sorrow much deeper than that of the other mourners. His face was pale, and his eyes were surrounded by dark rings that attested to nights of sleeplessness.

After I had comforted Elkanah and the others, I went to sit on the ground next to him; and Pninah joined us. Since Samuel had not seen Yeroham very often during his lifetime, we recounted little stories about what his grandfather had said and done on various occasions, and it seemed to ease his sorrow.

Before long, Efrath, Samuel's nurse in the Temple, entered the yard and sat down next to us. She asked Samuel if it was true, as she had been told, that he had known of Yeroham's illness some years ago, even though he had not seen him for a long time beforehand.

Samuel seemed uncomfortable and did not reply. Efrath persisted. She asked him if it was true that he knew things that he did not see with his own eyes.

He replied with forced lightness, "Yes. I know that Pninah is wondering why I am in such a deep despondency now, even though I hardly ever saw my grandfather when he was alive."

This seemed to be very true, for she blushed and asked what his answer to this question was.

It came in the form of a parable: "There once was a woman who wore sackcloth all her life, tears always flowing from her eyes. One day, as she walked on a country road, she met another woman just like herself.

"The second woman asked her who she was, and she replied, 'My name is Sadness, and my task is to enter a man's soul and make him sad. And who are you?'

"The second woman responded, 'My name is the same, and my task is the same as yours.'

"So the first woman proposed, 'Let's walk together and enter the same man and make him twice as sad as anyone else.' And this is what they did."

By now, Efrath had lost interest in the tale and went to sit with other mourners.

Pninah asked Samuel, "And who is that second woman called Sadness who has infiltrated your soul?"

This seemed a good opportunity for Samuel to pour out his heart before her, so I effaced myself silently, and went to sit some distance away, though not out of earshot, and to my shame, I eavesdropped on what they were saying.

"As we are sitting here," he responded to her question, "she has retreated into a corner."

"But why is she there at all?"

He merely shook his head.

Pninah did not relent. "This is not the first time that you've been troubled in recent months. I have seen you so before."

"Yes."

"And you don't want to tell me about it?"

"No."

"You look into my soul, but you never let me look into yours."

A smile could be seen in his eyes, but it was mirthless. "Perhaps one day I will."

"But not now?"

"No, and you should not demand it of me," he said in a disgruntled voice.

Pninah seemed hurt, and I was angry at Samuel for speaking so harshly to her.

After that Pninah could only report to me what I knew already, that her attempt to discover what was ailing my son had not met with success. I had pinned my hopes on her and was deeply disappointed.

Yet when I pondered their talk later, what persisted in my memory were not the unkind words with which he had rebuffed her approach, but something even queerer: the sad smile followed by a hurt accusing look that he had shot at her while he said them—as if he believed that she might wish to injure him, which he must have known was not so.

I felt piqued. Surely he could not still be holding against her whatever it was that had come to pass between them on his first visit to our house before the wars. What could it be that made him so cross at her?

In the following months, when Samuel came to visit us, he frequently sat in the yard under an olive tree. His brothers and sisters usually surrounded him, clamoring for his attention, the younger ones showing off their juggling of pebbles in the air, or their ability to throw them quite far, puffing up with pride at his praise. But when they left him, he would remain sitting bent forward, his knees supporting his chin, gazing unseeingly into the distance.

Whenever I noticed him like this I went to sit at his side, watching his green eyes, which were clouded over with the constant pain in his heart. I did not know what to say to make it flee. All I could offer him was my silence. He seemed to cherish it, but it worked no magic on him: His ache was still reflected in his eyes.

The Book of Pninah

O n one of my visits to Arnon some time after the grim harvest of the wars had come to its end, he met me in front of his house. "There is someone here who wants to see you," he announced.

I looked at him inquiringly, and he added: "It is Patrussim."

This was a surprise, and I was uncertain whether it was a welcome or unwelcome one.

As one of the commanders of the Philistine army, Patrussim had the blood of thousands of our youngsters on his hands. He could not claim innocence of this abomination and nothing could ever absolve him of it in my eyes.

But he had already been meted out his punishment from the Lord: During the terrible plague that had hit Ashdod, he had lost his wife and his youngest son and daughter. Then, too, who was I to judge the man who, together with Arnon, had saved my sons' lives? So my feelings toward him were first and foremost of gratitude and pity.

Patrussim was inspecting an array of small clay figurines on a shelf in the eating room. When he heard the door open he turned and came forward. After only a slight hesitation, I ran to him. He gathered me to him and I kissed him and wept loudly, as if he were not Arnon's kinsman but my own.

Only when I stepped back from him did I notice how much he had changed. He was stooped, his hair was almost completely white, and his face was creased with the deep furrows that old age had scored upon him before its time.

He welcomed me with kind words. "I am glad, Pninah, that my visit here gives me an opportunity to see you."

I tried to find words with which to console him, but I was not suc-

cessful. I tried to express my gratitude to him and I was not successful in that, either.

"It is not necessary," was his response. "You have already repaid
what I have done for you."

At that moment, refreshments were served and Bathanath came
in and called on us to sit down at the table.

As we did so, I asked in disbelief, "How can this be? I've done
nothing."

"A member of your family has, and that is almost the same
thing."

"Who is it?"

"Samuel, the son of Elkanah."

"What has he done?"

"Does he never come to visit his father and his mother?"

"He comes often, but he has not told us anything. What could he
have done for you?"

"In the last war thousands of our men were captured by the Israelites. My two eldest sons, who were officers in our army, were
among them. Your captains, eager to exact revenge for their previous defeats at our hands, ordered all captives to be felled by the
sword, but Samuel shouted that they must be allowed to live. At first,
your captains would not listen, but he threatened them with terrible
retribution from your God. They were gripped by fear and called on
their soldiers to stop."

I was stunned into silence.

"I would have you write a letter to him for me."

I wrote the letter, and he pressed his seal on it.

Then he turned to address Arnon. "And now, I will detain you
no longer, as you have only a little time together, and it is precious
to you. I hope that now there will be peace in the land, and that you
will come to visit us again."

I took my leave from him brokenhearted, for I knew that,
notwithstanding his invitation, I would never visit him nor would I
ever see him again.

The next time Samuel came home, I asked him to step into my
room. After we sat down he noticed the letter I was holding. "So
you've seen Patrussim," he said.

"Yes, he came to visit. I mean . . ." and I proffered the letter.

"I know what you mean," he replied, taking it from my hand.

Since his first talk to me before the wars, Samuel had never again reprimanded me for my visits to Sdeh Canaan. But he always made it disturbingly clear that he knew precisely what I was doing there.

Disregarding this, I said, "There are no words that could match what you have done."

He looked at me, a smile lurking in his eyes.

"Did you know that Patrussim's sons were there?" I continued.

"It was called to my attention."

"Why did you not speak of this?"

"It would have looked as if I wanted to earn your praise."

"You've earned not merely my praise, but my deep admiration."

For some time now, Samuel had been immersed in a puzzling dejection, whose source he was unwilling to divulge. Since his grandfather Yeroham's death, he had been plunged even deeper into it. Now, he drank up my words, savoring them as if they were some rare nectar; they seemed to revive him. "Pninah," he said in wonder, "you have never spoken words like these to me before."

"You have never done deeds like these before."

"This is true," he replied regretfully, overtaken by sadness once more. "Also, I'm afraid that you have not formed a high opinion of my . . . my . . . prophecies."

"How can you think so? I am aware that all you foretold for the people of Israel has come true. Not one thing has been missing."

"But this has been outweighed in your mind by the error I made when I talked to you of your own life. I have been deeply mortified, and only now have I found the strength to speak to you about it. I humbly apologize. I have realized as never before that the ways of the Lord are inscrutable, and that they cannot be understood by any human being."

"Not even by you?"

"Least of all by me," he said meekly. "Knowing only a minute part is sometimes worse than knowing nothing."

"You have saved thousands of human beings, and this is more important than anything."

"I'm glad that I have redeemed myself in your eyes."

I dismissed the matter from my mind, but something else was

bothering me. "Samuel, since that talk, I've wondered what you meant by your words at the end. When I complained that there would never be a man who loved only me, you replied that I would not make a successful prophetess."

His eyes lit up with laughter. "Are you striving to become a prophetess?"

"No, but what did you have in mind?"

He looked at me for longer than was proper, his gaze lingering on the cleavage revealed by my tight Ishkar dress before he lifted it back to my eyes. "I prefer to let you wonder."

Suddenly the door was flung open and Elkanah came in. My husband, who had recently arisen from his thirty days of mourning, had returned to his work in the fields. He must have come home just when Samuel entered my room. Since then, some time had passed, and he now had an angry look in his eyes. When he saw us sitting and talking, he seemed somehow relieved.

We rose to our feet and bowed to him, and Samuel stowed the letter I had given him in a pocket in his garment.

"What have you been talking about?" Elkanah asked.

Samuel's face was blank, as he replied, "We have been discussing my brothers' miraculous rescue on the battlefield."

"And what were you saying?"

"I told Pninah that the ways of the Lord were inscrutable." With these words he bowed to his father, then to me, and left.

Elkanah now turned to me. "Pninah, what has been going forth here?"

I thought these words hilariously funny. I clapped my hand over my mouth to stifle the laughter that was straining to burst from it. "Sir," I answered, "surely you cannot have forgotten that I am nineteen years older than he is, and almost the same age as his mother."

My words did not reassure Elkanah. "Age is nothing to him," he said with an edge to his voice. "He was never a child like other children, or a boy like other boys. By the time he was sixteen, he knew more girls than most men have known by the time they die."

I had been aware for some time that his words were true. "But I am not a girl," I averred.

"You have the slim and shapely body of a girl. I have seen him looking at you as if he wanted to swallow you."

"You cannot believe that I would be enticed by one who is younger than my own sons."

"Women lose their sanity around him."

"But surely not women of my age?" I protested.

Disregarding my objection, Elkanah issued his newest command: "From now on you will not sit with him in your room."

I bowed my head in acceptance of his decree. He observed me more closely, saw my dress and stiffened. "And you will not wear an arousing dress when he comes."

Again I bowed my head.

He looked at me again, and added: "And when *I* come, you will take it off."

I did as I was bid, and we were rocked by pleasure and release.

Afterward I reflected that Elkanah's jealousy was not pointed at the right target, and I was glad of it.

As for Samuel, he was indeed an outstandingly handsome young man. There was wild power radiating from his body and from his piercing green eyes. It was not surprising that so many women yearned for pleasure with him.

Yet Elkanah did not perceive that it was not so with me. My affinity with Samuel stemmed from something entirely different: his uncanny ability to trace every ripple in my soul, which pleased me.

I did not realize at the time how closely my soul and my body were linked.

The Book of Hannah

In the years after the wars, my other sons grew up, too, and Elkanah bought them a property that bordered on ours. All of his sons and daughters, except for Samuel, married and settled close by.

They all came to stay at our house for the first two days of every month, to welcome the new moon with us. We reveled in their visits, but no one as much as Elkanah. For through these gatherings it became evident for all to see that he was now the head of a great clan, as he had always dreamt he would be.

All of his daughters and daughters-in-law were gifted with plentiful fruit of the womb, which came rolling out of them as quickly as their previous infants were weaned. They were as fertile as the earth of the Jordan Valley in a rainy year.

And they always bore the new issue of their womb in their arms, presenting it to Elkanah as if they had brought it into the world expressly as a peace offering for him. He made a great show of accepting each of these offerings graciously. He nestled each little bundle in his lap with great joy, and blessed it with the triple blessing of the Lord.

In the course of time, Elkanah's progeny multiplied, and when they visited there were so many of them that tents had to be pitched to house them. He basked in the glory of his descendants, the issue of his loins, flesh of his flesh. These children would insure that his seed would be passed down from generation to generation, that he would continue to live through them forever, and that his name would not be blotted out for as long as the sun shone over the earth.

They all treated him with the greatest reverence. He would sit on a stone, and they would sit in a semicircle at his feet, thirstily absorbing the words of wisdom he voiced for their benefit, as if these words were water from a living spring. Or at least they pretended to, which was enough to make him feel that his cup was flowing over.

I, and Pninah, too, delighted in our children's and their children's visits. When they came, they brought much noise, much dirt, and much happiness. And when they left, there was much silence, and much cleaning up to be done.

Although Samuel dwelled at a distance, he came as often as the others—sometimes more often. I was jubilant that he, who had not lived at home since he was three years of age, wanted to see so much of us. Still, he looked forlorn as no man should, and I could not abide it. In my eagerness to come to his aid, I hatched a scheme.

There was a stableboy in our house, a young man I trusted. I sent him out as a spy to investigate what was transpiring in Samuel's house and in his life in Mizpah.

Having dispatched the spy I was as happy as an unruly child who, for once, had outwitted his parents.

Upon his return a week later, the young man came to my room. He recounted that Samuel's large house in Mizpah was always teeming with life, with hordes of people who had come from Dan to Beer Sheba, much like the bottom of the sea teemed with fish and other creatures.

In the morning his front yard was given over to shrilly arguing complainants, who came to Samuel to settle their disputes. The rumor was that they were so numerous because he never passed harsh judgment on anyone and his verdicts were such that both contenders went their way satisfied.

At noontime this crowd thinned, and was replaced by the poor and the ailing who came to seek succor from Samuel. His heart was as soft as butter, and his hand was always open to the poor. Anyone who shared his tale of woe or need could wheedle silver pieces out of him. No one left his house with an empty pouch.

The source of the silver that Samuel distributed so freely was the litigants, who were required to pay for the privilege of his judgment. Samuel's clerks exacted the same payments from everyone, and registered them so that no suspicion of bribery could be attached to them. The silver nonetheless accumulated, and it more than sufficed for his charity and for himself and his household.

The ailing were more difficult to deal with. There were those with incurable diseases, whom healers had given up on as hopeless, and those staring squarely into the face of death, unable to accept their approaching end.

With compassion in his face, Samuel was forced to explain to them that he had no miracle cures for them. All he could offer were the ancient words of the Lord's blessing. But they left appeased, convinced that a blessing from his lips was of more benefit than the ministrations of any healer.

In the late afternoon the help-seekers gave way to Samuel's young followers, both male and female. Those known as "sons of prophets," who yearned to be prophets themselves. They demanded nothing of Samuel but his closeness. He was tireless in their company, as fresh in the evening as he was in the morning. He would sit in the yard and talk to them, patiently, endlessly, caressing the whole lot of them with his eyes. And they him.

His maids would set out food and drink for them, though many brought bread and meat of their own to share with the others. Then, as darkness fell, some remained to camp down for the night. They sat singing or chatting well into the night, the noise of their songs and chatter gradually sinking into a hum, then into a hush, and then into silence.

On the sabbath, they trailed after him to the town square, where he read from the Torah. Thousands who had come from all parts of the land to listen to him were held spellbound with the fascinating speeches he delivered in his compelling voice.

At his home, there was also the neighbor. She was a hauntingly beautiful, black-haired young woman of a lithe and slender build, whose striking looks reminded the spy of me, except that she was younger, slimmer, and lighter of step.

While her husband, a master carpenter, was toiling at his workshop, the wife idled away her days, her maids bustling about, scurrying back and forth in an effort to carry out her numerous instructions.

Once or twice a day she would wander over to Samuel's house with an easy grace and a beguiling smile, bearing with her trays laden with the mute testimony of her maids' exertions: savory dishes for his delight.

She was clad in dresses as white as snow, the color of holiness and purity, but there was nothing holy in the clinging shape of those gowns, nor was there anything pure in the seductive glances she directed at Samuel. But, my spy could not tell whether Samuel was as smitten with her as she was with him.

Did Samuel admit any of his female admirers into his bedchamber to share the pleasures of the night? Or did the seductive white-robed neighbor sneak in under the mantle of darkness to dispel his loneliness while her husband slept in exhaustion from the day's labor?

My spy paused and cast a meaningful look at me to indicate that, as to this, he was at a loss; there was no way to tell. Short of peeping into Samuel's room through the cracks in the shutters of his window, which he was loath to do, there was no way to find out.

The young man continued: "I thought that Samuel would not notice me among the many who always crowded his yard, but I was mistaken. After a week had passed, he surprised me by coming to sit next to me, and saying: 'You may now go back to my mother and apprise her of the result of your mission. You may advise her that you have seen all there is to see. For no matter how much longer you remain, you will not see anymore than you have seen already.'"

After that my emissary fell silent, for there was indeed nothing left to reveal.

I thanked him for his report both in words and in silver, then remained seated in my chair, my head spinning in confusion. Could it be that the neighbor, a man's wife, prohibited to Samuel by one of the Ten Commandments, was the temptress whose allure had kept Samuel in misery for so long?

It was well known that many young men hankered after women who resembled their mothers. Could Samuel be one of those men?

I began harboring the fear that Samuel would not take kindly to being spied on and would be justly incensed at me. The next time he visited us I sought him out to offer my apologies.

"What I have done is detestable," I admitted. "I can justify it only by assuring you that my sole purpose was to help you. I beg your forgiveness."

He smiled. "I forgive you, as you say. Rest assured, my mother, that nothing you do could ever be unforgivable. Only . . . it was futile, for no one can help me. Not even you," he said with vehement sincerity.

It occurred to me that I might as well turn our talk to good account, so that sweetness would yet emerge from bitterness. "Is it the neighbor?" I probed.

His response contained no words but only laughter, with a touch of embarrassment in it. I took it to signify neither yes, or no, but "I refuse to tell you."

So I pressed on. "Samuel, are you so distant from me that you cannot open your heart to me? You may be a revered prophet and judge, but I am fuller in years and therefore in wisdom than you are, and my love for you is boundless, wider and deeper than the great sea. Reveal your trouble to me and see if I may not be able to try to help you."

Instead of opening his heart, he spoke baffling words to me: "My mother, rather it is I who am being tried."

In the following years I often turned those words over in my mind, but it took a long time before I grasped their meaning. And when I finally did, I also found out that I could do nothing to help him.

The Book of Pninah

As my father grew older, my sons moved in with him to help with the farm. Elroy built an enormous winery and produced such outstanding wines that they became famous in the land. Elhanan grew herbs endowed with rare healing powers. In time he became a skillful healer and people came from afar to seek his help. They both took wives and sired sons and daughters.

My elder daughter, Gilah, who resembled me, became a scribe and taught children and wrote letters for people. My youngest, Nehamah, found no joy in the written word, but she was as beautiful as her aunt Hagith had been in her youth. They both found husbands with good-sized properties in Ramathayim, and bore them children.

After they left our house, I took over the three rooms that had belonged to them. I turned one into a bathing room, one into a scroll room, and the third into a teaching room.

In due course my father lay down with his fathers. Since there were no sons to inherit his property, the elders decreed that I would inherit it. Hagith would have been an heiress, too, but she had lost her rights when she became the wife of a man from another tribe. So the property came to me, and I immediately bestowed it on my sons. But I made it a condition that they share their wealth with their sisters.

Since their families were growing, my sons decided that the time had come for them to part.

A good-sized property in Shaar Efraim came up for sale. My sons set their hearts on it but did not have the means to buy it. Elkanah gave them as much as he could, but he had six sons and four daughters to provide for, so what he gave was still not enough. Before long a man from a distant village came along and purchased it.

A few months later something odd happened. The man sent

word to my sons that he regretted having bought the property. He was eager to move back to his own village, hence he was prepared to sell the house and land at half the price that he himself had paid for it. My sons immediately struck a deal with him. He moved away and was never heard of again. Elroy became the sole owner of my father's property, and Elhanan became the owner of the new property, and they were both content.

For some time I was mystified by this occurrence. It did not make sense for a man to make such a poor deal. Why should he lose so much silver when he could have sold the property at the same price at which he bought it?

Suddenly the solution to the riddle came to me. When next I met with Arnon, I accused him of having instigated the whole affair. At first I could not induce him to confess, but when I declared that I could not accept such an enormous gift from him, he was amused and asked, "What are you proposing to do?"

I answered that I would pay him back bit by bit from the silver pieces I earned teaching. Then he got truly angry. "After all these years," he said, "how can you still not understand something so simple?"

When I asked what that was, he replied, "That I am involved in your children's welfare because they are like my own to me. Now, what little time we have together is too precious to be wasted on this foolishness. Let's enjoy the pleasure of being with each other."

As time went by, Hannah's beauty remained, but she grew large in all parts of her body. Wrinkles appeared in her face and white streaks in her hair. This did not diminish Elkanah's love for her, and in her sureness of this she was content. I no longer begrudged Hannah her happiness any more than I begrudged the almond trees their winter blossoms.

Following Bathanath's advice, I continued to eat wondrous herbs and, as my father had been, I remained slim. When white streaks began to appear in my hair, my friend gave me honey-colored dye to cover them. Thus my hair retained its rich color, and still tumbled down to my shoulders as prettily as it did when I was a shepherdess. My face was no longer that of a girl, but it was smoother than that of other women my age.

I salved my face and body with oils and sweet scents that pleased the nostrils and awakened the senses. Elkanah and Arnon were stirred by them, but the years exacted their tribute from them, too. The two men I loved now had more white hair, and less power to know a woman.

Yet the fire that could be stilled only by the act of love continued to burn inside me with a surprising strength. My two men could no longer extinguish it, and I was left in want. I became as restless as a wandering bird, and I could not be at peace with myself.

My life was rooted in the hills. I was born at their foot and was bred absorbing the rhythm of the seasons through their changing colors. Thus I escaped there, to walk and collect the herbs that Bathanath had taught me to gather from hidden crevices underneath the rocks, and to seek the peace I failed to find elsewhere.

It was during winter, on one of my walks, with my sheepskin cloak wrapped tightly around me and my eyes searching the ground for muddy patches to avoid, that Samuel came into view and halted in front of me.

He was once again in low spirits. I had not talked with him about this for a long time, but now I asked him what was amiss.

The words rushed out of him almost angrily. "It is a matter about which I cannot talk." Then, it seemed, he tried to direct my mind to other matters, adding, "There is something amiss with you as well."

I demurred at his words. "All is well."

Brazenly, he voiced his disbelief. "Pninah, don't disguise your soul. You should know by now that it is as an unrolled scroll open to my gaze."

I hung my head low, and cast down my eyes.

He murmured under his breath, "I wish that I might help you."

I sent him an indignant glance. "Samuel," I protested, "what are you intimating?"

"You are aware. But I regret my words. Forgive me," he said meekly.

I decided to swallow my anger, and instead of giving vent to it, I urged, "If you would tell me what bothers you, perhaps I could help *you?*"

He merely shook his head.

"Samuel," I persisted with urgency in my voice, "pouring one's heart out to another eases its burden. If a fire is burning in your heart, let me help you extinguish it. If water is flooding your soul, let me help you ebb it. If a sin is disturbing your peace, I will not condemn you. Why do you not let me share your burden?"

He remained silent, impervious to my appeal. Although he was so tall and broad shouldered, he resembled nothing so much as a little boy who had fallen down and bruised himself, obstinately refusing assistance in dressing his wound.

While I spoke to him, I raised my face to look into his and my cloak's hood slipped back from my head. He gathered my long hair in his hand, drew the hood over it, and tied its strings under my chin. Then he turned on his heels, and walked away to the far side of the hill.

All I had obtained for my efforts was a tender gesture, and his drifting off to seek solitude. I bit my lip and cursed my words.

The following week, I encountered Samuel on the hill again. That whole afternoon the sky had been dark, threatening rain. But the air was unusually clear and the colors of the hills were fresh, the trees and bushes presenting sharp contrasts of dark and light shades of green. Suddenly, I saw Samuel emerging from amid those shades.

Just as he came up beside me, the heavens opened up, and a torrential downpour began. He grasped my hand and we ran.

He led me to a large rock with a dent in it that formed a shallow cave, deep enough to afford us shelter. We sat, the heavy rain pouring down in front of us like a thick curtain cordoning us off from the outside. Behind this curtain we were isolated, sharing the magic of a world reserved for us alone.

After we had wiped off the rain from our faces, Samuel's eyes lit up with laughter. "I like you in your cloak. You look like a child."

I laughed at him in return. "I assure you that I'm not a child."

"I know," he said. "Nevertheless, there are still matters about which I could teach you."

At these words, my head shot up. He brought his face close and for a moment he hovered on the verge of fastening his lips to mine. I felt a quiver run through my body. I was ashamed and averted my face. He took it in both his hands, turned it back and tilted it up toward him.

But he withdrew his own face and murmured, "Don't be afraid of me. I won't touch you."

I was less afraid than puzzled. What could he teach me that my two teachers had not?

He responded to my intense curiosity by laughing again. "You would like to learn, but it cannot be taught through words."

I blushed to my neck, but there was nothing to be said in response, so we simply sat huddled together, watching the torrents pour down. I made an effort not to think of what I had just felt, and snuggled myself deeper into my cloak.

A short while later, I told Samuel that I enjoyed sitting like that, watching the heavy clouds and the rain they unleashed. I asked if he did, too.

The earlier laughter had fled from his face. He wrapped my cloak more tightly around me, and replied sullenly, "It brings more comfort to my soul than anything else I may hope for."

This was the type of enigmatic remark that left me confused. I raised my eyebrows inquiringly, but his infuriatingly blank face told me nothing.

The hush around us was broken only by the pounding of the rain against the rock above our heads. We sat there until it ceased; and when we reached home it was almost dark.

For several weeks I continued reliving what had occurred. But Samuel never referred to it; so I thought that I had been turning a hump into a mountain.

I would encounter him on the hills quite often. Though he never appeared to be looking for me, when we met he would shorten his steps to suit mine and walk beside me.

At times he discussed with me the weekly portion of the Torah he was to read on the coming sabbath in the Mizpah town square. He would tell me what he planned to say about it to the masses of people who came to hear him and I would offer my own reflections. He never accepted them, but the debate made his eyes glitter. Walking on the hills was apparently good for him, for afterward he always looked more cheerful, though not for long.

*   *   *

On a day in late spring, an unusual incident occurred. An easterly wind was blasting across the hill, bearing with it the blazing dry heat of the desert. Samuel, who was walking beside me, had opened his shirt to be cooler.

A gust of wind swept my hair over my eyes, blocking my view. As I could not see, I tripped over a stone. My left foot gave way under me and a sharp pain cut through my ankle.

I sank to the ground and raised my knees. I spread my legs apart, and drew my dress down between my open thighs, pulling my feet toward me. This enabled me to examine the inside of my left ankle, which had become sensitive to the touch.

Samuel bent over me and announced gruffly, "This must pain you. I will carry you home."

He placed his right hand under my shoulders and my right armpit, his left hand under my knees, and lifted me up in his arms. My cheek came to rest against his bare chest, and he began walking.

I told him that I could easily walk by myself.

"I want to carry you," he insisted.

I had never been so close to him before, and I was deeply disturbed, though I could not say whether I was frightened by his strength or my weakness.

"Samuel," I requested, "set me down."

He laughed, and his laughter sounded unfamiliar. His eyes were lit by a fiendish light, which became darker by the moment, until they were nearly black. I felt his breath, scalding like the fumes from a burning furnace, on my face. I shivered, appalled by the rush of his feelings, of mine.

"Put me down," I pleaded once more, but my voice was too soft to be convincing.

He spoke in a hoarse voice that sounded as if it came from the depth of his throat. "I could make you plead with me for something entirely different, if I wanted to."

He dipped his head; his burning lips found mine, and he began playing with them. His heat streamed into me from his lips, from his tongue, which penetrated my mouth, my being.

My body moistened with perspiration and my senses swam. I felt a powerful surge run through me, stronger than anything I had experienced before. I could scarcely breathe and had to gasp for air.

When he removed his mouth from mine I reached out and wrapped my arms around his neck. I drew down his head, until his mouth touched mine again. As we kissed I heard little wails, such as those of an infant, breaking from within me, while tears blinded my eyes.

We crossed the vineyard at the back of our house, which was covered by the shadows of the trees in front of it. There Samuel released me and admitted shakily, "I've been out of my mind."

Still struggling to catch my breath, I replied, "I have been, also."

"I know. I could have . . ."

"It was the heat."

"But not the heat outside. It was my fault, forgive me."

I felt the flames that had begun to subside inside me welling up again. I was in an agony of unfulfilled need, outrageously disappointed that such a fiery encounter had ended so tamely, that Samuel had given me a taste of what could have been, but had denied himself. I clutched at his hands and tried to pull him back up the hill.

But he stood as firm as a rock. I searched his face for a sign that he might relent, but there was nothing. He was willful and headstrong and obstinate. Nothing could sway him and he never did but what he himself wanted to do. And he did not want to do anything further with me.

Still half dazed, I released him. Glumly, reluctantly, I tried to banish my errant design.

Samuel spoke again. "I will take care of your ankle."

When we reached my room, he obliged me to sit down on one of the stones in front of it, in the shade of the big fig tree. He lifted my feet off the ground and placed them on the stone next to it. He brought some cool water for us to drink, a copper basin filled with cold water, and a lengthy cloth that dangled over his shoulder. He sat down, removed my left shoe, took my foot in his hand, and held it gently for a while, staring at my legs. Then his eyes sought mine, and he looked into them searchingly.

He dipped the cloth in the water, wrung it out and wrapped it tightly around my swollen ankle. Every few moments he removed it, immersed it in water and rolled it around my ankle again.

Guiltily, I enjoyed his handling of me. My cheeks were hot again, fed by my renewed fire. Still, I told Samuel that it was not necessary for him to care for my foot, because I could easily do it myself. I added that he must probably be bored by now.

"If you think so, Pninah, you know very little about me."

I was incensed. "If I know little about you, Samuel, it's because you refuse to tell me anything. Tell me now, that I may finally gaze into your soul." I looked straight into his eyes; and as I did so, my own eyes were bright with tears.

He responded to them by saying: "I have told you today in my own way." I could not mistake his meaning. I tried to unravel the tangled feelings that stumbled over each other in the darkness of my own soul.

That night, I stood at my window surveying the moonlit front yard. I watched leaves being blown by the still relentless wind, looking out beyond them for Samuel, but he did not come. Later, in bed, I tossed in anguish of want. Every fiber of my being sent out a call to him. I thought that he would hear it and use the darkness of the night to claim me. But the hush of the night was broken only by the rustle of the leaves in the wind.

After that day, when we met on the hills, he walked so close to me that our bare arms and our thighs brushed against each other, and I felt the pangs of hunger tugging deep inside me. The storm raging in him was reflected in his eyes, but whenever I attempted to talk to him of this, he rebuffed me with a sternly forbidding look. I wanted to reach out to him, to console him by holding his head between my breasts, by stroking it until I had smoothed out his unruly hair and kissed away the bruises from his soul.

Yet how could I comfort one who, though he sought me, adamantly rejected my tenderness—one whose heat radiated into me like that of the sun on a summer day, yet was as coolly distant as the moon on a winter night?

The Book of Hannah

When Samuel took a wife, his father and I were delighted, for she was the daughter of one of the most highly regarded families in our tribe. Then, too, I hoped that his bride would be more successful than we had been in healing his ravaged soul. The wedding was held in our front yard, and afterward the bride and bridegroom returned to Mizpah. Yet shortly afterward he was back, and his longtime sorrow still seemed to cling to him.

I found this deeply disconcerting. There was no reason why he should not be blissfully happy with his wife. His female admirers continued to surround him, and there had been hundreds, if not thousands, of girls for him to choose from. Not one of them would have refused him; and he had chosen Serach from among the multitude. With her lively, animated face, and her slanted black eyes framed by long, dark lashes, she was exceptionally pretty, and she had a soft, pleasant voice and a delightfully cheerful laugh that rang out like the little bells that were hung on the hem of the high priest's mantle. It was plain for all to see that her love for Samuel was bubbling over. What more could he ask for?

Yet it seemed that he remained unsatisfied.

Seven months after his wedding, Samuel's first son, Joel, was born. This made me wonder about the manner in which he had selected his wife, but I never spoke to him about it. His second son, Abijah, followed less than a year later, and we all went to Mizpah to celebrate the two circumcisions. After that he would tell me of his joy in his children, but even this did not seem to call him forth from the dark retreat in which his soul had taken refuge.

* * *

As we sat eating the evening meal during one of Samuel's next visits, he told us of his new plan. He had decided to move to Ramah, a town that bordered on Ramathayim.

I was overjoyed, but Elkanah's face was dark, and he asked Samuel what had prompted this decision. I knew that Elkanah loved Samuel no less than I did; hence it was strange that he should be displeased with his announcement.

It was Samuel's answer that offered a clue. At first he made no response at all. In the end, he replied: "Is it not obvious? I want to be near you and—"

I looked up sharply, just in time to see his gaze shifting to Pninah, as he added, "—the family."

There was nothing unusual in this, for Pninah *was* part of our family. What was strange was the manner in which he regarded her. It was not the look one would direct at a family member. It was a look a man gave a woman whom he wanted in his bed.

Ever since I had come to this house I had seen my husband directing looks at Pninah that alluded to the deeds of the bedroom. Now, to my chagrin, I saw my son do the same. But his was not merely the look of lust I was used to seeing in Elkanah's eyes before he disappeared into her room. It was the ardent look of a starved man who saw a loaf of bread in front of him, yet could not bring it to his mouth.

I was dumbfounded.

It now dawned on me, as it had not before, that Samuel had been circling around Pninah for years, in the manner of a mother-bird guarding her chicks. But because of his age and hers, I had not suspected his purpose.

It had not escaped me that he frequently walked in the hills with Pninah. He had been a hill walker even during his childhood at the Temple. And Pninah, too, had long been walking there on her own—as if the hills were the cradle of her childhood. So their walks appeared entirely innocent. Even now I still believed them to have been innocent in deeds, though heavy with the guilt of coveting and longing and dreams.

Yet how could this be? Numerous attractive girls were eager to do Samuel's bidding. And there was his wife, Serach, who loved him and was proud of him, and he seemed to be kind and gentle with her. In spite of this, he was starving for a woman who was nearly his mother's age—and his father's wife.

It had previously occurred to me that the lowness of his spirits might be connected to a married woman. But it had never entered my mind that it would be a woman of Pninah's age, or that she would be married to his own father. Now I understood why he had so adamantly refused to confide in me: He had known that I would utterly condemn his passion.

I had never understood why Elkanah lusted for Pninah as if he were a ram and she a ewe in rut. It was even more difficult to comprehend why Samuel did so. Whatever it was, I knew that nothing good could come from looks such as the one Samuel had cast her way.

Elkanah said nothing. I thought this very wise, for he could not well forbid our son to live in our vicinity.

I wanted to ask Samuel if he had consulted with Serach before he had made his decision to move to Ramah. But I knew that as she loved him, she would adopt as her own whatever scheme he had formed in his head. Even if he had set his mind on settling in Sodom or Gomorrah she would not have demurred. There was no sense in asking.

I thought of taking him aside and cautioning him, telling him that the path on which he was treading could lead only to disaster. But I was sure that he had done nothing. What could I accuse him of? So I decided against this plan, too.

Samuel had chosen a house that was large and well appointed, and Elkanah wished to give him a portion of the silver shekels required for its purchase; but Samuel had enough from what he himself had saved, and he refused to accept anything from his father.

Once Samuel had settled his family in their new house, he took to visiting us almost every day. And then, little by little, his turbulent soul became visible to my eyes.

The Book of Pninah

Shortly after Samuel came to live near us, Elkanah called me to his room.

"Pninah," he reminded me, "I have forbidden you to wear those indecent dresses of yours when Samuel is here. Recently you have been doing so again."

I showed him my customary obeisance. "Forgive me, sir."

"You will stop this. And you will remember that you are not allowed to sit with him in your room."

"I have not done so."

To his previous prohibitions, he now added another: "And you will no longer walk with him in the hills. You may continue to walk if you wish," he added generously, "but from now on, if you see him, you will come home directly."

The next time Samuel came to the house, we sat on the two large stones in front of my room.

Referring to the new prohibitions Elkanah had imposed on me, Samuel said that his father must have a poor opinion of him if he thought that he would transgress the Torah commandments that forbade adultery and prohibited a man to lie with his father's wife.

On another visit, Samuel announced to me, "I'm keeping the commandments that are the most difficult for me to keep."

"Samuel," I responded, "you speak as if I had no say in the matter. I would never . . ."

"Your words are foolish. I could take you any time I wanted to. You cannot have forgotten that I know how to excite you, as you know how to arouse me."

"You talk wildly," I said jokingly. "I know nothing of this."

"No? Then why are you sitting with your legs apart in a manner that, as you well remember, causes me to lose my sanity?"

I jumped to my feet and exclaimed, "It's a mistake."

He got up, too. His breathing was labored. "Have no fear," he said, "I am in control of myself. I will not touch you."

I saw Hannah standing some distance away, and I pointed this out to him. "Your mother is worried."

He quickly regained his composure and replied, "She has no need to be. I will go and reassure her."

When he returned and Hannah had left, he looked at me and said harshly, "Pninah, what are you trying to do to me? Why do you hold out this unspoken promise to me, always? I am but human. I cannot fend you off forever."

My sinful desire flared up inside me as he stroked my face.

"And now," he continued, "change out of your ensnaring dress, as my father has ordered you to do, lest I forget the commandments that have been holding me back from you all these years."

I stepped into my room to do this, but when I came out he was no longer there. I thought that he had fled from me, as he seemed to believe that I was provoking him to do something against his will. This stung me, for I feared that he would not return to see me again. But he came the next day, and then day after day, as if nothing had happened.

Often Samuel brought with him rare and precious scrolls recounting the tales of our people after the land of Canaan had been conquered, and placed them in my scroll room. At first I refused to accept them, but he would not take them back. Short of throwing them away, there was nothing I could do but keep them.

He also told me about his judgments, and about the people who came to him seeking miracles that he could not perform. Now that he lived in Ramah, he read from the Torah and held his speeches in this town's square, which was packed full every sabbath. Gradually, he said, he had reduced what he required of the people. Previously he had been adamant in his demand that they keep every commandment. He still urged them to abstain from committing adultery, but was now less vigorous in this exhortation.

Often I accompanied Elkanah and Hannah to the square to listen to him, but until now I had not noticed this omission. I asked why this was so, and this was his reply: "I am hesitant in demanding from others what I find so difficult to keep myself."

Samuel still had only two sons, and he told me of his disappointment as it became clear that he and his wife could not beget any more children.

I hesitated for some time. But when I saw how deeply upset he was about this, finally I asked if it would not be best for him to take a second wife.

"No," he answered, "because the only woman I would have wanted for my wife is not available to me."

One day, when I returned from seeing Arnon, I found Samuel waiting for me. He led me around the house where, behind the backyard, there were some trees and bushes that threw pleasantly cool shadows on those who walked under them, toward the vineyard beyond.

While we walked, Samuel reflected on my life: "When you were a girl you dreamt of having only one man whom you would love, and who would love you all the days of his life. If you wish to know why it was not so, it is useless to ask me. I don't know. But I do know that if you had met such a man *then*, I would not be standing next to you *now*, looking into your incredible eyes. And this would have been . . ."

I looked up at him inquiringly, and he added, ". . . unthinkable."

Saying this, his eyes met mine. And without touching me, just by looking steadily into them, he forced me to stand on the tip of my toes and bring my mouth close to his. I felt the passage to my womb contracting inside me, clenching inward, from my wanting of him. He brought his arms around me, but I barely had a chance to feel the heat of his body when he abruptly released me, and whispered, "Pninah, my love, I can no longer control myself. I must go." I saw tears filling his eyes, before he began walking away with his head bent.

I called after him in a choked voice. "Samuel!"

He turned back to face me, and I felt words I had not meant to say rushing out of my mouth. "Please don't be so unhappy. I love you more than the breath I draw to sustain my life."

The love for him, which I had nursed inside me in utter silence for I don't know how long, had finally found its voice. I had been moving toward this moment for years, and I felt no regret.

It was not so for him. He took a few hesitant steps toward me, halted, turned around once again, and fairly ran through the shadowy vineyard, then up the hill.

I returned to the backyard. When Hannah came out to look for him, I could only tell her, truthfully, that I had no idea where he had gone.

That night I sat in front of my room, nursing the ache inside that Samuel had caused. I was overwhelmed by the tenderness that had grown in me for him. Its strength had become terrifying.

I placed my arms on my drawn-up knees and rested my head on my arms. I remained so until the stars were being swallowed up into the paling sky, pondering what I finally recognized as the harrowing struggle in both our tormented souls. I could only wait and see what he might, or might not, decide to do.

The Book of Hannah

When Samuel began visiting us without respite, Elkanah talked to me of his suspicion that our son did not come to our house to see his parents and, like me, he was deeply perturbed. He told me that he had forbidden Pninah to meet Samuel in her room or on the hills, and I could see that she heeded his prohibition. So I tried to calm Elkanah by telling him (although I did not believe so myself) that Samuel and Pninah were apparently kindred spirits, and that he came to her in friendship.

He retorted with some asperity, "Hannah, my darling. You will not have me believe this. I am not that stupid."

He then told me that he would also forbid Pninah to sit with Samuel in front of her room.

I advised Elkanah against this. I told him that this might cause them to hold clandestine meetings, and that this could lead to worse than what they were doing now. I soothed him by convincing him that nothing much could transpire while they were sitting in the front yard, where I could always watch them, though in my heart I knew that much *was* happening.

Observing Samuel and Pninah from a distance, I saw him grow more reckless in his dealings with her, and that she reciprocated his feelings. I decided that I could no longer keep silent, that I must issue a warning to my son. I cautioned him that he was treading on dangerous ground. I reminded him of the relevant commandments, and of the curse and death penalty the Torah imposed on a man who did what he was set to do with his father's wife.

He reassured me, promising that he had himself under control. But when I looked at him, I saw tears glistening in his eyes. These tears rocked my heart, for despite the many admirers I had in my youth, I had never before seen a man cry from thwarted lust.

From day to day I watched him weaken, and soon he had lost control entirely. He began touching Pninah, and walking with her amidst the trees and bushes, where they could not be seen. I feared that it would not be long before they were joined together.

My thoughts took a new turn. I not only worried about Samuel, but I began to resent deeply what Pninah was doing. By failing to reject his advances, she was inexorably delivering him into the hands of evil. She should have made it plain to him from the beginning that she did not want his attentions. Instead, she had shown that she enjoyed them, and she was playing with him no less than he was playing with her.

I weighed the possibility of taking Pninah to task, but I knew from previous experience that it would be to no avail. Yet I could not but wonder what was going on in her mind. Did she think that I saw nothing? Did she expect me to remain silent, or even to protect her from Elkanah's suspicions?

She had dealt falsely with him and I had been screening her from his jealousy for many years. Whenever his suspicion had alighted on her, I had conspired with her to divert it. I had been loath to do this, but I colluded with her because I was grateful for her unfailing assistance throughout the years. I also still felt obligated to compensate her for the sorrow I had caused her. Most importantly, I cared for her, and I did not want to see her life crumble like a house built without a stone foundation. But now she was overreaching herself and was demanding too much of me. I was not going to do what she wanted.

If Pninah and Samuel knew each other, and if I told Elkanah about it, he would most certainly hand her a book of divorcement and send her away, and there would be nowhere for her to go. Were her father still alive, she might have gone to his house, but as it was, she would have to move to one of her children's homes. And although they could not refuse to offer her shelter, none of them would relish housing a mother who—as everybody would know by then—had strayed.

Yet Pninah was not a little girl. She must have considered all of this. Or, if she had not, she should have done so. I could no longer help her. My loyalty now had to be to Elkanah, the man I loved, the essence of my life. I would not let his wife and his son dishonor him. So far I had nothing to voice except suspicions, and there was no point in apprising him of those, because he had enough suspicions of his own.

But I resolved that if Pninah and Samuel did come together, and I came to know of it, I would not remain silent.

It was not long after these thoughts crossed my mind that I received a letter which greatly surprised and pleased me. It contained an invitation to visit relatives in Dan, a town in the far north of the land of Israel. It was sent by my mother's younger sister, who had moved there many years ago to become the wife of a prosperous resident. Since then we had lost touch with her. She had given birth to sons and daughters who were now grown-up, but so far we had never seen them.

My aunt was keen to renew contact with us and have us meet our young cousins. At first I thought of going without Elkanah. Yet it would be odd if all those who had husbands or wives brought them along, and I went on my own. So I asked Elkanah to accompany me.

He agreed, but since he knew that Samuel would not be able to come because of his reading the Torah on the sabbath, he insisted that I invite Pninah as well. I did his bidding, but, as I anticipated, she had no wish to accompany us. Elkanah considered ordering her to come, but I pointed out to him that it would be cruel to force her to do so against her will, being the only one there who did not belong to the family.

Elkanah thought of another plan: At our next evening meal he ordered Pninah to move in with one of her children for the duration of our journey. When she heard his new command, she almost choked on her food. After she managed to swallow it, she said, "Sir, as you know, I obey you in everything. But surely you cannot contemplate humiliating me so unbearably as to appoint my children to guard my steps. They would realize your intention, and I would be deeply shamed before them."

Elkanah opened his mouth, but before he could reprimand her for her disobedience, I nudged his elbow. He understood that he had overstepped the limits, and remained silent.

After Pninah had gone to her room, Elkanah said that if he

could not send Pninah to one of her children, it would be best if he stayed behind as well. I retorted, with hot tears in my eyes, that if he did not come, *I* would be deeply shamed before *my* children and my brothers, whose husbands or wives would all be there.

I suggested that he request Efrath to stay with Pninah. After she had been Samuel's nurse at the Temple, she had helped me with the other children. Now she was old, and Elkanah provided her with food and clothing. She was totally dependent on his support, so she could hardly refuse to come to our aid. She was a forceful woman, and I told Elkanah that we could trust her to keep Pninah in check.

At first Elkanah rejected my notion, but when he saw the tears in my eyes spilling over onto my cheeks, he began to hedge. He weighed the matter in his mind for several days. As the day of departure drew near, I told him that if he did not come with me, my relatives would take this as a sign that I was an unloved wife. When he heard the plea in my voice, his love for me bore more heavily upon him than anything else, and he did what I beseeched him to do. He visited Efrath and charged her to follow Pninah like a shadow for the entire week.

We set out with the stableboys who were to guard us on the way. Our three maids we left behind to see to the work that needed to be done in the house, in the hope that they, too, would deter Pninah from what might be her evil designs.

Even so, it was with a heavy heart that I left the house.

The Book of Pninah

A few days after Samuel had walked with me under the trees, Hannah requested that Elkanah escort her on a visit to her relatives in Dan. She dealt kindly with me and asked me to come along also, but I knew that she was glad when I refused. Her younger brothers, and most of her children and their families, would be there. It would be a family gathering, where I would stick out like a bramble among roses.

I was content to stay behind, as I had my lessons and my letter-writing and my children's children to occupy me, and I did not anticipate that I would feel lonely.

Elkanah and Hannah left with the rising of the sun. I gave my lesson to the children, and it was finished before noon. Efrath, whom Elkanah had appointed to stand guard over me, had not arrived. I sat in front of my room in the sluggish, hot summer air, enjoying my solitude, when Samuel arrived.

He approached, and said not a word as I rose to my feet. We entered my bedroom, locked and shuttered it. As his hands moved to strip me of my dress, he recited from the most famous of all love songs:

Love is as mighty as death . . .
Torrents of water cannot extinguish love . . .

My own love was even mightier than death, a flame unleashed from my innermost being, which even Noah's flood could not extinguish.

Suddenly, though, there was something that defied words—not a light, nor yet a darkness; not a sound, nor yet a stillness; not a presence, nor yet an absence—an irresistible compulsion to place my hands over his roaming ones. He must have sensed it as well, for his hands froze under mine.

I spoke words I did not know had been inside me: "Samuel, my love for you is like fire in the deepest recesses of my soul, and I will do as you wish. But it might be that afterward you would hate me for having led you into this abyss."

"I could never hate you. I will love you all the days of our lives on this earth and beyond."

"But something worse might come to pass. You might hate yourself. Then the sin would form its own punishment."

He removed his hands from my body and was silent. The silence wrapped itself around us like a blanket until it became unbearable, and the summer heat bore down on us all the more.

It was a long time before I broke it. "The portion of the Torah that is to be read this sabbath . . ." I said, and there was no need to say more, for we both knew that it could not be worse. "If we go over the brink, will you still be able to stand in the square and lift your eyes to the people and chant it before them?"

There were no words in his mouth. His gaze fixed itself on a point in the air, as if he was seeing a vision.

"What are you staring at?" I asked.

"My soul."

"And what do you see?"

"A woman. A woman named Sadness, and she is growing and growing, until she suffocates me."

"But she will shrink again and disappear. She will not always torment you, and you will not dwell in discontent forever."

He sat down on a chair, and his body convulsed in dry sobs. I stood before him, and I finally did what I had wanted to do for so long. I placed his head between my breasts, and smoothed his unruly curls with my hands, and kissed them with my mouth, and wet them with my tears, and the passage to my womb coiled itself into knots of desire and pity and love.

After that I must have fallen into a stupor, for what I remember next is lying on my bed, shivering yet hot as if in the throes of a fever, and the room filled with the emptiness of my loss.

For the rest of the week my suffering was dry and mute. Even the screams of my desire were soundless, yet I knew that Samuel heard them, as I heard his.

On sabbath morning I forced myself out of bed and went to listen to Samuel's reading of the Torah at the Ramah town square. When I arrived, he was already standing in its center, on the elevated spot on which the table for the Torah reading was placed.

He looked at me briefly—accusingly, or with relief, I was not sure—bent over the Torah scroll in front of him and began to read. As usual, his chanting carried from one end of the square to the other. Then for a moment he stood still, as immobile as a statue, before he continued with only the slightest tremor in his voice:

And Moses charged the people, that same day, saying . . .
Cursed be he who lies with his father's wife . . .
And all the people shall say, Amen. . . .

When the reading was finished, a hum of voices arose as the people waited for Samuel to speak. When he began, a hush fell on the crowd. He said that since the sixth month of the year was upon us, this was the time to return to the Lord, in anticipation of the Day of Atonement. But how was this return to be accomplished?

When he was still a boy, the matter was clear to him. He called on the people to renounce evil and keep all the commandments, even those that were the most difficult to keep. Those who transgressed even one, he judged harshly.

Now, there was more wisdom in his heart. There could be no forgiveness where idol worship, or murder, or incest was concerned. The poor and the strangers in our midst had to be cared for, and bribery was an abomination.

But in all else, no man or woman could be flawless. It was possible to return to the Lord even if one did not fulfill all the commandments, so long as one fulfilled more commandments more wholeheartedly than before. Human beings, including himself, were mere flesh and blood and therefore weak, and only the Lord was righteous in all his ways.

He illustrated his speech with tales and parables, and the people loved his newfound leniency. As soon as he finished, they besieged him and would not let him go for a long time.

I noticed Serach in the crowd, and she greeted me with the friendly smile of a kinswoman, which I readily returned. I saw how proud she was of Samuel, totally effacing herself before his eminence. And I wondered what she knew of his weakness.

Back in my room I lay on my bed as broken sunlight filtered through the trees in the yard, covering my body, bathed in sweat, until the shadows moved in and all was drowned in the darkness of my heart. My eyes were heavy with the sleep that would not come and the tears I could not bring forth.

A few days later, when Elkanah returned and came looking for me, I was in the bathing room reclining in the tub, the cool water reaching up to my neck. The sleep that had eluded me for almost the entire week had finally overtaken me, and I was immersed in its depths.

I have a vague memory of my husband lifting me up in his arms and, panting heavily with the exertion, carrying me, dripping with water, to my bed. He eased me down on it, and wrapped me up in a soft large towel. It seemed that he shook me, trying to force me to wake, but I could not. I did not even hear the door of my room closing behind him as he left.

I slept like an infant in its mother's womb until the light began draining from the room. As I emerged from my chamber, my drowsy eyes alighted on Elkanah. He was standing in the front yard, his right foot resting on a stone, examining one of the almond trees that had withered and would need to be felled.

He approached and asked what was ailing me. I told him that I had not been able to sleep much during the last few nights, and, for that reason, I had slept during the day.

My explanation, though truthful, sounded lame even to my own ears. I was not surprised when Elkanah stared at me with knitted eyebrows for a long time, harboring grave suspicions as to what had caused my lack of sleep. But before he could speak, Hannah was at our side and we went to the front room for our evening meal.

The Book of Hannah

The family gathering was all that I had hoped it would be, my aunt as affectionate as any aunt could be. But Elkanah had no peace of mind, wandering by himself in the dark of the evenings, uneasy even in his sleep. So we set out from Dan before everyone else, and reached home half a day before we had planned to arrive.

By that time, I had learned of two matters that I had not previously suspected. The first was that Samuel had been the one to re-establish contact between the two parts of our family, and that he had done so even though he knew well that he himself would not attend the family meeting.

My aunt had told me this when I was talking to her by myself, so Elkanah did not hear it. He was already so worried that I decided to say nothing to him about this as yet.

The second matter, of which I became aware as we entered our house, was that Efrath, who should have been there to be Pninah's guard, was nowhere to be seen. When I placed those two pieces of knowledge next to each other, I thought that I had a good notion of what had gone on in our absence.

As soon as we entered the house, Elkanah went into Pninah's room to look for her. While he was there, Efrath came hobbling into the front yard on her cane. Her eyesight had dimmed, and she did not see me from a distance. She sat down on a stone at the edge of the yard in the shade of an olive tree. She opened a bag she had brought with her, took out a small tapestry, pretended to work on it, and tried to look as if she had been sitting there for the entire week.

A short while later, when Elkanah emerged from Pninah's room, he saw Efrath. He asked how the week had passed, and she answered that the week had gone by, as it should have. He asked if there had been any visitors, and she replied (and of course it was the truth) that she had seen no visitors.

Elkanah asked if she had stayed at our house for the entire week. At that Efrath stiffened, her voice trembling with righteous indignation. "Sir, you seem not to trust me. I have been where I ought to have been, every moment of this week."

She yawned into his face with surprising insolence, feigning exasperation and boredom from the week she had been forced to spend in Pninah's company at his behest. Then she gathered up her tapestry, put it in her bag and, leaning heavily on her stick, limped out of the yard.

Though deeply enraged, I found what must have been Samuel's ruse very inventive. Yet I found nothing amusing in Pninah's part in it. My anger at her was kindled so strongly that I felt an urge to throw handfuls of earth and stones at her head. In my wrath, I resolved to reveal to Elkanah what had come to pass without giving her warning of what I intended to do.

But my heart was heavy for Samuel, so I decided to smooth his path to cast away his sin before I revealed it to his father. I had no doubt that he would come the following day, so I decided to hold back until then.

During the evening meal, Pninah looked pale and exhausted. I wondered what Samuel could have done to make her look so.

Elkanah paid no attention to her pallor, but probed her deeds during our absence by asking if Efrath had been a good companion for her. She glanced at him furtively before she bent her gaze to her food. Then she replied evasively that Efrath was a very decent woman, but that she was not her friend. He asked what had occupied her during the week, and she said that she had been at home most of the time.

I could tell that Elkanah was casting about in his mind for more questions to ask, questions that might provide clues as to what Pninah had been doing. Since I wanted to postpone the revelation of the truth, I decided to intervene, and did so by telling Pninah at length about our trip. She feigned interest, and from time to time asked some pertinent questions. In this manner the meal came to a successful conclusion. And it occurred to me that we must surely be the most unusual family in our entire tribe.

After Pninah had retired to her room, Elkanah asked one of the maids who came in to clear the dishes from the table if Samuel had been to our house while we were away. She replied that he had not entered the cooking room or the front room while she was there. At hearing those words, Elkanah's peace of mind seemed to be restored. I reflected that Samuel must have beguiled the maids, as he had done with Efrath.

I went to my room and sat on my bed to contemplate our fate. After a while, although I was still simmering with anger at Pninah, I decided that it would be unfair to inform Elkanah of what had come to pass before warning her. So I went to her room to talk to her.

She was in her night garment, and appeared to have been in bed, on the verge of falling asleep. But she put forward a chair for me to sit on, and since the night was creeping in she lit the oil lamp on her table. The spluttering lamplight struck into the darkness as she sat opposite me and I looked at her. Despite having children's children now, there was nothing grandmotherly about her and she looked surprisingly youthful. There were hardly any creases to mar her face, and her shape remained what it had been in her girlhood. There was a subtle allure in her eyes, and I could not entirely blame Samuel for succumbing to her appeal.

I blamed her, instead. I reflected angrily that she should have contented herself with the Canaanite man, instead of encouraging my son—a man of God—to commit such a grievous sin with her.

By now she must have become aware of my fury, and I expected her to show some anxiety. But she was as calm as a ewe grazing in rich pastures. How could she be so serene in the face of the disaster that was about to befall her?

We sat for a while, my rage almost choking me. If she was conscious of this, she did not show it. Finally she laughed. "What is your message to me, Hannah? Speak, for I am listening."

Her words conjured up memories of a talk I had held with her so many years ago, when she had voiced the same words. Only this time I scorned her in my heart even more than I had then, and I was determined not to support her.

I retorted, "My words, though not sweet to your palate, are sincere. Unless you promise to put a halt to this, I will have to speak to Elkanah."

"There is nothing to halt," she murmured with a drowsy smile, such as that of a little girl who expected her mother to sing her a lullaby and rock her to sleep on her lap. "It was halted before it began."

"Did he not come to you?"

"He came to my room but he did not come to me."

"I can scarcely believe it. Did you halt him because you were loath to dishonor Elkanah?"

"No," she demurred. "He who rolls a stone up the hill will have it roll back at him."

My anger, which had begun to ebb, now soared again. "Taking a second wife is not the same as your sin."

She looked at me thoughtfully. "A second wife? No . . . it's not only that. I have loved Elkanah from the beginning, and all I dreamt about was to be close to him and be loved by him. Even now I still love him, and if he had loved me, and not cast his eyes at any other woman, I would never even have peeked at the sleeve of the garment of another man. But he has scorned my love."

My mind flatly rejected this notion but I was not about to argue with her. "Then why did you halt Samuel? Did you find that you did not love him as much as you thought you did?"

Pninah seemed to be lost in thought for a while. She replied, "I love him more than anyone. And had I been able to heal his wounded soul with my love, I would have done it and I would have been in bliss for it."

"Then what was it? Did you realize how wrong it would have been to bring a great sorrow into the life of Serach?"

With a thin smile on her face, Pninah retorted, "Do you think, Hannah, that you should be the one to lecture me on the evil of bringing sorrow into another woman's life?"

I had momentarily forgotten what I had done. I caught myself and blushed and apologized. "Forgive me. I should not have rebuked you."

"Forgive me, too. I should not have scolded you either. I know now that I cannot blame you for what you did, because you could have done nothing else. In any case, it happened many years ago and it no longer bothers me."

With these words, Pninah rose to her feet, to indicate that our talk was at an end.

Somehow she had dodged my questions and, once again, I was furious. "You still have not told me what stopped you. In truth, I don't believe that you rejected him, and I will reveal this to Elkanah."

"I speak the truth, but do as is good in your eyes. I have only one request of you: Wait until tomorrow, by which time I will have gathered my strength and I will be able to face him."

I was still plagued by disbelief. "I'll wait until tomorrow," I conceded, "and I will also warn Samuel. But after that, I'll open my mouth as surely as the threshing of the wheat follows the harvest."

Pninah remained unperturbed. As a warm smile played over her face she said, "I am sure that when you open your mouth it will be with wisdom. And I wish you to know, Hannah, that whatever you tell Elkanah will not make any difference to me. I will never say or do anything to hurt you."

"Because I am Samuel's mother?"

"Yes. And also—as you told me many years ago when you rescued me from an abominable fate—despite everything, I still love you, and I am still your friend." Pninah then embraced me and kissed me on the cheek, as she had done only once before.

At this moment Elkanah admitted himself into the room, and he saw Pninah hugging me. Even after all these years, he was still delighted with any sign that she had accepted me, and that we were getting on well together, and now he showed this by favoring us with a benign look.

We both bowed to him. He turned to me. "Hannah, I will now escort you to your room." Then he said to Pninah, "I'll be back soon."

It was the last thing she wanted. "Sir, I am tired, and I would like to go to sleep."

A withering flash crossed his dark eyes, as he issued his order: "You will wait for me."

In her customary deceptive servility, she replied: "I will do as you command, sir."

Elkanah put his arm around my waist and almost shoved me out of the room, stepping into the night with me, leading me to my door. Then he turned, and with brisk steps strode purposefully back to Pninah's room.

After he had shut the door behind him, I tried to divert my thoughts from what was happening in there at that very moment. I lay awake on my bed for a long time, and gradually my anger at Pninah dissipated. I reflected that life had led the two of us into this collision. Our childhood friendship had collapsed under the weight of our love for the same man; we had been pettily jealous of each other, hostile strangers forced to live in the same house. But for years now we had been friends again, the bond between us as strong as that of blood sisters. Even so, I would not let her nor Samuel demean the man I loved, or lessen him, even in my own eyes.

Perhaps when I saw Samuel tomorrow I would be able to convince him to renounce the evil he seemed to have embraced. But if I could not, I would do what I had to do: apprise Elkanah of what had occurred, even if it destroyed the life of Pninah, my rival and my friend.

The Book of Pninah

After Elkanah and Hannah's return, Elkanah spent the night with me. His previous suspicions seemed to have abated, but he did not have much to say to me. He wanted simply to fulfill the need that had built up in his body while he was away. Although I wished for nothing but sleep, I resolved to make him enjoy this night with me, for if Hannah carried out her threat of denouncing me, however unjustly, she might succeed in convincing him of my guilt, and thus it might be the last night we spent together in his house.

Hence, I did not allow his release to come too quickly. I teased him to build up his need even more. I undressed in deliberately maddening slowness to make him watch me, touch me, until he gasped in excitement. To test his patience even further, I demanded his caresses and his kisses. Then my tongue found the secret fold that I knew about in his familiar member, which tantalized him more than anything, making him writhe in anticipation.

I made him moan with impatience until he pleaded, "Please, let me come into you."

I allowed him in only little by little, and even then, I was in no rush to let him complete our act, slowing down his movements inside me, so that they would go on for a long time. When his release finally came, it was as shattering as any he had ever experienced, even in his youth. He roared out his joy, like the roar of a bull, with a wrench of agony at the end. And he rocked back and forth like a leaf blown by a storm.

When it was over, he tousled my hair in gratitude, and said, "I've had to wait for this too long. The next time I go anywhere, you will go with me."

"Were there no maids in Dan, sir?" I teased him.

"Not one who pleased me. On top of which she demanded silver of me, which my own maids would never dare to do."

As he hovered between wakefulness and sleep, he was moved to give vent to his thoughts about me. "I did right to marry you, Pninah. Your breasts still look untouched—when I see you naked I am still enthralled, as I was when I first set eyes on you stepping out of that pool. You possess unbelievable passion. You please me more than any maid. You were rebellious at first, before I bent you to my will. But you have learned to submit yourself to me, as you should. And you have borne me sons and daughters who bring us joy and do us honor. I am satisfied with you in every way."

He had now spoken more words to me than he had done for a long time, and he must have felt that he had said all that I could have wished him to say. He evidently sought a response from me, for he opened his half-closed lids and eyed me expectantly.

So I said with the submissiveness he expected of me, "Thank you, sir, for regarding me with favor." Then, for the first time in my life, I called my husband by his name. He was startled at this breach of custom, but did not object. "Elkanah," I said, "despite the many humiliations you have visited on me, I still love you as much as I loved you when I first met you on top of that hill. It is important to me that you know this—that you believe it."

A smile of contentment crept onto his face as he murmured, "I enjoy your love. I need it." Then he drifted into a heavy sleep of satiation and said no more.

I dwelled briefly on what he had left unsaid. Not a sound about what *I* needed. Not a shred of a word about his love for *me*.

I counted myself fortunate to have found elsewhere the love I thirsted for, which Elkanah was unable to give me, and soon I followed him into slumber.

When I woke up in the morning, I had recuperated from my exhaustion. During my talk with Hannah the night before, I had been too tired to care what she would or would not say to our husband, or about what would happen next. But now I was feeling some disquiet as to what he might do if Hannah maligned me. I was anxious for Samuel to come, so that I could voice my worries in his ears.

* * *

When Samuel arrived, though, he was unperturbed about this, and had entirely different matters on his mind. He brought with him a large, oblong package that he placed on the table in my scroll room. Elkanah had prohibited my meeting with Samuel in my room, but I thought that this prohibition did not pertain to my scroll room, so I followed him there.

I saw him remove the outer wrapping from the package, and I perceived that what he had brought was a very large Torah scroll. He said it was an ancient scroll that he had purchased some years ago from the Temple in Shiloh, before it was destroyed. He brought it to me as a present, as he surmised that I would like it better than jewelry.

I was touched, for Samuel had given me what was, without doubt, his most valuable and cherished possession. Through this sacred gift, he had offered me his heart more clearly than he could have done in any other manner. And by accepting it, I had offered him mine.

Only later did it dawn on me that by bringing me this Torah scroll he had also delivered to me the key that would unlock the remaining recesses of his soul.

The Torah's holy radiance suffused my humble scroll room, elevating it into a small sanctuary, and I stepped back from it in awe. Samuel removed its cloth covering, and motioned to me to come closer. I asked if I was allowed to touch it. He assented, but I could not bring myself to do it. He waited patiently, and finally I gained courage, and I put my hand on it. Since I had never handled a scroll of this size before, he showed me how to roll and unroll it, in order to reach the passage that I wanted to read.

He rolled it until the passage he sought, the Ten Commandments, came into view.

"The Day of Atonement is approaching," he said, "and in order to atone for my sins, I have to win the forgiveness of the persons against whom I have sinned. I would like to win yours."

"Samuel," I said with laughter in my eyes, "I cannot think of any way in which you have sinned against me, so there is nothing to forgive."

"Look at these commandments," he said. "By transgressing one of them, I have also transgressed against you."

"But you have not broken any one of them."

"Look again."

I looked and I understood him, and remained silent, and he continued: "'You shall not covet your friend's wife.' That is, you shall not covet someone else's wife. Yet, Pninah, I have coveted you, and loved you, since I was fourteen. I remember when I came to visit here for the first time. You wore your violet dress, and I came to talk to you in your room, and you were in turmoil because I looked at your body and because I knew all about you. I told you then that I loved you, but the words I used were such that you couldn't understand me. Since then I have been carrying your image before my eyes at all times.

"I performed daring feats of bravery on the battlefield so that you would hear of them, yet I escaped unharmed so that I could see you again. You were my reason to do good by saving the enemy's captives. But you were also my reason to sin. You have caused me to covet that which belongs to another man. The sins of adultery and of lying with my father's wife were always before my door, waiting to be committed. And because I wanted you, I inflamed you and made you suffer more than you were suffering already, for . . . other reasons. For this I seek your forgiveness."

"If there is anything I cannot forgive it is that you did not talk to me of this from the first. Why did you let your sore fester inside you for so long?"

"What would you have me say?" he queried gruffly. "That I loved you but could not decide whether I loved the Lord's commandments more? I preferred to keep my torture to myself, to wrestle with it in silence, in the darkness of my soul, as the third father of our people, Jacob, wrestled with the angel—probably a like torment in his own soul—in the dark of night. The dawn brightened for him, as it has not for me."

"The brightness of your dawn is in another domain. The people revere you and your destiny lies in leading them."

"In this, too, my life will not run through still waters. There will be mighty storms I must brave. Already I can feel the winds of change. The people are getting restless and yearning for a strong leader, one who will rule over them with an iron rod, as I have no wish to do. The day will come when they demand that I anoint a king for them. Yet the Lord is our king and we need no other."

"But I will be at your side and will lend you all the strength I have for as long as it lasts."

"It will last for as long as I live, for I will not live one day without you."

His words were meant as a solemn pledge, like placing a ring on my finger under the canopy, something he would never be able to do. They were like a sweet melody to my ears, yet I smiled inside myself in silent disbelief.

"And I will guard you like the apple of my eye," he continued, "and shield you and protect you as fiercely as a lion, and I will not let a hair of your head fall down to the ground, as long as my eyes are open to perceive the light of day."

At that moment I heard the door to my bedroom open. Then the connecting doors to the scroll room were flung apart and Elkanah, who had just returned from the fields, stood on the threshold. As Hannah had not been home since morning, I knew that she could not have spoken to him yet. But he had a look of fury in his eyes nevertheless, and seemed on the verge of scolding me.

Yet when he saw Samuel and myself seemingly reading the Torah together, he was so astounded that he said nothing.

We both bowed to him. Samuel greeted his father affably and inquired how his trip had been. I noted with approval that he did not lower his gaze, but looked straight into his father's eyes in a calm, friendly manner, as if nothing were amiss.

After he had chatted with Elkanah for a while, Samuel wrapped up the Torah scroll and placed it on a shelf, saying that he now wished to greet his mother. She was due to return shortly, so he stepped out into the front yard to wait for her. Before long she arrived and bore him off to her room.

Elkanah went to his room to wash off the day's sweat from his body, and I stepped into my bedroom. I felt no apprehension. Samuel was there and I felt protected by his presence. Still, there was no certainty of anything, and I stood gazing out of my window, wondering what lay in store for me.

The Book of Hannah

On the day after we returned from our trip, as I knew that Samuel would not make his appearance until the afternoon, I went to visit my father and my mother in Shaar Efraim. Both were old and frail now, and were unable to come to Dan with us. My younger brothers, with their wives and children, lived with them, and they would have given them an account of our journey. But I was sure that they would want to hear it all from me as well. So I relayed everything from beginning to end.

When I returned home, the heat of the day had passed and a cool breeze began to blow through our yard. Yet I was bathed in sweat, at the prospect of the fateful talk with my firstborn now looming before me.

Samuel was standing in the front yard waiting for me. I put my arm around him as I used to do when he was still a boy and, without uttering a sound, I led him to my room.

I was fully intent on giving him the scolding he deserved, and apprising him of my resolution to reveal his deed to his father. But when I regarded him, he looked so despondent that I did not have it in my heart to say anything.

I remembered the years of his childhood that I had forced him to spend away from me, among strangers in the Temple. I remembered how, even as a child, he had suffered from an oppression of the spirit, because of his forebodings of disaster. I recalled his terrible distress before the wars, and his deep mourning and lamentations afterward. And that even afterward, his mood continued to be downcast for years. I remembered the tears I had seen in his eyes in the past months because of his craving for Pninah. And now he was not at peace either. I was torn, and I could not decide what to do next.

We sat down on two chairs facing each other, and I waited for him to speak first, which he did: "My mother, what can I say? Whatever I might tell, you would not believe."

"Truth has its own voice. Let it speak."

"The truth is that I have struggled with myself for many years. In the end—"

"How many years?" I interrupted.

"Since I was fourteen, and came for my first visit here. You may remember that on that day I went to talk to Pninah in her room. When I came out, you asked me why I was so upset. I could not bring myself to tell you then, but I had a reason. For during that talk a flame was kindled in my body and soul, and I came to realize that I loved her and wanted her. It was a love born in sin, a hopeless love. Yet I knew that I would bear it with me for as long as I lived and that there would never be any respite, or any other woman, for me."

I raised my eyebrows in disbelief. "So you did not know any of those lovely girls who adored you?"

"I did not refrain, but it was nothing to me. Pninah knew about it and she did not condemn me. I wanted Pninah. I continued to yearn for her."

"But you did take a wife."

"Serach was one of those lovely girls. I knew that she was pregnant before she did. There was no sense in delaying the wedding. Still, my heart was with Pninah."

"Until you came to live here, I was not aware of what was in your heart."

"No."

"Was Pninah aware of it?"

"Not entirely. I only spoke of it to her today."

"And while we were away?"

His face radiated no happiness. "I did not mean to put a barrier to my love, and neither did she. The barrier came from . . . elsewhere."

Samuel's words had the ring of truth in them, and it spoke louder than his voice. In my heart I sighed with relief, yet what he had said rankled me and I was not entirely satisfied. "Samuel, surely you did not require the one who sets a barrier to the sea to put a barrier to you. You could not have slighted your father and desecrated his bed."

He remained silent. Unmoved.

I felt bound to say, "Apart from your breach of the commandment to honor your father, you have much to lose. Your reputation would be in the dust, and his and ours would sink to the ground with it. Besides," I continued, "would you have felt no guilt toward Serach?"

He gazed at me unflinchingly. "No more than any other man who is unfaithful to his wife or wives."

Samuel's words hit me like a slap in the face. I had no doubt that there was an unspoken message in them, and I was in deep shock. Samuel always knew everything about us, but he had never insinuated that his father might be doing something illicit. Yet such acts were implicit in his seemingly innocuous words.

And Pninah, did she know as well? I remembered several occasions over the years when she was on the verge of revealing something unpalatable to me, but then drew back. Or had I been the one to recoil, the one purposely to misinterpret the hints she was sending out to me, because I did not wish to know? Was this what she had meant yesterday when she assured me that she would never say anything that might hurt me? Even then I had ignored her hint.

But now I could no longer deceive myself. My head dropped in shame to be so slighted by the man I loved, and the ground felt shaky beneath me.

Samuel looked at me with concern, his knit eyebrows and creased forehead reminding me of his father's, and said, "My mother, what are you thinking of? Many men are unfaithful to their wives."

I paid no heed to this, but voiced my thoughts aloud. "My hurt is of no importance. I still love him very much."

Samuel made no reply, but I noted that he was getting fidgety, shifting back and forth in his chair like a little boy in one of my lesson, waiting impatiently for it to be over. He kept looking out into the front yard, apparently hoping to see Pninah pass by.

I could not help but smile. "You have seen her a short while ago. Are you so anxious to see her again?"

"Forgive me," he said humbly.

Briefly setting aside the shock that had just been visited upon me, I beheld his eager, youthful face and my heart melted. I dismissed him gently, while showing my love for him. "Samuel, you may go now. But perhaps you would like to bring your family to share our sabbath meal with us?"

His eyes lit up. "I would like that very much. Thank you, my mother."

He bowed to me and went off to look for Pninah.

When Elkanah came out of his room a while later, I was sitting at the edge of the front yard, lost in black thoughts. I no longer harbored suspicions about Samuel and Pninah, but was plagued by an entirely different sorrow. My body was shivering with a cold that had been present, unrecognized, longer than I could remember, and my eyes were wet with the tears of insult. Elkanah approached and I examined him more closely than I had in a long time.

His bushy hair was still lustrous, but now it was speckled with the gray of the years gone by, years in which the sun had also etched creases in his face. He was heavier, and thicker around the waist, than he had been when I became his wife. But this only made him look more distinguished. Elkanah was the prosperous head of a flourishing clan, a highly esteemed man in our tribe, and people mentioned his name with respect. He looked entirely like the dignitary he was. Against my will, my heart swelled up with pride and love at the sight of him.

He regarded me apprehensively, and the grooves between his eyes deepened when he realized that I was in distress. As he came close, I averted my face from him, something I had never done before. Hence he knew immediately what the bitterness in my heart stemmed from.

He sat down next to me, took my hands in his, and said softly: "Hannah, my beloved, who has besmirched me in your eyes? Was it Pninah?"

"So Pninah knew?"

"Of course she knew. But I ordered her to remain silent so that you would not be hurt."

"It was not Pninah."

"Then it must have been Samuel. He always knows exactly what one would wish he did not."

I was taken aback. "He didn't say a word about this. You know well that he would never voice such despicable words."

"If it was not Samuel, then who was it?"

"It was nobody. I just understood it by myself when he spoke of men who are unfaithful to their wives."

"He wanted you to understand it by yourself," Elkanah said sourly.

I rushed to the defense of my beloved son. "No, you wrong him. It is not what he wanted me to understand. It just happened. In my heart I must have known it all along, but I didn't want to admit it."

"And now you are grieved," he said mournfully.

Elkanah put his arms around me and kissed me long and lovingly. The kiss was like our first kiss, many years ago. I looked at him and my eyes welled in tenderness. Despite his iniquities I loved him as much now as I had then. I was angry, humiliated and degraded, but sick with love for him.

"Hannah, I love you."

I did not doubt his words, but thought them singularly inappropriate. "Then why do you do this? Since I became your wife I've had to resign myself to your lying lustfully with Pninah. Now I have to face the sad truth that you have been treading heedlessly over me, committing this abomination with other women as well."

His voice was silkily caressing as he said, "It is only with those maids in the fields, who are always available. I live in the midst of my people, and I promise you that I'm not worse than the other men around me. All the landowners I know, who have maids working for them in the fields, do the same. And I don't do it by far as much as I used to. In any case, the maids are as unimportant to me as the day before once it has gone by."

"And Pninah? Is she also that unimportant?"

"No. Pninah is different. I must be honest and say that I need her and I don't think I could do without her."

I kept quiet and he continued. "I always thought that she was completely mine, and that she had learned to accept all I did. But no longer. A short while ago I suspected her of a grievous sin and I was ready to mete out to her a dire punishment. It was not so. But I've come to realize that she is elusive, and that I have no notion of what is in her mind. I would not have believed it had I not seen it myself, but Samuel has brought her a huge Torah scroll, and earlier in the afternoon when I entered her scroll room, they were standing there, learning the Torah together."

"You have known all along that she is a scribe and a scholar."

"I have been concerned with her other attributes, and have paid no attention to this. Perhaps I should have."

I gathered my courage and finally asked Elkanah the question I had wanted to ask him since I became his wife: "What are those attributes? What is it that drives men—I mean you," I amended hastily, "mad with passion for her for years?"

But his reply left me no wiser than I had been before: "She . . . No matter. All this has nothing to do with you. I love you on a much higher level, the level of the spirit. You are a gracious lady of great refinement. There is an elegant air about you, which I adore. I love the serene expression in your heavenly face. Even when we are in bed together you are calm, and I can't think of anything more restful than holding you in my arms, with your cool cheek against mine. You are the queen of my soul. I love you more than I love anyone in the world, and I always will love you so, and you know it."

I noted that Elkanah did not promise to cease what he was doing, nor did I have the effrontery to demand it of him. I merely replied, "I have never thought otherwise."

After that we sat next to each other, and he put his arm around me, and my heart melted like wax under fire at his touch, and we watched the magic of the sun setting in a red glow over the hills of Efraim, painting the clouds in its own color, the blue of the sky darkening, until the glittering moon emerged and the hills were shrouded in a silvery mist.

I knew that despite Elkanah's infidelity, I would still draw strength from his love for me, and mine for him. I foresaw that the river of our life would flow calmly in the golden joy of our autumn years together.

I broke the silence and said, "Despite what you are doing with those women, I love you very much. There has never been another man for me. No man but you has ever known me, and no man but you ever will."

"I have never thought otherwise."

The Book of Pninah

I had told Hannah that Elkanah had scorned my love, and it was true. Not so Arnon. After his one attempt to rupture his ties with me, his love for me had never wavered. I had demanded nothing, but he had given me everything. Without his unfailing love I would not have survived Elkanah's perfidy; I would have shriveled away like a flower torn from the earth that nourishes it. He had also been a true friend. He had rescued my sons from death and given them more from his wealth than their own father had been able to give them.

Throughout the years my love for Samuel had grown imperceptibly, moment by moment, but I had not felt guilty before. Only now did I realize that I had come to love him even more than I loved Arnon. So, after all that had been between us for so many years, how could I face my lover now?

I had grave misgivings. Arnon knew me in depth and, unlike Elkanah, he was always sensitive to my moods. He might learn about the tidal wave flooding my heart simply by looking at me. And so it was.

We were lying in his bed, but for the first time ever he did not come to me. He was supporting his head on his elbow and studying my face intently with his clear gray eyes as he asked, "Pninah, why are you not looking into my eyes as you usually do?"

I lifted my eyes to his, but only briefly.

"I sense that there is something weighing on you. Something has changed in your life. Is there another man?"

"I have not been unfaithful," I mumbled feebly.

His voice hardened. "Nonetheless, there is a man and it makes you feel guilty."

"Why should I feel guilty?" I asked with a sob.

"Because even if he has not invaded the innermost shrine of your body, he has invaded your innermost being."

It was not a question but a pronouncement, and I could not rebut it. Not even with my eyes.

When I finally lifted them again, I saw that he was shaken. His jaw was clamped tightly; love for me had visibly ebbed from his eyes and they were as hard as stone. "You have betrayed me with every one of your heartbeats. From now on, I will always be tormented with the doubt of whether your body has followed your soul into infidelity."

"It will not be."

"I no longer trust you."

I sat up on the bed. "Do you wish for me to go?" I asked, my temples throbbing.

There was a long, unpleasant silence.

"Not yet," he finally retorted stiffly. "I want to understand you better before I decide."

He sat up, too, took hold of my shoulders and pushed me down on the bed, flinging himself down beside me. As was our custom in his bedroom, we wore nothing. But now he pulled the bed sheet over me to cover me up to my neck, as if he could not bear to look at my body.

Quietly, almost in a whisper, he asked, "Have you not been happy with me?"

My heart broke for him as I truthfully replied, "I have been profoundly happy."

He drank up my words as the dry summer earth drinks up the dew of the night, and for a while we lay there, immersed in silent memories of our many years of happiness together.

"Then why has our love not been sufficient to satisfy you?"

"He . . . I . . ." I could not go on.

His voice was heavy with hurt. "You have no explanation?"

I did—that my love for Samuel was not something I had chosen, but had forced itself on me, and that I was starved for him in my body and my soul. I did not think that this is what Arnon wanted to hear, so I remained silent.

"Who is the man?"

"As you said on the first day we met, you won't find this out from me."

This made him smile in an unfriendly fashion. "No matter. I already have a notion of who he is. During my travels in your parts, I've heard rumors that he visits his parents' home surprisingly often and I have wondered about this for some time. You are still so beautiful that you could easily have attracted so young a man. And you are shameless enough to wish for it."

Once again, I could not think of any reply.

Suddenly Arnon rose out of the bed, turned his back to me, and walked over to the window. He opened the shutter a bit, and stood looking out in silence.

I tossed the sheet that was covering me to the floor, and went to stand next to him. "Do you want me to leave?" I asked again.

Nothing tangible bound me to Arnon. He was not my husband; he could not hand me a book of divorcement and banish me from his house. But he could banish me from his heart, from his life. So I waited in trepidation to hear what his response would be.

There was none.

I slipped on my dress, shoved my feet into my shoes, and left. Later, as I sat in the carriage, tears flooded my eyes and streamed into my mouth, their taste as bitter as poison.

I thought of Arnon as I had seen him a short while ago at the window of his room. He was still overpoweringly handsome. The copper-red of his hair had begun to fade into a yellowish white, and his features had become sharper than they were in his youth. Fine lines radiated from his eyes, but he had not put on fat across his waist, as Elkanah had done. He was still lean, tall, broad-shouldered, and manly.

He could no longer know me as often and as forcefully as he had done before. What had been a cascade gushing down a mountain after the snows had melted, had turned into a spring flowing calmly, intermittently, down a gentle slope. But no less than before did I long for the thrill of his body against mine, and for the comfort of his words of love in my ears, which I was sure I would never hear again.

As these thoughts crossed my mind, one of my guards turned

around and said, "Lady, I hear the noise of carriage wheels. Ought we to stop and wait for it?"

My heart gave a leap; I asked him to halt. Soon Arnon caught up with us.

He called to me to move over to his carriage and instructed the guards to take the other one home.

When we were alone, he drove his carriage to the side of the road and stopped. "And now, Pninah," he said, "tell me this. Do you still wish to continue your meetings with me? You need not feel compelled. Once, when I thought that it was no longer convenient for me to continue, I tried to put an end to them. You may do the same. What I did for you later on, I did because I love you and because I am your friend, and not for anything that you give me in return. You are free to decide whatever is good in your eyes."

"Do you still want to meet me?"

"I will not conceal from you that I am deeply disappointed. Nevertheless," he began stroking my hair, "you are still the light that shines before my eyes. Years ago, when I loved another woman, I still loved you so that I could not live without you. Perhaps you will feel the same toward me now."

"You are as dear to me as you were before," I spoke truly.

"So I would like to continue. But only if you do it not because you feel obliged to repay what I have done for you, but because you truly love me."

"Yes," I said. "Yes."

He enfolded me in his arms, I nestled myself against him, and he locked me in an embrace and kissed away my tears.

My meetings with Samuel continued as well, but they were of a different order. Often when he came we would go into my scroll room and, leaving the door ajar so that Elkanah could not object, we would read from the Torah scroll he had given me.

With my father I had learned the Torah in a straightforward manner, but with Samuel we explored difficult passages, their hidden meanings, and their lessons for our people. At those times I was standing tall as a cedar in the Lebanon, my head touching the stars, and I could think of nothing closer to heaven.

It was enough for me. Throughout the years heavy storms had

broken over my head, and I had known adversity and despair. But whenever I had walked in the valley of the shadow of death my shepherd had led me into life again. The dream I'd had in my youth of finding a man who would be for me alone, and I for him forever, had not come true, but I had still found shelter under the mantle of love, and the strength to give shelter to those I loved.

I had found rest for my soul, if not for my body, and I was thankful to the Lord and at peace with myself.

The Book of Hannah

The fast of the Day of Atonement had passed, and almost the entire crop of grapes in the vineyard had been gathered in. The summer was drawing to an end, but toward the middle of the day its heat still lay heavily over the house and a hot easterly wind hissed at the bushes surrounding it. I stepped out of my room on my way to the midday meal, to the sight of Elkanah entering the front yard, leaning on one of his workmen.

As I approached, I noticed that his brown head-covering had been dislodged and was hanging limply down his left shoulder, making him look like an eagle with a broken wing. The sky was on fire with the rays of the sun, scorching his bare head. The workman brought him to a halt and sat him down on a stone, and Elkanah bent forward and leaned his face on his hands. I ran and knelt next to him.

"My head," he said, and nothing more.

By this time Pninah had run out of her own room, and she was kneeling on his other side. "Sir," she exclaimed, "you must come out of this burning sun and into the shade."

"My head," he repeated, clutching it and gazing at her blankly.

The workman had left by then, so in silent unison we placed our hands under his armpits and attempted to lift him up, to guide his steps to his room. He was heavier than I would have believed possible and we could not budge him.

As we looked around helplessly, Samuel, who had just ridden into the yard on his donkey, came to our aid. He raised his father from the stone singlehandedly and, making him lean against his own chest, walked him slowly to his room. As they stepped over the threshold Elkanah almost slipped from his arms, but Samuel's grip was strong, and he half carried him to his bed.

Elkanah lay inert, his eyes bleary, beads of sweat springing out and gathering like heavy dew on his forehead. Pninah rushed out and returned with a pitcher of water and a cup, which she filled and put to his lips. She tried to pour it into his open mouth, but the liquid spurted out and ran down his chin. I wet one of his shirts with the remaining water from the pitcher, and wiped the sheen of sweat off his face and head and arms, while Pninah peeled off his shoes and bathed his sweaty legs and feet. This seemed to do him good for he immediately sank into a deep slumber.

Wary of waking him, we left his room and conferred in front of his door.

"Elhanan," I said.

Pninah's second son was a renowned healer and Samuel immediately ran to the stable and charged one of the boys there to ride to his house and bring him immediately. But Elhanan lived in Shaar Efraim and it would be some time before he arrived. So Samuel went off to bring another healer who lived closer by.

This was a long-bearded man, about fifty years of age, heavy with a belly almost as large as that of a woman about to give birth, heavy also with confidence in his own skills. He sat down on Elkanah's bed and placed his ear against his chest, listening for a while, as we stood nearby, awaiting his verdict.

Finally he sat up and said, "He has exerted himself too much by working in the fields in the blazing sun, as he should not have done at his age, and this is the result."

We looked at each other, for we knew it to be far from the truth: Elkanah no longer did any work in the fields himself, and he had long made a practice of reclining and dozing in the shade of a tree in the heat of the day, resuming his task of overseeing his working men and women only when the sun had begun its travel downward, to meet the hills.

"But there is no need to fear for him," he continued, "his heartbeat is strong. He needs merely a good potion to steady it. I have it with me."

He removed a skin from his basket and handed it to me, saying: "This potion has a genuine essence of grapes' peel mixed with pomegranate nectar and cinnamon. Make him drink a few sips whenever he can, and he will soon revive and laugh at his own weakness. I will send my daughter later to find out how he is, and if need be I will come again."

Apparently feeling that he had faithfully earned the pouch of silver that Samuel pressed into his hand, he left contentedly, carrying his gigantic belly, which seemed to contain his entire wisdom, proudly before him.

By the time Elhanan arrived, Elkanah had become restless and a thick sweat was once again pouring down his ghastly, pallid face. Elhanan knelt beside his father and after listening to his heartbeat and his breathing, gently opened his eyelids with his fingers, regarding his apparently sightless pupils, one of which seemed to be much larger than the other.

When he arose, the color had drained from his own face. He called on his father to open his eyes, but although Elkanah's eyelids fluttered, they remained shut. Elhanan opened his father's mouth and placed what looked like a tiny ball of compressed herbs under his tongue.

We waited expectantly to see what would happen. After a few moments my beloved opened his eyes, then his mouth. He spoke in a low voice and his words were slow and slurred: "I am not well. Call Elha— Elha—"

Elhanan bent over him. "I am here, my father."

"All is dim. Your face is shapeless and spotted such as . . . a leopard," he continued to slur.

"Raise your hand to touch my face and you will know who I am."

Elkanah lifted his left hand and ran it over Elhanan's face. "Are you . . . are you . . . my firstborn . . ."

"No. Elroy is your firstborn. Now lift your right hand to touch my hair."

My husband lifted it a little way but it fell heavily back on the sheet. "It's weighed down with lead," he murmured, and his voice was feeble like that of an old man.

Then he began babbling words that made no sense at all. Elhanan, whose face was like that of Elkanah but with Pninah's blue-gray eyes, sat down at the table at the foot of the bed, and from the bag he had with him he removed a container with a liquid in it.

"What is this concoction?" Pninah demanded.

"It is a blend of crushed hyssop and pure myrrh and it has been known to be beneficial when a man is seized with this . . . affliction. But he is in a bad way, my mother. I can only try."

Elhanan knelt at the side of the bed again and lifted his father's head by cradling it in his arm, managing to pour some of the liquid down his throat, with only part of it streaming out of his mouth.

Soon Elkanah was deep in sleep again, his head bent sidewise, saliva drooling from his mouth onto his shirt, his sheet. While we sat around him, I watched in horror as slowly, little by little, my beloved's mouth bent itself sidewise, and his face froze in an ugly contortion, the like of which I had never seen before.

The room had become dusky, and all of our sons and daughters, who had been drifting in one by one, stood around us. I looked at their faces, and they held no comfort for me.

The following morning, the sun had risen warily, but an almost translucent moon still floated in the sky, not quite ready to give way before the overwhelming light of the sun. Elkanah's room was still cluttered with bowls half filled with the various potions and nectars that had been administered to him during the night. I gathered them up and took them to the cooking room, leaving Pninah to watch over him.

On the way back, I encountered Samuel, who, together with El-hanan, had spent the night in our house. I grasped his hand and dragged him to my room. "Samuel," I said, "you will not let your father die."

"I am not a healer like Elhanan," he replied in a low voice, "and neither can I work miracles."

My heart plunged. In my agitation I shook his shoulders. "You can, if you set your mind to it."

He raised his eyebrows in disapproval, as he said sharply, "My mother, I honor you deeply, but your despair leads you to utter words that have no merit. If ever the Lord grants me the power to perform a miracle it will be for the sake of the people of Israel, and not for the sake of my own family."

"You are performing one every day," I shouted at him, my voice shrill with anger.

He looked at me in silent puzzlement.

"For Pninah," I said. "The way she looks, so young still as if she were her own daughter, can be nothing but a miracle."

He flushed and turned from me. I lifted my hands to his shoulders and turned him around to face me again. His green eyes were fiery with wild fury, as if I had invaded the innermost recesses of his soul against his will. "I have only the power of prayer. Like you. Like everyone. Nothing else."

"Then gird up your loins and pray for your father and intercede for him in heaven."

"How can you think that I have not prayed for him already? At times the gates of heaven are shut to my pleading."

A chill ran through my bones. "Are you telling me that he is about to die?" I asked miserably.

He gathered me in his arms and stroked my graying hair and whispered, "You have six sons and daughters and three times as many children's children, all of whom adore you, and many still to come. They will sustain you."

I pushed him away and clenched my hands into fists and beat them on his chest. He grasped them gently in his big hands, then brought them to his lips. "Our years are numbered. Life on this earth does not last forever," he said.

I thought of how quickly the years had fled, as if they were fugitives from a battlefield. And all they had left behind was scorched earth, with nothing to hold on to.

"Except the children," he said as if he had read my thoughts, "your descendants. My father's descendants, who will keep his name alive for all the generations to come."

For the next five days, Elkanah hovered between wakefulness and sleep, between speaking sense and emitting meaningless sounds like an infant suckling at his mother's breast. His beard, which had always been neatly trimmed, had grown into wisps of surprisingly white hair, and his face was nearly as pale as his beard. Pninah and I took turns keeping a vigil over him, and Elhanan and two or three more of our children were always there, taking turns among themselves as well.

By the fifth day, having eaten and drunk almost nothing, Elkanah had thinned to the bone, and the shadow of death hung over him. As the day drew to a close and I was there with him, he lifted his left hand, and rubbed his forehead and moaned. His eyes, which had not opened the entire day, remained shut, but pain was visible on his contorted face.

Elhanan was kneeling at his side, attempting to pour a newly brewed potion into his mouth, but my husband could swallow nothing, and every last drop of it was pouring onto his bearded chin. His breath was becoming more and more labored, and his face even whiter than snow. Elhanan arose, as pale as his father, and put his arms to his sides, to indicate that there was nothing more he could do.

My man's life, my own, was visibly seeping out of him. I felt an uncontrollable desire to shake him back to consciousness, but Samuel, who just entered the room at that moment, restrained me by gripping my shoulders. Pninah came in, too, and we stood side by side.

As I watched my beloved, I felt something deep, as old as if it had been there always, waiting for this moment to burst out: the fear that had engulfed the sons of Adam ever since the expulsion from the Garden of Eden. The fear of death. My heart beat my alarm for Elkanah, and Pninah's trembling arm around me only made it pound in even greater terror.

Suddenly Elkanah opened his eyes. We both knelt at the side of his bed and clung to him. He could hardly see anything, and his hands groped for me blindly. "Hannah," he said. His voice came out in harsh gasps and his words were broken, like pieces of a shattered bowl of pottery. "I love you . . . even in death."

"So do I love you, my husband, with all the might of my soul," I said. "But you are not in the clutches of death," I lied, and sobbed. Pninah's face was alight with anguish, and in my heart I willed him to say words of love to her also, but they would not shape in his mouth.

"Pninah," he whispered, "Pninah . . ." It was the last word he ever voiced. He fell into a sleep as deep as death.

By the time night had descended all our sons and daughters had assembled again. Then, as if he had been holding out until they came, he twitched, his breath gave out, and his face turned into a lifeless mask; and I felt myself sinking into a void with him.

Later I found myself reclining on a chair on which my children had placed me, with tears falling like heavy drops of rain from my eyes. And there was nothing left for me to do but rent my clothing, as others had done before me.

When later I looked back on the month of mourning for Elkanah, I remembered very little of the first few days. My chest, run through with deep, bloody furrows, and my fingernails, under which there was still skin and blood, remained as the only testimony to what I was later told had been my wailing and screaming and cursing the day on which my mother had given me birth, and the tearing at my own skin and flesh in a rage of agony. Even my old and frail parents' hands on me could not restrain me.

It must have been four or five days before I became lucid, and it is only then that I began to truly confront the depth of my loss: the knowledge that Elkanah had been my strength, my light, my being, and in losing him I had lost myself.

As the days of mourning dragged by, and more of our relatives and friends came to sit on the ground with us to share in our bereavement, I could not ignore them. They spoke words of comfort to me, and I had to respond so that they would not feel insulted. They said that Elkanah's way had been paved with success and that he had attained all he had yearned for. I could not but accept their words. They said that his death had been ordained in heaven, and I voiced my agreement to these words, too, as did Pninah, who was sitting at my side.

Of the hundreds who filled our yard each day, I remember particularly our pupils, those we had taught throughout so many years. Except for those fallen in the wars with the Philistines, none was missing. They filed by, one after another, generation after generation. The older ones with their children, many of whom were now our pupils as well—the young ones with their fathers and mothers, who had placed their trust in us to teach their children, sons and daughters alike. Their sight was like the balm from Gilad to me, reminding me that we were blessed to be teachers in Israel, spreading the word of the Torah to the multitudes.

I drew comfort not only from our former pupils but also from the prospect of those in the years to come, for because of them, we would not want. As widows Pninah and I would not inherit our husband's property, but neither would we live in dire need as so many other widows did. Our children would not be obliged to hand out bread for us to eat and clothes for us to wear. The fees from our lessons would be more than enough to fill our storerooms with whatever we might wish for, and to pay the maids' and stableboys' wages as well.

Nonetheless I found myself in a lethargy from which even the first rains of the year, refreshing the earth after its summer dryness, could not resuscitate me. My sons and daughters spoke words of comfort to me, but their words were like voices calling in the wilderness; they could not touch my heart. Only Pninah, the sister of my soul, had that power, and by comforting me, she comforted herself.

"We have given life to others," she said, "and they are giving life to us. All our children have prospered. None have become mere woodcutters or waterbearers. We can draw consolation from our pride in them. We have each other, our petty jealousies forgotten, our friendship as sturdy as iron. Most important, we have ourselves. We will be our own shelter from adversity. The strength coursing in our veins is sufficient even to lend to others, so they can lean on us." And I knew her words to be true.

She spurred me on to assume the task of holding our family together, as Elkanah had done for so long.

"You are the first wife. Why should it not be you?" I queried.

"I am not carved out for it, nor am I worthy of such greatness," she responded earnestly, "but you were born to be exalted. You were aware almost as soon as you came out of your mother's womb that you had a special mission in life. And now you recognize it not only to be the mother of Samuel, but also the mother of Elkanah's family. Like Sarah, Rebecca, Rachel, and Leah who, each in her own way, built the house of Israel, so will you build the house of Elkanah that it may flourish even without him."

It was the first day of the ninth month, the first time our clan gathered to welcome the new moon after my beloved's death. I had summoned them to come to our house as they had always done during Elkanah's lifetime. But now, as the lot of them with their wives and husbands and children began filling our yard, I was gripped by panic. In my mind's eye I saw Elkanah sitting on the large elevated stone in the center of the yard, welcoming his descendants with hugs and kisses and gracious words, as he had always done. Would he not be furious if he knew that I was about to usurp his place? And would I not let them down by performing poorly what he had done so well?

But already Samuel was propelling me to the stone that had been Elkanah's seat and gently pushing me down onto it. After they all greeted me with the deference that was really due to him, not me, I sat mutely, wondering what I should say next.

The family sat down at my feet—even Samuel, even Pninah. I looked at the two of them, and it was plain to see that his ardor for her had not waned. He still regarded her as if he were a wanderer in the desert, parched by thirst, and she a spring of living water with which to quench it, yet out of his reach. Then the notion struck me, like thunder on a clear day. Now Pninah was no longer his father's wife, but his widow. If he came to her in the coming months or years, the curse imposed by the Torah on a man who lay with his father's wife would no longer fall upon him. And neither would the death penalty to which they would have been subjected under Torah law. All was shrouded in doubt; the days ahead would tell their own tale.

I recalled myself from my straying thoughts, back to what lay before me. Elkanah's property would have to be divided among our sons and they would be looking to me to make this happen, but there would be time for it later. Now there was another matter, more urgent by far, at hand.

A week before, Pninah's younger daughter, Nehamah, had given birth to a girl, her fifth child. She now placed the little bundle in my lap, so that I might bestow my blessing on it, as Elkanah had always blessed his newly born children's children. I kissed the little creature that was greedily sucking the corner of the milk-soaked blanket her mother had placed in her mouth, and, my voice shaky, I blessed her with the triple blessing of the Lord.

Then the voices around me melted into a hazy hum like that of a swarm of bees. I felt a bitter sting of sorrow in my heart, but when the tears rolled down my cheeks into my mouth they held the sweet taste of honey, the taste of life.

Hannah's Epilogue

My scroll on Samuel's birth and youth had been deposited in the Temple in Shiloh and in scroll rooms across the land of Israel. When the Temple was demolished and razed to the ground, I had no doubt that one day copies of it would be deposited in a new temple, to be built wherever the Lord chose to have his name dwell. But this scroll told only a small part of our tale.

Pninah and I resolved to each write a book that would tell the rest of it, two that would later become one. When all was ready, we would make ten copies of the whole and seal them. Pninah's daughter, Gilah, who was a scribe, was to keep them and pass them on to our children's children, who would open them only when everyone concerned had gone the way of all flesh. It would then be their task to make more copies, and pass them down to their children, and so it would continue. Thus our combined scroll, although it would not be deposited at any temple, would still be read by generation after generation, for countless generations to come.

So one evening I sat down at the table in my room, and I began to write:

What hurt before, no longer hurts. The grief of years gone by no longer clings to me. The pain I have inflicted and the pain inflicted on me then, the horrors of the wars—all these are long gone, overtaken by a new grief. Yet the memories are still as clear as the water that flows down the river Jordan, as strong as the blazing sun was on that day, in the month of the Festival of the Wheat Harvest, the day that determined my life . . .

HISTORICAL NOTE

This novel is set in ancient Israel, an agricultural-pastoral society, which also created the peerless compilation of books known as the Bible. Ancient Israel's high regard for the written word is evident also in the fact that written records of laws, events, or prophecies are mentioned many times in the Bible itself.

At the time described here (the eleventh century BC) literacy was not yet widespread. Scribes (as well as priests) acted as teachers to limited circles, and made a living also by writing letters for people.

There was some literacy among women, especially those of high social standing: The Bible ascribes important literary works—The Song of Deborah and The Song of Hannah—to women. It also ascribes the writing of letters to Jezebel, the wife of the Israelite King Ahab in the ninth century BC. Women's literacy is also attested to by archeological evidence showing that some women owned seals inscribed with their names, which were used to seal written documents. Hence, there may well have been women scribes who taught children, as did both Hannah and Pninah in this novel, or who wrote letters for a fee, as did Pninah.

There is no substantiated knowledge as to who wrote the various books of the Bible that follow the Torah. Some commentators raise the possibility that women scribes may have participated in writing them, a possibility I have also taken up in this novel.

There were scroll rooms (libraries) in existence. The Temple in Jerusalem, which most scholars believe was built in the tenth century BC, contained a scroll room; so it is feasible that there was one in the previous Temple at Shiloh, described in this novel, as well.

Ancient Israel was a polygamous society, but many anthropologists believe that even in such societies only a small minority of men could afford to take more than one wife. Thus, jealousy usually ensued from the taking of a second wife, as is evident in several stories, including that of Hannah and Pninah, in the Bible itself.

Adultery was apparently widespread in Israel, as we learn from the reference and condemnation of the practice by various prophets. "All of them commit adultery . . ." (Hosea, 7:4). "[E]ach neighs at another man's wife . . ." (Jeremiah, 5:8). Hence the adultery committed by both Elkanah and Pninah in this novel was not unusual.

Men's attraction to their fathers' wives or concubines other than their mothers was not an unknown phenomenon either, for which two such instances mentioned in the Bible may serve as evidence. Ruben, the son of Jacob, had relations with his father's wife, Bilhah. David's son Adonijah, wished to take his father's concubine, Abishag the Shunamite, for his wife after his father's death.

There is no evidence in the Bible for Samuel's attraction to his father's wife, Pninah. But I found it suggestive that although Samuel had grown up in the Temple and afterward became a judge in another town, and thus had not lived in his father's town of Ramathaim/Ramah since he was an infant, for no apparent reason, he subsequently moved back and made his home there.

ACKNOWLEDGMENTS

I would like to express my profound gratitude to the people who have read previous versions of this book and made major contributions to its improvement in both content and style: Olivia Marks-Woldman, Heddi Keil, Michael Newman, Yehiam Padan, F. J. Gibbons, Tamar Fox, Jane Cavolina (who corrected many flaws), Judith Riven (who has also been most supportive as my agent), my daughter-in-law, Ruth Etzioni, and my son, Ethan Etzioni.

My deepest thanks to Julie Saltman, the book's editor, for guiding me through the final stages of the writing process and for her excellent work in polishing the final version of the book.

Finally, thanks to my husband Zvi Halevy, my son Oren Etzioni, and my daughter Tamar Halevy for their unfailing patience and encouragement.

ABOUT THE AUTHOR

Eva Etzioni-Halevy is professor emeritus of political sociology at Bar-Ilan University in Tel Aviv. She has written fourteen academic books and published numerous articles. Born in Vienna, she spent World War II as a child in Italy, then moved to Palestine in 1945. She has also lived in New York City, and spent time at the Australian National University in Canberra before taking her position at Bar-Ilan. Eva lives in Tel Aviv with her husband; she has three grown children.